Advance praise for Donna Grant and *Mutual Desire*

"A unique, sensual, and exotic read."
Kate Pearce, author of *Simply Sexual*

"A collection you can lose yourself in. Sexy! Sexy! Sexy!"
Jenna Petersen, author of *Lessons from a Courtesan*

"Donna Grant masterminds tales of timeless passion."
Two Lips Reviews

Books by Donna Grant

THE PLEASURE OF HIS BED
(with Melissa MacNeal and Annalise Russell)

Published by Kensington Publishing Corporation

MUTUAL DESIRE

DONNA GRANT

APHRODISIA

KENSINGTON BOOKS
http://www.kensingtonbooks.com

APHRODISIA BOOKS are published by

Kensington Publishing Corp.
119 West 40th Street
New York, NY 10018

All Kensington titles, imprints and distributed lines are available at special quantity discounts for bulk purchases for sales promotions, premiums, fund-raising, and educational or institutional use.

Special book excerpts or customized printings can also be created to fit specific needs. For details, write or phone the office of the Kensington Special Sales Manager: Kensington Publishing Corp., 119 West 40th Street, New York, NY 10018. Attn: Special Sales Department. Phone: 1-800-221-2647.

Aphrodisia and the A logo Reg. U.S. Pat. & TM Off.

ISBN-13: 978-0-7582-3207-6
ISBN-10: 0-7582-3207-1

First Kensington Trade Paperback Printing: May 2009

10 9 8 7 6 5 4 3 2 1

Printed in the United States of America

To Mary O'Connor for knowing just what I need without me ever asking. For offering your house to my family when we had nowhere else to go because of the hurricane.

To Georgia Tribell for always being ready and willing for anything and being there to listen.

To Robin T. Popp for the daily e-mails and always sharing a room with me at a conference, even if you do freeze me out of the room.

To Steve Grant. You're my one, my only. My everything.

Contents

SPELLBOUND

1

Highlands of Scotland, Winter 1592

Kate thought outliving two husbands would prevent her from being married off. Again.

She should have known better.

It didn't help that her father had wanted an alliance with a Highlander for as long as she could remember. Living on the border with England, Kate never thought he would get that union since Highlanders thought them nothing more than Sassenachs.

Now, her father had the pact, but at the cost of Kate's hatred.

Twice she had married the decrepit men her father chose for her. Twice she had suffered their pawing on her body. And twice she had buried her husbands.

Luck, it seemed, had been on her side. Both men had died within months of their marriage, saving Kate from years of agony and loneliness.

Kate had assumed her father would allow her to choose her

next husband, should she ever want one, after she had been such a dutiful daughter. It came as more than a shock when her father announced she would marry Laird Ewan MacDonald.

A powerful—and feared—Highland lord.

Da told her nothing of this Highland laird other than the fact the laird was in need of a wife. For nearly two weeks, Kate had traveled across Scotland to reach the remote castle of her new husband. The brute hadn't even shown for their marriage, preferring instead to marry her by proxy.

Just thinking about it sent her into a rage. If there had been any chance at a friendship between them, Ewan MacDonald squashed it by not deeming her important enough to fetch himself. Kate couldn't wait to give him an earful once she finally met this Laird MacDonald. Maybe he would be as old and feeble as her previous husbands and find an early grave.

A smile pulled at the corners of her lips. "I can but pray," she murmured.

Maybe this time she wouldn't have to return home after her husband died. She'd already decided she would enter a convent before she returned to her father and was forced into yet another marriage for his alliances.

"Did ye say something, milady?"

Kate glanced at Rory Campbell as she pulled her cloak tighter around herself to help ward off the frigid temperatures. As his laird's loyal man, he had stood in for Ewan during the wedding. Several times on their trip she had tried to get him to speak of Ewan, but Rory was closemouthed. Yet it never hurt to keep trying.

"Tell me of my husband, Mr. Campbell. Was he married before?"

Rory chuckled. "Nay, milady. Me laird has nev'r married before now. Ye needn't worry of having another woman's children running aboot."

The mention of children always made Kate heartsick. For so

long she'd yearned for bairns of her own, but even that had been denied her.

"That is good news," she said and looked between her horse's ears to the road before her. Since Rory was now answering her questions, she decided to try for another. "Is he a fair man?"

Rory's hazel eyes swiveled to hers. "Fair? He's as fair as a Highland laird can be, milady. It takes a strong man to rule a clan as large as ours."

"I see."

"Doona fear though. Yer husband will protect ye should any of our enemies attack."

Kate's lips parted in shock. She knew there were Highland clans who were at almost constant war with each other, but she hadn't thought to ask of the MacDonald clan.

"Do the MacDonalds have many enemies?" she asked hesitantly, unsure if she really wanted to know.

Rory and the men around her laughed. "Aye, milady," Rory answered. "The MacDonalds are a powerful, proud, and rich clan. Our lands are huge, and there's many who want what we've worked hard for."

"Interesting." Kate could see her future of watching the men leave to battle a different clan every day. Or worse, battle at the castle.

This could be a way out of your marriage.

Kate cringed inwardly. Had she come to hate life so desperately that she was now praying for her husband's death, a man she hadn't even met? She wanted out of the marriage, but she could never live with herself if she came by it while turning into someone vengeful and malicious.

She had faced each of her marriages with the knowledge that there was nothing else for her to do. Women didn't have a choice in these kinds of situations. Men held the upper hand. From father to husband, a man would always rule her life.

It didn't seem fair, though she had always been an obedient daughter. But this latest act by her father, it went beyond her own reckoning. Not once had she fought him on his choice of husbands for her.

And this is how he repaid her?

She had learned of the marriage a scant half hour before the ceremony. There hadn't been time for her to run away to a convent or to even talk to her father.

Her hurt and anger had grown as the priest performed the marriage. During the few hours afterward in the poor excuse of a celebration meal, her belongings had been packed. Kate had a sharp tongue and a vicious temper, so her father had stayed away from her for fear of causing an uproar.

His betrayal had cut deep. So deep she hadn't bid him farewell. She hadn't even glanced at him when he wished her Godspeed. She regretted her harsh attitude now. With the distance of her old home on the border with England and her new home in the Highlands, she doubted she would ever see her father again.

Tears stung the backs of her eyes. She wasn't sure who she hated more, her father or Ewan MacDonald.

"Ye'll get to see yer first glimpse of the castle over this next rise, milady. Ye'll understand then why so many clans want what we MacDonalds have."

She gave Rory a brief nod and tried to feel some excitement about her new home. At least she hadn't married a weak man. She had seen firsthand on her journey to the MacDonald lands just how powerful the clan was. Everyone knew of Ewan Mac-Donald, and many feared his wrath should something happen to his men or his new wife.

There should be some satisfaction in that knowledge.

Yet there was nothing.

When their small group crested the rise, she stopped her mare beside Rory. The castle rested on the edge of the cliff, its many towers reaching toward the clouds while a thick stone wall enclosed the massive structure. She looked at the churning sea and its dark, cold depths that set the backdrop for the Mac-Donalds' land. The wind was harsh and cold as it swept from the water across the land, blowing through the few trees that dotted the rolling hills.

The gray stones of the castle matched the sky and her mood. From where she sat, she could see the men at the gatehouse watching them. The tartans the men wore spoke louder than any banner ever could, proclaiming them MacDonalds.

"What do ye think? Isn't it a magnificent sight?" Rory asked, pride dripping from every word.

Kate inhaled the sea air and blinked against the wind that stung her eyes. " 'Tis larger than I imagined." *And more ominous.*

"It's taken the MacDonalds many generations to build such a grand castle. Ye should be proud to be one of us now."

Kate began to doubt if she could ever find happiness in such an uninviting place. "Oh, aye, Rory. I'm very proud of that fact."

Rory gave a snort, indicating he didn't believe her, and nudged his mount forward. "Come, milady. Yer laird awaits ye."

Kate was tempted to stay where she was. She licked her lips to hide her smile as she wondered what the all-powerful Ewan MacDonald would say when he was told his wife refused to enter the castle.

Do you really want to find out?

Kate groaned inwardly. That wasn't the way to greet her new husband and his clan, but then again, he had insulted her pride by marrying her by proxy.

Get your revenge another way. Use your head instead of letting your anger consume you.

She knew her conscious was right, but it still gnawed at her to be nothing more than an afterthought. Ewan *needed* a wife because he *needed* heirs. She would be used for nothing more than that.

"Come, milady," Rory called over his shoulder.

Kate lifted her chin and clicked to the horse, her mind already forming a plot for revenge. Highlander or not, Ewan would learn soon enough that she was more than someone to breed his children.

The other MacDonald men followed behind her as she trailed after Rory. Every step of her mare took her closer to a man and a castle she wanted no part of. She was tired of traveling, but she wasn't ready to meet her new husband. In fact, she doubted a few years would be enough time to prepare her for Laird Ewan MacDonald.

The only thing her father had said of her new husband was that Ewan MacDonald was a very powerful laird. Power in her mind meant he had to be controlling. And Kate hated to be controlled. She wanted to live her own life, make her own decisions—something that baffled her father to no end.

With her head turned away from the vicious sea wind, Kate trusted her mare to follow the others. If Kate were more adventurous she might kick the mare into a run and try to escape.

But that wasn't something she could do. Kate had given her word when she had taken Ewan as her husband. She was well and truly trapped. The only escape she would find would be in her daydreams.

2

All too soon they reached the impressive gates to MacDonald Castle. Kate's mare stopped next to Rory, and Kate had to tilt her head all the way back for her gaze to follow the tall wooden gates to the gatehouse above. The guards stared down at her, whispering among themselves.

She sighed. This would be another place where she would be treated as an outsider. She was a Lowlander, and thus nothing more than English to these Highlanders. Was it too much to want a husband she didn't mind looking at, one that she could laugh with, and children to bring light and hope into her world? Had she done something in a past life to force fate into giving her such misery?

There were no answers for Kate, and there never would be. She knew that, but she couldn't help but ask every once in a while. She had survived two marriages. She would survive another or make the most out of it.

She was a realist, and as such, she knew her place in life, as much as she hated it. In the meantime, she would pray that one day women would have the right to choose their own husbands—or not choose one at all. Maybe one day women could do whatever they wanted and be beholden to no one but themselves. It was just a dream, but what a glorious day that would be if it could be so.

The gates swung open and they rode into the bailey. People began to gather as they rode toward the castle. Kate let her gaze wander the large bailey, and she spotted a blacksmith's shop and the chapel close to the castle before her mare halted.

Once Rory stopped at the steps of the castle, she swung her cold and numb leg over her mare's neck and dismounted. The stares of MacDonalds made her uneasy, and to make matters worse, it appeared her husband wasn't at the castle to greet her or introduce her to his people.

Just what kind of brute was her husband?

A savage most likely. Everyone said Highlanders were.

Kate took a steadying breath as she looked at the faces that surrounded her. Her lips pulled back in a smile as she winked down at one of the children who gazed up at her with wide eyes. She kept the smile on her face as she turned and followed Rory up the steps to her new home despite the whispers of "Sassenach" and "Lowlander" that ran through the crowd like fingers of lightning.

This was their home, and she was the stranger. She couldn't blame them for their wariness or for the curious stares. She was thinking the same thing as they were: *Why had the laird chosen a Lowlander as a bride?*

Her curiosity got the better of her sometimes, but she wanted to know. Why her? She had never met Ewan, or seen him for that matter.

Kate sighed and lifted her cloak and skirts and climbed the steps. There would be plenty of time later to wonder why she was a laird's wife. For now, she just wanted out of the cold.

After such a long journey, Kate was looking forward to a

warm fire and a good meal. Even her gloomy new home would be welcomed after being in the frozen weather for so long.

Whether she wanted it or not, MacDonald Castle was her home now. As large as it was, it must have plenty of servants to keep it clean. But when she walked into the castle, she came to a halt as her eyes registered the filth around her.

"Somethin' wrong?" Rory asked.

Where did she start? It looked as though the castle hadn't been thoroughly cleaned in months. The stink of old rushes filled the air, making her breathe through her mouth. Scraps of bones were piled near four wolfhounds that slept before a hearth that needed to be cleaned of its ashes.

Rory walked into the great hall and filled a goblet with ale. He lifted the drink to his mouth and drained it in one long swallow.

After he belched and wiped his mouth on his sleeve, he turned to her. "All right. Let me show ye to yer chamber."

Kate fought not to roll her eyes as she trailed after Rory yet again. Everywhere she looked, layers of dust and dirt could be seen. She prayed her chamber was cleaner than the great hall, but she wasn't holding out any hope.

She stood in the doorway of the master chamber and barely suppressed a shudder. The bed was unmade and ashes spilled from the hearth, not to mention that there was even more dust. There was no way she was sleeping in a chamber so filthy. There would have to be cleaning done before she could relax.

Kate turned and found a woman with flame red hair and gentle green eyes watching her from behind Rory. Kate gave her a smile. "My name is Kate. I'm your laird's new wife."

"Welcome, milady. Me name is Beth."

"Thank you, Beth. Tell me, when was the last time the castle was cleaned?"

Beth glanced at Rory and licked her lips. " 'Tis been a while, milady. When the laird is gone, things tend to . . . slow."

"That's not going to happen as long as I'm here," Kate said as she pushed up her sleeves. "Gather some women. We've got some cleaning to do."

"You're going to cl—clean, milady?" Beth's eyes rounded and she buried her hands in her skirts.

Kate bit back a grin at the girl's surprise. "I am, and I'm going to start in this chamber. We best get started."

"Aye, milady. I'll gather some more help," Beth said and hurried away.

Rory looked around the chamber and shrugged. "I doona see what's amiss."

"Are you married, Mr. Campbell?"

His brow furrowed and he took a step back. "Nay, milady."

"When you do find yourself a wife, you'll understand."

Rory stood in the doorway for several moments before he stammered something about helping Beth and walked away. It wasn't long before Rory and Beth had gathered a large group of women. Kate dispersed them throughout the castle to begin cleaning.

She rolled up her sleeves and began to strip the bed. Just like at home, she was alone again. In some ways she looked forward to the time by herself to get used to the castle and her role as wife.

A sound at the door drew her attention. When Kate glanced up, she found Beth watching her. The girl gave her a shy smile and took a step into the chamber.

"I hope ye doona mind me help, milady. I doona think the laird would like ye cleaning."

"I don't care what he thinks," Kate said. "But I'm glad for the help."

Beth began to clean the hearth. "We're all verra happy to see Laird Ewan finally wed."

Kate shook out the new linens and kept her mouth closed since her reply wouldn't be kind.

"Yer verra lovely, milady. The laird has made a good match."

Kate looked up, startled by the servant's kind words. "Thank you."

She smiled and returned to the linens, but Kate now had a warm glow in her heart. Maybe this time it would be different for her.

The time passed quickly as they worked, and soon the master chamber was spotless. Kate stood back and looked at their effort. The feather mattress had been plumped, and with the deep green velvet bed hangings shaken out, the bed looked utterly inviting. A MacDonald plaid had been folded at the end of the bed, reminding her it wasn't just her chamber.

They had even cleaned the sword and shield that hung over the bed. Both weapons looked ancient, and Kate wondered who they had belonged to.

"The laird will be grateful for what ye've done, milady."

Kate crossed her arms over her chest and turned to Beth. "Maybe, but this should have already been done. Who's in charge of the castle?"

"That would be Bridget, milady," Beth answered softly.

Kate knew she needed to find this woman and set her straight on how the castle should be cleaned, but first she wanted something else.

"Would you show me the castle?"

The servant's eyes lit up. "Aye, milady. I'd be delighted."

There were many twists and turns and several sets of stairs she was shown as Beth led her through the castle. Kate tried to memorize them all, but she knew it would take some time before she truly learned her way around. As Beth walked, she told Kate the history of the MacDonalds and how they had come to have such power in the Highlands.

"Many wanted a match with Laird Ewan," Beth said. "If a smaller clan could have had an alliance through marriage, it would have kept some of their enemies away."

Kate shook her head. "Is that all the men do?"

"Milady?"

"Battle each other? Can the clans not live in peace?"

Beth smiled as if she were talking to the village idiot. "Ye'll soon come to learn our ways, milady. We Highlanders are verra proud people, and our men are some of the best warriors."

Kate found herself wondering if her husband was such a warrior, young and powerful and strong. But she knew she wouldn't be so lucky. If Ewan was young, he would have his pick of women just as Beth said, and since she had never met him, she couldn't imagine him choosing her, a Lowlander no less.

Another old man, then.

"This is the best view from the castle," Beth said excitedly.

Kate chuckled and followed her up the winding stairs of one of the many towers. When she reached the top, her steps slowed as she walked to the window. She could only stare in amazement at the grandeur before her.

" 'Tis me favorite spot," Beth admitted. "I think ye'll like it here."

Kate nodded, lost in the sight of the sun sinking into the horizon as if the dark waters of the sea swallowed it whole. The sea reflected the vivid pink and purple that streaked across the sky. Time stood still as she watched the sun sink into the horizon. The dark fingers of night crept over the land, but just before the light faded completely, a sound from below drew Kate's attention. She turned as Beth leaned out the window.

"What is it?" Kate glanced below, afraid they were under attack. The gates had been swung open wide though, so it couldn't be an assault.

"The laird has returned," Beth screeched. She whirled around, a huge smile on her face as she rushed from the tower.

Kate stared after Beth's retreating form as she nibbled her lip in apprehension. So, her husband had returned. She peered out the window and looked for the eldest man in the line of Highlanders that rode through the gates, but her gaze was riveted on the black-haired man who rode at the head of the warriors.

He sat upon his steed as if he owned the world. She gripped the window and shifted to try and get a better look at him. It was too bad she was so high up because she would have liked to see the warrior's face.

You're married, Kate.

And it wasn't something she was likely to forget, not with her husband now at the castle.

Her stomach fell to her feet. She turned away from the window and glanced down at her gown, which had become dirty from the cleaning. She couldn't meet her new husband dressed as she was. If only there were time to get cleaned.

Kate groaned as she tried to rub away spots of dirt on the hem of her gown. The spots proved too difficult. She straightened and put a hand to her head. As much as she wanted to delay the meeting, she couldn't. Laird Ewan had arrived home, and he would be expecting her.

She took her time as she descended the stairs. If she was fortunate, maybe she would get lost on her way to the great hall.

Somehow, she managed to navigate the corridors with only a few mishaps and soon arrived at the stairs to the great hall.

Kate glanced down at the people milling about, trying to get a glimpse of her husband before she was introduced to him. She wiped her clammy hands on her skirts and squared her shoulders.

"Milady," Beth said with a gasp as Kate descended the stairs. "I'm sorry I left ye."

Kate waved away her words. "Think nothing of it."

Servants and the men who had accompanied her to the castle stood in the great hall as if waiting for the king of Scotland. Kate swallowed nervously and looked about. It was as if everyone was arranged just so, and she didn't know where to stand.

Since she didn't want to move to the front, she gradually walked to the side until she stood next to the hearth and the blazing fire.

Kate clasped her hands in front of her and wished some of the heat would come back into her bones. She liked her new spot. It would give her a chance to view her husband first and see him interact with his people before she made her presence known.

Two heartbeats later the door to the castle flew open, and the black-headed warrior filled the doorway. His gaze scanned the hall, passing over Kate twice before he stepped inside and moved into the great hall.

"Welcome home, laird," Rory greeted him.

Kate's heartbeat quickened when she realized her new husband was not the frail man she expected, but a young, viral warrior. She glimpsed her husband's wide shoulders and thick arms. His saffron shirt gave her a glimpse of his chest and the black hair that curled there.

His sleeves were rolled up, exposing tanned, muscular forearms. Her gaze traveled down his trim waist to the end of his kilt. Slung across his back was a vicious-looking sword, reminding everyone he was a warrior. And laird.

She couldn't help but notice he wore the MacDonald plaid like a king wore a crown. And to the MacDonalds, he was king.

"I was told my wife arrived." His deep, clear voice filled the hall. "Where is she?"

Beth's eyes widened as she turned her gaze to Kate. Kate took a deep breath and tried not to let the sting of his words affect her.

He had no idea what she looked like. She wasn't sure what hurt worse: the fact that he hadn't wanted to know what she looked like or that she wasn't worth his time.

Both only fed her anger. She wanted to storm from the hall, gather her belongings, and leave. She had known she would get a good idea of her husband by watching and listening, and she wasn't at all impressed with the powerful Laird MacDonald.

Yet she couldn't leave. If she didn't do something soon, Beth or Rory would point her out, and Kate was too proud to slink away.

"I'm right here," she said and stepped forward.

He swung around. Bright, clear blue eyes fringed by thick, black lashes looked her up and down. His black hair hung loose about his shoulders in waves and was pulled away from his face by several tiny braids.

That face was enough to make any woman melt. He had a square chin and an angular face with wide, full lips and black brows that slashed over his eyes.

As he walked toward her, Kate had to tilt her head back to look at him, he was so tall. The sheer bulk of him, from his height to the width of his shoulders and the muscles bulging in his arms, gave her pause. She had seen big men before, but this Highlander commanded power like nothing she had ever seen.

Her body reacted with alarming speed as his gaze roamed freely over her. Her stomach fluttered and her heart pounded in her chest.

He's certainly not old.

She hadn't expected her husband to be so young or so disarmingly handsome. When his eyes stopped at her breasts, her nipples hardened and her sex clenched. For the first time in her life, she wanted her husband to take her to his bed and make love to her.

She swallowed and met his gaze, refusing to let him know how her body reacted to him. Her anger faded to something deeper, something stronger . . . something wanton.

His forehead furrowed and he crossed his arms over his chest. "You're not the wife I chose."

For a moment Kate thought he jested, but the anger sparking in his blue eyes told her otherwise. His words lashed across her like a whip. The hall went deathly quiet as they waited for her response. She might have considered being intimidated by her husband's size and obvious power, but her fury overrode everything.

She drew herself up as tall as she could and glared at him. "Well, I'm the wife you got."

3

Ewan blinked, unable to comprehend that the petite woman standing before him dared to talk back. She was attractive, with her dark blond locks and amber eyes that flashed in fury.

She was slim, and her curves were in all the right places. Her heart-shaped face gave the impression of an angel, but the stubborn tilt of her chin spoke volumes.

"Nay," he said. "The woman I chose had golden blond hair and blue eyes."

The woman snorted. "That is my sister."

"Sister?" Ewan got a sick feeling in his gut. This couldn't be happening to him, not after all the trouble he had gone to. "That's the woman I paid for."

His wife laughed, the sound devoid of humor. "Ah, then Da duped you. You foolishly thought he had only one daughter. You never gave him her name did you?"

"How could I give him a name when I didn't know it? And no one calls me foolish," Ewan growled. He dropped his hands and took a step toward her. Instead of running away or cowering as most did when he let loose his temper, the woman's spine straightened even more, if that was possible.

Amber eyes glittered dangerously. Her gaze moved over him in much the same manner as he had subjected her. "It would have been simple courtesy to ask her name. Also, I never called you foolish. I said you 'foolishly thought.' "

"Do not mince words with me, wench." Ewan knew he should walk away until his ire cooled, but he was captivated by the spitfire.

"I have a name," she said between clenched teeth. "Though you haven't deigned to ask it. Instead, you'd like to stand there and make me feel inferior for your mistake."

Ewan blinked. He was so taken aback he could only stare at her. Before he could form a response, she turned on her heel and stiffly strode away. He watched her leave, amazed she had dared to try to put him in his place.

Amazed . . . and excited.

She hadn't only dared it, she had done it.

He should have been irate, but he found himself more stunned and even slightly admiring of the wench. He had always treated women decently, and his only excuse for not doing so now was that he had been deceived. Her father had known exactly which woman he wanted for his wife. Why the man would send this shrew to him when Ewan had never aggrieved the man was just . . . wrong.

"What are ye going to do?" Rory asked as he came to stand beside Ewan.

Ewan turned to his first in command. "Didn't you realize the wrong woman was standing up as my intended bride?"

"In truth, nay," Rory answered. "I only saw the girl from a distance, and even then only briefly. Munro produced her and the marriage was promptly performed."

"Shite," Ewan cursed. It was then he realized the castle was cleaner than it had been since the death of his mother. Had

Bridget gotten everything in order for his new bride? "It's clean."

Rory and Beth opened their mouths to speak, but another voice, a seductive voice Ewan knew all too well, reached him.

"I told ye I'd take care of yer home, laird."

Ewan turned to find Bridget leaning against the wall with her pert breasts thrust toward him. She gave him a sly grin, her lips full and pouty. Her dark hair hung down her back thick and loose, and her eyes all but undressed him.

"I've missed ye." She straightened and walked toward him, her hips swaying seductively.

"I'm married now."

She laughed softly. "It doesna sound as though she meets with yer approval. I told ye, ye should've taken me as yer wife. I'd have made ye happy."

Ewan held up a hand to stop her from coming closer. It had taken him a few years, but once he realized Bridget's claws dug deep, he made sure to stay as far away from her as he could. Though his body didn't always listen to his mind.

Despite Bridget's charms, Ewan could think of only one woman, and that woman had amazing amber eyes and a temper that might match his own. He'd set Bridget straight about sharing his bed later, once he spoke with his new wife.

"See to my men. They're hungry." With that, he turned and took the stairs two at a time to look for his wife.

He strode to his chamber to find the door slightly ajar. With a little nudge of his hand, he pushed the door open and found his wife standing before the hearth. Her arms were wrapped around herself and her gaze was fastened on the popping red orange flames.

Ewan took a deep breath and reminded himself to stay calm. With her temper and his own they wouldn't get anywhere shouting at the other.

Exactly what I didn't want in a woman.

Somehow he would get them out of this. There was always the possibility of an annulment, but he would have to see to it immediately.

She's certainly passionate. And most likely passionate in bed.

Ewan grimaced. She wasn't the woman he had chosen. She'd make his life a living hell. So why was he thinking of what their bedsport would be like?

He stepped over the threshold. She didn't raise her head to acknowledge him or even appear to know he was in the chamber. He closed the door behind him and leaned against it, wondering how he should begin. Women liked it when men apologized. Despite the fact he didn't have anything to be sorry for, it would help him gain the information he needed.

"I should apologize."

"Don't bother," she said without looking at him. "I'm sorry my father duped you, and I'm doubly sorry you won't have my beautiful sister as your wife."

Ewan let out a breath. He'd let his temper rule him below, and he had hurt her in front of his clan. He should have known better. "You have the advantage of knowing my name. Will you tell me yours?"

"Kate."

He liked it. She was a woman with spirit, which she had proven in the great hall. He grinned as he recalled the sight of her face flushed with anger and how her chest had heaved. She would stand up against him on anything she believed she was right on.

In other words, she would disrupt the quiet I demand in the castle.

He wanted a biddable wife, a woman who would agree with everything he said and wanted, a woman who would smile graciously and do as he told her without argument.

Kate was the opposite of his idea of a perfect wife.

Ewan ran a hand down his face, his mind frantically trying to speak of ending the marriage without hurting her delicate feelings even more.

"The only way out for either of us is an annulment," Kate said, as if reading his mind.

He pushed away from the door and walked to his bed, noticing how clean his chamber was. "Aye. There is that option."

" 'Tis our only option," Kate said and turned toward him. "You haven't bedded me. I'll move to another chamber, and we can start the annulment process immediately."

Ewan's eyes narrowed as he sank onto the bed. It seemed he wasn't the only one disappointed with his marriage. Since he didn't want her, he shouldn't be angered that she was so quick to want to get rid of him. Even if he was a prize catch in Scotland.

"I'm not what you expected then?" he asked.

"Nay. Let me explain just what my father has done to you. This is my third marriage."

"Third?" Surely he hadn't heard her correctly.

She nodded. "I was wed for the first time when I was four and ten. It lasted six months before he died. A year later, my father married me off again. That marriage lasted all of two months before he died choking on a chicken bone. I had expected to never marry again. Aye, I had even expressed that desire to my father who obviously didn't take my wishes into account."

"I'm your third husband?" Ewan looked at the young woman before him, unable to believe she'd been married twice before.

"Aye."

"Did you kill your first two husbands?"

She stared at him a moment before she burst out laughing. When she straightened, she wiped at the corners of her eyes. "Both of the men had one foot in the grave when my father chose them for my husband."

"And you had no choice but to return to your father because both men had heirs already, I suppose?"

"Precisely."

He studied her a moment. To have a father marry her off for a third time seemed beyond cruel, especially when Ewan had chosen the other daughter. "You want out of this marriage?"

"I was hoping you were another old man, except this time without heirs."

"Wouldn't you want me to get you with child to ensure you always had a home?"

As soon as the words left his mouth an image of Kate, her head thrown back in abandonment as he plunged into her, filled his mind. His balls tightened and his cock thickened.

She hesitated a moment. "That thought has crossed my mind."

"But no more?"

She shook her head and let her gaze fall.

"Why?" he asked and rose from the bed to walk to her. "Am I not pleasing enough for you?"

"You please me fine enough."

She was uncomfortable—that much was obvious by the way she refused to meet his gaze. Her arms crossed under her breasts, drawing his gaze to the full swell of her chest. He wondered what her breasts would feel like in his hands and if she would like it when he suckled and pinched her nipples.

His cock jumped just thinking about sinking into her slick heat. A few moments ago he had been angry at having her as his wife, and now he wanted her with an intensity that frightened him.

Women had always come to him, eager for him to love them. But there had never been a woman that he had desired above all others. Not once had he lusted after a wench so desperately that she was all he thought about.

There was something about Kate that brought out the primal urge in him to claim her, to throw her on the bed and seduce her one kiss, one touch, at a time until she screamed his name, her body shaking with her climax.

His hunger for her grew with each moment he looked at her. It gnawed at his gut, urging him to take what was rightfully his.

She shifted from one foot to the other. Ewan tore his gaze away from the swell of her breasts and forced himself to think of something else—anything other than bedding her.

Because if he stayed near her, he was going to do just that.

"When did you arrive?" he asked when he noticed the dirt on her gown.

"Just after midday."

"Was your journey difficult?"

She shrugged. "Not terribly. My cloak kept most of the chill from me."

Ewan clenched his jaw as suspicion gnawed at him. "And what did you do while you waited for me?"

"I gathered the women and we cleaned the castle."

Just as he thought. A slow, steady stream of anger sizzled through him. Bridget had lied. Most likely she hadn't even helped with the cleaning.

"Thank you," he murmured. "I've needed a wife for some time to keep up with the duties of the castle."

"Any number of women could have taken that duty until you found a wife."

Bridget had assumed that role, a role he should never have allowed her to have. Ewan licked his lips as he stared at Kate.

"You've never been to the Highlands before, have you?"

Her head swiveled to him. "Nay."

" 'Tis much colder here, and living next to the sea will make it even colder."

"I'll survive."

He had no doubt that she would. With a grin, he turned and headed to the door. "I'll have a bath sent to you. I must give my men orders, then I'll have our supper brought up so we can be alone."

Her brow furrowed as she took a step toward him. "We are going through with the annulment, aye?"

He stopped and looked over his shoulder at Kate, his hand on the door handle. "We'll talk about it more over supper."

Ewan left before she could argue. As he walked down the corridor, he found he wasn't as disappointed as he had first been upon finding Kate as his wife. The hunger she elicited in him was enough to make him contemplate keeping her.

You want quiet, though.

But with Kate in his arms, he wouldn't care about anything else. She was passionate, and that passion could burn him as no other woman had. How he'd longed to find a woman whose passion met his own, but he'd given up that hope long ago.

Maybe, just maybe, he had that woman now.

By the time Kate finished with her bath, she had no more calmed herself than when Ewan had left the chamber. She had been so sure he would give her the annulment since he wasn't happy to find her instead of her sister as his wife, but there had been something in his blue gaze that made her blood burn and her body ache with an unfamiliar need.

There would be no annulment if she let him bed her. But, oh, how she wanted to feel the weight of him atop her, to taste his kiss and run her hands over his broad back. She'd heard from her friends that sex could actually feel good for a woman. The few times she's experienced it, it had brought her either pain or . . . nothing.

She would stare at the ceiling and think of the next day's meals or she would bite her tongue to keep from crying out in pain. She hated bedsport as much as she hated being married. It was just one more way a man ruled a woman.

As Ewan's wife, he had every right to take her, sealing their marriage. She shuddered as she recalled the gnarled, shaky hands of her previous husbands as they pawed at her body.

Ewan's hands didn't shake. They were large, tanned, and calloused. A warrior's hands. A laird's hands.

She swallowed and licked her lips as she wondered what his hands would feel like on her body. She had seen his anger, knew he was quick to rile, but he hadn't raised a hand at her. He had shouted enough to alert the entire clan of his ire, but she would rather that than be struck.

Her first husband had often backhanded her, but it didn't make her cower as he had hoped. Instead, it gave Kate the strength she needed to get through each day. Those six months had been like six lifetimes.

There were many differences Kate could see already between Ewan and her first two husbands. But it wasn't enough to make her change her mind about the annulment. Besides, it hadn't been her he had chosen. It had been her sister.

Her father had known it, too. Why had he done it to her and Ewan? Why trick such a powerful laird and risk so much? Why put her life in danger?

He'd had desire in his eyes.

Kate had seen the desire for sure in Ewan's eyes, but that didn't change anything. Though, she wondered if Ewan would be a different kind of man—a man who let her be herself.

She rose from the water and began to dry herself. Her hands grazed her breasts and her nipples puckered and sent a stab of longing between her legs. Her sex throbbed, and for a brief instant she thought of allowing Ewan to bed her, to see if he could bring about the wonderful feelings a woman could experience.

Yet, did she dare to give into her own desires? She wasn't the bride he wanted. He had chosen her sweet, beautiful, biddable sister who was the exact opposite of her. Kate didn't think she could stand to see his disappointment again.

She dressed and took the MacDonald tartan from atop the bed, wrapping it around herself in a vain attempt to find warmth. She couldn't stop shaking. The bath water had been hot, but the castle stones soaked up all the warmth, leaving little for her. Even the fire she huddled in front of couldn't generate enough heat.

The only warning she had that Ewan approached their chamber was the sound of his voice. Kate rose and braced herself for his arrival. He opened the door, barely sparing her a glace, and motioned in Beth who carried a tray of food. He moved the table and chairs that sat beside the window nearer to the fire and motioned for Kate to take a seat. Kate sat and curled her legs beneath her skirt.

She noted Ewan's damp hair and fresh saffron shirt beneath his kilt. Beth gave her a grin as she set out the food, but Kate was too nervous to return Beth's smile. Kate kept her eyes on her food instead of Ewan, for that would make her think of other things, things that made her sex ache and her breasts swell.

The sound of the door closing told her Beth had left. Now she was alone with Ewan.

"You really want out of this marriage?"

Kate's gaze snapped to Ewan. "Don't you? I'm nothing like my sister. Besides, my father deceived you. That in itself is enough to get an annulment." She speared a bit of meat, smiling inside at her quick thinking.

"I might have been a wee hasty in stating my annoyance at being tricked."

She nearly choked on the delicious roasted meat as he lowered himself into the chair opposite her. "You don't even know me. How can you say you might have been hasty?"

"Exactly my point," he said casually as he ate. "Let's get to know each other. Maybe we'll see that we are definitely meant to be apart."

Or meant to be together.

He hadn't said the words, but Kate realized his intentions. His blue gaze met hers. He smiled and reached over to fill her goblet.

She chewed and swallowed before she trusted herself to answer. "All right. What kind of woman are you looking for?"

"I thought I knew. Now, I'm not so sure."

A look of pure desire centered on her, scorching her with its intensity. Kate's stomach fell to her feet with a thud. She couldn't catch her breath, and her heart pounded loudly in her ears.

"What do you want?" he asked.

You.

Thankfully, she didn't blurt it out. "I want the impossible."

"What might that be?"

"A man who understands me, a man who will laugh with me, share his life with me, and grow old with me. I want lots of children so their laughter can fill my home. I want a man who will let me be me." She shrugged and took another bite. "As I said. Impossible."

She couldn't tell what he was thinking, but she knew no man could ever live up to what she dreamed of having, especially not this Highland laird who was used to commanding everyone. There would be no compromising with him.

"The weather will take some time for you to become accustomed to it."

His words were like a bucket of ice water doused on her. She knew then that her hopes of being free were gone. "You won't give me the annulment?"

"In truth, I don't know. I want you in my bed first."

4

Ewan watched the dismay, then anger, flash across Kate's pretty face. She wanted out of the marriage, and he would let her go if he was wrong about the passion he sensed between them. But if he was right, he would do anything to hold onto her forever.

"You can't be serious." Her voice came out in a strangled whisper, but he saw the flush on her cheeks.

She was tempted.

A slow smile pulled at his lips. "I would never jest about something so serious."

Her hands, which shook slightly, moved to lie atop the table. "I'm begging you. Give me the annulment."

"What are you afraid of, Kate? My bed? Or what I'll do to you in that bed?"

"Please."

"Were your two previous husbands that lacking?"

She rose from her chair and made a dash for the door. Ewan was quicker and put his hand against the door so she couldn't open it.

Kate spun around to glare at him. "You would force me?"

Her pupils dilated, and her chest rose and fell quickly, drawing his gaze to her lovely, full breasts. By the saints, he couldn't wait to see them bared, her nipples straining for his mouth.

He moved closer to her, pinning her against the door with his body. His other hand came to rest beside her face, her hair teasing the back of his hand. "I won't have to force you."

At his words, her mouth opened in surprise . . . and her amber eyes darkened with desire. Ewan leaned down and gently ran his mouth over hers. When he could take it no more, he gave her lip a tiny lick.

She moaned softly, and his control snapped. He claimed her lips in a kiss meant to prove the depth of the passion between them. He wasn't prepared when her lips parted, but he didn't waste any time slipping his tongue inside her mouth.

Her body sagged against his. Ewan's arms instantly came around her, molding her to his chest as he pushed her against the door. His body hungered for more of her enticing body.

She returned his kisses with as much ardor as he had expected. What he hadn't anticipated was his body's instant, and ravenous, response. The longing, the craving, consumed him, demanding he take her and make her his own.

He lifted her in his arms and carried her to his bed, a place he wanted to keep her for the next fortnight. Once he reached the bed, he let her feet drop to the ground, and he broke the kiss.

Her lips were swollen and her breathing ragged as her lids lifted. She stared up at him with confusion and pleasure mixing in the depths of her amber eyes. "What have you done to me?"

"I've awoke the woman inside you."

He didn't give her time to speak as he began to undress her at his leisure. He kissed and licked each expanse of creamy skin that he exposed. Her skin was as soft as down, as smooth as the sea on a calm day.

His hands caressed her silky skin, learning the curves and

contours of her delicious body. He inhaled the clean, passionate scent of her and groaned as his balls tightened.

Desire, hot and true, burned through him like lightning. His hunger for her overwhelmed him, making his hands shake as he pulled her gown over her head and tossed it aside. When she was finally bared to him, he sat on the bed and pulled her between his legs.

"By the saints, you have a magnificent body," he whispered as his gaze raked from her rosy-tipped nipples to the swell of her hips and the patch of dark blond curls that hid her sex.

He swallowed and reined in the lust that threatened to drown him. His hands moved leisurely down her sides, enjoying the simple feel of her. He glanced at her face to find her eyes closed and her lips parted, her chest rising and falling rapidly. His cock jumped, eager to bury inside her hot, slick sex.

He cupped her breasts, lightly skimming her nipples with his thumbs. She sucked in a breath and put her hands on his shoulders to stay upright. A soft moan passed her full lips as her head fell back and her hair tickled his legs.

Never had just touching a woman left him with such a burning need before. He bit back a moan as her nipples hardened before his eyes. Unable to wait a moment longer, he covered a nipple with his lips, swirling his tongue around the tiny bud and suckling it deep in his mouth.

She gave a breathy cry and sagged against him. Ewan steadied her, unwilling to release her for even a heartbeat. He moved to her other nipple and glanced at her as he flicked his tongue over the bud. Her pupils dilated as she watched him, and her nails dug into his shoulders.

It was nearly too much for him. His hunger turned into a ravenous craving he feared might never be quenched.

Kate couldn't breathe. Flames of desire licked her body as Ewan laved her breasts while his hands stroked her back and bottom. Just his touch was enough to make her crave more, but when his mouth began a delightful journey over her skin with his kisses and licks, she came undone.

Her body was no longer her own. She couldn't control her reaction to him, and all thought fled except one—Ewan. All she wanted was for him to continue touching her, awakening her. The passion and pleasure swirling through her were too much to bear and impossible to ignore.

Her breasts swelled and her nipples ached as he continued to feast upon her breasts. She had never known they could be so sensitive. Ewan gently bit down on her nipple and her sex throbbed in response. Her hands moved to thread into his mane of raven locks, holding him close so he didn't stop the exquisite torture.

Chills raced across her skin in stark contrast to the blood that pumped like fire in her veins. She couldn't remember why she hadn't wanted him to touch her. Not once did it ever enter her mind to ask him to stop. It felt too glorious to think of walking away.

And she wanted to see what he would do to her next.

She arched her back, silently begging him to continue the wonderful agony. Unable to help herself, she ground her hips against his rock hard chest and felt a bolt of desire spear through her.

Suddenly, he wrapped his arms around her waist and lifted her to place her on the bed. The cool air of the chamber met her nipples and caused her to hiss in a breath, but it was Ewan's desire filled gaze on her sex that made her squeeze her legs together in anticipation. She bit back a moan and watched hungrily as he pulled off his boots and unclasped the brooch over his heart that held his kilt.

The tartan fell in a whoosh to his feet. Kate rose up on her elbows when he jerked his shirt over his head. His body rippled with muscles and a commanding power that even a blind woman would see.

She couldn't wait to run her hands over his wide shoulders and solid arms and chest. But it was his cock, thick and hard, that made desire blur her vision and her sex grow damp.

He placed his hands on the bed near her feet and crawled over her until he was even with her face. Then he settled his weight atop her and took her lips in a slow, sensual kiss that melted any resistance she might have had.

His hands were everywhere, touching every inch of her skin as if he were memorizing her. Kate took advantage and let her own hands roam over his broad back and shoulders. His muscles moved and bunched under her hands, reminding her of his power.

The feel of his rod pressed against her belly spurred her longing. She wanted him inside her to quench the growing hunger, but she could tell by his leisurely kisses that he had other plans.

His mouth moved down her throat and across her chest to the valley between her breasts. Breathing became impossible when he began to thumb her nipples while his hot mouth continued its trail down her body. Raw desire ripped through her and caused her to grind her hips against him as her need grew.

A moan she wasn't able to stop escaped her lips. He lifted his head to give her a sly, devilish grin. He knew exactly what he was doing to her, and God help her, she loved every moment of it.

His kissed down her stomach to her navel, which his tongue circled before he moved to her hips. He nipped the skin over her hip bone and then ran his hot tongue over it.

Pleasure consumed her, intense and vibrant. There was no turning back now, not that there ever had been. She wanted to know what he would do next, but at the same time, she was frightened of what she might feel.

When his hand covered her sex, she couldn't stop herself from grinding into his palm. She gasped at the exquisite longing that exploded through her.

Kate wanted more. All she wanted was the wonderful feelings inside her to continue. And she wanted Ewan.

Her hands dug into the bed coverings when he slipped a finger inside her. His finger moved within her, stroking her expertly. Desire began to tighten inside her, building with each touch, each kiss.

Suddenly, he rose over her. She gave a startled cry when he removed his hand from between her legs. Nothing had ever felt so wonderful, and she wasn't ready for it to end.

"Kate," he murmured and captured her gaze.

She saw the raw hunger, the passion, in his gaze. Her stomach flipped at the knowledge that it was for her. Ewan, a stranger and her husband, desired her. It was there for her to see . . . and accept.

His cock rubbed against her sensitive sex. Ripples of pleasure washed over her. Her back arched, searching for something that could quench the ache inside her. The tip of his cock found her entrance. Kate lifted her legs, and he slipped inside her. He moaned as his eyes closed, his arms shaking.

Kate waited for the pain that always came when she'd been forced in the marriage bed, but this time there was the most wonderful sensation. She let the tension drain from her body as Ewan continued the rocking of his hips until he was buried to the root.

He moved her leg until it was wrapped around his waist, and she hurried to shift the other since it brought him farther inside her. When he began to thrust, Kate gasped at the spike of pleasure.

His thrusts grew faster, deeper, until all Kate could do was hold on to him as he showed her what it meant to be loved by a Highlander.

The desire that had begun to build with his first kiss tightened, pulling her toward something. And then she shattered.

She closed her eyes as her breath locked in her lungs and bright lights popped behind her eyelids. She dug her fingers into Ewan's arms as her body convulsed and took her spiraling down an abyss of unimaginable pleasure.

As the last of her climax drained away, she felt him plunging deep inside her, prolonging her orgasm. He gave a final thrust that touched her womb before he threw back his head with a shout as his seed emptied inside her.

Kate watched him, amazed that he had found the same pleasure she had. She held him, her arms wrapped around his wide shoulders, when he fell atop her. His breathing was ragged, hoarse, and his heart thumped loudly against her chest.

For several moments they stayed as they were. With her body sated, her eyes drifted close. The peace that surrounded her was amazing. It was as if the world had suddenly righted and everything was as it should be.

Then Ewan rose up on his hands and stared down at her.

His brow furrowed as he regarded her a moment, as if he wanted to say something. He must have thought better of it, because he rolled onto his back with a sigh.

Kate stared at the canopy as the beautiful feelings began to fade away and reality returned. She wasn't sure if she should leave. This was her bedchamber as well, but only a few moments ago she had asked for an annulment.

By the saints, what he must think of her. Kate decided it was best if she did leave. She needed to think, and she couldn't do that with Ewan near her. Just as she rose to leave, Ewan reached over and pulled her against him.

For a moment she thought about refusing, but his heat stilled her. She had never slept with a man nor had one hold her as Ewan did. She quite liked resting her head on his chest and listening to the rhythmic beat of his heart.

She was also stunned. Stunned that he had wanted her after

declaring she wasn't the bride he paid for, and astonished because he had taken her to his bed and shown her the most wonderful experience of her life.

To say Ewan was a conundrum was putting it mildly. She didn't want a husband, but she couldn't ignore that her body had ignited under his expert hands and mouth. She wondered how it would be the next time they made love.

There can't be a next time, not if you want the annulment.

But how could she refuse such marvelous and delectable yearnings of her body when she knew the outcome would be pleasure beyond her wildest imaginings?

And how, in the name of all that was holy, did she get herself in such a predicament?

Ewan ran his fingers over Kate's back as he thought of their lovemaking. The fire he'd seen in her had told him sex would be good. He hadn't expected it to be great—possibly the best he had ever had. That in itself gave him pause.

She had touched him in a way no other woman had. Not once had she held back. She had opened herself to him, and in doing so, had made his climax marvelous. Even afterward, when he usually preferred to be alone, he found himself needing to hold her.

And to make matters worse, he knew deep in his bones that each time he bedded Kate it would only get better.

She was a passionate woman, in and out of the bed. He had thought he wanted a docile wife, but now he knew he would have been bored with such a woman. With Kate by his side, she would make his days interesting, and their passion would never wane.

He looked down to find her sleeping contentedly in his arms. She might have given in to his seduction, but that didn't mean she would understand why he would no longer entertain the idea of an annulment. Despite her previous marriages, no man had shown her the joys of sex.

Although he would have preferred to have initiated her to sex, he was content to be the one to begin her instructions in the joy of sex. He smiled as he thought of all the ways he could take Kate.

It was up to Ewan to show her what their life could be like. He, for one, was up for the challenge. Already his cock hardened, wanting more of her. He had become addicted to her with just one intoxicating, delicious taste.

He shifted his hips and groaned as his desire grew. He was like a lad after his first roll in the hay, she excited him so much. There was nothing Kate could say to disprove that she had enjoyed what he had done to her. Her scream of pleasure still echoed in his head. It had been the feel of her sex clenching around him that had made him peak.

If he had to keep Kate in his bed for a fortnight to prove they were meant to be together, he would. There was nothing she could say or do that would make him give her the annulment. She was his now.

He smiled as he began to plan the complete seduction of his wife.

5

Ewan awoke to find himself curved around his wife's delicious body and his rod pressed into her back. His lips lifted in a grin when he discovered his hand held one of her breasts.

He loosed his hold and let his thumb circle her nipple until it puckered, straining against him. Then, he pinched it. She stirred, a soft moan passing through her lips. His cock jumped as his hunger grew. He licked his lips as he caressed down her side and over the swell of her hip.

His fingers brushed her sex and his balls tightened. He took her leg and gently moved it atop his so he could have access to her slick heat. Once she was settled, he ran his fingers through her curls to her sex. He fondled her slowly, tenderly, until she became damp and his fingers glistened with her moisture.

His breathing grew harsh as his cock thickened, the longing for her drowning out everything. All his life he had looked to find a woman who could make his blood sing. He'd finally found her.

When he realized how he had almost let her slip through his

fingers, his chest ached as though an iron band had wrapped around him. But now that he knew, he wasn't going to make that mistake.

He slipped a finger inside her tight, hot sheath. She clenched around him, and he was unable to hold back a moan of pleasure. In and out his finger moved, stroking her. After a moment, he added a second finger. Her back arched and her hips ground against his rod. Her chest heaved with her ragged breaths, and her soft moans only spurred his desire.

When he could take it no more, Ewan shifted his hips until the tip of his cock met her damp flesh. He closed his eyes and pushed inside of her. She moaned low in her throat and gripped his hand. Finally, she was awake.

"Ewan," she said with a breathless sigh.

His hand moved to the pearl hidden in her curls, and he swirled his finger around it. "Shh. Don't think, just feel."

He didn't give her time to answer before he began to thrust. Her sighs became little cries of pleasure as he worked her pearl with his finger and continued to plunge inside of her with long, hard strokes.

His climax was close, but he refused to peak before Kate. When she began to meet each of his thrusts with her own, he gripped her pearl between two fingers and gave it a gentle squeeze.

A scream tore from her throat as her orgasm claimed her. The feel of her body clenching around his cock pushed him over the edge again. He was blinded by the force of his climax. Ewan gripped her hip and plunged deep within her, his seed pouring from him.

He knew that if he couldn't convince Kate with words that she belonged with him, he would tie her to the bed and make love to her until she admitted he was right.

For several moments, neither moved. He loosened his hold

on her and let out a deep breath. Just before he gave into sleep, her soft voice reached him.

"This changes nothing."

Ewan sighed and turned her toward him. With his thumb on her chin, he moved her face until her amber gaze was locked with his. "This changes everything. You canna tell me that you deny the passion between us."

"Just because you are the first man to bring my body such . . . pleasure . . . doesn't mean we should spend our lives together."

He knew he could demand her silence on it. It was his right as her husband, but he recognized the fiery spirit within her. To break her would break the fire that drove him wild. He had no wish to do that.

"You doona think I can change your mind on the matter?"

"Nay."

He smiled at her sure manner. "Give me a month to prove otherwise."

"A month is too long. No one will give us an annulment after a month. A week?"

"Not nearly long enough." He dislodged a strand of her hair that was caught in her lashes. "Give me a fortnight."

"Done."

He smiled. She had unknowingly given him exactly what he wanted. He hadn't been fool enough to think she would give him a month.

Her gaze narrowed suspiciously. "You smile as if you've already won."

"Nay. I see a woman who loves to be pleasured, and I intend to make sure you are pleasured thoroughly. And often."

She blew out a breath and shrugged. "Just because I like what you do to me in bed doesn't mean I will want to spend the rest of my life with you."

Ewan was dangerously close to losing his temper. His wife was more than stubborn. He couldn't understand why she didn't see what was between them. After having two husbands she hated, he had expected her to know that the pleasure and desire with him was different. Lasting.

"Suppose I agree to the annulment, what will you do? Return to your father and let him force you into another marriage?"

"Never," she all but spat. "I want to be in charge of my own destiny."

He leaned on his elbow and rested his head on his hand. "Few women are in charge of their own lives, Kate. Men rule the world, and in doing so, we rule you."

"I know that all too well. I'll enter into a convent once you annul the marriage," she retorted sharply. "No man will rule me there, and I'll be safer inside those holy walls than here where there are constant battles between clans."

He hid his grin at her assurance that he would give her what she wanted. "You would become accustomed to the Highlanders' way of life. Somehow, I doona think you'll find life as a nun as appealing as you might think."

" 'Tis better than being a man's chattel. I would make my own decisions."

"Nay, you wouldna. You would answer to the mother superior, doing her bidding just as you would your husband's."

He could tell by the way her brow furrowed that she hadn't thought of that possibility. Her teeth worried her bottom lip as she thought over his words.

If he were a gentleman, he would let the matter rest, but Ewan hadn't become such a powerful laird by being a gentleman. "At least with me, you would get some say. And I would give you the children you want."

"How do I know you aren't lying? You could be saying this just so you wouldn't have to hunt for another wife."

"You doona." He shrugged a shoulder. "In truth, lass, your best alternative is staying here as my wife. If you think over it carefully, you'll see I'm right."

She rolled over and rose from the bed before padding barefoot around to his side, where she reached for her clothes. He didn't want her hiding her magnificent body from him, but it had gotten significantly cooler in the chamber since the fire had died.

Once she was dressed, she turned and faced him. "Is it that you don't want to admit a mistake was made? That I'm the wrong woman for you?"

"Of course not." He sat up, waiting for her next barb.

"You're a handsome man. You could easily find another wife."

He grinned then. "You think me handsome?"

She shrugged but didn't comment.

"In truth, Kate, I could find another wife. However, I'm nay so stubborn that I would walk away from a woman that has as much passion for life as she does in bed."

She turned her back to him and moved to the hearth where she stroked the fire to life once more.

Though Ewan was loath to leave her, there were things he needed to see to. The most important one was to make sure Bridget was no longer in the castle. She could only mean trouble for him. Since he was trying to convince Kate to forget the annulment, the last thing he needed was a former lover causing a bigger rift. Not to mention Bridget had to be punished for her lie.

He rose from the bed and quickly dressed. The air helped to cool his desire and focus his attention on the plan he had for Kate. When he finished fastening the brooch over his heart, he found his wife watching him.

"They say you are a formidable and influential laird."

He gave a slight nod of his head.

"A man in your position shouldn't have so quickly and easily chosen a wife."

Ewan walked to stand in front of her. He grasped a strand of her hair and rubbed his fingers over the silken locks. "I did have my choice of women. Many families wanted to align themselves with me, but none of those women interested me."

She glanced down. "Then you saw my sister."

"Aye. I was in the Lowlands seeing King James. Your sister was pretty and not connected to any Highland family. A perfect solution for me."

She nodded and turned her head to the window. " 'Tis dawn."

He paused at how vulnerable she looked. Her voice was low and her eyes troubled, as if she wasn't sure she was happy at how they had spent the last few hours.

Ewan couldn't imagine how angry he would be if he were in her shoes. Three husbands she had been forced to wed. No wonder she wanted her freedom so desperately.

'Twas too bad he wouldn't be able to give it to her.

"I'll have Beth fetch you when 'tis time to break our fast."

She didn't spare him a glance as he left the chamber.

When the door closed behind Ewan, Kate let out a shaky breath and bowed her head. He was right. Only a fool would deny the deep attraction between them, but she wanted her freedom so desperately she was willing to sacrifice such passion for it.

Kate wished the yearnings in her body would stop. It had been a huge relief when Ewan had left the chamber. Being so close to him made her remember how it felt to have his hands and mouth on her, and how her body came alive under his hands. The desire overwhelmed her, made her forget everything but feeling more of the ecstasy Ewan's touch promised.

How could one man do that to her?

Surely there would be other men whose mere touch could make her cry out with pleasure. It was a chance she was willing to take. Just for once, she wanted to make her own decisions.

Her father's betrayal was a wound that might not ever heal. Always she'd been a good daughter, never arguing either time he had sent her off to marry. But this time, it had been too much.

She had begged him to leave her be after her second marriage. When he had told her of Ewan, she had railed against him, shouting things at him a daughter should never say to her father.

After the wedding he'd told her the real reason. He had found her sister a very prosperous match with an Englishman. It was a match that would align their family with the crown, just as her marriage to the Highlander would align them in another way. She had been too angry then to argue more.

Kate pushed thoughts of her father from her mind. Being angry at him would not solve her current problem. She had no doubt she could convince Ewan to give her the annulment. After all, she wasn't the bride he had paid for.

Though, if he ever found out her sister had gone to another man, Ewan would never agree to release her from their marriage. She hated secrets, but she didn't have a choice. Not this time.

He had asked for a fortnight in which to prove she wanted his body. There was no need for it since she had craved his body from the first touch of his lips. The fact he had brought her such exquisite bliss made her yearn for him even more.

But she could never tell him.

Her eyes closed on a moan as her sex clenched at the memory of his cock sliding in and out of her. Hesitantly, her hand covered her breast. Beneath her hand, her nipple grew hard and ached for Ewan's mouth.

Desire surged through her and centered at her sex, which

had begun to throb in earnest. She wrapped her arms around her middle and bent forward. But nothing she did made the hunger go away. Ewan had turned her into a wanton in one afternoon.

And God help her, she loved it.

6

By the time Beth came for her, Kate had managed to get herself under control, though the desire never went away. With her hair braided and falling in one thick plait down her back, Kate walked to the great hall to find every seat filled.

She stood at the base of the stairs and let her gaze wander the hall as laughter and conversations deafened her. A sea of Mac-Donald plaid worn by every man, woman, and child only made her stand out as a stranger even more. Ewan might have taken her to his bed, but he hadn't given her a tartan of his clan claiming her as his wife.

I thought you didn't want to be his wife?

She didn't, but as long as she was, he should have welcomed her.

Kate told herself she wasn't hurt by it, that it merely proved he was still considering their annulment. She wouldn't feel comfortable wearing the tartan anyway, not when she planned to leave in a fortnight—sooner if she were able.

She hid her hands in her skirts so no one would see how they shook. How she hated meeting new people, especially a large crowd that would be staring at her, analyzing everything about her. How could she have forgotten that dining in the great hall would mean eating in front of nearly the entire Mac-Donald clan?

Because Ewan had well and truly bedded you.

It was a disturbing fact that she hadn't remembered much of anything while in his arms. He could have asked her for eternity, and she would have given it to him. A man shouldn't have that kind of command over a woman's body.

Her gaze shifted to the dais. She found Ewan reclining in his chair with a small smile on his too-handsome face as he watched his people. His love for his clan was evident in his blue gaze.

As for the clan, their happiness was obvious, stating again what a powerful and true leader Ewan was. The men respected him and the women admired him. It would take a special kind of woman to be able to stand by his side. Something she certainly wasn't.

It was then she realized eating in the great hall would be a disaster. Ewan would introduce her formally as his wife, which would make their annulment that much more difficult for him.

But you want him to acknowledge you.

Kate didn't know what she wanted anymore. Ewan had confused everything by making love to her. She should have been stronger and turned him away. She should have known what his touch would do to her.

You did know.

She turned and made her way back up the stairs to the next floor and the balcony that overlooked the hall. She quite liked her vantage point where she could look down at the clan without them noticing her, and if she stayed in the shadows, not even Ewan would be able to find her. She had no doubt he would send someone to look for her soon. Until then, she was content to stay as she was.

Ewan's bark of laughter made her look to see what had caused such humor. She spotted two lads running around the great hall avoiding one of the servants giving chase and scolding them for getting into the kitchen and the sweetmeats. The entire hall erupted in laughter, all except for the lads' mothers who caught them before they could escape.

Kate chuckled at the scene. The laughter had put her at ease, erasing some of her fears. Maybe she could dine with Ewan. She was hungry, and it would give her more time to speak of the annulment without worrying if he would seduce her again. She turned to the stairs when a woman with dark hair stepped in front of her.

"So, ye think ye've won," the woman snarled, transforming her beautiful face into nastiness.

Not to be cowed, Kate raised her brows. "Do I know you?"

"I'm Bridget." When Kate didn't respond, the woman continued. "I was supposed to be his wife."

Kate crossed her arms over her chest and studied Ewan's would-be wife, instantly disliking the woman for trying to take her place.

I thought you didn't want Ewan as a husband.

She didn't want Ewan, but for now, he was hers. "Apparently, Ewan thought differently or he would never have looked outside the clan for a wife."

"I'll kill you," Bridget screamed and flew at her.

Just before she reached Kate, something jerked Bridget to a stop.

"What in the name of all that's holy are you doing?" Ewan bellowed at Bridget. "I told you to stay out of the castle now that I have a wife."

Kate needed an outlet for her anger, and the fact that Ewan and Bridget had been together only spurred her rage. She stepped toward Ewan and put her hand on his arm. "I'll take care of her."

Ewan's blue gaze swung to her. "You doona know what she's capable of."

"Maybe, but I do know what kind of woman she is. Release her."

For a moment, she didn't think Ewan would do as she asked, but then he released Bridget.

Bridget immediately launched herself at Kate again. Kate ducked the nails aimed at her face and grabbed hold of Bridget's long dark hair. She pushed Bridget to her knees and yanked her face up to look at her.

"Your laird told you not to come back to the castle. I suggest you do as he has commanded, because if I see you in the castle again, I will cut off your hair."

Bridget's eyes grew huge with fear and fury. To cut off a woman's hair was a sign she had been disgraced. "Ye wouldna dare. My laird would never allow it."

Ewan stepped toward her. "I'll cut it off now, Bridget, and put all questions to rest."

Her gaze moved from Kate to Ewan. Reluctantly, she nodded. Kate released her, and two men she hadn't seen stepped forward and took Bridget by her arms to lead her from the castle. It was then Kate realized how quiet the great hall had become. She didn't need to look over the railing to know that everyone watched her.

Kate fisted her hands and drew in a deep breath. She wasn't sure what had come over her with Bridget. It couldn't possibly have been jealousy of the woman. Ewan had chosen her for his wife, not Bridget.

But he didn't.

Nay, he hadn't chosen her. He had chosen her beautiful, graceful sister. Why then did Kate forget that, and why did she feel the need to make it known Ewan was hers? Twice in his bed and she couldn't think straight.

"You've got quite a temper." Ewan moved in front of her,

one side of his mouth lifted in a grin. "Are you sure there are no Highlanders in your family?"

Kate couldn't stop the smile that pulled at her lips. "Thank you for doing as I asked. It felt good to be able to handle Bridget myself."

"Everyone needs to know you're their mistress."

"For the next fortnight at least."

He ignored her remark and offered her his arm. "I've been waiting for you. Are you hungry?"

"Famished."

They descended the stairs to the hall and walked to the dais. Kate didn't need to look around to know all eyes were on her. It made her distinctly uncomfortable, but she had to admit she would have been as curious in their place.

Ewan sat her beside Rory and took the chair at her right while an older man sat on Ewan's other side. Food was served as soon as Ewan gave a nod to the servants.

The meal was full of strange dishes that Kate had never sampled before, but she tried them all and discovered she liked most of them. The noise in the hall grew once more as the food was served. Once most had their attention on their platters instead of her, it was easy for Kate to relax and enjoy her meal.

Ewan leaned close, his breath brushing her ear. "My clan watches you. They're curious about my new lady."

She shivered and felt her breasts grow heavy as his warm breath caressed her neck. She swallowed and licked her suddenly dry lips. *His lady.* It had a nice ring to it, but not enough to throw away her chance at freedom.

"If you doona want me to haul you over my shoulder and take you to our chamber to make love, you'll remove that look." His voice was low and thick with emotion.

She glanced at him to see his eyes smoldering. "What look?"

"The look that says you're remembering my hands on you. That you want me again."

She could deny it. But she didn't want to, not when her body yearned for him so. "Would you?"

"What?"

"Take me over your shoulder?"

His eyes darkened with desire. "In a heartbeat, lass."

Could he really want her that desperately? Was he lying about the passion between them? What was it about him that made her blood heat and her heart pound in her chest?

Answers to those questions no longer mattered. All she wanted was to have his skin next to hers, his rod filling her, and his incredible mouth kissing her.

Her lips parted and moisture gathered between her legs just thinking of how he might take her next.

"You want me," he said.

It wasn't a question. "I want you."

He grinned and reached for her hand. She didn't hesitate when he stood and pulled her up beside him. Her gaze never left his as he walked her to the stairs.

By the time they reached his chamber, her body shook with the anticipation of his touch. Her heart raced and her body hungered for one man—Ewan. She didn't try to deny it or even understand it.

He barred the door behind them then pulled her against his chest. She raised her face to his, desperate for his kiss. His hands cupped either side of her face, caressing her skin, while his gaze roamed slowly over her face.

Finally, his head bent to claim her lips. Kate rose up on her toes and wrapped her arms around him as his mouth slanted over hers. His kiss was long and slow, burning her with his hunger and intensity.

Kate let her hands wander down his back to his firm bottom. A low moan vibrated through him before his kiss turned fierce, heated. He crushed her to him and backed her against the door before lifting her. He wrapped her legs around his waist and ground his hard cock against her aching sex.

She sunk her nails into his back, her need swallowing her. She gasped, the hunger so great it frightened her. Her head fell back against the door and his mouth trailed down her throat, kissing and nipping her delicate skin.

When he yanked at her skirts, Kate was all too ready to aid him. She pulled them up around her waist as he reached down and jerked up his kilt. Excitement made them rush and fumble with the clothes, but once the tip of his cock brushed against her damp sex, clothes no longer mattered.

He entered her with aching slowness. "Please," she begged. "I need you, Ewan."

"You have me."

She shook her head. "Nay. All of you. I need all of you."

"Then take me." His lips kissed her jaw before he filled her. Then he stilled.

Kate was delirious. She tried to move her hips, but Ewan's grip was strong as he held her immobile. When he pulled out of her with the same leisure as he had entered her, she thought she might die from desire.

"Ewan. Please," she begged.

He rotated his hips so his cock rubbed against her swollen flesh, igniting her when he grazed her pearl. She held his shoulders, her body quivering with each touch. Surely such pleasure was a sin.

Then he plunged inside of her, his thrusts deep and hard. Kate sank her nails into him. Desire coiled tightly, and all too soon, she felt herself reaching her climax. A heartbeat later, she shouted his name as she succumbed to the delicious pleasure.

With each thrust, he extended her orgasm, taking her to unbelievable heights of joy. It took a while for her to come down from such a high. She laid her head on his shoulder and dimly felt him move before she realized he hadn't peaked. Ewan pulled out of her as he walked to the bed and laid her upon it before he began to undress her.

"What are you doing?"

He gave her a wink full of wicked promise. "What does it look like?"

She smiled and helped him. While she was with him for the fortnight, there was no need for her to refuse the exceptional satisfaction he could provide her. Besides, she told herself, she would have no trouble walking away from him when the time came. Pleasure was nice, but it wasn't everything.

Once she was naked, he hurried to remove his own clothes, but when she opened her arms for him, he turned on his heel and walked away.

Kate rose on her elbows and saw the tub she had used earlier sitting before the fire with ribbons of steam rising from the water within. He was still hard, still wet from being inside her.

He glanced at her before stepping into the tub. "Care to join me?"

Kate sat up and eyed the tub and Ewan. To her utter dismay, her body wanted more of him. Again. Thrice already she'd had him, but she wanted more. What had he done to her? And did it really matter?

She swung her legs over the bed and padded across the cold stones to the rug next to the tub. He held out his hand, silently waiting. With chills racing over her skin, Kate accepted his hand and stepped into the water.

A sigh escaped her as she sank to her chin. Her eyes closed and she leaned her head against the edge. She wasn't surprised to feel Ewan's hands on her legs, his fingers caressing her. He ran his hands up her calves to her knees and nudged her legs apart. Once she complied, he moved her feet on either side of him.

She cracked open an eye and watched as he lathered the soap between his hands and lifted one leg to slowly wash her. Kate moaned contentedly, loving the feel of his hands on her and the way he knew just where to touch her.

He repeated it again on her other leg before lowering it into the tub. The water moved around her as he leaned forward, his hands caressing up her thigh to the juncture of her legs.

Her breath lodged in her throat as he came close to touching her aching, swollen sex. Again and again his fingers moved near her, teasing and tempting her. Her sex clenched, ready to feel him inside her once more.

"Ewan," she murmured when it became too much to bear.

"What do you want?"

She licked her lips and gripped the side of the tub. "I want you to touch me."

As soon as the words left her mouth, his hand cupped her sex. She burned for his touch, desperate to ease the growing ache inside of her. But Ewan had other ideas.

He used his finger to circle her heated flesh before easing the tip of his finger inside her. She shifted her hips, seeking more of him, but he held her still.

Her eyes opened when his hands left her. He lathered the soap before he reached for her. His hands gently moved over her sex, using the soap to bathe her.

Kate gasped when he pushed a finger inside of her and swirled it around. Her hips began to move against him while the water lapped against her breasts. Her nipples, already hardened by the chill, ached with the touch of the water.

His other hand cupped her breast and began to massage it. She moaned at the onslaught of desire that shot through her. Suddenly, his finger pulled out of her to caress her with the barest of touches across her pearl while he pinched her nipple with the other hand to mix pleasure with pain. Her sex pulsed with need from the delicious torture.

"Ewan," she cried out, ready to climax.

Instantly, his hands were gone. She whimpered as her sex clenched. He pulled her atop him so that his cock rested against her throbbing flesh. His blue eyes were ablaze with desire, and his breathing was as strained as hers. Her eyes rolled shut when he cupped her breasts and began to thumb her nipples into tight peaks.

She moved her hips in response and moaned at the feel of his rod against her. She reached her hand between them and stroked his cock, loving the feel of how smooth and hot he was.

He groaned and thrust upward in her hand. As much as she wanted to explore more of him, her body needed release. Next time she would be sure to have her turn discovering his glorious body.

She rose up on her knees and moved over his rod. Her gaze met his as she slowly lowered herself onto him. He pinched her nipples before he leaned up and began to suckle them.

Kate dropped her head back, unable to stand the pleasure a moment more. She moved her hips and cried out at the sensations that shot through her. She quickly set a tempo. The water splashed over the sides of the tub as she braced her hands on his chest and he held her hips, rocking her against him.

"Kate," he rasped.

She barely heard him as her climax claimed her. It was just a heartbeat later that he bellowed and plunged deep before he spilled his seed.

For several moments they stared at each other, lost in the pleasure of their bodies. Each time she made love to him was a different experience, stirring her in ways she didn't know were possible. And though her body was sore from his attention, she couldn't wait until he took her again.

"You're insatiable," he whispered as he brought her head down for a soft kiss.

"As are you."

He chuckled. "Let us bathe before the water turns cold."

Kate hurried to wash and dry before making a dash for the bed. All she wanted to do was warm up before she put on her clothes, but she should have known Ewan wouldn't allow her to retrieve her clothes so soon.

7

Ewan lifted the covers and crawled in beside Kate. She had surprised him with her eagerness to delve into their passion, and he was most thankful that she had. He had been prepared for another seduction, but when her gaze had filled with desire, all he had wanted to do was get her out of the great hall and into his chamber where he could explore more of her beautiful, amazing body.

No woman had ever touched him as deeply as Kate, and she seemed to do it without even trying. He could spend the rest of his life wondering what it was about her that drew him to her, but he was content simply to have found her. There was no use questioning it, not when he needed to convince her to stay with him willingly. He would force her if necessary. She was his wife, after all, but he didn't want to start off their marriage with her hating him.

He rolled onto his side and stared at her. "How many kids do you want?"

She laughed at his question, then blinked and licked her lips.

"I don't know. I haven't really thought about an exact number. It has always been just my sister and me. We were five summers apart, so we were never as close as some siblings."

"A dozen then?"

She grinned and shrugged as she turned to face him. "Maybe. Would that be too many? I just wanted as many children as God decided I should have."

"And if we've already started?" He watched her smile soften and her eyes get a faraway look in them.

"I don't know," she answered. "I hadn't thought of it. I wasn't able to conceive with my previous husbands."

Ewan couldn't help but be thankful for that, because it had allowed him to find her. "Maybe it just wasna your time, Kate. Maybe you needed to find the right husband."

"Will you force me to stay if I am carrying your child?"

He clenched his jaw. His immediate answer was yes, but he knew that wouldn't bring her around to his way of thinking. "I married because I need an heir, Kate. I would ask that you stay until the child was delivered."

"And then you would take my child?"

"Our child," he corrected her. "I could provide a life for the child, whereas you couldna. A convent wouldna allow you to bring the child with you."

Her gaze lowered. "I hadn't thought of that. You're right, of course. The child would need to stay with you. I know you would look after him."

With as many times as they had made love, and the many times Ewan planned to take her, it would be a miracle if she didn't conceive. "When will you know?"

Her amber gaze met his. "Next week."

Ewan held in his sigh. He had hoped it would be longer than their agreed fortnight to keep her near him that much longer. It seemed fate had conspired against him.

"And you?" she asked. "Do you want just the one heir?"

He paused at her question, unsure of how to answer since he had never thought of it. His title demanded an heir, and though he liked children, he had never wanted one the way a woman did. "It is my duty to marry and supply an heir for the clan. I haven't thought about children other than that."

"I don't think men give much thought to children at all unless it suits them. For women forced into marriages they don't want, the children grant them the opportunity to experience love in ways that would otherwise not be given to them." She tucked her hand beneath her cheek when she finished.

"So you don't think a man could love his wife?"

"Nay," she answered confidently. "Commoners are allowed to marry for love, but for the nobility, we don't have that luxury. We marry for wealth or power and nothing else."

"Love may not be an option for us," he said and scooted closer to her. "But great sex is."

He tugged the covers down to her waist and flicked his tongue over her nipple. She moaned and threaded her fingers in his hair.

"Aye. There is that," she murmured.

He lifted the blankets away from her body and moved over her, settling between her silky thighs. Her feet touched his lower back before sliding down his buttocks and the backs of his legs.

His lips covered a nipple and he ran his tongue over the tiny bud while his hand played with her breast. He scraped his teeth over her nipple, causing her to arch her back and dig her hands into the blankets. She moaned and whispered his name.

How he loved her response to him. Her breasts were incredibly sensitive. A mere touch could make her moan. He moved to her other nipple, suckling and teasing it until she cried out and ground her hips against him.

He kissed the valley between her breasts and began to move down her chest when she suddenly rose up and pushed him onto his back.

" 'Tis my turn at your body," she whispered and crawled on her hands and knees between his legs.

Ewan's breath locked in his lungs at her words. Excitement poured through him with the knowledge that she wanted to touch him. He was powerless to do anything other than look at her parted lips and eyes filled with desire.

Her breasts swayed as she moved. He longed to reach up and tweak her nipple, but he yearned more to know what she would do to his body. His cock swelled in anticipation, delighted to feel her touch.

She knelt between his legs and ran her hands over his chest and stomach before leaning forward and kissing his chest. He sucked in a breath when her breasts rubbed against him, sending his blood shooting like fire through him.

A few women had touched him thus, but only after he had asked them. None had done it on their own, which is what kept Ewan on his back and his hands fisted in the blankets instead of burying himself deep inside her.

His breath hissed through his teeth when her hands moved down his thighs. His cock jumped, yearning for her touch like the grass yearns for the sun.

She sat up and slowly unbraided her hair to let the dark blond locks fall around her shoulders. When she bent forward, the brush of her hair on his rod and balls sent a tremor rushing through him.

Her lips continued to tease and torment as she moved down his chest. Meanwhile, her hands had stopped at his hips, just inches from his straining cock. He moaned when her hand finally closed over his rod. Breathlessly, he waited, his body shaking from the effort to keep his hands off her.

With her mouth moving closer and closer to his cock, Ewan found it impossible to breathe. Her breast touched his rod, and he lifted his hips, hanging onto his control by a ribbon.

Her hair hid her face from his view, but he didn't need to see her to know what she was doing to him. Her hot breath fanned his cock, and she teased him with the barest touch of her lips while one hand stroked him and her other cupped his sac, rolling his balls in her hand.

And then she took him in her mouth.

Ewan cried out her name as the pleasure consumed him. Her hot tongue swirled around the tip of his rod before she took him deep in her mouth, sucking him.

It was too much. He had to touch her, had to feel her heat until they both shouted with their climaxes. Ewan sat up and reached for her.

"Wait. I'm not done."

"Trust me," he said with a groan as he felt the dampness betwixt her legs.

When she was straddled over his chest, her back to him, he lay down and reached for her hips to pull her toward his mouth.

"Have your way with me," he murmured, "while I have my way with you."

He licked her sex before swirling his tongue over her pearl, teasing her until she was panting.

"I . . . I cannot concentrate," she whispered.

"Aye, lass, you can."

He parted her sex with his hands and pushed a finger inside of her as her mouth once more covered his cock. He closed his eyes at the delicious torture her mouth and hands brought him. The deeper she sucked him in her mouth, the faster his tongue moved over her pearl. The more she played with his sac the deeper his finger went inside her.

Her soft cries filled the chamber to mix with his moans. Her hand around his cock gave a little squeeze before she began to move it up and down his length.

Ewan stiffened as he felt his orgasm building. He added a second finger to the first and began to thrust faster into her, stroking the raised spot inside her that would give her the greatest pleasure.

Suddenly, her mouth lifted from his rod. "I'm not done with you, but if you don't stop, I'll peak." She was breathless, her hips moving back against him.

He reluctantly released her, but before she could take him back in her mouth, he lifted her off him. He turned her onto her hands and knees and came up behind her. She looked over her shoulder, her eyes half-closed and swimming with need.

Ewan nearly spilled his seed at the look she gave him. He guided himself to her slick heat and pushed inside as she moaned. He began to thrust deep, her soft moans filling the chamber. Ewan gripped her hips and slammed into her, his orgasm rising once more, but he refused to climax. He reached around and found her pearl, strumming it.

"Ewan," she screamed.

"Come for me."

She gasped and her body stiffened with her climax. No longer able to hold onto his control, Ewan gave in to the pleasure and succumbed to his orgasm, letting Kate's body milk him dry.

He pulled out of her and fell onto the bed. Kate rolled to her side and snuggled against him as he wrapped himself around her. He knew the moment she found sleep. But there would be no sleep for him.

Something had happened. Each time they had been together, he had felt it, but this last time the connection between them had solidified, reaching all the way to his soul. It had bound them together for eternity.

And he knew if he made her stay the entire fortnight, he

would never be able to let her go. Though every fiber of his being told him she was the one for him, the thought of keeping her against her will made him sick to his stomach.

It was his right to keep her since she was his wife. Yet there was something uniquely special about Kate that would be destroyed if he forced her. He might be able to woo her with sex over time, but she would hate him for months, perhaps years.

He didn't want that for either of them.

If there was any chance of him granting her the freedom she desired above all, he had to do it. Just one day with her had changed his life forever. He couldn't imagine what two weeks with her would do.

And if she carries your child?

Ewan sighed. Her greatest wish was for a child to love. He wouldn't take that away from her, nor would he allow her to enter into a convent where she would have less freedom than she did now.

He had enough coin to make sure she would never want for anything, and he would make sure she never had to marry again unless she wanted to do so. He tried not to think about the way his gut twisted when he thought of her with another man.

Mistress of her own destiny, just as she wanted.

Can you let her go? Can you really let her walk out of your life?

He was going to have to. He gazed down at the temptress who had turned his life all to hell in a matter of hours. Mercy wasn't something he was known for, but it was something he would grant Kate because she had given him what no one else had—her passion.

Plenty of women had shared their beds with him, but not a single one of them had given him such passion and joy and pleasure as Kate had.

She had spoken of love earlier. Though he knew some of his men loved their wives, love had never factored into his idea of a marriage. Yet, being around Kate had made him realize that if there was true emotion between two people, the experience could be sublime.

He wasn't sure what love felt like, but he knew enough to know he felt something special for her.

It was too bad he wouldn't be able to explore it more deeply.

8

Kate opened her eyes to see the sun shining through the window and a fire in the hearth. She had half-expected Ewan to wake her by making love to her again. Maybe she had woken first, and this would be a great time to explore more of him. She grinned just thinking of taking him in her mouth again. He had liked it, and she had enjoyed pleasuring him.

She rolled over only to find his side of the bed empty. Kate blinked and reached out to touch the linens. They were cool, which meant he had been gone a while.

His absence bothered her more than she wanted to admit. She rose from the bed and reached for her clothes. When she had dressed and plaited her hair, she left the chamber and walked to the great hall.

But she didn't find Ewan.

She sat to break her fast, trying to ignore the unrest in the pit of her stomach. Ewan was laird and had many responsibilities that couldn't be ignored, or at least that's what she tried to tell herself. Since he had spent so much time with her yesterday, surely he had much to catch up on.

Surely. . . .

But it didn't stop her from thinking his absence was more than just clan duties. She ate, contemplating the future and Ewan's assurance that she wouldn't want to leave him. She certainly liked the sex, but the contentment would soon wear off, leaving her longing for her freedom once more.

Stay in his bed for a fortnight and you could very well get with child.

That was almost enough to make her stay. How she wanted children. She had always dreamed of holding her own children in her arms, watching them grow and learn and live. She had thought herself unable to have children, but with a man such as Ewan, there was hope.

But she couldn't have her freedom and a child. Alone she could make her way in the world, even if her only alternative was to become a nun.

Ewan was right: They wouldn't allow her to bring her child to the convent. At the same time, she would never be able to give up a child if she was lucky enough to conceive.

What do you really want? Freedom or children?

There wasn't an easy answer. She wanted both, but it was impossible. She would stay her fortnight, and if she wasn't pregnant, she would leave without a backward glance.

But if her stomach did swell with a child, there were decisions she would then have to make. Maybe she could strike a bargain with Ewan. As soon as the thought crossed her mind, she realized he was too proud of a man to accept any sort of bargain that didn't include her being his wife in every way.

She hadn't expected to find herself in this predicament, but then again, she hadn't expected to find her body yearning for her husband. It was ironic, really. She had thought of nothing but her freedom from the moment of her marriage to Ewan, and now, when it was within her grasp, she didn't know what she wanted.

If only she could know for certain what type of man Ewan really was. He was a considerate lover, aye. He hadn't forced his will on her. Instead, he had offered her a compromise. He had every intention of seducing her during their fortnight together, and God help her, she wanted him to.

Part of her wanted him to tell her he wasn't entertaining thoughts of an annulment any longer. That she was his wife, and she needed to get used to the idea.

But he hadn't.

That should tell you what kind of man he is.

It most certainly did. Ewan had respected her enough not to force his will on her. He was giving her a fighting chance, though he seemed to know he would win in the end. And blast him, he probably would with the way he could work his magic on her body.

Kate's eyes burned with tears. She blinked them back and pushed her unfinished meal from her. A talk with Ewan was in order. She couldn't stand indecision, and she needed to know what he was going to do. No more teasing, no more bargains. It was time for the truth.

She walked out of the castle and into the bailey. The sky was heavy with low, thick gray clouds. The bite of the cold stung her cheeks, and she wrapped her arms about herself to keep warm. She wished now she had grabbed her cloak.

The bailey was full of people, but the one person she searched for she couldn't find. Her gaze scanned the battlements, but again, nothing.

"Milady," Rory called as he took the steps two at a time. "Ye shouldna be out without yer cloak. We've got a bad storm comin' in."

"I see that," she said as she glanced at the sky once more. "I'm looking for Ewan."

Rory's gaze dropped. "Didn't ye know, milady? He left before dawn."

"Left? To go where?" She didn't care for the disappointment that filled her abdomen and left a bitter taste in her mouth. Why hadn't Ewan woken her? Why hadn't he told her?

"There was an attack last night on one of the neighboring clans. We've an alliance with them, so when a rider came begging for help, the laird was quick to respond."

The wind whipped around her, stinging her eyes. Was this how her life would be if she stayed? Always wondering where her husband was or if this battle would be the one to claim his life? How did the Highland women bear it?

"Why aren't you with him?" she asked.

"The laird left me in charge. He doesna want the castle left undefended, especially with you."

"Is he expecting someone to attack us?" Kate's mind was in a whirlwind at the thought of being attacked. She glanced at the gate and found it closed and barred.

Rory chuckled. "There are few clans who would dare to try, but with ye here, the laird wanted to be safe."

That should have made her feel better. But it didn't. "How long will he be gone?"

"If all goes well, he should return tonight."

Her heart fell to her feet. "What do you mean, if all goes well?"

" 'Tis a battle, lass. If the injuries are serious, they will travel slowly."

Kate's mouth went dry. Injuries? What if Ewan got injured? Who would look after him?

"Doona worry, lass," Rory said, as if reading her mind. "Laird Ewan is one of the finest Highland warriors I've ever seen. He's strong as an oak, too. 'Twill take more than a sword to bring him down."

Kate thought she was going to be sick.

* * *

Ewan wiped the blood from his sword and sighed. He had arrived just in time. The MacDuffs were a small clan, and they depended on him. What worried him was that the number of raids on the MacDuffs had grown with each passing month. Few clans raided during the winter months, preferring to wait until spring, but not these attackers.

Why were the MacDuffs being singled out? The entire Highlands knew the MacDuffs were aligned with the MacDonalds. If he ever found out who was doing the raids, his wrath would be quick and fierce.

Normally he would search out the band of men, but he had another duty to see to. Still, he would make sure the bandits were caught, because these weren't simple raids. The attacks had escalated, and this last time children were killed.

"Laird!"

Ewan turned and found one of his men kneeling beside a fallen warrior. He trotted his horse to his clansman. "What is it, Angus?"

"It's the MacDuffs' laird."

Ewan jumped from his mount and lifted the MacDuff tartan away from the dead man's face to find it was indeed Thomas MacDuff.

"I didn't think he left the castle. I told him to stay put."

"I'm sorry, laird," Angus said and rose. "I'll inform his clan."

"Nay," Ewan stopped him. "I'll do it."

He dreaded it. Thomas had been old and frail, but he had been a good laird for his people. With no heirs of his own, Thomas's title would go to his nephew.

"Angus, find Colin for me."

Angus nodded and turned on his heel to find the new Mac-Duff laird.

Ewan blew out a breath. He wiped the sweat that had formed

on his brow despite the cold temperatures. Hot or cold weather, battle always wreaked havoc on a body. The sky would likely open up any moment with a fierce storm, and he still had one more stop to make before he could return home to Kate.

Kate.

He had wanted to wake her that morning making slow, sweet love to her. That had been ruined with the call for help from the MacDuffs. Ewan had contemplated waking Kate to tell her where he was going, but had decided against it at the last moment. He hadn't wanted her to worry.

His wife had most likely been happy to wake without him beside her. He knew his touch confused her. She wasn't ready to admit they were meant to be together, and he feared she might never be ready. Not that he blamed her. In her place, he would crave freedom as deeply as she did.

"Laird."

Ewan turned to find Colin MacDuff before him. Colin was younger than Ewan by at least ten years. He was a few inches taller and still growing into his body. Colin would be a man to be reckoned with in a few years when he reached manhood. Ewan imagined Colin, with his blond hair and dark eyes, had captured many a wench's heart.

"Colin, I'm sorry to be the one to tell you, but you're now the laird of the MacDuffs."

"What?" Colin asked, his brow furrowed.

Ewan pointed to the body at their feet and waited for Colin to see for himself. After Colin looked at his dead uncle, he stood and ran a hand down his face.

"Who attacked your clan?" Ewan asked.

Colin shrugged. "I don't know."

"Who had dealings with Thomas over the past few months?"

"Only one clan. The Campbells. Uncle was trying to arrange a marriage for me with the laird's youngest daughter."

Ewan nodded. He would have to speak to the Campbells,

but not now. First, he had an errand to undertake. "The alliance between the MacDuffs and the MacDonalds still stands, Colin. If you need me, just send word."

Colin nodded, his eyes glazed. He lifted his uncle over his shoulder and walked to the castle.

Ewan mounted his horse, eager to set out. "Angus, have a few men stay behind and help the MacDuffs. Then ride for home."

"Are you going to the Campbells, laird?"

"Nay. Not yet. I'll be back as quick as I can." He spurred his mount into a run just as the snow began to fall.

Kate swallowed a knot of dread and wrapped her cloak tighter around her as she stared out the tower window. This time her gaze wasn't on the sea but on the rolling hills now covered in a thick layer of snow.

When the men had returned from the MacDuffs' without Ewan, Kate had known something was wrong. Even now she wasn't sure if she believed the men when they told her he was unharmed. But no one knew where he had gone. Or how long he would be. Rory seemed to think Ewan had gone to the Campbells, but she had seen the faces of the other men. They knew he had not.

So where was Ewan? Why hadn't he sent a message back for her?

What did you expect after telling him you didn't want to be his wife?

The truth was, she had a suspicion she knew exactly where Ewan had gone—to get the annulment. Elation should be pumping through her, but all she felt was disappointment and regret. Which didn't make sense. She wanted her freedom; she had even begged for it.

Then why did the thought of leaving Ewan make her feel as if her heart were being ripped in two?

Kate didn't know how long she stood in the tower, and it didn't matter. All her life she had known what she wanted. She had known what direction to go in to achieve that goal. And then she had met Ewan.

Everything she thought she wanted now didn't seem to matter. The glorious lovemaking she had explored with Ewan, lovemaking she knew deep in the marrow of her bones she would never experience again, had changed everything.

Ewan had respected her enough to seduce her. He had shown her his worth in every kiss, in every touch. And she had been too blind to see it. It saddened her that she had been ready to give up Ewan and the promise of their future for her freedom. And for what? To enter a convent? She would be no freer there than with Ewan. At least with Ewan she had hope of children and the possibility of a good life.

Rather, she'd had that chance. It had slipped through her fingers like water because she had been too stubborn to admit to Ewan that he might be right.

He asked for a fortnight. He didn't give you enough time.

And that was her own fault. Ewan was a powerful laird, a man who could have any woman he wanted. Why would he spend time seducing her when he could have another, willing woman?

After three husbands, Kate had finally found a man she could have a future with—and she had destroyed that tiny grain of hope. She didn't blame Ewan, though. He was giving her what she had asked for.

How he must hate her to give her the annulment before they even learned if she carried his child. If his seed was growing in her, she wouldn't enter the convent. She would make her way in the world somehow. Her child would know nothing but love. They might not have much, but they would have each other.

It would be enough.

It would have to be.

Kate's hands were numb when she realized she could no longer see into the growing dusk. Night had taken over the Highlands.

She walked the castle corridors like a ghost. She only had a few days in the majestic structure, but it had been long enough to admire the craftsmanship and learn much about the Highlanders that others called savages.

Maybe she would stay in the Highlands. It was a wild, untamed land, as she had seen on her journey to Ewan. There were long lochs and beautiful valleys. The winters were brutal, but she could survive it.

When she returned to Ewan's chamber, the tub was gone and the fire was long dead. There were no signs of the exquisite night they had shared together. Kate flexed fingers numb with cold and stoked the fire to life before she curled up on the rug in front of the hearth. She didn't even have the energy to make it to the bed, a bed that smelled and felt of Ewan.

She forced her thoughts away from Ewan and turned them to her father. He would be furious at the annulment, but then again he had tricked Ewan. Besides, she didn't intend to return to her father and give him another chance to marry her off. If she ever married again, it would be to a man of her choosing or she wouldn't wed at all.

Tears pricked her eyes as she thought about a child growing within her. If she had taken Ewan's offer, there would have been much joy between her and Ewan as they set about making a child. But what about afterward? Would he still be the man he was now? Would he still want her?

You know he would.

Did she? Her parents' marriage had been arranged, and though there had been no great love between them, they had been deeply fond of each other before her mother's death. Her father wanted to marry again, which is why he had set about making advantageous matches for his daughters. He wanted his new wife all to himself without sharing his home with his daughters.

Kate didn't begrudge her father his happiness, she just didn't like being discarded as if she meant nothing, as if her feelings didn't count. Though she and her sister weren't close, she would have liked to be in attendance for her marriage. That wasn't possible now. Kate would never be able to get across Scotland on her own and in time for her sister's wedding.

Would Ewan have taken her, she wondered? There was so much for him to do as laird that she doubted he would have had the time. She smiled as she recalled the first time she had seen him from the tower window. Even then she had recognized him for the warrior he was. Proud and commanding. Just one look at him and she knew he would do anything for his clan.

Though she knew her father loved her, she longed to have someone who would do anything and everything for her love. At one time she had been sure she would eventually find that man, but after a while she realized it had only been a dream.

Until Ewan.

He was the kind of man that would die for the woman who held his heart. It was too bad she wasn't that woman.

9

Ewan pulled his mount to a stop as he crested the hill and looked over his lands and his castle darkened by the night. The MacDonalds had held the land for hundreds of years, and God willing, they would hold it for several hundred more.

He had always been proud of who he was and what he stood for. Not once had he thought he was lacking. Now, he wasn't so sure. Sacrifice was something he was ready to do for his clan, but he had never thought he would sacrifice for himself.

Ewan lifted his face to the sky, the bitter cold slicing over his skin and whipping his hair around him. His mount's sides heaved from their long trip, and though the animal was anxious to get inside the stable, Ewan wasn't ready to see Kate quite yet.

It had taken him longer than he wanted, but he had secured the annulment. After calling in several favors and making promises, he would be able to give Kate what she desired most.

His gaze shifted to his chamber. No candlelight could be seen, and he wondered if Kate waited for him. Had she figured out where he had gone? Was she angry that he had left without waking her? Had she worried about him in the battle?

Ewan ran a hand through his hair and cursed himself for being ten kinds of fool. Every instinct in his body told him not to let her go. But his heart told him he had no other choice.

When he had made his decision to give her the freedom she so craved, he had acted on it immediately, else he would have changed his mind. Letting Kate go would be one of the hardest things he had ever done. Or ever would do. Yet it was something he knew he had to do.

Selfish he may be at times, but Kate made him realize it was more than his feelings and wants that mattered when it came to a marriage. He had been tricked, and she had been forced into her third marriage. Freedom seemed only fair for the both of them.

He nudged the horse into a walk. He was weary down to his bones and just wanted the comfort of his own bed and a hot meal. And Kate. By the saints, how he wanted Kate in his arms, to kiss her, to caress her. Her body was made for his touch.

He greeted his men as he approached the gates to the castle. After he reached the castle steps and dismounted, he tossed the reins to a stable lad.

"Give him extra oats," he told the boy before taking the steps two at a time.

He let out a sigh as he entered the castle and stepped into the great hall. Each time he left, he couldn't wait to return. Because of his position, he was often called away to aid with other clans or even King James. There was a price to pay for the kind of power he held.

The hall was filled with sleeping men and a few couples whose moans of desire drifted through the castle. He made his way to the stairs and climbed them. Kate was going to be deliriously happy. At least he could give her that.

His steps slowed as he neared his chamber. He hesitated a moment before he opened the door. The only light inside came from the fire that was dying down. He smiled when he spotted her curled on the rug. He opened his sporran and took out the document to lay on the table by the bed.

For long moments he stared at the simple piece of paper. Then he took out the ring and set it beside the parchment before he turned and moved to the hearth. He added more logs to the fire before he sat and looked at his wife.

She wasn't his wife anymore, he reminded himself. He still recalled how angry he had been at finding her instead of her sister. Now, he realized, it had been fate that had sent Kate to him. Fate had known what he needed more than he had.

From the time he walked out of the chamber yesterday until now, all he had thought about was Kate and making love to her. Despite his exhaustion he wasn't going to pass up an opportunity to claim her.

Especially when it might be the last time.

Kate was on her side with an arm tucked beneath her head and her glorious dark blond locks spread out behind her. The red orange flames of the fire bathed her skin in their glow. She was so damned beautiful it made his heart hurt.

Ewan rose and removed his clothes before he lifted Kate in his arms and carried her to the bed. She stirred against him, her hand resting against his chest. His heart squeezed painfully. He prayed he had done the right thing and that she would be happy.

He laid her on the bed and pulled off her shoes before he lifted her skirts and rolled down her wool stockings. He was covering her feet with his hands to help warm them when he heard his name.

"You've returned," she said.

He smiled and looked into her sleepy eyes. "I have. 'Tis awful weather we have. You didn't stay warm as I warned you."

" 'Tis difficult when there's no warmth to be found. I contemplated jumping into the fire I was so cold."

"I'm here now."

"Aye, you are." She sat up and removed her gown.

A slow smile spread over his face as his gaze moved up and down her marvelous body. He watched as her nipples hardened in the cool air and felt his already rigid cock jump in reaction. Chills raced along her skin, but he would heat her up soon enough.

Ewan moved onto the bed at her feet and slowly shifted her legs open until he could kneel between them. He gave her a wink and parted her woman's lips to feast upon the beauty of her sex. With his tongue, he softly licked her from the bottom to the top of her sex, stopping to tease her pearl for a moment.

"Saints, Ewan. You torment me so."

"Nay, love. I pleasure you."

Her breathing quickened with each flick of his tongue. Ewan smiled inwardly and resumed his tonguing of Kate. When he moved a finger to her entrance, he was amazed to find her already wet and ready for him.

"Ewan."

His head jerked up to find her watching him. "Relax, Kate." She nodded. "Don't stop. Please, don't stop."

He was all too happy to return to pleasuring her. With his fingers holding her sex open, his tongue licked and sucked her pearl while he stroked deep inside her with the fingers of his other hand.

Her soft moans filled the chamber while her body writhed in need. His own desire was nearly too much to bear, and his hunger to plunge inside her soon overwhelmed him.

He leaned up and wrapped his lips around a pert nipple while his fingers continued to fondle her. He gently scraped his teeth over her nipple. She let out a soft cry and wrapped her arms around his neck to anchor him to her.

"I need you inside of me," she whispered into his ear. "Please, Ewan. I need to feel you."

He wasn't about to deny her, not when it was something he craved as well. He shifted and leaned over her, using his hands to brace himself on either side of her head while the tip of his cock rubbed against her. She closed her eyes and moaned before she reached between them and took his rod in her hand, slowly stroking up and down his length.

Ewan swallowed and fought for control. "I'll spill if you doona stop."

"I can't stop," she said. "I love the feel of you in my hand."

He nearly died right then at her words. But he was so close to peaking that he could no longer stand to have her hands on him. He entered her with one thrust, burying himself to the root.

Kate cried out and sank her nails into his back as he filled her. She felt herself stretching and sighed at the wonderful sensations. At first she thought she had been dreaming, but when she had woken to find Ewan nude and wanting her, she had never known such joy. Maybe she had been wrong about the annulment. Maybe there was a future for them after all.

Her sex throbbed with need from his tongue and fingers. She had thought to give the same pleasure he had given her, but he hadn't let her fondle him for long. The hunger to feel him inside her, pumping long and hard, consumed her. And finally, he was.

Kate wrapped her legs around his waist and heard him moan as he leaned down to kiss her neck, lightly biting her skin before running his tongue over the nibbled area.

She shivered, eager to drown in the climax that had been steadily building since his first touch. Now, her blood sang with the heat and desire he had filled inside her.

He pulled out until just the tip of him filled her before he thrust deep. He repeated the action several more times, and each time brought Kate closer to her climax, coiling the desire tighter and tighter.

"Ewan, I cannot take it," she cried.

Only then did he begin to thrust hard and fast. With her ankles locked at his back and her arms around his neck, he plunged within her until sweat glistened on their bodies.

The more he rode her, the more she wanted to put off her orgasm, to enjoy the sweet pleasure. Yet, all too soon, her body exploded. Her eyes rolled back in her head as she succumbed to the desire.

Pleasure sucked her under, washing over her body in a tide of bliss. Slowly she came back to herself, her body still trembling from her climax.

She opened her eyes to find Ewan still moving over her, his eyes closed and his jaw clenched, as if he, too, were holding off as long as he could.

Kate ran her hands over his back, loving the feel of his muscles moving beneath her hands. She cupped his bottom as his hips shifted. He gave a grunt before he pumped twice and stilled over her, her name whispered from his lips.

Tears pricked her eyes. He fell forward, his head buried in her neck. Kate held him close, unprepared and unsure of what was ahead for them. A few days ago she had been confident she wanted her freedom at all costs, but now she was willing to give it all up.

She had laughed when Ewan claimed his touch would change her mind, but she realized almost too late how right he had been. His soft caresses and fiery kisses had awoken the true woman inside of her, a woman that liked to make love and needed a man's touch.

Ewan had left his mark on her, unintended though it might have been. Until the day she died, she knew she would never forget the wonderful way he touched her body and brought her fulfillment.

All too soon he raised his head and looked into her eyes. The blue depths gave a hint of his sadness before he hid all emotion from her. Was he about to tell her it was over? Was it then when he would hand her the annulment and send her on her way?

Kate's heart pounded as she waited. She was grateful when all he did was lean down and kiss her. He threaded his fingers with hers and slowly pulled out of her. She smiled up at him when he broke the kiss. There were no words, and by the satisfied look on his face, there wouldn't be. Then he shifted to reach for something from the table by the bed.

"Hold out your hand," he bade her.

A niggling feeling of foreboding washed over Kate, but she gave him her hand. She watched as he dropped something into her palm. She opened her fingers to find a stunning gold ring with the largest garnet she had ever seen. Her gaze jerked to his.

"I meant to give this to you yesterday," he said. "I picked it out after I signed the marriage contract with your father, but as soon as I saw you, I knew the garnet belonged to you."

She looked down at the stone and couldn't resist putting the ring on her finger. It fit perfectly, as if it had been made specifically for her. She released a pent up breath as the gem glistened in the firelight. She smiled, because she had been so very wrong about the annulment. She was still his wife.

" 'Tis . . . magnificent, Ewan."

"I'm glad you like it. I have another gift for you."

Kate sat up when he leaned for the table once again. Another gift? What else could he possibly have for her? She spotted the roll of parchment in his hand and dread filled her. The smile faded from her face and her blood turned to ice. She wanted to run from the chamber, to act as though she never saw the parchment.

But she couldn't. She had faced everything life had thrown her; she would face what she had pleaded for.

"You know what this is?" he asked.

She took a deep breath and met his gaze. "The annulment."

"Aye. I'm giving you your freedom, Kate."

"Why? You asked for a fortnight. 'Tis only been a few days."

He ran a hand down his face, showing his exhaustion. "I knew the moment our lips touched the first time that our joining would be like nothing I'd ever experienced. And with each time after, it became more and more difficult to even think of letting you go."

She inhaled a shaky breath. "If there's a child?"

"There willna be a convent for you, nor will I take the child you've always dreamed of having. I will give you enough coin that you will never need to worry. All I ask is that I get to see the child during his or her life. I want to know our child, Kate."

He was giving her everything she wanted, yet she didn't want to take it. Her vision blurred with tears. Whether she wanted what he offered or not, he had given it to her. As soon as the annulment had been signed, their marriage had ended.

"You willna have to return to your father," Ewan continued. "Nor will you have to worry about being forced into another marriage ever again. You are free, Kate."

"Why are you doing all of this for me?"

"I could have forced you to stay with me, and it crossed my mind. But I couldna do it. You are a unique woman with unbelievable passion. Neither should be destroyed, and that's what would happen if I forced you to stay."

She looked at the parchment he now held out to her. Her hands refused to take it.

Tell him you've changed your mind. Tell him you want to be his wife. Tell him!

But she recognized it was too late for that.

Slowly, she reached for the parchment and let it drop in her lap. "You've given me everything. How can I ever thank you?"

"Nay. To give you everything, I would have been the man you could have lived your life with."

His words were like a punch in her stomach. She moved to kneel before him with her hands on either side of his face. "You are everything a woman could ever want. You've shown me what it's like to have a real man touch me, and I . . . I've . . ."

"What, lass?" he asked, his blue gaze searching hers. "Tell me."

"I'm not sure I want to leave."

For a moment he didn't respond. Then she felt his hands on her back. "I'm giving you your freedom from marriage and your father. Not many women would pass that up."

Now that she had told him her feelings it was as if a huge weight had been lifted from her shoulders. "I'm not most women, nor have most women been pleasured by such a powerful, handsome laird."

"You want to be my wife?"

She licked her lips and nodded her head. "I knew when I found you gone this morning that you had left to get the annulment. I should have been happy, but I wasn't. I've had the entire day to realize that I've made such a terrible mistake, Ewan."

He pulled her against him, his arms wrapping around her. "At least you've told me."

There was something wrong, Kate realized. She had expected him to be excited at her announcement. And then it hit her. Maybe he had just been nice, not wanting to hurt her. Maybe he had found another woman.

She pulled out of his arms. "You have your freedom now as well."

"I suppose so." He shrugged and wrapped a strand of her hair around his finger.

"You could find you another wife, one that wouldn't change her mind as I have done."

"I could."

Kate gritted her teeth as anger rose up within her. He had been playing her all along. How could she have been such a fool?

"Or," he said, "I could ask the woman kneeling before me in all her naked glory if she would be my wife."

She blinked. "What?"

"We'll do this the proper way. No one will stand in my stead, no proxy marriage. You and I will stand before God and the clan and pledge ourselves to each other."

Kate's heart pounded so hard she feared it would leap from her chest. She threw her arms around his neck as the tears fell down her cheeks.

"Is that an aye, lass?" Ewan asked worriedly.

She nodded, unable to find the words with her throat clogged with emotion.

"About time," he ground out before he pulled her arms from his neck and lowered her to the bed. "I've a mind for more time loving my future wife before dawn."

She giggled through her tears. "Shouldn't we wait?"

"Nay," he said between placing kisses around her nipple. "You want bairns, and I'm going to ensure we try as much as possible."

Kate let out a breathy sigh when he suckled her nipple. Maybe her father hadn't tricked them. Maybe he had seen something in Ewan. But he was hers now, or would be as soon as they could be married again. Until then, she planned to enjoy the pleasure he brought her.

"Concentrate," he murmured.

Kate groaned when his finger pushed inside of her. There was no doubt in her mind that their days and nights would be filled with hours of pleasure.

No more freedom for her. She wanted to be well and truly tied to her Highlander.

10

Two days later . . .

Kate smoothed her hands down the MacDonald plaid draped across her chest and down her skirt. Ewan had given it to her the day before as a surprise. Ever since he had asked her to be his wife, he had been giving her small gifts.

First the ring, which hadn't been such a small gift. Then there were the ribbons. How he had come to have so many ribbons, and in so many colors, Kate would never know. After the ribbons there had been a fur-lined cloak. Then, the tartan.

"Ready, milady?"

Kate started and whirled around to find Beth in the doorway. "Aye. Ewan is there?"

Beth chuckled. "Of course, milady. I think he's more worried about whether you will come down or not."

"Silly man." Kate hurried past Beth, anxious to see Ewan. She had slept little the night before. Between Ewan's loving and the wedding, sleep hadn't been an option.

"See, milady?" Beth said when they reached the great hall.

Ewan stood facing the stairs, his hands clasped behind his back. His long, black hair hung free, just as hers did. He smiled and winked at her, a wicked gleam in his blue eyes.

Kate made her steps slow, savoring each moment. When she reached him, he took her hand in his and raised it to his lips.

"You look divine, Lady MacDonald. The tartan suits you."

"Even though I'm a Lowlander?"

He shrugged. "I'll turn you into a Highlander yet."

"I fear you already have."

"Just what I wanted to hear."

She bit her lip to keep from laughing as he guided her out of the castle and onto the steps. The entire clan had gathered in the bailey and on the battlements to watch the wedding.

Even the weather was cooperating. There were no clouds in sight, and the sun shone bright above them. Uncharacteristically, the wind had died down to just a breeze.

"Do you need your cloak?" Ewan whispered.

She shook her head. There was no way she was going to hide the tartan, not after it had finally been given to her. "I'll be all right."

Ewan stopped them in front of the priest. "Last chance, love?"

She glanced up at him. "Nay. You cannot back out now. You've already asked."

"Kate."

At the seriousness of his tone, she faced him. "What is it?"

"Are you sure? You wanted your freedom so desperately."

She caressed his cheek, the love in her heart warming her. Her Highland laird had asked her the same question every day. The only way he would ever know she meant it was for her to take the vows.

"I'm yours, Ewan. I was the moment you rode through those gates the first day I saw you."

"My Kate."

"Aye, Ewan."

The priest cleared his throat, and they both faced him to begin the ceremony. Kate didn't hear any of the words, she didn't need to. The only words that meant anything to her were the words of love Ewan had whispered the night before after he thought she had gone to sleep.

Suddenly, Ewan grinned and jerked her to him. "There's no escaping me now, love."

His mouth descended on hers in a scorching kiss that set her blood on fire. A great cheer went up around them, and the clan shouted their names.

Kate broke the kiss and pulled away. "You really thought I would change my mind?"

"I let you go once, I wasn't about to do it a second time."

She put her hands on his chest and studied him. "When I came here, I thought I knew what I wanted, but I didn't. You showed me what it could be like as your wife. I'd be an utter fool if I walked away from that."

"Not to mention the bedsport."

Kate laughed and licked her lips. "I love you, Ewan Mac-Donald."

He stilled, the smile falling from his mouth. "You do?"

"I do. I don't know how, and I don't care. We have a future ahead of us, and it's going to be full of ups and downs, tragedies and joy. But we will have each other."

"I don't know how I lived without you."

"Tell me what you whispered last night."

He jerked. "You heard?"

"Aye. I want to hear the words every day for the rest of my life."

"I love you, Kate MacDonald."

Kate laid her head on Ewan's chest and sighed as she looked out over her clan. She would wait for the morrow to give Ewan her surprise. Her lips pulled back in a smile as she imagined his delight when he learned about the child growing inside her.

ENTHRALLED

1

Aldvale Kingdom, Azure Province

Linarra seethed with rage and stared at her king. She fisted her hands in an effort to keep from hitting him. "Nay."

Usotae laughed, the sound hollow and malicious, much as he was. His bejeweled fingers drummed lazily on the arm of his throne as his gaze raked over her. They were alone in the vaulted-ceiling chamber with its gilded pictures and jeweled throne.

Linarra had always thought the throne room of Aldvale Palace a majestic place. Until Usotae had been crowned. His cruelty and abuse had dusted the entire kingdom in a grimy film that might never wash away.

If she were a man, a warrior, she wouldn't hesitate to kill him. She'd lift her sword and sink it into his black heart. Maybe then Aldvale could return to the grandeur that once claimed their peaceful kingdom.

"Oh, Linarra. How you disappoint me." Usotae rose from

his throne and slowly walked around her. "You are so predictable."

Linarra refused to cower before him despite the fact her life hung in the balance. There was only so much she was willing to do for her kingdom. What he asked of her was ... impossible. She had the power to refuse, and there was nothing he could say that would convince her to go through with it.

He stopped behind her and bent close to her ear. "Did you really think you had a choice in the matter? Did you really think you, a mere ... woman ... could outwit me?"

She had to keep control of her temper. "I won't do it."

He chuckled as he moved to face her once more. His black eyes flashed dangerously, giving him a malevolent look she saw more and more often. So many in their kingdom thought their young, handsome king with his black hair and dark coloring was just what the kingdom needed. Only a few knew the truth about Usotae.

Those who did ended up dead.

"I'm merely asking you to spy for me, Linarra," Usotae said with a tsk. "Don't make it sound as if I want you to murder him."

But murder him they would. Linarra didn't know the Kellian king, but she had heard numerous rumors of the warrior king's skills and the skills of his men. If she walked into the Kellian jungle, she would never return. The Kellians did not tolerate outsiders.

"Find someone else to do your spying. I owe you nothing." Linarra turned on her heel and made for the door. She got five steps from Usotae when his voice halted her.

"But you do owe me. Or have you forgotten your sister so quickly? I told you she would hinder you, but you didn't listen."

Linarra sighed, the weight of the world on her shoulders.

One of her worst mistakes had been begging Usotae for help when her sister had been charged with murder. She had always known Usotae would use it against her. It had been too much to hope he had forgotten, but she should have known Usotae would never forget.

"I had the charges against your sister dismissed," he continued as he walked toward her, the heels of his boots clicking on the white stone floor. "However, new evidence can be found."

Her sister's life for her own. Linarra would never condemn her sister to death, not when her sister was innocent. And Usotae knew it. Linarra's knees threatened to buckle. She had never felt so helpless, so powerless.

He brushed his hand against her hair to finger the end of her braid. Linarra fought the urge the slap his hand away. How she hated him, hated everything he stood for. The kingdom would perish because of him, and there was nothing she could do about it.

She kept her gaze on the door, wishing she could take her sister and leave Aldvale, never to return. But she knew Usotae too well. He would never allow them to leave. They would be hunted for the rest of their lives until his men found them. When they were finally caught, their deaths wouldn't be quick. Usotae liked to torture his prisoners and watch the life drain from them in slow drops.

Nay, if there was ever going to be a chance of being free of Usotae, Linarra had to do as he asked. Once she was finished, she planned to take her sister as far from Aldvale as she could. If Usotae dared to stop them, she would kill him. And damn the consequences.

If you survive the Kellians.

She would. She had survived her parents' deaths, and her king's abuse and betrayal. She was nothing if not a survivor.

Usotae caressed a finger down her neck to the swell of her

breasts. "The assignment is easy. You will be given to Falcor as a present of goodwill. Falcor won't be able to refuse your exotic beauty. No man can."

"What is it you want me to do, exactly?"

He smiled and cupped her breast. "Use this body to gain his trust and discover his weakness."

"You would give me to a man when you have kept me from all others?" There was something that nagged at the back of her mind, something that she should puzzle together.

Usotae had wanted her for his queen, and when she had refused, he had seen to it that no man in Aldvale would want her by staking his claim on her. She was destined to spend her life alone, but it was better than being his queen. Death was better than having Usotae as a husband.

"I think sending you to Falcor is the least of what you deserve," Usotae said.

She should have known he would punish her for refusing him. She should have been prepared for it, but this had taken her by complete surprise.

"The Kellians are barbarians, Linarra. He will use your body until there is nothing left. You will be broken, just a shell."

"Ah, this is my penalty for refusing to marry you?"

"This is only the beginning. You will pay again and again until I grow tired of you." He stepped away from her, his lips pulled back in a sneer. "There will be another spy waiting for you to deliver the information."

Linarra whirled around to face him. "Once Falcor discovers what I've done, he'll kill me."

"Maybe." Usotae shrugged. "But I doubt it. Use your charms wisely, my dear. Also, let me put aside any doubt in your mind about going to Falcor for help. If any Kellian steps foot in Aldvale, I'll kill your sister myself."

"You think I would trust a Kellian?"

"I think you would do anything to get your sister out of Aldvale."

It disturbed her that he knew her so well.

"To be sure there is no miscommunication, I'll have your sister kept at the palace until your return."

Linarra swallowed, loathing Usotae with each beat of her heart. "How will I know who to deliver the secrets to?"

"There are Kellians who have contacted me, men who want to see Falcor overthrown. You won't have any problems finding them."

"What do you want Kellian for? It's just a jungle."

Usotae grinned and crossed his arms over his chest. "There is more to Kellian than people realize. The Kellians have had it long enough. It's my turn now."

"You're just going to take over the kingdom after you kill Falcor?"

"Leave the decisions of a king up to me. You worry about staying alive and gaining those secrets."

"And once I deliver the secrets to your spies?"

"I'll get you out as soon as I can. Maybe."

"So you'll leave me in Kellian?"

Usotae brought her body up against his own. "I might be more willing to extract you sooner if you let me have a taste of that lovely body of yours."

Linarra jerked out of his arms. She glared at the man who had once courted her, the man she had once thought to marry—until she had seen him for the monster he really was. His eyes no longer held the joy of youth, for once he had ascended the throne, he had fed off the power.

The handsome man who had nearly won her heart so long ago had died the day the crown had been placed on his head. And in his place stood a ruthless, power-hungry tyrant who would do the unthinkable to get what he wanted.

"You may blackmail me into spying for you, but I would sooner hang myself than let you touch my body," she said.

Usotae's hand snaked out and gripped her long braid, yanking her against him. "Never doubt that I will have you, Linarra. For too long you've rejected me. You could have been my queen, but now you'll be a whore."

He shoved her away from him. Linarra tried to keep upright, but she tripped over her skirts and landed on her hands and knees. Pain lashed through her body. She bit her tongue to keep from crying out. With deliberate slowness, she rose to her feet and lifted her chin. Usotae might have backed her into a corner, but that didn't mean she had to do everything he wanted. There had to be some way to get free of him.

Linarra hurried into her home and quickly shut the door behind her. She leaned against it, her heart pounding as hatred burned deep within her.

"Linarra?"

She opened her eyes to see her younger sister, Narune, standing in the doorway that led to the kitchen. "Everything is fine."

"It's not. You can't lie to me. He wanted to try and make you wed him, didn't he?"

If only that had been all Usotae wanted. Linarra took a deep breath and pushed away from the door. She'd been followed home by one of Usotae's guards. She had no doubt more watched the house just in case she decided to try to run.

"You're scaring me," Narune murmured.

Too much was at stake to lie to her sister, as much as she wanted to. "I have to go away for a while."

"Why?"

"Usotae has something he needs me to do."

Narune gave a snort. "He would be sending one of his emissaries if it was important. Just where is he sending you?"

"To the Kellian jungle."

Narune slammed her hand against the door jamb, her slight body trembling with anger. "I don't believe this. Usotae is punishing you, isn't he? Doesn't the man understand you don't want him?"

"It isn't so simple." Linarra walked past her sister to her chamber where she stood and stared absently. She had so little time to explain things to Narune, so little time to plan.

"By the gods, he didn't," Narune ground out. "He's calling in his favor."

"In a way."

Narune sat on the bed and took Linarra's hands in her own. "We can run away. I should have agreed long ago when you tried to talk me into it, but I was young and scared. We'll leave tonight. As soon as I can pack."

Linarra cupped her sister's face in her hands. She looked so much like their father with his hazel eyes and light brown hair. "I cannot. There are guards watching the house, watching us. I have to do this, because if I don't, Usotae will find new evidence to charge you again."

All the blood drained from Narune's face. "But . . . I thought that was finished. The charges were dismissed. I didn't kill him."

"I know." Linarra knew better than anyone.

Narune bit her lip as her brow furrowed with worry. "I don't understand."

"Usotae is king. He can do whatever he wants."

"Gods. What do we do now?"

"I do what I'm supposed to do." Linarra swallowed as her anxiety grew.

"What is that, exactly?"

Linarra paused. "It's probably better if you don't know."

"I need to know," Narune stated. "If he is using me against you, I have a right to know."

As much as Linarra wanted to keep her sister innocent, it

wasn't going to happen. And she had a good point. She was part of what was going on, and she deserved to know. "Usotae will tell you anyway."

"How bad is it?"

"I'm being given to the Kellian king as a gift."

Narune's mouth dropped open in surprise. "Nay."

"It will only be for a short while," Linarra lied. "I'm going to spy for Usotae."

"You'll be killed. We've all heard stories of the Kellians, especially their king. He's a barbarian, Linarra. They'll kill you on sight."

She smiled at her sister's dramatics, despite their grain of truth, and took her hand. "I will get into the castle, and I will get close to the king. I have no other choice, because if I fail, Usotae will kill you."

"I didn't think I could hate him more than I already do," Narune said as she rose to her feet and paced the chamber.

"Listen to me. Usotae wants Kellian for his own. I don't know why, and it doesn't matter. If an attack should be sent on Kellian, run as far from here as you can. We've coin hidden in the bottom of my drawer. Take it and run. Don't look back."

"What about you?"

Linarra's heart tugged at the fear that shone in her sister's eyes. "I'll find you. I promise."

2

Kellian jungle, Kellian palace

Falcor watched from his chamber as another summer storm drenched the jungle. He longed for the days when he used to run through the tropical forest carefree and unknowing of what it meant to rule a kingdom. He missed the days where his only worry was how soon he could escape the castle and explore the wilds of Kellian. His greatest fear then had been facing his parents after sneaking away from his studies.

How things changed when childhood melted away. He blew out a harsh breath. Life had been simpler then, but a man had to make sacrifices when he was king. Falcor's sacrifice had been his own wants, especially that of a wife and family.

By the time his father was his age, Falcor had been three summers already. But if Falcor was truthful with himself, he doubted he'd ever find a woman for his bride.

It wasn't that he couldn't find a woman. There were several in Kellian that were beautiful, but none stirred his blood.

Bringing an outsider into Kellian in these turbulent times wasn't a viable option.

Already provisions had been made for the next in line to take over, and that next in line just happened to be his cousin, Yarrow, who lived in the neighboring kingdom of Shadowhall.

There was no way Falcor would leave Kellian without a king, and with a group of men who saw to it that Kellian was fighting every kingdom that bordered their jungle, Falcor knew it was only a matter of time before he was challenged by one of his own.

His people thought there was no heir, that if anyone killed Falcor they would gain the crown. The secret of Yarrow's birth had been well hidden by Falcor's father and uncle, but documented well. Yarrow would be an excellent king for Kellian. He was a good man, honest and wise.

A knock brought Falcor out of his musings. He turned to find one of his guards. "Aye?"

The guard bowed. "Your Highness, an emissary from Aldvale is requesting entrance to the jungle."

Falcor was immediately suspicious. Aldvale's king, Usotae, wasn't known for his kindness. His cruelty had spread far and wide. "What do they want?"

"They have a gift from King Usotae to you. A gift of peace, I'm told."

The fact Falcor desperately wanted peace helped him make his decision. "Give them an escort through the jungle. We'll see if it is indeed a gift of peace or some trick of Usotae's."

The guard bowed again and hurried to carry out Falcor's orders. Falcor looked through the rain and wondered just what kind of gift Usotae would give him. He wasn't callow enough to believe it was a true gift of peace, not when the sender was one such as Usotae.

Still, Falcor held out hope.

* * *

Linarra shifted in the rug. Her feet had gone numb, and it was difficult to breathe. Thankfully the guards carried a canopy that protected her and the rug from the downpour that had begun before they ever reached the jungle.

She turned her head and peeked through the opening to find that the dense green of the jungle had swallowed them. She stifled a scream when she saw a small tougar move in the trees. Her heart squeezed painfully as she waited for the animal to pounce and the screams that would follow. When nothing happened, she closed her eyes and decided it would be better if she didn't look. It was going to be difficult enough facing the warrior king without worrying what predators awaited her as well.

The guards carried her for hours, and with each of their steps Linarra berated herself for not leaving Aldvale years before. Narune had tried to run but a group of Usotae's men kicked down their door and took a screaming Narune with them to the palace.

Linarra had been held by other guards, unable to do anything to help her sister. Narune's screams begging Linarra to help still echoed in Linarra's head.

If only she could.

It hadn't surprised her when Usotae had walked into her home a moment later. He had shackled her to the bed, giving her enough room to stand, but just.

The humor in his gaze had made her dig her nails into her palms to keep calm. She would never do anything to give him a reason to execute her sister.

Usotae had kept her and Narune separated while Linarra received her instructions from one of the castle whores. Her mother had told Linarra the joys of making love to a husband, but Linarra was so disgusted with the thought of giving her body to a man she didn't love she didn't know how she was going to seduce Falcor.

Despite her misgivings, Usotae was positive Falcor would

want her. She prayed that was the case, because it would take every ounce of her courage to give her body to him.

At least Usotae didn't force you.

It had come close, though. He wanted her, but he hated her too much to take her. Her jaw still ached from his backhand the night before. It was a good thing she didn't bruise easy or they would never have left for Kellian.

"The castle has come in view," one of the guards whispered to her.

Linarra couldn't help wanting a peek of the castle. Few had seen the Kellian stronghold for themselves. Many said it was nothing more than a crumbling pile of rocks while others said it was a magnificent piece of architecture.

She wished she wasn't enclosed in the rug so she could see for herself, but she'd have to be content with whatever brief look she got.

One of the Aldvale guards let out a low whistle at the same time that she spotted a round tower of black stone that rose out of the jungle like a god.

"I've never seen anything so massive," a guard said.

"And black stone," said another.

The guards continued to comment, Linarra hanging on their every word. Could the Kellian castle be larger than Aldvale's palace? Surely not. The Kellians were barbarians, or so they had been told. No one really knew much of the Kellians. They preferred to stay in their jungle, and few ventured into the deadly area.

Linarra took a deep breath to ready herself. She was about to come face-to-face with the warrior king.

Falcor was sitting in the crowded great hall listening to a dispute between two of his commanders when the Aldvale entourage arrived.

Word had spread quickly through the castle that an envoy

was coming, for the hall was jammed full of his people. They parted as their visitors entered.

Four men, Aldvale guards by the look of their sleek navy tunics, carried what appeared to be a large rug. Falcor waited for one of them to step forward and speak, but none did.

He rested his elbows on the arms of his throne and steepled his fingers. The storm had finally passed and the sun broke through the canopy of trees to pour light through the windows that lined the top of the walls of the massive great hall.

A whisper rippled through the hall. His personal guards stood near, their hands on their swords. Still the Aldvales stood silent, their heads bowed and their gazes lowered. Just what did they have, Falcor wondered.

"You have been sent by King Usotae?" he asked.

The men at once fell to their knees and lowered the rug to the floor with a little push to unroll it. The rug stopped at his feet, but he wasn't prepared for what was in it.

Of all the gifts he might have expected, a stunningly beautiful woman staring up at him clad in see-through material so he could make out the outline of her nipples wasn't one of them.

The exotic woman rose to her feet with the grace of royalty. "King Falcor," she said and dipped into a low curtsy.

He shivered at her smooth, melodic voice. Her lower face was covered by sheer black fabric, hiding her from him. Her unusual almond-shaped eyes that were tilted up at the corners were the most vivid, and unusual, shade of gold.

She turned about on the rug, and Falcor had eyes only for her and her thick waves of tawny tresses that fell well past her hips. Her long, sheer black skirts whirled about her legs, tempting him with peeks of sleek, toned legs. Her top was molded to her full breasts like a lover's hand and stopped just under her breasts, leaving her stomach bared along with the large golden jewel that nestled in her navel.

"What you see before you is a gift from my king, Usotae," she said.

Falcor took a deep breath. He'd never felt lust so pure and true before, and it took everything he had to rein in his desires and not lay her down on the rug and ravish her as he longed to do. "My men were told it was a peace offering from Usotae."

She smiled, her full lips teasing him through the fabric. "Aye, Your Highness. Many kingdoms bicker over land and few have managed to go a year without feeling the effects of war. King Usotae wants you to know you can regard him as an ally."

"Is that right?" Falcor stood and stepped on the rug, its blue and gold mosaic unnoticed. "The same Usotae who told me not two years ago that he would one day have my kingdom for himself? The same Usotae who is, right now, sending men to his borders to attack neighboring kingdoms."

If his words unnerved her, she never showed it. She inclined her tawny head. "I see the rumors have reached even as far as Kellian."

Falcor folded his arms over his chest. Around the hall, his people had grown quiet, eager to hear what their visitors had to say.

"Rumors? I wouldn't call them rumors." She had no need to know he had spies in Aldvale who reported back to him on a daily basis. He knew all about Usotae's hunger for power, as well as Usotae's designs to take over neighboring kingdoms.

"Usotae is a strong king, a man who wants to keep his people safe. If that means he must send men to our borders to protect us from invading forces, he will do it. A few kingdoms such as Pereth and Hesione, and even Shadowhall, have managed to find peace in our war-torn provinces. Would you not seek the same?"

She had hit upon one of his greatest desires, but for all her cool words, he didn't trust why she had been sent. Her king might have told her all that she had relayed to him, but Falcor knew the truth.

Usotae was an intelligent man. He knew what to tell his kingdom to keep them from revolting. And he knew exactly what to tell other kings to put fear in them. Falcor didn't scare so easily, though. He had been waiting for Usotae to attack, and he'd just made the first move.

"You may return to your king. Tell him I appreciate the beautiful rug, and I will think on his words." He turned from the hall, eager to find the quiet of his chambers to think over the woman's words.

And cool the lust from his blood.

"King Falcor," she called. "It is I who am your gift."

Falcor felt the breath rush from his lungs as he halted. Slowly, he faced her. "Usotae would send a woman as a gift?"

Her gaze lowered, but not before he saw them blaze with emotion. "I am Linarra, daughter to one of the oldest families in Aldvale. I am yours to do with as you wish."

"Ah. A prize many in your kingdom seek, I presume?"

She lifted her gaze hesitantly to his, refusing to speak.

Falcor walked to her and held out his hand. "I think the rest of this conversation can be held in privacy."

She placed her hand in his. The shock of her touch went through him like lightning. He jerked his gaze to her to see if she felt it too, but her gaze was once more on the floor.

He escorted her from the hall and through the winding corridors to the tower stairs that led to his chamber. It was privacy he wanted, and that was the only place for it.

Once at the top of the tower, he opened the door and waited for her to enter before he closed it behind them. She walked around the chamber, looking at everything.

"It's very beautiful."

Falcor chuckled at her amazement. "You say that as if you're surprised. Did you think we Kellians were a savage lot?"

Her brow furrowed as she turned away from him.

"Ah. You did." Falcor moved from the door. "This tower, called King's Tower, was built specifically for the kings of Kellian. This chamber is where I hold private audiences."

"A long way to climb to have a private meeting."

"It's not just for that. These are also my chambers."

She looked around the spacious chamber again, at the table with six chairs, at the hearth large enough to stand in, and at the two oversized chaise longues. Falcor tried to see the room through her eyes, and he wondered what she really thought of it.

He had always thought the tower perfect in its simple elegance, but maybe she saw it as austere, unadorned—savage. He, like his father before him, preferred a simple style. There were no statues of marble or adornments of gold in his tower. That was saved for another chamber, one he used only when another king visited.

The tapestry above the hearth had been made by his mother. The weapons on the walls were from each king that had ruled Kellian. There were a few luxuries to be seen, such as the rug he'd had imported from Pereth and the silver trenchers from Shadowhall. Even the candelabras, though made from simple iron, held candles scented with sandalwood and spices.

"Where is your bed?" she asked.

An image of him gazing down at Linarra with her tawny hair spread around her as he thrust deep inside her hot sheath flashed in his mind.

Falcor cleared his throat as his cock swelled. "My chambers are above us."

She looked at the ceiling then at the door they had come through. A smile pulled at her lips. "I see. The stairs stop at this chamber so anyone who comes to see you must go through here before your chamber."

"Exactly. We Kellians like our privacy."

She laughed, the sound completely unexpected and musical. He suddenly wanted to hear more of it.

"Why did you bring me up here?"

"I'm not in the habit of receiving women as gifts. Though you are very beautiful, I must return you to your king. I didn't wish to do that in front of a hall full of my people."

Her eyes widened at his words. "You wanted to save me embarrassment?"

"Aye. I will take you to your guards in the morning. It isn't safe to travel the jungle by night."

"My lord, I don't think you understand. King Usotae didn't send me to you for a bride. I am to be used however you see fit."

Falcor's fury roared to life. "Your king cares so little for your wishes that he would give you to me to turn you into a whore?"

Her hands clasped together in front of her. "I am a gift, Your Highness. It is rude to return a gift."

"It's rude to return a rug. A woman is something entirely different."

"Nevertheless, I cannot return."

In truth, Falcor was ecstatic to hear it, but deep in his heart he knew no good could come from her being in Kellian. She was an outsider and from Aldvale. Not a good combination.

Yet, his body wasn't listening. All he cared about was the beautiful specimen standing before him, offering herself to him. No man with a pulse could have turned her away. And Falcor was very much alive.

3

Linarra didn't quite know what to think of the ruggedly handsome king of the Kellians. Falcor wasn't what she expected, that was for sure. His regal bearing collided with his simple soft leather pants and dark red tunic.

Long, straight, flaxen hair was pulled away from his face and tied in a queue at his neck. Gray eyes similar to a turbulent winter sky seemed to peer into her very soul and call to her again and again.

His face was all hard planes and angles, giving him a potent, powerful look. He had a straight, narrow nose, strong jaw, and wide mouth. His full lips, tilted in a slight grin, looked as though they knew how to kiss.

Linarra shook herself. Only one man had ever tried to kiss her, and Usotae had made a muck of it. So why was she suddenly thinking of kissing now? And the enemy, no less?

Could it be because of Falcor's wide shoulders or his thickly muscled arms and chest? Or the way his eyes looked her over from head to toe, as if he contemplated devouring her.

Falcor exuded command and excitement, sensuality and passion—a heady combination, to be sure. Her stomach flipped and her blood heated as his hungry gaze swept over her again. Usotae had wanted her, but he had never looked at her with such . . . craving . . . as Falcor did.

To help dispel images of Falcor kissing her—touching her—Linarra turned and licked her lips. "Please, King Falcor, do not return me to Aldvale."

She was prepared to beg, to do anything to make sure she stayed in Kellian. When Falcor didn't answer, Linarra made herself face him. His stormy gray gaze caught and held hers, seeking the deepest recesses of her mind. She stood straight, refusing to bend under his stare.

"Something tells me you aren't being completely honest with me, Linarra of Aldvale. Why should I allow you to stay?"

"You might find me entertaining."

He chuckled. "I'm king. I have plenty of entertainment in my castle. What makes you so different that I would give you access to my castle and my people?"

This was the time for her to begin her seduction. If she didn't say something quick, he would send her back to Aldvale and Narune would be lost.

Think!

"You may have plenty of entertainment, Your Highness, but trust me when I say, you've never had anything like me."

For a long moment he stared at her, as if contemplating her words. Finally, he nodded. "I'll let you stay, but don't do anything foolish like try to spy for Usotae."

Linarra's blood ran cold at his words. How could Falcor already know why she was sent? She let her fingers caress her thigh before she rested her hand on her hip. "Do you really think he would send a woman to spy?"

"I don't put much past Usotae. I've already caught four of his spies over the past month. Now he sends me a very lovely, very enticing present as a peace offering." Falcor shook his head slowly. He dropped his arms and moved toward her. "Now do you understand why I think he's up to something?"

Linarra couldn't believe how easy it was to act the seductress. Of course it helped that Falcor was so devastatingly handsome. She held her position, eager to feel his touch and at the same time wanting to run away.

Falcor was dangerous, more dangerous than she could have imagined. She silently cursed Usotae for his stupidity. If Falcor had caught four spies, he would be on his guard against anyone, including a woman meant to seduce him.

He stopped a foot from her. "I will protect you while you are in Kellian, but if you try to spy for Usotae, or worse, try to murder me or another Kellian, it will be my sword you feel. Do you understand?"

Linarra nodded woodenly. Now both kings had threatened her. One with her sister, the other with her life. Though, to be fair, she'd do the same in Falcor's position. A king had to protect himself and his kingdom.

"I will have your guards return to Aldvale and have a servant find you a chamber," he said and started to turn away.

Linarra reached out and touched his arm. He froze then turned back to her. She swallowed to work up the courage that had deserted her. A separate chamber would not get her the secrets she needed.

"Do I not please you?"

His gaze once more raked over her, sizzling her with its intensity. "You know you do."

"Then why don't you want me?"

"It's not a question of want, Linarra."

Her name on his lips made her heart quicken. Her name had never sounded so sensual, so beautiful, as it did at that moment.

"I will see to your chamber. I gather you brought no more clothing?"

She glanced down at the black silken skirt. "Nay. I was told I wouldn't be wearing much once I arrived."

A smile pulled at her lips when Falcor's gray eyes darkened. She had to seduce him, and it was easier to do now that she had seen him, had felt his heat, fleeting though it had been. She didn't know why he hadn't sent her away. All she could do was be grateful she had the chance to carry out what Usotae wanted.

There was one thing she knew for sure: She would have no problem making herself kiss the handsome warrior king. In fact, she yearned to feel his mouth on hers. His nearness caused her breath to quicken and her blood to race. What would it feel like when he did kiss her?

"You caused quite a stir dressed as you are. I cannot allow you to wander the castle like that. The men will come to blows fighting over you."

She laughed. "Not if they know I'm yours."

He motioned to the left with his head. "There's a door that leads to my private bathing chamber. Feel free to use it while I see about a chamber and clothes. Are you hungry?"

"Aye, thank you."

He nodded and walked from the chamber.

Linarra let the smile drop and released a long breath. Falcor was cautious of her, which was going to make him difficult to seduce. Even more so because she liked him. There was something about him that seemed decent and fair. He didn't deserve Usotae's tricks.

But Linarra had to think of her sister.

She walked to the door he had motioned to and opened it. Pleasure erupted in her as she stepped into the lavish bathing chamber. The same black stone that the castle was built from was also in the chamber. Every shade of red could be seen in the chamber, from the lavish rugs of varying sizes scattered throughout to the vibrant flowers whose scent filled the air to the wide chairs that were placed near the windows.

Her gaze turned to the tub, though in truth the sheer size of it made it almost a small pool. It stood in the center of the chamber, about three feet high. Upon closer inspection, she saw that there was a pattern to the black stones that made up the tub. Every fourth stone had a beautiful design painted in a deep red.

Unable to resist the call of the water any longer, Linarra swiftly undressed and climbed into the steaming water. She let out a sigh and sank to the bottom.

The hot water soothed her muscles, which she had kept tense since leaving Aldvale. Gradually, she began to relax. The tub was so big she could literally swim back and forth in it if she so chose. She sank under the water to wet her head. When she surfaced, she wiped the water from her face and smiled.

She could get used to such splendor. No one in Aldvale, not even Usotae, had anything so marvelous. Linarra found a seat in a corner and sat.

The exhaustion of the day had taken its toll on her. She rested against the side of the stones and closed her eyes. But all she saw were incredible gray eyes darkened with desire. Her lips parted as she imagined him kissing her, holding her. She bit her lip as her nipples hardened, and she yearned to have his hand cup her breast.

A sound made her eyes fly open as her stomach clenched with fear . . . and excitement. The prickling of her skin made her aware she was being watched.

Linarra turned her head to the door and saw Falcor staring at her. He stood motionless, his gaze unreadable. And she found that she ached to touch him, to seduce him. A man she didn't know, a noble king she shouldn't believe, yet her body wanted him, *knew him* . . . trusted him.

And that's when she realized she was in danger of losing more than just her life.

* * *

Desire had never rushed into Falcor's body so swift and true as it did when he saw Linarra in his tub. Her bronzed skin, heated by the warmth of the water, glowed as droplets ran down her body.

Her golden eyes were riveted on him, waiting to see what he would do. But he didn't sense any fear. Instead, he sensed . . . desire.

Falcor inhaled deeply as he tried to calm his racing blood and a need so great, so intense, that it blinded him. Many women had turned his head, several had even held his attention for a while, but none had ever made him wild with such need.

None had ever made him . . . hunger . . . for just a taste of her.

The urge to feel her skin, to sample her lips, to claim her, was so powerful that he took a step toward her. The corners of her mouth lifted in a smile that was pure delight.

Who was the bigger fool? A man who sent such a woman as a gift? Or the man who received such a gift and turned it down?

Falcor had always thought himself able to see through deceit, but with Linarra, all he saw was the promise of pleasure beyond his wildest imaginings.

His feet moved slowly to the edge of the tub, his fingers just grazing the top of the black stones as he stopped. "Are you enjoying your bath?"

"Truly. I've never been in a tub so large or so beautiful. There is much about the Kellians that isn't known."

"Aye. We aren't the cruel barbarians people would believe us to be."

With a little push, she glided toward him, her magnificent tawny mane floating elegantly behind her. Long, slim fingers gripped the black stone and pulled her forward. Her gaze moved over him until she returned it to his face.

"Not a barbarian in the least, my king. I see before me a grand king, handsome and wise and powerful. A man that could have any woman in his kingdom but sleeps alone."

He didn't know how she knew he slept alone, and it didn't seem to matter. Not when she was so close to him and his need was so great. All he could see, and feel, was Linarra.

She stood, droplets rushing over her luscious breasts and down her flat stomach to the water below. Falcor lowered his gaze to stare at a body most men only dreamed about, a body that stood before him, asking—nay, begging—for him to take her.

Falcor considered himself to have a will of iron, but it was crushed when faced with the beauty before him. He desperately wanted to touch her, to run his hands along her skin and learn each curve of her body.

"Tell me, King Falcor," she said, her voice husky and seductive. "Why is it you are alone?"

"No woman has yet claimed me."

She smiled and ran a finger over his jaw. "Foolish women."

He was unable to stop his hands from reaching for her. The instant his skin made contact with hers, he felt a jolt of something raw and primitive move through him. Her eyes widened a fraction, but she said not a word.

With his hands on her waist, their bodies were mere breaths apart, separated only by the black stones and water. Water ran over his hands from her hair, teasing him to touch more of her, to *feel* more of her.

Her gaze lowered and her lips parted. Chills raced over her skin as her head lifted toward his. And for the life of him, Falcor couldn't think of a reason not to sample her full, ripe lips.

The first touch of her mouth against his was like the rays of the morning sun after a long, dark night. It beckoned him, urged him to taste more of her. Falcor ran his tongue over her lips, learning her, savoring her.

He took a deep breath and inhaled the scent of lilies, orange-wood, and sensuality. Scents he would forever associate with the wildly exotic woman in his arms, a woman whose very essence pulled at his soul.

His hands moved around her waist and up the delicate arch of her back. Strands of long hair clung to his skin as if seeking to mold him to her. But Falcor didn't need any assistance; he had already given in to the temptation she offered.

While his mouth and tongue learned her lips, her hands circled his neck and her fingers worked loose the queue to free his hair.

Just the feel of her nails raking over the skin of his neck sent chills down his spine. He could stand it no more. He slanted his mouth over hers as his tongue slid between her lips to mate with hers.

A small moan left her lips as she melted against him, her wet skin dampening his tunic. The more he kissed her, the more he wanted her. He deepened the kiss, urging her to give all she had.

She moved to kneel atop the stones, molding her body to his. It was too much for a man who was already on the edge. Falcor gripped her hips, rubbing his straining cock against her. She broke the kiss and leaned back to look at him. Her chest heaved with her erratic, labored breathing. Her gaze searched his, as if she hoped to find something in his depths.

"What are you looking for?"

She licked her lips. "Nothing."

Falcor let her lie, for he needed much more than explanations right now. "You taste extraordinary."

"Do I? Since we are confessing, let me say you are the first man to kiss me so wonderfully."

Falcor couldn't have been more shocked. "Usotae sends a woman to seduce me and she hasn't kissed properly before?"

"You won't be disappointed in me, my lord. I was given instruction on how to pleasure you."

Falcor closed his eyes as he imagined her mouth on his cock. He swallowed and forced open his eyes. "I should send you to another chamber."

"But will you? Even an inexperienced one such as I can feel our mutual desire. I'm yours to take," she said, and she guided his hand to cup her breast.

One feel of the exquisite weight of her breast and her dark nipple hardened. It undid Falcor. Without another word, he lifted her in his arms and turned from the chamber.

4

Linarra wrapped her arms around Falcor's neck as he carried her to a hidden set of stairs that took them to his private chambers.

The room was massive in size, with every luxury a king could want. A large bed stood against a far wall. Columns of black stones stood at the four corners of the bed and were draped in silky gauze of black and red. Pillows of every size and shape littered the black bed covering, each pillow covered in black and red.

He didn't slow as he took her to the bed and gently laid her upon it. Linarra tried to recall the training she had received before leaving Aldvale. But all she could think about was the man standing before her, a man with desire and need shining boldly in his gray eyes. Her lips still throbbed from his kiss. That kiss had curled her toes and made her stomach clench in anticipation of what was to come.

His hand caressed her hips before moving upward to stop just short of her breasts. Her nipples hardened and her breasts swelled at the thought of him touching her. Her heart raced and her blood pounded in her ears while her body screamed for him.

She had been more than bold when she had moved his hand to her breast in the bath, but she didn't regret it. Even now, remembering the way his nostrils flared and his eyes heated sent shivers of delight over her skin.

Yet, instead of cupping her breasts, Falcor plucked a strand of her hair from her chest. He rubbed the strand between his fingers before he brought it to his nose and inhaled.

"You smell as exotic as you look."

His words sent chills down her spine. Many men had called her beautiful, but only in the reflection of Falcor's eyes did she truly believe it. He made her feel attractive and interesting. His hunger only fueled her desire until she was drowning in it.

Her body wasn't her own. She no longer had control over it. As soon as she had laid eyes on the warrior king, she had known deep in her soul that he was unlike any man she had ever met. He oozed sensuality mixed with sheer power, and it caused her heart to skip a beat.

She opened her mouth to ask him, beg him, to touch her, but her voice refused to work. He dropped her hair and ran his fingers down her cheek to her neck and then to the valley between her breasts.

Her back arched, silently urging him to touch her breasts and give her some relief from the ravenous need coursing through her. A breath hissed through her teeth when he rubbed his palm over her nipple with the lightest of touches. Desire shot to her sex, causing it to swell and throb with need.

When he straightened and pulled off his tunic, Linarra rose to her knees. Her breath rushed from her lungs as she looked at his broad chest that rippled with muscles and tapered to narrow hips.

Her hands itched to touch him, to feel the valleys and hills of his muscles. But before she could, he kicked off his boots and unbuckled his sword. She noticed a large ruby in the hilt of his sword as he laid it next to the bed, but she soon forgot it as he reached for the waist of his pants. Her mouth watered as he unfastened his pants and tugged them off.

Linarra licked her lips in eagerness. He was magnificent, like one of the ancient statues she had been made to study as a young girl. Perfectly proportioned, burning with power and leadership, Falcor was like the early kings who had once fought over the kingdoms before they had been divided.

And for the night, he was hers.

He bent forward and his flaxen hair fell over his shoulder as a lock dropped into his eye. Linarra reached up and swept aside the strand of hair.

"Tell me again why no woman has claimed such a fine warrior as you?"

He chuckled. "I've yet to find a woman that stirred my soul as well as my blood."

His words made her stomach flip. She got lost in his gaze. She almost told him why she was really in Kellian, but she didn't want to spoil the wonder that surrounded them, not when there was a chance he wouldn't believe her.

"No more talking. I've something else in mind," he said just before his mouth claimed hers and he laid her back.

Linarra was more than willing to kiss him again. His kisses sent her spiraling into a place filled with pleasure and desire, a place where Usotae couldn't harm her or threaten her.

His hands caressed each side of her face as his kiss deepened. It scorched her with its intensity and kindled her growing desire until a bright flame of need swept over her.

Only then did his mouth move from her lips to her neck, leaving a trail of kisses with his hot mouth. Linarra basked in the feeling of his hard body against hers, tempting her, teasing her. His rod, thick and rigid, brushed against her stomach as he continued to nibble her skin.

When he came to her breasts, he paused for a brief moment cupping each of them in his hands and staring into her eyes before he bent and took a nipple in his mouth.

A soft cry tore from her throat at the wonderful bliss that ran through her as his mouth and fingers teased her nipples. He suckled one nipple as he thumbed the other until she was panting, the need between her legs growing with each breath she took.

She ground her hips against him and felt a jolt of pleasure. When she tried to repeat the movement, he stopped her with a hand on her hips.

"Nay," he whispered.

Linarra pushed aside her frustration as he reached between their bodies and cupped her sex. She sighed and pushed against him.

"Already hot and wet," he murmured. He kissed her stomach and his tongue traced her navel, which still held the golden stone. "A woman made for pleasure."

She had a hard time concentrating on his words with his hand on her sex and his mouth kissing her stomach. Her fingers curled into fists as she fought to keep from begging him for more.

But he didn't leave her wanting. His fingers parted her curls and he pushed one inside of her. She groaned and arched her back. In and out his finger moved, slowly stroking her, awakening her.

When he added a second finger, she felt him stretching her, moving deeper and thrusting faster. A strange sensation began to build inside of her, pushing her toward some unknown force.

He leaned over her, a strange light entering his eyes. "You surprise me."

She licked her lips and fought to concentrate on his words. "What's wrong?"

"You are a maiden still?"

As he asked this, he pushed his fingers deep inside of her. Linarra pressed her lips together and nodded.

"I should get up and walk away."

"Nay," she said and gripped his arms. "Please. Don't stop this wonderful torment."

He swallowed, his jaw clenching. "This isn't right. I shouldn't be the one taking your virginity. That right belongs to your husband."

"That right belongs to you." She let out a shaky breath as his finger stroked her. "I want you."

"I couldn't walk away now if I tried." He bent down and kissed her, a wild, fierce kiss that left her breathless and her mind in a whirlwind.

Heat ignited inside of her. His kiss revealed his hunger and his need, and it awoke in her the desire to please him, to touch him as he had touched her.

When she would have shifted, he moved her arms above her head and held her wrists in one hand. He stroked her sex and suckled her nipples until she writhed with need. Her sex clenched, eager to have his cock inside her.

His fingers withdrew and caressed her sensitive flesh, heightening her need with his teasing touches. Then, his finger swirled over her pearl with the slightest of movements.

A cry tore from her throat at the sheer bliss that consumed her. He added pressure as his finger moved quickly back and forth over her pearl. Linarra was panting, the desire making her body shake as she felt the need coiling within her. The pleasure was intense, exquisite.

The sensations that had been building within her suddenly came together, and in an instant, washed over her. A scream stopped in her throat as the wonderful, powerful vibrations ripped through her, erasing everything but the man holding her.

When the last of her tremors left, she opened her eyes to find Falcor watching her.

"By the stars, you are beautiful."

She smiled and touched his face. "Nay."

He grinned as he moved to cover her body with his. She sighed at the feel of him against her, his cock rubbing the sensitive flesh of her sex.

"You aren't supposed to argue with a king," he said just before he kissed the spot below her ear.

"I must have forgotten that." Her fingers ran through his thick, silken locks.

With the slightest shift, she felt him penetrate her, stretch her . . . fill her. The desire which had never left her flared to life again.

She wrapped her legs around his waist as he pushed deep inside of her. In and out he moved, each thrust sending waves of delight rolling through her.

The deeper he went, the harder he thrust. When he came to her maidenhead, he didn't hesitate before he pushed passed the barrier that marked her a maid. The pain was minimal as he tore through the membrane, and it quickly faded as he buried himself to the root.

He stilled, his arms shaking as he held himself above her. Linarra couldn't stop touching him. He was warm, hard. She loved the feel of his muscles moving beneath her hands.

His hips shifted as he began to move within her. She was blinded by the pleasure flowing through her. Linarra gripped his arms and met each of his thrusts, their desire feeding off each other until they felt as if they were the only two people in the world. The passion was fierce, the need strong.

When she opened her eyes to find Falcor watching her, Linarra knew she was lost. Whether it was Falcor or the exquisite pleasure he had given her, things had gotten extremely complicated.

She gasped as she peaked again. Each time he plunged inside her, he prolonged her pleasure. As the last of her orgasm faded, he pushed deep and stiffened as his seed poured inside of her. His head tilted back, and he gave a shout as he climaxed.

He rolled off her and tugged her against his chest. Linarra snuggled against him, content to lay quietly in his arms while their passion still filled them.

Falcor had been nothing like what she had expected, which made it all the more difficult to deceive him. However, no matter how much she might like him, her sister's life was more important.

There has to be a way.

But there wasn't, and she knew it. Usotae didn't threaten carelessly. He meant what he said. He would kill Narune without a second's hesitation. It made it worse that he had taken Narune to the palace. She would be locked in a dungeon and kept as a prisoner.

Linarra didn't even know Kellian's traitor or where to meet him. Usotae had just told her the spy would find her. She had no doubt that if she failed to bring information, Usotae would kill her sister. There was nothing Linarra could do to get out of her predicament. Nothing at all.

She would play the seductress and gain Falcor's trust as she must. A fool she wasn't, though. She had no intention of telling the Kellian traitor all of Falcor's secrets. She would keep some to herself to ensure she was kept alive.

Usotae would demand she tell him everything, and she would, once Narune was freed and out of Aldvale. With her sister safe, Linarra had only once choice. She would have to kill Usotae. If she didn't, he would forever control her life through her sister, and if either of them were to be free, he had to die.

She'd killed before, although the first time she hadn't meant it. This time, she wanted to kill. Narune could never know, though. No one could ever know.

"You are deep in thought," Falcor murmured.

Linarra shrugged and closed her eyes as his hands caressed

her back. "It's not every day that a woman makes love to a king."

"So that makes you special."

She smiled and laid her hand over his heart. "I think it does. At least for tonight."

"Tell me, Linarra, for a woman as beautiful and passionate as you, why hasn't Usotae wed you for himself?"

Slowly, she sat up. His question worried her. Falcor was an intelligent man. She had seen how quickly he had worked through things when she had rolled to his feet. How much had he guessed already? He had been reluctant to take her, and she knew he didn't trust her, but had Usotae let him know what she really was? Was this all an elaborate scheme to kill her?

She studied Falcor, suddenly worried. If she made the wrong decision, it could ruin everything. With nothing else to do, Linarra followed her heart. "I could tell you something that was half-truth, half-lie."

"You could. I would never know the difference."

"Maybe." She turned until she faced him, her knees drawn to her chest. "Usotae courted me once. For many years, the kingdom thought we would wed."

Falcor moved his arm under his head. "Did he find someone else?"

"Actually, it was me. I decided I couldn't marry him."

"He was heir to the thrown. I've known women to kill to be in your position. Why would you turn it down?"

"I wasn't afraid of being queen, if that's what you're thinking. I just didn't want to be his queen."

"There has to be a reason. He had to have done something. You tell me that he's changed. That Usotae wants peace. I know the Usotae that's been in power for the last several years. He's harsh with his people, brutal with others."

"Aye. He turned from the boy I knew and thought I wanted

to spend my life with, to a man I didn't recognize. A man I wanted no part of."

"And now that he's changed, as you say? Why not take him now? I'm sure he still wants you."

She laughed. "Would Usotae send me as your gift, to be used as your whore or your slave, if he still wanted me for his queen?"

"Or my wife."

She stilled.

"Ah, yes," Falcor said as he sat up. "That was in Usotae's missive. He suggests that if I find you appealing, I could wed you."

"What? He sent a missive?"

Falcor nodded. "I was given it this morning not long after you and your guards asked for entrance into the jungle."

"He actually said you could take me as your wife?" Usotae had said nothing to her about such a statement. She had always assumed she would leave once she had the secrets Usotae needed.

"He said nothing to you, then?"

Linarra shifted and rose from the bed. Her legs shook and threatened to buckle beneath her, but she stood straight. "Nay. He said nothing."

"Interesting."

"Why is that?"

"Why indeed? I saw the surprise in your eyes, but it wasn't just surprise. There was anger there as well."

"You're mistaken."

"So, tell me, Linarra. What secrets were you sent to pry from me?"

She whirled to face him, her heart thumping wildly. This couldn't be happening. "I was sent as your gift. Nothing more." Even to her own ears her voice was shaky, unconvincing.

"No man, king or not, sends a woman such as yourself as a gift unless he is after secrets, secrets to bring down a kingdom.

As wonderful as you are to pleasure, and as beautiful as you are to look at, you won't get any secrets from me."

Linarra couldn't breathe. Her sister's face flashed in her mind, her screams begging Linarra to help her reverberating in Linarra's head. She had vowed to Narune to get them out of Aldvale once her mission was done.

She had never lied to her sister before, but now she feared the absolute worst. Now she feared she might never see her sister again.

5

Falcor watched Linarra carefully. He could see the terror in her eyes, the uncertainty. It was obvious Usotae had blackmailed her, but why? Could it be because Linarra had refused to be his queen? Falcor had known vengeful men before when it came to women. It could be something that simple that pushed Usotae to send Linarra.

It was a bold move, and one that would have worked if Falcor hadn't had his own spies. His lust for Linarra was so deep it frightened him at how easily he had given in to her.

Linarra, however, had been a virgin. If Usotae had wanted to find the secrets he needed, he would have sent a courtesan who knew how to seduce a man. It was Linarra's beauty and exotic nature that had pulled Falcor under her spell.

Why then, was Usotae using Linarra as his spy? Her eyes showed everything, which meant she hadn't spied before. Usotae knew Falcor had killed all four of his spies, and only a fool would send another so soon.

Unless Usotae wanted her dead.

Still, that didn't make sense. None of it made sense. Especially why Linarra was helping Usotae. Why hadn't she just said no? Whatever Usotae was using to blackmail Linarra was strong.

Falcor had to discover what that was. Though he knew he would be better served by sending her back to Aldvale immediately and forgetting about her, he found that he wanted to help her. He didn't fully understand why, nor did he dig deeper to find the answers. It was enough that he wanted her with him.

You want her in your bed.

Without a doubt Falcor wanted her in his bed for many days to come. Linarra responded to his touch like no other. She didn't hold anything back, and she gave as much as she received.

It had been a long time since he had been so sated after a bout of lovemaking. Usually, he felt as if something were missing. But not with Linarra. With her, everything seemed . . . right.

"You are after my secrets, aren't you?" he asked again.

"I don't know what you mean."

He chuckled. He had expected just such an answer. "I have not kept my people safe by being naïve, Linarra. Be honest with me. I can be merciful, but I can be vicious if I feel my people, or my kingdom, are in peril."

She bit her lip and glanced away as if debating her options. Finally, she took a deep breath. "Just tell me something small, something I can send Usotae. Anything so he will think I'm doing what I am supposed to."

"Why don't you let me help you be free of Usotae and whatever hold he has over you?"

Her head lowered as she closed her eyes. "You can't."

Falcor rose from the bed and moved to her. Just as he opened his mouth to speak, he heard the door open below. "Supper has arrived as well as clothing for you."

He turned and reached for his pants. As he tugged them on, he couldn't help but wonder what was going through Linarra's mind. She acted desperate, and desperate people did desperate things.

Once his pants were buckled, he took his cloak and wrapped it around her. He then led the way downstairs. His servants had everything laid out on the table by the time they arrived. On one of the longues, the servants had arranged the clothes he had requested for Linarra.

Out of the corner of his eye he saw her walk to the gown and touch it. He turned to her. "They aren't as fine as the silk you wore, but I hope they will suffice."

Her head snapped up. "The gown is perfect."

She didn't hesitate as she pushed the cloak from her shoulders. It puddled at her feet in a whoosh. Falcor's body stirred at the sight of her luscious form. Her tawny tresses hung in damp waves to her hips.

He longed to run his fingers through their length, to feel the strands graze his thighs as she straddled him, to have her hair fall around his face like a curtain as she leaned over him and he thrust inside her.

Kellian women rarely let their hair grow midway down their back, so Linarra's locks were something that excited him in a way he couldn't explain but wanted to explore.

She pulled on the simple gown, unaware of Falcor's turmoil. The gown was a pale red and hugged her full breasts and small waist before falling smoothly to the floor. The neck of the gown dipped just enough to hint at the swell of her delightfully sensitive breasts. She touched her shoulders where the sleeves fluttered about her arms, making her look more sensual, more exotic than ever. She faced him and raised her brows in question.

Falcor nodded with a smile. "You look delicious. The Kellian dress suits you."

She laughed and walked toward him. "The gown is so soft. I feel as though I'm wearing nothing."

"It is made from a special thread from the wool of the ucas that graze throughout the jungle. They are difficult to catch, but their wool is the finest to be had."

He pulled out a chair for her and waited until she sat before he took his own. He handed a platter of boiled twinega eggs to her.

"Have you ever thought to trade the wool?" she asked after placing one of the eggs on her platter.

Falcor shrugged and passed her a piece of roasted fegan. "The meat is from one of the best-tasting foul in the jungle. I think you'll like it. As for trading, there have been occasions we've given the wool to a kingdom as a gift. Why do you ask?"

"I know the market at Aldvale, and I know that my people would pay handsomely for fabric such as this."

Falcor considered her words as he chewed his food. "Kellian is a rich enough kingdom, but it is something to consider."

"It would also allow other kingdoms to know the Kellians instead of fearing you."

"Sometimes fear is good."

"Why would you say that?"

"Because of the jungle. Too many people die each year because they don't know the dangers."

"So it isn't because you don't want visitors?"

Falcor thought over her words as he chewed. "My people don't care for visitors, but we do have them on occasion. We've gone so many generations mostly by ourselves that it has become our habit."

"Yet, if you start selling the wool, people can learn of the jungle and its dangers."

He grinned. "Were you sent to take the wool then?"

Her answering smile was genuine. "Nay, but I may ask if I can keep this lovely gown."

"Consider it yours."

She blinked, the smile slowly fading. "Truly?"

"Truly. Now, eat. The roasted fegan is one of our specialties."

The moon hung full in the sky, and the jungle was alive with sounds, even in the dead of night. Falcor sat on the window seat in the king's tower and thought of his evening with Linarra as he looked over his home. She was a rare gem, a woman pushed into being a spy by a man who had once sought her hand.

The message from his man in Aldvale had given him a brief warning that a spy would be coming to Kellian just before Usotae's missive arrived. Falcor had known Usotae would try something unexpected.

What continued to worry Falcor was how caught he would be had he not been warned of Linarra. He'd been unable to think of much else but her since the moment she rolled from the carpet in all her beauty. His lust was so strong, Falcor began to doubt if he could have kept anything from her.

Linarra's exotic splendor had captured his attention, but it had been her body that had pulled him completely under. Falcor had never likened himself for a fool, but he knew Linarra would have made him one. He just thanked the gods he'd been cautioned ahead of time.

"Do I keep you from your bed?"

He turned at her voice and found her beside him. "Nay. The jungle often draws my attention."

"I suppose having grown up here, it doesn't frighten you?"

Falcor laughed. "There is much about the jungle that would frighten anyone. There are carnivorous plants big enough to eat a grown man."

"Nay."

He nodded. "I do not jest. I've seen them, and they are vicious. There are predators who, with a swipe of one paw, could sever your head from your body, and small bugs whose bite can kill you."

She shuddered and wrapped her hands around herself. "I'm amazed I made it to the castle in one piece. Had I known ahead of time what awaited me, I don't think I would have come."

"I'm glad you did come." He hadn't spoken truer words in a long time. Despite her being a spy, he was glad to have her with him, even if it was only for a short while.

She clasped her hands together and leaned her head to the side. "I think I believe you."

"As you should."

"Tell me more of the jungle," she said as she sat beside him. "Were we in great danger coming to your castle?"

"Nay. My men brought you here. Without them, you might very well have ended up somewhere you shouldn't be. If you know what to look for, you can walk just about anywhere in the jungle. It's one of the reasons visitors who don't have my men escorting them usually end up dead."

"And you ran the jungle freely as a child?"

"Oh, aye. Every day."

Her brow furrowed. "Did your parents never worry? I don't think I would allow a child outside these walls."

He glanced out over the tall trees and thick foliage as he recalled the long days of his youth when he hadn't had the worries that rested on his shoulders now. "My parents most certainly worried. Especially my mother."

"You miss those youthful days."

He looked at her and gave a brief nod. "When you have such carefree, wonder-filled days, it's hard not to miss them."

"Where you ever injured in your outings?"

"Nearly every time," he replied with a smile. "My father would laugh and tell my mother to get used to my ways, but she never did. She was always waiting for me when I returned, ready to clean the wounds I had sustained. She didn't scold, though."

Linarra sighed. "She sounds like she was a great woman."

"The very best. She was kind and giving, and willing to open her heart to anyone in need. She was a good match for my father."

"What was he like?"

Falcor crossed his arms over his chest and chuckled. "Tall, stern, unforgiving as kings have to be at times. He was also honest, fair, and wise."

"Sounds like you learned a lot from him."

"I did. He often told me my mother made him a better man, that she softened his edges."

Linarra smiled as he spoke. "They sounded as though they were meant for each other."

"My mother often said as much."

"What happened to them?"

Falcor took a deep breath and felt the familiar stab of pain that accompanied thoughts of his parents. "My father was wounded by a tougar. His men weren't able to get him back to the castle before an infection set in. For three days he hung on, a fever raging in his body, before he died. My mother went a month later from grief. I think she died the moment he did, it just took her body a little longer to realize it."

"I'm so sorry," Linarra said, and she placed her hand on his.

Falcor stared at her hand against his. Her touch was soft but sure. "It was a long time ago."

"Tell me of your childhood," she said as she dropped her hand. "Did you have any brothers or sisters?"

"Nay, only me. What of you?"

She glanced away from him. "My mother died eight years ago, and my father just last year."

"I'm sorry."

She waved away his words. "My father was very sick. It was for the best."

"Siblings?"

"Aye, I have one. A sister."

Instantly, he knew she was the eldest. "She's younger?"

"How did you know?"

He shrugged. "A guess. Does she know where you are?"

"Aye."

Falcor pushed a strand of hair behind her ear and looked into her golden eyes. "I cannot help you return to her if I don't know why Usotae is using you."

She put her hand to his lips. "Don't," she begged. "I like you. I wasn't expecting to, but no matter what my feelings are, Usotae has to think I've succeeded."

"Or you die?"

She shook her head.

Falcor snorted as he leaned his hands against the railing of his window. "He has your sister, doesn't he? He's using your sister to get you to spy for him."

When she didn't answer him, he looked at her. "I can help you, Linarra. I can get your sister out of Aldvale."

She laughed then, her eyes wild with panic and resignation. "If only you could."

"If I could, would you trust me then?" She hesitated, and he took her by the shoulders. "Linarra?"

"Nay," she said softly. "He'll be expecting you to try to take her. I know him, Falcor. I know just what he's capable of. If you try to take her, he'll kill her."

"He wouldn't dare, because if he does, he knows he has no more hold over you."

Her brow furrowed as she thought over his words. "Maybe, but I cannot be sure. You're asking me to betray my people."

"Nay. I'm asking you to trust me."

"I don't know you."

"Your body knows me," he said just before he pulled her against him and claimed her mouth in a fiery kiss that set his heated blood raging.

One taste of her had only teased him. Her body was like a

drug, one that he wanted to return to time and again. The taste of her sweet lips made him only want her more. And the more he sampled her, touched her, the more he felt the stirrings in his soul.

She melted against him, her breasts pressing against his chest. His body, inflamed with need, wanted her immediately. He clawed at her gown, eager to have her body bared to him. Once it was pulled over her head, he tossed it aside and stared down at the beauty before him.

With a groan he fell to his knees and cupped her breasts, loving the way they filled his hands. Her bronzed skin was smooth and unblemished, warm and alive at his every touch.

He leaned forward and bent her to take a nipple into his mouth, letting his tongue swirl around the tip until it hardened and she pressed her chest against his mouth. His tongue ran back and forth over the tiny bud, making Linarra moan and her hands clench in his hair.

His mouth then moved to the valley between her breasts and down to her navel. He nudged the stone, eager to see it gone and replaced with a ruby to match his sword. But he didn't linger. His hands moved to her hips, kneading and caressing her.

Her legs parted when he kissed the tawny triangle that hid her sex. He lifted her in his arms and placed her on the window seat, then he opened her legs and flicked his tongue over her pearl.

The startled cry that tore from her lips made him smile. He settled between her legs and pushed a finger inside her. Her liquid heat nearly made him spill.

Linarra leaned back on her elbows and gloried in the feel of Falcor's mouth on her sex. His tongue was doing amazing things while his finger stroked her. Her body tingled with desire as she closed her eyes and let the feelings engulf her.

Rapture spread through her as she felt her orgasm building.

Each lick of his tongue and push of his finger inside her sent her toward the precipice of desire.

Hunger for Falcor consumed her. She wanted to touch him, to feel him, but when she started to rise, he pushed her back. Linarra gave in, certain she would have her turn.

She spread her legs wider, loving the feel of his tongue on her pearl. Her eyes closed and heat centered on her sex. She felt herself building, and she eagerly sought the release. She cried out as his fingers pushed deeper.

And then she climaxed.

Her world went black as her body convulsed with the orgasm. She drifted on a sea of pleasure, her body awash in ecstasy.

When she opened her eyes it was to find Falcor kissing the inside of her thigh as he watched her.

"I love watching you peak."

She smiled and sat up. "Do you?"

"Aye."

She knelt beside him and reached for his pants. "Twice now you've touched me. 'Tis my turn."

He stood and let her pull down his pants, freeing his thick, hard cock. She reached up and took it in her hand. He was smooth and hard and hot.

His eyes watched as her fingers encircled him and slowly move up and down his length. He sighed and briefly closed his eyes when her tongue flicked out to lick the head of his rod.

Linarra loved the feel of him. Legs of thick muscles held him still as she rose on her knees to place tiny kisses up and down his cock. When she reached his tip, she raised her gaze and took him into her mouth.

He let out a loud moan and gripped her head as her lips closed over him. Remembering her instructions, she cupped his sacs and gently rolled them in her hands while her mouth moved up and down his length.

This was one instruction she had thought never to use, to never to *want* to use. But with Falcor, everything was different. She couldn't get enough of him, and the more he pleasured her, the more she wanted to satisfy him.

His fingers threaded through her hair as he urged her to take him deeper in her mouth. Linarra widened her lips and took him deep in her throat. His moan was enough to tell her she had done just what he wanted.

She knew he was close to climaxing when he began to move his hips faster, his hands holding her head harder. And with a shout, he came.

Linarra licked her lips and leaned away as Falcor fell back on the window seat. She hadn't expected to enjoy having his rod in her mouth, but seeing how much he liked it made her want to do it again.

He touched her face, his eyes tender. "No one has ever done that before."

Bliss filled her. She shouldn't want to please a man who was supposed to be her enemy, but she couldn't stop the feelings within her.

Nor did she want to. Not when he promised such pleasure, such . . . surrender.

6

Falcor scratched his chin as he listened to Eldon. They sat in the great hall, which was empty except for a few servants. His commander began to recount what he had learned while spying in Aldvale.

"You're right, my king. Usotae is gloating about how Linarra will seduce secrets out of you."

Falcor sighed. "What did you learn of her? Anything?"

"She was once betrothed to Usotae. She called off the betrothal, but reports conflict as to the reason."

"Anything else? Why did Usotae send her?"

Eldon smiled, his dark blue eyes full of hate. "Several lords have asked for her hand, but Usotae refused them all. She won't have him, but he won't let anyone else have her."

"Then why send her here?"

"Punishment, I imagine," Eldon said. He clasped his hands behind his back. "Usotae isn't in favor with all of his people. I don't think I've seen, or heard, of a king as brutal as he."

Falcor leaned forward in his chair. "You said he sent Linarra here as punishment. Why? Because she wouldn't marry him?"

"That is part of the speculation. It is well known in Aldvale that she is here. Many expect her to fail, for Usotae has given her a daunting task, especially given how you've discovered the other spies."

"Only with your help, old friend. Now what happens if she fails?" Falcor had an idea, but he wanted to hear it from Eldon.

His spy let out a long breath. "She has a younger sister that Usotae is holding. She was suspected of murder several years ago, but before the trial could begin, he released her. Now, it is rumored that should Linarra fail, her sister will be tried for that crime and hung in one day."

"Well before Linarra could return to save her," Falcor said. He rose and walked the empty hall. "Did the sister commit the murder?"

"Some say nay, others say the evidence doesn't prove anything."

"For a man who refuses to allow anyone to have Linarra, I find it extremely odd that he would send her to seduce me." He turned to Eldon. "Would you send a woman you wanted, a woman that you had kept from everyone else, to sleep with your enemy?"

"Nay," Eldon said. "But then again, Usotae isn't a normal man. He wants power. Lots of power. He's looking to Kellian first, and afterward he plans on using the same strategy as he works his way through Hesione, Pereth, and all the small kingdoms. From what I hear, he even has his sights on Shadowhall."

Falcor snorted. "He'll never get Shadowhall." He paced the hall a few moments, gathering his thoughts before he stopped next to Eldon. "Can you get to Linarra's sister?"

Eldon's eyes widened. "You mean take her from Aldvale?"

"Aye. And bring her here?"

A slow smile spread over Eldon's face. "Aye, my king, I can. I've been waiting for an excuse to enter Usotae's palace."

"He'll be expecting you."

"He won't be expecting what I have in store for him."

"If he thinks any Kellians are in Aldvale, he will kill Linarra's sister."

Eldon lifted a brow. "He's never known I was a Kellian before; he certainly won't now. Narune is kept at the palace. He's keeping her in the dungeons. I'll get in as soon as I can."

Falcor ran a hand down his face. "This mission calls for more men."

"I cannot bring many more in lest Usotae get suspicious. I may be able to bring a few of our men into Aldvale, but I'd never get them in the palace."

"Do what you can, old friend."

"I'll bring her to Kellian, Falcor," Eldon vowed.

Falcor watched one of his most trusted personal guards leave, confident that Eldon would return with Linarra's sister. Eldon never made a vow he couldn't keep. Falcor just hoped he returned in time.

He blew out a breath. Now, he had to make Linarra trust him enough to confirm all of what Eldon had heard.

Linarra rose from her bath and dried off. Falcor had left early that morning before she woke. When she had come downstairs, food had been waiting for her.

She had gone to bed with a smile on her face that was still there. Falcor had delved into her past, wanting her to open to him, but she had been afraid of the consequences. He might be able to free her sister, but would he still want her once he knew the extent of why Usotae had sent her? Would he still look at her with such passion and desire if he knew what she had done?

She wished she could explain what the feelings inside her were regarding him. He had been gone but a few hours and already she missed him—his warmth, his smile, his strength. He was a man unlike any she'd ever met. And ever would meet.

Deep in her heart, she knew had they met under different circumstances there could have been a future for them. But now, now she wasn't so sure. She had come to Kellian as a spy, to seduce him and earn his trust. The fact that he knew it only made things more difficult.

Falcor wanted her trust, but she didn't know who to trust. She wanted to believe him, but after what Usotae had done to her, it was hard for her to confide in anyone.

Would he be able to see past that to the woman she truly was? And if he could, what would he do when he learned that she had killed a man? Would he kill her as Usotae expected him to?

She didn't think Falcor would, but he might throw her out of the castle, letting the jungle kill her instead.

A shiver raced down her spine. She pulled on another gown that had been laid out for her. The gown was a beautiful shade of pale gold. A gown fit for a queen, she mused.

Linarra smoothed her hands down the front of the dress before reaching for a comb. She walked to one of the chaise longues near the window and looked out over the jungle that fascinated Falcor so.

She was so engrossed in combing out her tangles that she never heard the door open. There was only the stir of the air and the smell of sandalwood that told her Falcor had returned. She lifted her gaze to find him leaning against the door watching her, his arms crossed over his chest.

Her lips lifted in a welcoming smile, but the little jump her heart gave at the sight of him gave her pause. "You left early," she said as she finished and set aside the comb.

"I did." He pushed off the doorway to walk toward her. "You were sleeping, and I didn't wish to wake you."

There was almost a desperate look in his gaze that told her

he searched for something. But what, she didn't know. "Is something wrong?"

"I discovered some news recently."

She waited for him to continue. When he didn't, she raised her brows in question. "And?"

"Despite the wonderful lovemaking last eve, you haven't given me a reason to trust you."

"Trust me?" she repeated. "I . . . I told you the truth."

"Nay. You told me part of the truth. I'm offering you my aid, Linarra, not something I do lightly. You have nothing to lose by trusting me."

"I can lose my sister," she cried and rose from the chair. "That is something."

He nodded slowly. "My offer was to get your sister out of Aldvale. Alive."

Fear and anger throbbed in her heart. She had come to trust Falcor, a trust she had given him by the way he had touched her body, but it was a trust she had given too early. She should never have let down her guard.

"Nay."

He was at her side in a moment. "You don't have much of a choice."

"I have more than you realize."

She tried to move past him, but his hands were quick. He pushed her against the wall, his body molding to her as his lips descended on hers.

Linarra told herself to push him away, begged her body not to respond, but she could no more have ignored Falcor than she could have stopped breathing. She moaned as her arms snaked around his neck, accepting his kiss and the power his touch had over her body.

His hands were everywhere, touching her, teasing her . . .

tempting her with a passion that he alone had awoken, a passion that she wanted only with him.

She let out a small cry as he lifted her in his arms and moved toward the stairs, taking them two at a time. Excitement filled her as she realized he wanted her again, wanted her as she wanted him.

Just looking at him, remembering how his body stroked hers, filled her with hunger. He lowered her legs and held her until her feet touched the floor. Then, his hands moved to her gown, slowly drawing the fabric up until it bunched in his hands at her waist. With one tug, he pulled the gown over her head.

Linarra tried to reach for his tunic, but he quickly grabbed her hands. "Not yet," he whispered and nibbled behind her ear, sending delicious chills over her skin.

She wondered what new pleasures he would give her as he placed her on the bed. His hand moved to her shoulder and gently caressed her arm as he moved to her wrist. It wasn't until he pulled out some rope that she stiffened.

He raised a blond brow. "You'll enjoy this."

Linarra hesitated but relaxed and let him tie first one wrist then the other to the columns on either side of the bed. A fission of alarm filled her stomach when he began to tie her ankles to the columns at the foot of the bed.

"Falcor?"

He glanced at her over his shoulder as he stood and moved to the table and chairs near the bed. He sank into one of the chairs and leaned forward, resting his elbows on his knees as his head dropped forward.

Linarra pulled at her bonds. The knots were tight, not giving an inch as she tugged. Falcor hadn't moved, and she wished she had her gown on at least. She felt exposed, stripped . . . frightened.

"I didn't want to do this," Falcor finally spoke. His voice was low, softly spoken.

"Untie me."

He shook his head and raised it to look at her. "You gave me no choice."

"Untie me," she yelled and pulled harder on the bonds.

"Stop. You'll only harm yourself."

A sob stuck in her throat at the tenderness in his voice. Here was the king she had feared, the man who held her life in his hands.

"I'm going to ask you one more time to tell me why Usotae sent you here," he said.

Linarra briefly closed her eyes. She would rather die at Falcor's hands than let her sister die for her crimes, or worse, allow Usotae to kill her.

She took a deep breath. "I've already told you."

His chair creaked as he leaned back, drawing her attention. He studied her for several long moments that seemed to stretch into eternity. His hand reached out and took a small orange jar from atop the table.

"Long ago, my people stumbled upon a flower that, if ground and combined with certain ingredients, can make a person wild with desire. An aphrodisiac. Depending on how much, or how little, is applied, the hunger can last for hours. Even days."

Linarra swallowed as she looked at the small, seemingly harmless jar.

"The cream is saved for special circumstances. It can take lovemaking to another level if used with caution, but more times than not, too much is used, sending the person into a wild ride of need where they think they are satisfied only to find the need upon them again, stronger each time."

He turned the jar around in his fingers, staring at it before he rose to his feet.

"Put anywhere on the body, the cream will react almost immediately. But if I put the cream on your sex," he said and reached down to lightly run a finger through her curls, "you'll need instant satisfaction."

"And if I don't get it?"

"The need will grow, pushing out reason and thought. Your sole need will be to peak. You'll do anything, say anything, for release."

7

Falcor watched Linarra's gold eyes widen and panic take hold. He had hoped—nay, prayed—that she would see him to be the fair king that he was, a man that she could trust to keep her and her sister safe.

"You're going to use that on me, aren't you?"

Though she tried to sound calm, he heard the break in her voice. Every fiber of his being wanted to throw the jar out the window, but he knew he had to do this to learn the truth so he could save her.

"I am."

"Why?" Her brow furrowed and her lips pressed together.

He let his finger trail over her thigh, the bronze skin smooth and toned. "Because it's the only way I'll learn the truth."

"Please. Don't."

It pulled at his heart to hear her beg, but he turned a deaf ear to her. "I can help you, but not if I don't know the details, Linarra."

She shook her head. "Don't do this, Falcor."

"Will you tell me what I need to know?"

She closed her eyes and swallowed. "I can't."

"Then you leave me no choice."

He moved to the foot of the bed and took the lid off the jar. His finger moved to dip into the cream, but he hesitated.

"Linarra," he said and waited for her gaze to meet his. "I'm not a bad man. I don't know you, but it's almost as if I know your soul. If this is the only way I can save you, then I'll do it. Even if you never forgive me."

"You're doing exactly what Usotae wants you to do." She blinked, her beautiful gold eyes filling with tears.

"He wants me to interrogate you and discover the truth?" He lowered his hand. "Why? So I'll invade Aldvale and give him the reason he seeks to retaliate?"

"How . . . Aye," she said reluctantly. "I don't understand how you know that."

"In order to rule a kingdom and keep your people safe, you have to think like your adversary and your friend. Usotae hasn't tried to keep his ambitions quiet, so when word came that he was sending me a peace offering I was immediately skeptical."

"You have spies in Aldvale." It wasn't a question.

"I do."

"If you knew he sent me, why did you allow me in Kellian?"

He shrugged. "I was curious to see what sort of gift Usotae would bring. It also allowed me to learn more of him and how far he would go to gain Kellian."

"You used me just as he did."

"Nay." It came out harsher than he intended, but it infuriated him for her to compare him to Usotae. "I had no idea he had sent a woman until you rolled out of that rug."

She turned her head away, refusing to look at him. Falcor took a deep breath and dipped his finger into the cream.

When he'd first been crowned king, he had tried some of the cream to understand just how it felt. He had gone insane with want, his body searching for release after just spilling his seed.

It had been a vicious cycle he thought would never end and an experience he hadn't forgotten.

"One last chance, Linarra."

"Nay."

That one word sealed her fate. He set aside the jar and moved toward her parted legs. Just before he touched her, he recalled the easy way she had gone into his arms, the eagerness of her kisses and her cries of ecstasy as he brought her to climax.

That would be forever gone once he put the cream on her. But if he didn't, if he didn't learn the truth and save her sister, she'd be just as lost to him.

The thought of never having Linarra in his bed again was like a dagu to his gut. From the first time he had seen her roll seductively out of the rug to his feet, he had known their souls were connected in a way that defied reason.

Before he lost his nerve, he opened her woman's lips and applied the cream to her pearl. It was only a small drop, but it would be enough to make her body scream for about an hour. Enough time for him to learn what he needed.

Linarra closed her eyes at the contact of Falcor's hands on her body. But she knew instantly he had applied the cream for there was a current like lightning that snaked through her and came to rest between her legs like a fire. The need was instant and intense and demanded release.

She tried to ignore it. She focused on her breathing and not the way her nipples hardened as the breeze blew over them from the opened window. She tried to count backward instead of feel the pulsing in her sex. She clenched her hands into fists to keep her hips from moving.

But it was all in vain, for the cream wouldn't be ignored.

She cried out as a wave of desire washed through her, making her buck from the bed, seeking anything to rub against her to ease the need.

Suddenly, Falcor was beside her, touching her with his body from head to foot. She strained against her bonds wanting to caress him, needing his hands on her heated flesh.

He didn't speak. His hand moved to cup her breast and tweak her nipple, making her arch from the bed as her sex clenched and throbbed.

Each breath she took made the need grow higher, and each touch of Falcor's hand made her body yearn for more. She grew restless as his hand moved from one breast to another, teasing, stroking but never touching her sex.

She cried out and tried to turn toward him, but her bonds held her immobile. She moved her hips into the bed, trying to find whatever relief she could, but there was none to be found. Only Falcor could ease her.

The realization made her scream with fury.

"Tell me."

Distantly she heard Falcor's voice, and it took everything she had to listen instead of letting the desire drive her mad.

"Why did Usotae send you?"

She tried to answer, but the need was too great. All of a sudden, his hand was on her sex. His finger parted her curls and caressed her heated flesh. Linarra moaned and shifted her hips to feel more of him. He moved a finger over her pearl, using the barest of touches. But it was all she needed.

The climax, when it came, poured through her like liquid fire. Her body bucked with the force of the orgasm. She let out the breath she had been holding when the climax finally faded. When she opened her eyes it was to find Falcor on his side, his elbow braced on the bed and his hand holding his head, staring at her.

"Why, Linarra?"

Even as he asked the question she could feel her body begin to stir again. All he had said had been the truth. She would be in this torment until she answered all his questions. She had little choice.

"He wants Kellian. I told you that already."

"Why did he send you? Why did you agree?"

Linarra gritted her teeth as her sex convulsed. Falcor's hand was no longer on her, and she needed the contact.

"He wanted to punish me for refusing him."

"Why did you agree?" Falcor was relentless.

"He has my sister, and he threatened to kill her if I didn't do his bidding."

"Why? Why didn't you just run away?"

She sobbed and shifted her hips on the bed. "My sister was going to be tried for murder, a murder she was innocent of. He stopped the trial, but threatened to start it up again should I fail."

"How were you to relay the information to Usotae?"

"Falcor," she whispered as the desire once more consumed her, drowning out his voice.

Instantly, his finger was inside her, thrusting deep and quick. She sighed as the pleasure mounted. Just as before, the climax was quick, but more powerful.

Time was lost as the world went black while her body spasmed with pleasure. She licked her lips and took a deep breath. Falcor's hand still moved inside of her, giving her the friction she hungered for.

"Linarra?"

She nodded and moaned as he added a second finger to the first. "I was to meet a spy in the jungle."

"Usotae planned to leave you here for me to mete out justice, didn't he?"

"I think so," she said weakly. Her nipples ached and she

wanted to feel his lips on them again. She opened her mouth to ask him when he interrupted her.

"Did he plan on releasing your sister then?"

"He said he would."

Falcor's voice moved closer, his mouth near her ear while he began to move his fingers faster. "And you believed him?"

"She's my sister, all that I have."

Even before the desire could build, Falcor had stroked her into a frenzy. Before the last word was out of her mouth, she peaked. Her breath came in great gasps as her chest heaved, but still Falcor was unyielding. Her climaxes were growing shorter, the need more forceful with each one.

"He's counting on you telling me of your sister, isn't he?"

She nodded and arched her back, hoping his mouth would find her nipple. "His men will guard my sister constantly until I bring him your secrets. Only then will she be released. I think he plans to kill you."

"Interesting," he said just before his tongue flicked over her nipple.

The desire fell tenfold on her. "Falcor."

"Is that everything?"

"Nay. He has spoken with some Kellians who want to overthrow you. They are the ones I was supposed to contact with the information."

"By the stars, Linarra," he whispered before his body covered hers.

She didn't know when he had removed his clothes, nor did she care. The feel of his heated skin on hers was wonderful. She longed to touch him, kiss him, hold him, but he still refused to remove her bonds.

His lips claimed her mouth the same time his cock entered her. He plunged deep, touching her womb. His kiss was rough, demanding, and there was no doubt in her mind he was laying claim to her.

He ended the kiss and rose over her while his thrusts quickened. Linarra's gaze was caught by his. She looked deep into his gray eyes and for a moment thought she saw his soul just before her world was ripped apart by another climax.

She must have fallen asleep for when she opened her eyes, her bonds had been removed and Falcor stood at the window with his back to her.

She curled onto her side and watched the easy way his lethal body moved. He hadn't put on his clothes, and his contemplative mood told her he was weighing what she had relayed to him.

Her sex clenched, the aftermath of the cream still resonating in her body. Of all the tortures she could think of that he could have done to her, that had been by far the kindest, but not one she wanted to repeat anytime soon.

"I'm so sorry, Linarra."

She didn't wonder how he had known she was awake. "It is I who am sorry. I should have trusted you."

"But you still don't?"

"I've found that trusting someone is most difficult."

He turned to her. "This morning I sent a group of my men to Aldvale to free your sister."

She bolted upright, her heart falling to her feet. "You didn't? He'll kill her and your men."

"My men are very good at what they do. One of them has stood right next to you while you were at Usotae's palace and you never knew it."

She swung her legs over the bed. "All I asked of you was for you to tell me something so that I could help her."

"You said yourself that he wouldn't free her until he had all my secrets. No amount of secrets would have satisfied him. He would have told you to come back for more each time."

It was then she realized he spoke a truth she had refused to see. Her throat welled with emotion. "I just want to be free of him."

"Then trust me."

Linarra hesitated for a moment before she rose and walked to the man who had somehow managed to steal her heart. "I can get you the names of the Kellian traitors."

The look of wrath on Falcor's face made her tremble, but when he enfolded her in his arms, she knew if there was any chance for her to have a future, she needed to put her trust in the king of the Kellians.

8

Falcor's first instinct was to keep Linarra locked safely in his chamber, but he knew if he was to learn the names of the traitors, she had to venture out. He couldn't wait to learn who the men where, though he had an idea of who might be involved.

It had been a long time since he had felt such wrath, and the need to mete out justice was strong. This had to end soon lest it tear apart his people. He refused to be the king who couldn't keep his kingdom together. The Kellians had stood for too long for a power-hungry king and a group of traitors to rip it apart.

Falcor would die before that happened. He was prepared to pay that price—anything to keep Kellian out of Usotae's clutches. Falcor had sent a missive to his cousin Yarrow detailing all that he knew. Shadowhall was one of the largest kingdoms, and Kellian had always been on good terms with them. The fact that his cousin was the right hand of Shadowhall's prince had only helped them in the past.

Falcor didn't want to involve Shadowhall, but sacrifices had to be made. A call for help was the least of his problems. He knew Yarrow would come, and when he did, Marak would be with him. With his cousin and Shadowhall's prince at his side, he could face anything Usotae tried.

He glanced out the window and saw two men sneaking through the dense foliage near the gate to the garden below. His arms dropped from Linarra as he moved to his clothes.

"What is it?"

"'Tis begun." He buckled his pants and reached for his sword.

"Begun? What has begun?"

He heard the tremor in her voice as he finished pulling on his boots. He raised his gaze to her and shrugged. "The beginning of the end, Linarra. There can be only one victor. Either me or Usotae. It's time we discovered just who the traitors in Kellian are. They must be stopped."

She moved woodenly to the bed and dressed. "My sister—when will we know?"

"Soon." He yanked on his tunic and reached for the dagu that he kept hidden in his boot. "Ready?"

"Nay," she answered as her fingers combed through her hair.

"Leave it down."

Her hands stilled. "It gets in my way."

He moved to her and plunged his hands into her thick tresses. "I've never seen hair as long as yours. It teases me, tempts me. Much as you do. Leave it. For me?"

"How can I refuse such a request?" She rose up on tiptoe and kissed him.

He wrapped his arms around her and pulled her against him, eager to taste her once more. His body begged him to take her again, but he had waited too long to end the dissension in his kingdom to put it off any longer. He ended the kiss and offered her his arm.

"I will protect you."

She licked her lip. "I'm going to hold you to that oath. What if they suspect I've told you?"

"Oh, they will."

"What?" She halted, refusing to leave the tower. "What do you mean?"

Falcor blew out a breath and raked a hand through his hair. "Usotae knows that he has put you in a difficult position. Anyone in your situation would ask for my help. He's counting on you to do just that."

"So he can kill me?"

"I don't know."

She leaned against the door, her amber eyes filled with anger and doubt. "I knew he wanted to punish me. He made that very clear."

"And he knows you'll do anything for your sister."

She nodded. "He never intended for me to leave here. He expects me to die, doesn't he?"

"I believe so. He will then call upon Aldvale and demand revenge for your death. He'll invade Kellian in days."

"By the gods. What do we do?"

Falcor smiled, for he had a plan. "Do you trust me?"

"Absolutely."

"Good."

She hesitated before taking his arm again. "What do I do?"

"Exactly as you've been instructed by your king, my love. You will tell the traitors my secrets." He steadied her as she stumbled on the stairs. "Easy."

She shook her head, her brow furrowed with confusions. "Falcor, you cannot be serious."

"I've never been more serious."

"I can't do this."

"Aye, you can. You'll not only save your sister, but thousands of lives."

She visibly swallowed. "You're sure this can work?"

"It will work."

"Gods help us," she murmured.

Once they were seated in the great hall, Falcor bided his time. As usual, the hall was filled with his people. As soon as word spread that he had Linarra with him, they wanted a look at her. Many craned their heads to see the woman who sat at Falcor's feet with her long tawny hair hanging loose about her hips.

He hadn't wanted her on the steps. He had wanted her in the chair beside him, the chair reserved for his queen, but he knew it was imperative that everyone think she was his slave. The traitors were there, watching. Word would travel back to Usotae, just as Falcor wanted. Let Usotae think he held the upper hand.

Falcor's gaze returned to Linarra again and again. She sat facing him with her back straight and a slight smile on her face, as if it were an honor to be near him. Every now and again she would reach over and touch his leg, giving everyone the idea that he had bedded her properly. And repeatedly.

He caught sight of a group of men that he'd been suspicious of for some time. After a nod to his personal guards, he kept his eyes on them. They had been part of Cryoe's group. Cryoe had led the men, intent on taking over as king until Falcor killed him. Cryoe's men were a mean-spirited lot that loved to kill and plunder, and who desperately wanted Falcor off the throne. Falcor refused to allow them to continue their ways. They wanted to turn Kellian into a place for murderers and thieves, and he had put a stop to them immediately.

They were the best candidates for the traitors, and the fact that they couldn't keep their eyes off Linarra gave him the advantage he needed.

"Let's take a walk." Falcor stood and held out a hand to Linarra. "I'd like to show you our garden."

"Garden?" she asked with raised brows.

He felt the tremor run through her as she put her hand in his. He gave her a slight squeeze of encouragement. His vow to keep her safe would stand. His guards knew to take down anyone who threatened her.

"Falcor," she whispered.

He kept his gaze forward. "Trust me, Linarra."

They didn't speak again as they walked from the hall and out the door. The sun's rays blinded them as they exited the castle. Falcor hastily turned her off the path.

He chuckled and leaned close. Anyone looking their way would think he was nibbling her ear, not giving her instructions. "Once in the garden you'll walk away to look at flowers, giving the traitors time to find you. I will make sure I'm occupied and unaware of what you're doing."

"What shall I tell them?"

"Tell them Kellian has an heir if something should happen to me."

She glanced at him. "Dangerous information."

"Information that has been kept quiet for too long. Ready?" he asked as he led her into the garden.

"Nay." She gasped and stopped to stare. "By the gods, this is a paradise."

Falcor let her look her fill at the unique flowers only found in the jungle. They had been transported to the castle where a grand garden had been designed with giant wir trees, beautiful flowers, and an array of vibrant vegetation.

It was a haven his mother had loved dearly. His parents had spent hours in the garden, holding hands and whispering to each other. Their love could still be felt in every petal and leaf. It had been a solace to him once his parents died. There wasn't a day that went by that he didn't visit the garden.

His gaze swung to Linarra. She was as exotic as the flowers that surrounded her. It was almost as if she belonged there, that they had waited for her. Now that she was with him, he couldn't imagine letting her go. No other woman would ever be able to replace her in his bed or in his heart.

When it was all over, if he survived, he was going to make sure Linarra had a reason to stay in Kellian. As much as he wanted to plan how he would take her, he had more pressing matters to think about—namely Usotae and the traitors.

The wheels had begun to turn as the plot thickened. He had assured Linarra she and her sister would live. Now he prayed he could keep that promise. Usotae was a formidable foe. Any man as power hungry as Usotae would stop at nothing to get what he wanted.

There was only one reason he could want Kellian so desperately. And it wasn't the ucas' wool.

Falcor fingered the ruby on the hilt of his sword and moved to sit on the bench his father had constructed under one of the giant wir trees. Just as Falcor had expected, one of Cryoe's men entered the garden and came toward him. Falcor forced a smile in greeting, and out of the corner of his eye, he saw Linarra step close to a group of talm trees.

Linarra couldn't believe the beauty before her. She knew without asking that every flower in the garden had come from the jungle. There were plants of every color and design, some growing in clumps, others climbing, but they were all spectacular.

Just as with everything else she had experienced with the Kellians, she hadn't expected this . . . grandeur. She was so engrossed in inspecting a small star-shaped lavender flower that when someone whispered her name, she jumped.

"Come closer," the voice said from a clump of tall swaying talm trees.

Linarra glanced at Falcor to find him speaking with a man. This was the chance they had been waiting for. She pushed aside her fear and walked to the trees. Her hands trembled and her stomach tingled with dread, but she stood straight and gazed into pale blue eyes through the foliage.

"Do you have something for me?" the man demanded.

Linarra wasn't about to divulge any information until she had a name to give to Falcor. "What do you mean?"

"Do not play coy with me," he ground out. "I know Usotae sent you to spy. Have you learned anything useful?"

She nodded and pulled one of the talm leaves closer to her face to look at the long fronds. "I do, but how do I know the information will get back to my king as it should?"

"There are seven of us. We will make sure he gets it."

"I was told not to trust Kellians."

He growled. "You had better trust me. If I don't deliver the information, your sister dies."

Linarra glared at him. "I suppose I must trust you."

"Exactly. Now, what secrets have you learned?"

"An important one."

There was a loud, impatient sigh. "Tell me."

"Not until I know your name. Usotae said you would give me your name," she lied smoothly.

He snorted. "Why would I do that?"

"As a way of establishing trust. Usotae told me to tell you nothing until I had a correct name. I wouldn't lie to me either. He whispered a name in my ear, and if you don't answer correctly, you will hear no secrets from me."

For a moment she thought he might actually strike her. His gaze narrowed as he clearly considered whether to believe her words or not. Linarra prayed she had done a convincing job, because if she hadn't, everything Falcor was working toward would be ruined.

"Mylar."

She had no idea if he lied or not since Usotae had told her nothing. Linarra licked her lips and raised her brow. Her heart pounded so loudly she was sure the man heard it. "I guess you really don't want to learn what secrets I've discovered."

"Wait," he hurried to say as she turned to leave.

She turned back to face him. Her blood felt frozen in her veins she was so frightened. "Tell me truthfully this time, or I walk away."

"Tracor. My name is Tracor."

Unwilling to take another chance that he lied, Linarra stared at him a moment. His gaze held hers, telling her he wasn't lying. "There is an heir to the throne."

There was a slight pause before she heard him issue a long curse.

She began to move away when he whispered, "Find out more. I will come to you soon."

By the time Linarra returned to Falcor, her stomach was in knots. Fear for her sister's life, as well as Falcor's, consumed her. He played a dangerous game, one that could get him killed at any moment.

She waited until Falcor stood and dismissed the man he spoke with before she went to him.

"I gather someone found you?" he said as he led her from the garden.

She nodded. She welcomed his hand upon her arm as he guided her around the castle. Though she would have loved to look closer at the outside of the castle, there were more important matters at hand.

"His name is Tracor."

"I should have known," Falcor growled. "He was Cryoe's right-hand man."

"Who?"

"Someone who had wanted my throne but was too afraid to challenge me for it."

"What happened to him?"

Falcor smiled. "He was killed."

She took a deep breath as thunder rumbled in the distance. "He said there were seven of them."

"Aye. I know who they are. My men are already watching them, but I'll double the guards. Did he say anything else?"

"He was angry when I told him you had an heir. They hadn't been expecting that."

"Nay, I suppose they weren't."

"He also said that he would find me again soon. They expect more secrets."

He stopped and faced her. "There won't be a need. I plan for this to be over by tomorrow."

"Falcor," she began, but he hushed her.

"All will be well, Linarra."

She looked into his gray eyes and saw a future for her . . . for both of them. A future of happiness and joy. Hope kindled in her heart, and she grabbed hold of it with both hands. Until she thought of the consequences. "You could be killed."

"So could you, but I won't allow that to happen."

"You aren't a god," she reminded him.

He grinned, showing a wicked side that she hadn't seen before. "Oh, you'd be amazed at what I can do," he whispered just before he lowered his mouth to hers.

9

Falcor made sure Linarra was safe in his chamber before he found his personal guards. These were men he had trained with since they were boys, men he trusted with his life. A king did not pick his personal guards lightly.

"Your Highness," they said as he entered the small chamber beneath the castle. Only he and the guards knew of this chamber. It led to a hidden doorway that would get the king and his family out of the castle should there be an attack.

"It's begun," Falcor said as he accepted the goblet of ale.

Dunlain blew out a breath. "About time. I'm tired of waiting for it."

Falcor grinned at the auburn-haired giant. Dunlain was one of the tallest Kellians. He stood head and shoulders above everyone. "Easy, friend. You'll get your chance at battle."

The captain of the guards, Wigar, leaned forward. "What happened, my king?"

"I've learned the truth from Linarra. Usotae sent her here to spy, as we suspected."

The men grumbled, their ire already high.

Falcor raised his hand to quiet them. "Contact was made with Linarra by Tracor. All seven of Cryoe's men have aligned themselves with Usotae."

"Are they that dim-witted?" Dunlain asked. "Usotae will have no need of them if he gains control of Kellian."

"I know," Falcor answered with a smile. "That isn't going to happen, though. Now, Wigar, what have you heard from Eldon."

"Eldon and his men made it into Aldvale without a problem, my king. It was his plan to have Linarra's sister out of Aldvale and in Kellian before nightfall tomorrow."

"Not soon enough," Falcor said. "Take a dozen men and rendezvous with Eldon."

"But, Your Highness—" Wigar hesitated. "You will need all of us if we are attacked."

"There are plenty more men, and I have the rest of my personal guards. I've doubled the men on patrol and set up men hiding in the trees. If Usotae attacks, we will know it well before he gets here."

"And Tracor and his men?"

Falcor smiled, eager to begin. "I thought it would be best to confront them before they can cause too much commotion."

The men smiled and nodded.

Once the plan was set for Tracor and his men, Falcor dismissed all but Wigar and Dunlain.

Falcor stood and rubbed his neck where an ache had begun at the base of his head. "Tracor may have swayed some of the younger men to join him. He told Linarra there were seven of them, but I know it has to be at least three times that amount."

"Aye," Wigar said. "He would lie to her just in case she told you."

"Exactly."

Dunlain leaned forward, the blade of his dagu gleaming in the candlelight. "I'd rather seize them tonight before they can do more damage."

"I thought of that," Falcor admitted. "However, we need to know everyone that Tracor has turned. Not to mention, Usotae must believe all is still going according to his plans."

Dunlain nodded. "A sound decision, my king."

"Keep an eye on the men. If any look as though they are on Tracor's side, seize them."

"Aye, my lord," Wigar and Dunlain said in unison before they bowed and walked from the chamber.

Falcor rested his hands on the cool black stones and hung his head. "If any of the gods are listening, give me the wisdom of my father and the courage and strength of my forefathers."

If he failed, if one of his men had one misstep, it could very well kill Linarra.

"My king," Dunlain shouted as he ran into the chamber.

Falcor's head jerked up. "What is it?"

"Usotae is here. You need to leave. Now."

He clenched his hands. "Not without Linarra."

Linarra couldn't sit still. She tried to sleep. She tried to eat. She even took a bath, but nothing stopped the growing terror inside her.

Usotae would kill Falcor, of that she was certain. The thought of the warrior king dead left her heart in pieces. He told her everything would be all right, but he hadn't been able to hide the worry in his own gray gaze.

And her sister. What of Narune? Was she already dead? Usotae had placed her in the palace before Linarra had departed for Kellian. Usotae had assured her Narune would be alive when she returned, but he never intended her to return.

Usotae had to be stopped, and the only one that could do it was Falcor.

She paced the chamber, straining her ears to hear Falcor's approaching footsteps. She had no idea what he planned, but she knew it was going to be dangerous. It drove her mad not know-ing what was going on.

She walked to the large window where she stared out over the jungle. The thunder had grown closer, and she could see even now in the dark, ominous clouds that moved steadily to-ward them.

It was just by chance that she glanced down and caught sight of a group of men moving through the jungle toward the castle. Slowly she rose to her feet to get a better look at them, but she couldn't tell if they were Falcor's men or not.

She turned to race down the stairs when the door below banged open and Falcor yelled her name. She flew down the stairs and found him with his sword drawn.

"Here. I'm here," she said and rushed to him.

"We have to leave."

"What's going on?" she asked as he pulled her toward a mas-sive tapestry that hung from floor to ceiling.

He pushed aside the tapestry and opened a hidden door. "Inside," he said.

With her skirts lifted in one hand and her other holding onto Falcor, she followed him into the dark tunnel. Her breathing was loud, even to her own ears. She had never felt so frightened in her life, not even when she had killed.

"Usotae is here."

"What?" she gasped.

"He and his men began surrounding the castle about fifteen minutes ago. My men are following them, but before I engage him in combat, I wanted to make sure you were safe."

Emotion choked her, and though she had many more ques-tions, she couldn't speak. Instead, she worried about keeping upright as they raced through the tunnels.

When they finally reached the end, Falcor slowed to a walk and edged toward the opening. Linarra held her breath until

Falcor motioned her forward. Then they were running once again, this time through the jungle.

"Where are you taking me?"

"To the river," he answered. "Once you cross it, go to the castle and ask for Yarrow. He'll know what to do."

She pulled on his hand to stop. "I don't want to leave you."

He sighed and stepped toward her. "I don't want you to, Linarra, but I don't have a choice. I will return for you."

She wanted to argue, to tell him that she could help, but she knew he was only doing what he thought would keep her safe. How could she argue with that?

All her worries over the animals of the jungle vanished as she heard shouts from men who had begun fighting. She felt Falcor's urgency as he tugged her after him over the terrain.

She could hear the river roaring when Falcor came to a halt and jerked her behind him.

"Running away?" asked a voice Linarra knew all too well.

Falcor's body tensed. "Never. If you want a fight, Usotae, I'll be more than happy to accommodate you."

Usotae laughed. "Oh, I don't fight, Falcor. Only barbarians do that. Now, why don't you tell me who you're hiding behind you? It wouldn't happen to be Linarra, now would it?"

Linarra moved to stand beside Falcor and glared at the man she hated.

"It *is* you," Usotae said in mock surprise. "My, Linarra, you do work fast. I didn't expect for you to use your charms quite so effectively."

Falcor's hand squeezed her arm. "Leave her out of it, Usotae. Your fight is with me."

"As I said, Falcor, I don't fight." Usotae's smile vanished, replaced by an evil sneer.

Men moved from behind the trees to surround them. Linarra looked at Usotae's men, shocked that he had found them so quickly.

"I warned you," Usotae told her. "As we speak, your sister is being executed."

"You said if any Kellians came to the city she would die. None came."

He shrugged. "A king can change his mind."

Linarra lunged toward him, but Falcor grabbed her about the waist and pulled her against him.

"Not yet," he murmured. "When the fighting starts, run for the river and get across. Don't stop, and don't look back."

He was asking the impossible, but she would do it. For him. With a small jerk of her head as his answer, he released her.

Falcor knew the odds of his survival were slim, but if he could distract all of them and allow Linarra time to make it to the river, she had a good chance of getting across and finding Yarrow.

He stepped in front of her, blocking her from Usotae's view. A quick glance told him there were twelve Aldvale men. They would rush him at once, giving Usotae the time he needed to chase after Linarra.

Falcor slowly released a breath as he focused on Usotae. He had one chance to end it, one chance to kill Usotae. Linarra's hands moved against his back, reminding him she was there. He gave her a little push toward the foliage and leapt at Usotae.

Falcor raised his sword, a Kellian war cry sounding from his lips. Usotae's smile faded as terror widened his eyes. Falcor landed just steps away from him, but before he could get to him, Usotae's men attacked.

Falcor winced as he felt a blade slice through his tunic and across his back. He stepped and brought his sword down and across to plunge into the man's stomach.

Before he could withdraw his blade, he saw a weapon come at his head. He ducked and turned to come up behind a guard. Falcor smiled when another Aldvale soldier's sword sunk into the man.

Falcor pushed the dead guard away and kicked out at the other before the soldier could grab another weapon. Falcor's foot made contact with the guard's stomach, doubling him over. Then, Falcor raised his knee, crushing the man's nose into his head and killing him.

Falcor wiped the blood from his face and spotted Usotae. Pain ripped down Falcor's back, but he ignored it as he moved toward Usotae.

"Kill him," Usotae bellowed.

Falcor stopped and moved his gaze around the remaining nine men who seemed more hesitant than before to attack. He didn't wait to see what they would do. He took another step toward Usotae.

The guards swarmed him. Though he blocked many thrusts from weapons and hands alike, he felt many more sink into his skin. He lifted his arm and swung his sword in a wide arc to the side, slicing a man's throat.

Falcor gritted his teeth when a blade pierced him, sliding between his ribs. Blood poured down his side. His legs began to buckle, no longer able to hold his weight. He fell to his knees, each breath burning his lungs.

His gaze rose to Usotae's. The need to kill was strong, so strong that Falcor tried to stand but lost his balance and fell to the ground.

Leaves and limbs slashed at Linarra's face and arms as she raced through the jungle. Tears blinded her, making it difficult to see. She tripped over a root and landed with a thud on her stomach, her hands barely stopping her face from smashing into another root.

"Falcor," she whispered.

The river was in front of her, but the sounds of swords clanging made her rise and turn around. Falcor didn't stand a chance against so many men.

She glanced toward the river and the safety it offered, but she knew she couldn't go. To live without Falcor would be to live in darkness. She'd rather death than be without him.

Her decision made, she started back toward the man that had stolen her heart, and the vile scum who threatened the happiness she had found.

When she reached the small clearing, she peered through the leaves. Her heart fell to her feet as she took in the scene before her. All of Usotae's men were either dead or critically wounded, but it was the sight of Falcor lying on the ground with blood soaking his clothes that shook her.

She ran from the foliage and fell down to her knees beside him. She moved aside a lock of flaxen hair streaked with blood and looked into his gray eyes.

"You . . . were supposed . . . to leave."

She bent down and kissed him. "Shh. Don't worry about that now."

"Linarra," he said and shifted his leg toward him.

She looked at her hands and found them covered in blood—Falcor's blood. He was losing too much. She had to stop it, or he'd die. She turned to rip her skirts when someone grabbed her hair and yanked her away.

"Nay," she screamed and clawed at the hands that held her.

Usotae wound her hair around his hand until she had no choice but to stand. He leaned close to her ear. "You would save him rather than yourself? You didn't fall in love with the barbarian, did you?"

Linarra struggled against his hold. "I would. And I did."

He gave a vicious jerk and punched her in the side. "Hold still, whore."

Linarra's gaze moved to Falcor. She could see him weakening with each heartbeat. A tear slipped down her cheek for all that could have been.

"I told you I would kill him," Usotae boasted.

"You didn't, you filth," Linarra sneered. "Remember, you don't lift a sword. I'll make sure everyone knows that you were too much of a weakling to fight him yourself."

A blade pressed against her neck, digging into her skin and bringing a drop of blood that ran down her neck and into the valley of her breasts.

"You won't be alive to tell anyone anything," Usotae ground out. "I should have killed you the moment you refused to marry me."

"If you had, I wouldn't have been able to save my sister from the mongrel you sent to rape her."

There was a pause before he forced her head back as far as it would go. "It was you who killed him. I knew it."

Linarra smiled. "Oh, aye. It was me."

Falcor gripped the dagu in his hand as he listened to Linarra and Usotae. It was all he could do to keep his eyes open, but he forced himself to stay conscious, for he knew Linarra would need him.

He took a deep breath and pushed past the pain of his body. He focused on Linarra's face, a face that had come to mean too much to him in a short time. Never had he believed in souls recognizing another, but there was no doubt his soul had known what Linarra was instantly—his mate.

It seemed to take forever, the moment he had waited for. Usotae continued to blab about ways he'd kill Linarra, jerking her hair with every other word. Falcor could see the pain in her eyes and the way her lips pressed into a thin line, but he continued to wait.

He knew the type of man Usotae was. He would move at just the right angle, giving Falcor the time he needed to raise up and use the dagu.

Falcor smiled inwardly, for each time Usotae tugged Linarra's hair, she stepped away from him, bringing them closer to Falcor. A few more steps was all Falcor needed.

And then it happened.

Usotae pulled Linarra's hair and turned, leaving his side vulnerable. Falcor gathered all his strength and pushed up on one knee to plunge the dagu in Usotae's side.

Usotae gasped and stared dumbfounded at Falcor. "You . . . were dead."

"Dying," Falcor said. "Not dead."

The last of his strength gave out, and he fell onto his back. Blackness blurred his vision, and in the distance he could hear Linarra calling him.

Each breath became more and more difficult to take, and knowing that Usotae was dead and Linarra was free gave him the peace he needed.

"Falcor," Linarra whispered. She touched his face as the rain began.

He smiled and closed his eyes.

10

No matter how many times Linarra called to Falcor, he didn't answer. She heard something crashing through the jungle, but she didn't care if it was more of Usotae's men or a tougar. Her only thought was Falcor and keeping him alive.

"Let me see," she heard a voice to her left.

Linarra looked through her tears and the rain to find a man with light brown hair leaning over Falcor.

"Marak," he called. "We need to get him to the castle immediately."

The man, Marak, knelt on the other side of Falcor. "Nay, Yarrow. He won't make it. We need to do something now."

Linarra picked up Falcor's hand and held it as Yarrow and Marak began to staunch the flow of blood from Falcor's many wounds, with the rain helping to wash away the blood. She aided them when she could, but mostly she stayed out of their way. It seemed an eternity before they declared it safe to carry Falcor to the castle.

Even then Linarra didn't let loose Falcor's hand. She had to stay connected with him somehow, and the warmth of his hand told her he was still alive.

Inside the castle, Linarra was pushed aside as Falcor's personal guards and the two men undressed him and bandaged his wounds.

Linarra walked to the window Falcor loved to watch the jungle from. She glanced at her hands to see them still stained with his blood.

"I gather you're the woman who stole my cousin's heart?"

She turned to find Yarrow beside her. "Cousin?"

"Aye. Let me introduce myself properly. I'm Yarrow of Shadowhall and designated heir to Kellian."

Linarra forced a smile. "A pleasure. I'm Linarra, previously of Aldvale."

"And where do you hail from now?"

She took a deep breath and looked at the rain. "Kellian."

"It's a good thing Falcor is so strong then."

"What?" Her gaze snapped to him. "What do you mean?"

Yarrow grinned. "If there is no fever, he should be all right. He's lost a lot of blood, but we were able to get to him in time."

"How is that exactly?"

"How is what?" the man named Marak asked as he walked to them.

Linarra gazed at the blond, blue-eyed man. "How did you get to Kellian so quickly?"

"Shadowhall borders Kellian. Only the river separates us. With Yarrow being cousin to a king, we keep a watch on the river."

"And Falcor sent me a missive," Yarrow added.

She shifted her gaze to Marak. "I see. Are you related to Falcor?"

"I'm not so lucky." Marak gave a grand bow. "I'm Shadowhall's prince."

Linarra sank onto the window seat and began to laugh.

"My lady?" Yarrow asked as he took a step toward her, his brow furrowed.

She waved away his words. "I find it rather amusing Usotae thought Kellian so barbaric, so backward, that it never entered his mind that Kellian might be connected to other kingdoms."

Marak shrugged. "Usotae should have known better. Some men let the power of their position consume them."

"And some don't." Her gaze moved to Falcor. He looked so pale against the black linens.

"Go to him," Yarrow urged.

Linarra hurried to his side and took his hand in hers once more. Blood stained his bandages and dark circles ringed his eyes. "Don't leave me," she begged. "Not when I've just found you."

For days Linarra, Yarrow, and Marak took turns cleaning Falcor's wounds and changing the bandages. Each day Linarra prayed Falcor would wake and look at her with his lovely gray eyes.

A slight fever took hold of him on the second day, but they were able to keep it down. She didn't miss the exchange between Marak and Yarrow. They were worried.

Linarra rarely left Falcor's side. She talked to him, urging him to wake and whispering all the ways she would make love to him. A few times he moaned and turned his head toward her, but not once did he open his eyes.

By the fourth day, Yarrow no longer tried to hide his concern. "Linarra, there's something wrong."

"He just needs to rest." She smoothed back Falcor's hair and touched his whiskered cheek. "He'll wake soon."

"And if he doesn't?"

She glared at Yarrow. "Are you so hungry to be king you would step into his shoes before Falcor is dead?"

Yarrow stepped back as if slapped. "I don't want to be king.

I never have, but as the only heir, I am named. I'd much rather he marry you and sire a dozen children to take my place."

"I'm sorry." Linarra laid her head on the bed and sighed. "I just don't understand why he won't wake."

Marak rested a hand on her shoulder. "He had several wounds. I've seen men die from less, but Falcor is strong and he has much to live for. Don't give up hope."

Hope was all Linarra had been living off of since she had seen Falcor lying on the ground. She wasn't about to let go of it yet.

She let her eyes close, intending to rest them for just a moment. She didn't know how much time had passed when she was woken by something tugging her hand. Linarra raised her head from the pillow of her arms to find Falcor's fingers moving against hers.

Instantly, she was on her feet. "Falcor?"

His eyes opened slowly and met her gaze. She pressed her lips together as emotion welled within her.

"I'm. Here," he said hoarsely.

She wiped away her tears and brought a cup of water to his lips. He drank a few sips and laid back on the pillow with a groan.

"Don't do that to me again," she chided him. "I thought I had lost you."

He swallowed and grimaced. "You nearly did."

She smoothed back his hair from his face. "I know. If it wasn't for Yarrow and Marak, I don't know what I'd have done."

"Ah, so Yarrow got my message. Are they still here?"

"I'm here, cousin," Yarrow said and moved beside the bed. "As is Marak."

Falcor grinned. "Marak."

"Falcor," Marak said as he stood beside Yarrow. "We're glad to see you awake. You had Linarra quite worried."

"Not my intent."

Yarrow snorted. "You always were the dramatic one."

Linarra smiled at the exchange and watched the color return to Falcor's handsome face. She had never been so happy.

"Were you worried?" Falcor asked her.

She shrugged nonchalantly. "Not at all."

Marak and Yarrow burst out laughing at her lie. Linarra couldn't stop the smile that pulled at her lips when Falcor gave her a wink.

"We must leave now," Yarrow said. "We'll return in a few days."

"Good," Falcor said. "We'll have a feast then."

Linarra bid farewell to the men of Shadowhall. When the door clicked behind them she licked her lips, desperately wanting to fling her arms around Falcor. "You saved me. Thank you."

"I promised you I would. You promised to go to the river."

"I couldn't leave you. I . . . I've come to care greatly for you."

He took her hand in his. "You are free now, Linarra. Free to live your life however, and wherever, you like. Though, I had hoped that you would choose to stay here. With me."

She laid her head upon his chest. "There's nowhere else I'd rather be."

EPILOGUE

Falcor hated the weakness in his body. It had been nearly a week since he'd woken after sustaining the injuries, a week of pure bliss where he had come to know a great deal about Linarra. He had shared details about himself as well, secrets he had never told another soul.

He smiled as he remembered how nervous she had become when he mentioned her killing the man who had tried to rape her sister. It had taken a while, but he had finally convinced her he thought she did the right thing.

It was almost difficult to believe he had finally found the woman to be his queen, and a more perfect woman he couldn't have asked for. She was everything he wanted in a woman and more. She made him laugh, she made him angry, and she battled him on every front. But it made him a better man. Kellian was fortunate to have her, as was he.

As he gazed out his window in King's Tower, Falcor spotted the small band of men making their way to the castle. He had precious little time until they arrived.

He rose and grabbed the small black bag from a nearby table. "Linarra."

"Hmm?" she asked as she raised her head from the book she'd been reading on the bed.

"I want to give you something." Falcor lowered himself on the bed. He pushed her onto her side from her stomach and lifted his tunic she wore to reveal her navel where the gold stone still rested.

"What's in the bag?" she asked.

Falcor ignored her. "For many years I looked for you, hoping that one day I would find you, a woman worthy enough to be my queen and rule the Kellians by my side. I knew the moment I saw you roll out of that rug that you were her." He dumped the bag to reveal dozens of rubies of various cuts and sizes. "I don't want you to just fill my bed, Linarra. I want you to fill the roll as my wife and queen."

He lifted an oval ruby. "Say you'll be mine."

She blinked, her golden eyes full of love and hope. "There's only one answer I can give you. Aye."

Falcor smiled and removed the gold stone from her navel and replaced it with the ruby. "The ruby is the stone and color of the Kellians. All of these are yours to use however you wish."

"Mine?" she repeated and smoothed her hand over the stones.

"Aye. The jungle is full of them."

She laughed. "No wonder you didn't care about selling your wool to other kingdoms. The rubies give you all that you need."

"Nay," he said and pulled her to him. "You give me all that I need." Their lips met and desire swelled within him. Soon he would be able to claim her body once more.

"I have one more gift," he said and pulled her from the bed, tossing her a gown.

Linarra laughed. "You've given me more than enough."

"Get dressed. You'll enjoy this one most of all."

After she dressed, they walked from the tower and out of the castle. All the while she asked numerous questions to guess what it was he would give her. Falcor watched her closely as he stopped in the garden. It took her a moment to spot the group of men and the woman with them. The look of shock and delight on Linarra's face when she spotted her sister filled his heart with happiness.

The sisters ran to each other, their smiles and tears mixed together. They talked as one, each talking over the other with their questions. Their laughter and their joy was infectious. Falcor nodded to Eldon and Wigar. He would reward all the men who rescued Narune and returned her to Linarra. Kellian was safe, and his heart had been claimed. Soon his kingdom would be celebrating his marriage, and what a grand celebration it would be.

"How?" Linarra asked him. "How did you ever find her? Usotae told me she was dead."

Narune rolled her eyes. "He threatened it every day."

"Usotae had hidden her in the dungeons in Aldvale. It took my men some time to find her," Falcor explained. "Apparently, he anticipated I might send men to get Narune."

Linarra walked into his arms, the smile gone from her face. "I have something I need to tell you. I've wanted to tell you for some time."

"What is that?" He didn't like the serious look of her eyes or the way her brow furrowed. She should be happy, not worried.

"I love you."

Falcor smiled, his heart swelling with pride for the woman he called his. "I've known for some time."

"Have you?"

"Oh, aye."

"And?" she prompted.

Falcor shrugged, trying to hide his grin. "And what?"

"Don't you have something to tell me?"

"You mean, that I love you?"

She sighed and rested her cheek against his chest. "That's what I've longed to hear."

"I'll make sure you hear it often."

"I'll hold you to that vow, King."

He kissed her forehead. "Aye, my queen."

ENCHANTED

1

Amazon Jungle, April 1864

Arian de Busso, princess of Tulso, looked over the immense Amazon River from the safety of the bank. It had taken what had felt like an eternity to reach her destination.

After a year wasted as she convinced her parents to allow her to leave the kingdom, she was finally here. Her parents hadn't been happy about her decision to travel before she married. But Arian wanted an adventure. She wanted to feel alive before she was shackled to Tulso and her monotonous duties as a wife and royal.

Arian lifted her face to the sun and let the warmth drench her. A smile pulled at her lips as she thought about her older siblings huddled beneath layers of clothing in the frigid climate of their kingdom.

Tulso warmed enough during the summer months to allow them to wear a light sleeve, but never did one go with bare arms as Arian did now. Her body was accustomed to the harsh winter weather she had grown up with, so the heat and humidity of the Amazon left her body soaked in sweat.

But she loved every moment of it.

She glanced at her pale skin that had already begun to darken after just a few days in the sun. Now that she had a taste of the Amazon, she feared it would be harder to leave than she anticipated.

Who would want to return to the cold when she could have the splendor of the Amazon? Or even another amazing location. This taste she had of adventure had only whetted her appetite for more. There were so many other countries to see and experience. She might have to take a few detours before she returned to Tulso.

Her parents might never forgive her, but she would never forgive herself is she didn't take this chance, her only chance, at having an adventure. She needed as many good memories as she could to look back on in the long years of life at court.

It wasn't that she didn't know how fortunate she was to be a princess. It was told to her nearly every day of her life, but that didn't mean she had to like it. She didn't get to choose anything of her own, not even the color of her gowns. There was always someone, whether it was her mother or her father, who usurped whatever power she might have as a royal.

If anyone knew the truth of what it was like to be a princess of Tulso, they might think twice when they wished they could have her life.

She would gladly change positions with a commoner. She might be poor then, but at least she could make her own decisions instead of having someone make them for her.

It was one of the reasons her trip to the Amazon had been so important. It was the first time she had refused to let her parents ignore her. Her siblings kept telling her she would never get to leave Tulso, but Arian hadn't given up hope.

And now look where she was.

Arian bent to look at the dark waters of the river. She glanced across to the opposite bank and guessed it was easily several miles across. The sheer width of the river left her in awe. Nothing had prepared her for the exotic and wild beauty of the Amazon.

"Princess, be careful!"

Arian glanced down to see the toe of her boot below the water. She smiled at Vlad, her personal bodyguard who had been with her for several years.

"It's just water," she said and kicked it with her toe as she straightened.

Thomas, their guide while in the Amazon, stepped toward her. "You might want to heed your man, Your Highness." Thomas went down on his haunches by the riverbank and held half of a fish out in the water.

Arian leaned close to Thomas. "You've told me the Amazon has some very dangerous creatures. I understand that we must be careful."

"Watch, Your Highness," Thomas said softly.

No sooner had the words left his mouth than Arian noticed the water began to move. She spotted the fins of fish as they raced toward Thomas and the dead bait.

Arian stumbled backward when something began to tear at the fish in Thomas's hand. The water splashed and bubbled with the force of the fish beneath the dark depths. It wasn't long before there was nothing left of the bait but bones. Thomas released the bones and stood, his brows raised.

"What are those things?" Arian swallowed and looked at the river. Suddenly, the thought of cooling off in the water didn't sound like such a good idea.

"Piranhas, Your Highness."

Arian nodded. "Thank you, Thomas. I had no idea such a fish existed."

Thomas inclined his head. "The Amazon is so beautiful that many do not heed the warnings of danger. The piranhas are dangerous, but there is much more in the water to be cautious of."

Arian took a deep breath and decided she could live with the sweat that was layered on her skin for another day or so. There was no way she was getting in the river now. She shuddered just thinking about the small fish and the damage they had done to the bait in such a short amount of time.

She turned to the rain forest and let out an excited breath. Inside the canopy of the trees were creatures she had only seen in books and flowers she had only heard about. The Amazon had a beauty that could only be understood and appreciated by someone walking amid it.

"Come, Your Highness," Thomas beckoned as she stepped into the tree line. "Come and let me show you the Amazon."

Arian glanced at Vlad. His lips compressed and his jaw clenched as his eyes darted about. "All will be well, Vlad. You'll see."

"I don't know," he mumbled while his gaze scanned the trees limbs above them. "There is too much that can happen."

"Vlad, I have you, Thomas, and a dozen guards. I don't think another person has ever been so safe in this rain forest. Now come. I've dreamt about this too long to wait another moment."

Arian didn't look back to see if Vlad followed; she knew he would. Vlad was always there.

As soon as she walked into the rain forest, she gasped. There were trees so tall they seemed to touch the clouds. The trees' broad, dense leaves stretched for miles across the forest, blanketing everything below in shade and shutting out all but tiny rays of the sun that filtered through the crevices.

For a heartbeat, Arian could almost believe she had stepped into another world. It was so different, so amazing from anything she had ever seen that it couldn't be her same world.

Thomas moved to stand beside her. "I know. I had the same reaction my first time, Princess."

"It's . . . I cannot even describe the sheer beauty of it."

He chuckled. "There's more, Your Highness. Shall we continue?"

"Yes, please."

The many birds and animals were so loud they drowned out her thoughts. Arian closed her eyes to listen to the sounds of the rain forest and soak in the wildness. The adventure she had been dreaming of since she was a little girl awaited her, beckoning her.

Arian opened her eyes and hurried to follow Thomas. Her skin prickled with excitement. She couldn't wait to begin her exploration.

"Your Highness, wait a moment, please," Vlad said and rushed to her side. "I must stay near you."

Arian laughed. "It's only us and the rain forest. I sincerely doubt you will lose me."

"Don't forget the tribes," Thomas said over his shoulder.

Arian's gaze jerked to the guide. "You told us the tribes would leave us alone as long as we didn't harm them."

"Or venture into their villages," Vlad added.

"That is true, Your Highness," Thomas said. "However, the tribes are like the animals. You never know what they will do."

Arian sighed as Vlad laid his hand on the huge knife at his waist. "All will be well, Vlad. I think Thomas just wanted to caution us. Or frighten me into not venturing off alone."

"Did it work?"

"I've been warned, Vlad. I won't be going off alone anywhere in his jungle. I promise."

Vlad nodded and held back a limb so she could walk ahead of him.

"Did Thomas frighten you?" she asked the hulky guard. She didn't think anything could scare Vlad, but she knew he hadn't wanted to come to the Amazon. His duty to her had made him, however. Vlad preferred Tulso's cold climate, not to mention he didn't like wild animals.

Vlad sighed loudly. "As much as I hate to admit it, yes, Princess. He succeeded in frightening me."

She had an idea that Vlad had been anxious before they ever left Tulso. Her parents had made the tutors show him the dangerous plants and animals that could harm her. After that, Vlad had tried his best to talk her out of going to the Amazon and talk her into picking somewhere safer, instead.

Arian glanced at the dozen men that accompanied her. She had no doubt they would keep her safe. Vlad stayed by her side as she followed Thomas deeper and deeper into the jungle.

Anticipation poured through her. She could barely contain herself in her skin she was so restless to begin her great adventure. Yet, the more warnings Thomas called out about poisonous plants and the various treacherous animals, the more Arian began to doubt herself and the adventure she had craved.

As it was, she would be lucky to leave the rain forest without some type of bite or scrape that could very well kill her.

Vlad is with you. He would never let anything happen to you.

She kept repeating that in her mind to help keep calm. Eventually it worked and she was able to once more enjoy her amazing surroundings.

As they moved through the forest, birds with vibrant colors swooped down from the limbs above, their calls echoing through the trees. Several times Arian caught sight of animals through the foliage, but they stayed mostly hidden, as if they were watching her.

Each time she thought to take a closer look, she remembered Thomas's words about spitting venom and sharp claws and decided against it. Vlad's raised brows each time told her he knew exactly what she had been about to do.

Arian threw him a bright smile over her shoulder. "Admit you're having a grand time, Vlad."

"Princess, I'm having a grand time."

She chuckled at his dry tone and complete lack of enthusiasm. "Do try to contain yourself, please."

"As you wish, Your Highness."

Vlad was a powerfully built man. Many feared him because of his size alone, but only Arian knew he had a wonderful sense of humor and loved to play jests on others.

They traveled for about three hours when Thomas suddenly stopped and looked around.

"What is it?" Vlad asked.

Thomas shrugged. "I'm not sure."

"What does that mean?"

Thomas turned to him. "It means exactly what I said. I'm not sure."

Vlad fisted his hands at his side. "Then find out."

The hairs on the back of Arian's neck stood on end, as though she were being watched. She let her gaze wander over the jungle, but she could see nothing through the dense foliage.

As if sensing her fear, Vlad moved near her. "Princess, stay near me."

Arian crept closer to her bodyguard as out of the corner of her eye she spotted something dart through the trees. She tried to follow it, but lost it in the shadows of the jungle.

"What is it?" Vlad whispered.

"I saw something."

"Damn."

A cry from one of her guards at the rear of their group made them jerk around in surprise. Arian watched as the guard fell to the ground, his hand holding his neck. Her mouth fell open in surprise as she saw the dart with bright red feathers attached to it.

Vlad put a hand on her arm while he reached for his knife. "They won't get you while I'm still standing, Princess."

Arian knew he had said it to help ease her fears, but it only added to them. If anything happened to Vlad, she didn't know what she would do. He had always been there to help her, to aid her. She had done nothing alone since she had been old enough to walk.

She gripped his arm, her gaze scanning the thick branches of the trees above them. And that's when she caught her first glimpse of the warriors.

A scream welled up inside her. Before Arian could warn the men, they were surrounded. Warriors grabbed her, yanking her away from Vlad. He fought them until he was knocked unconscious to the ground by a vicious club to the side of his head.

"Vlad," Arian screamed, terror turning her blood to ice as she saw the blood trail down his face from his wound.

It was the last thing Arian saw before the warriors turned her away from the scene. She struggled against them as they bound her hands and feet. Behind her she could hear her guards fighting the warriors as they tried to get to her.

She screamed, and something was stuffed into her mouth, silencing her. She fought against the gag that was tied at the back of her head. Tears welled in her eyes as she realized how helpless she was to defend herself against such an attack. She had no weapon or any other means to try to get free.

Suddenly, she was lifted and carried through the rain forest as if she were some prized animal the warriors were bringing to their village as a trophy.

Vlad . . .

2
_____

Jensen D'Argent wiped his sweat-soaked forehead with the back of his arm and sighed. Even after four years, the heat still had the power to drain him. He sheathed the knife in his boot and reached for his canteen of water. He drank deeply, letting the cool liquid quench his dry throat, before he stood.

The bird he had been following had flown away before he could see its direction, but he had gotten a good sketch of it. After all this time, he continued to find new species of plants, animals, and birds. He was quite sure he would find many more species in the river, but the thought of a piranha getting ahold of him kept his feet firmly on land.

Jensen blew out a breath as he patted the notebook in his bag. That notebook listed all of his finds over the past months. Every couple of months he would send his notebooks to a friend at Harvard University who classified and documented Jensen's findings.

When he could, Jensen even sent samples. Harvard had dispatched a letter asking him to return to teach a course on the Amazon and his findings. It was a terrific opportunity, but the thought of leaving the Amazon wasn't something Jensen was ready to do.

It was odd. After all his travels and his restlessness, the Amazon had given him something nowhere else had been able to do. It had given him roots. There was nothing that could make him leave.

A group of monkeys in the trees above him began to yell at each other as they fought over some fruit. Jensen chuckled and turned toward the village.

It had been treasure that first brought him to the Amazon. Once he had found it, he had been unable to sell it and seek the fortune and glory he had longed for.

That treasure had belonged to a tribe of the Amazon, the Yanomami. Someone had stolen it from the tribe decades earlier, and they had thought it had been lost forever.

Instead of selling it, Jensen restored it to the Yanomami. In return, the tribe made him a member and gave him the honor of an elder. He chuckled every time he thought of that. As an elder he received special treatment, which only meant women were always throwing themselves at him.

He was just a man after all, and a man had needs. When those needs became too much to bear, he would relieve himself with one of the women. It was never more than that, despite the fact the women wanted much more.

But for Jensen, there was only one woman who had ever claimed his heart. A dark-haired temptress with amazing violet eyes. Those eyes held the promise of glorious passion for whoever dared to claim her.

Yet, for all his wanting of his temptress, he could never have her. She was a princess, and he was far below her in social status.

However, it hadn't stopped him from telling the tribe of his travels around the world and meeting this special princess.

Even after four years, he could still see her face as vividly as if she were standing in front of him.

She had been just a young woman, but he had seen the stunning, rare beauty she would be even then. He hadn't spoken to her, but when her gaze had passed over him, his heart had given itself to her.

It was idiotic for him to love a woman he didn't know, a woman he could never have. He had tried many times to find someone else to hold his attention, but it all came back to those violet eyes.

By the time Jensen reached the village, all he wanted to do was sit in his hut and dream about his princess and a life that could never be. He would speak of his finds to the tribe the next day, after he drowned his misery in a bottle of whiskey.

He was two steps into the village, and he knew instantly something was amiss. He hesitated, wondering if he should turn back into the jungle lest they try to marry him off again. But something prodded him onward.

When he noticed the people surrounding his hut on the outskirts of the village, he became concerned. As he walked to his hut, he nodded to the men as he passed. To confuse him even more were the number of smiles and whispers he heard.

What in the hell was going on?

He stopped outside of his hut where two of the Yanomami's most feared warriors, and his closest friends, stood by his door. They leaned upon their spears and smiled.

"Yuso, Magwi," Jensen said. "Tell me the reason you're gathered here isn't because you've found another woman you think would be perfect as my wife."

The men exchanged a glance. "No," Yuso said.

Jensen waited for him to say more, and when he didn't, Jensen clenched his jaw. He didn't like the apprehension that snaked down his spine. "Is there a jaguar in my hut then?"

Magwi's grin widened. "No. Something much better."

Jensen sighed. The warriors obviously weren't going to tell him. There was only one way to find out what was inside, and that was to have a look himself. He began to reach for his knife when Yuso's laughter stopped him.

Jensen fisted his hand. He was tired and in no mood for jests. "What is so funny, Yuso?"

"Trust me, Jensen. You won't need a weapon."

Jensen glanced at the warrior before he pushed past them and opened the door to his small hut. He stilled instantly, letting his gaze slowly move around his home while he took stock of everything.

And that's when he heard it—the soft breathing of a woman.

Jensen set his satchel by the door and moved to the back of his hut. Whereas the tribe slept on the ground, he had built himself a bed. He could envision any number of the tribe's women inside his home hoping to catch his eye and attention, but he wasn't prepared to see a woman sitting on his bed, her hands bound to the bedposts.

The sunlight from the opened windows poured into the small shelter, casting shadows throughout. A stream of light landed across the woman's face, and he noticed the gag in her mouth.

He started toward her, thinking it was another jest by Yuso and Magwi to get him married—until Jensen spotted hair as black as pitch draped over the woman's breast.

His cock hardened. He shifted, recognizing it had been quite a while since he had bedded a woman. Still, the thought of a woman's breast shouldn't send blood to his rod so quickly.

Then her gaze swung to him.

Jensen felt as if someone had punched him in the gut. He stared into violet eyes that had haunted him for four long years. Before he could speak, Yuso and Magwi walked inside. Jensen faced his friends, his heart pounding so fiercely he thought it might burst from his chest.

Violet eyes. Raven locks. If he hadn't been thinking of his princess, he could almost believe she was tied to his bed. But surely he was mistaken.

"What is this?" he asked in the Yanomami's native tongue.

"I knew as soon as I saw her," Magwi said. "She's the woman you've described to us, isn't she?"

Yuso snorted. "Of course she is. All you have to do is look at his face to know it's her."

Jensen ran a hand down his face. *It is her. My God.* "You can't just take her. She's a princess and important to her people."

"But we did," Yuso said. "It's the least we can do after you returned our treasure."

"She's a princess," Jensen argued again. "She'll have people looking for her."

Magwi chuckled then. "No, I don't think she will."

"You didn't kill them?"

He shook his head. "There wasn't a need. It was a small group, and we took them by surprise. While the men were fighting, Yuso and I ran off with your princess."

"She isn't mine," Jensen said with a sigh. *Though I wish she was.* He put his hands on his hips and squeezed his eyes shut. When he opened them, his friends were no longer smiling.

"You aren't pleased," Yuso said. "We thought you wanted her."

"I am pleased," he said. "Too pleased. That's what is so damn hard. I've wanted her for so long, and now that she's here, I still cannot have her."

Magwi clasped his shoulder and grinned. "Why not? It's no use to fight your destiny, Jensen. It wasn't coincidence that brought her to the Amazon after four years."

Yuso nodded. "When a man wants something as desperately as you've wanted her, why question the reason she's here. Take what is given to you."

Jensen watched his friends leave, their words echoing in his mind like a drum. Jensen's body flared with white hot desire just knowing she was near. He couldn't quite believe the princess was in his hut. Tied to his bed.

He groaned as his balls tightened. Now that she was with him, all the things he had dreamed of doing to her sent his heart racing and his blood to boiling.

Jensen closed his eyes and tried to make himself walk out of the hut. If he could leave, he would have Magwi return her to her people. She wasn't his. She was stolen.

For you.

But she wasn't *his*. She was a princess. He was nothing more than a commoner, and not even from her country. She was most likely married or promised to another by now.

Only one way to find out.

Jensen made his hands relax from fists. He tried to control the hunger for her that clawed at his belly, begging him for just one taste of her.

Like Magwi said, it isn't mere coincidence that brought her to the jungle.

Those words were his undoing. No matter how hard he tried or how much he pleaded with himself, Jensen couldn't make his feet move toward the exit.

He turned to face Arian and felt his gut constrict as he gazed at her beautiful oval face. Her expressive eyes regarded him with a hint of panic as he moved toward her. He knelt beside the bed and removed her gag so he could look at her wide, full lips—lips he could imagine gliding over his cock.

He bit back a moan and lowered his gaze. Which was a mistake since he found himself staring at her breasts. Her cream-colored gown was soiled and thin and molded to her curves by her damp skin.

To his agony, he saw the dark outline of her nipple through the material, and it was everything he could do not to reach out and thumb it until she begged him to take her.

"Who are you?"

Her voice snapped his attention to her face. He sat on the bed and cleared his throat. "My name is Jensen D'Argent. I was born in England but raised in America."

"Which explains your accent."

He shrugged. "I suppose it does."

"Why are you here?"

"I'm an explorer. I visited nearly every country before coming to the Amazon in search of a treasure."

"Did you find it?" she asked casually as if they spoke over tea.

He glanced at her bound wrists. She was scared, but she hid it well. *Brave princess.* "I did."

"Yet you are still here."

"The treasure belonged to the Yanomami tribe. I returned it to them."

She swallowed and looked around the hut. He could only imagine how dirty and dingy she thought his home.

"Still," she said, "if you are an explorer, why stay in the Amazon?"

He was intrigued as to why she wanted to know so much about him. His opinion of her grew at how easily she handled the situation. There were no tears or demands as he had expected from her, a princess. She was calm, her gaze direct.

"I'm not ready to leave," he answered after a moment. Life in the Amazon was simple. The tribe didn't expect anything from him. They accepted him for what he was and welcomed him. "I find I quite like it here."

They sat in silence for a few moments before she blew out a breath. "You haven't asked who I am."

"You haven't asked why you're here."

"No, I haven't. I assume you will get to that soon enough. Why don't you ask who I am?"

"I don't need to. You are Princess Arian de Busso of Tulso."

Her eyes widened in surprise. She regarded him silently a moment as she gathered her thoughts. He could almost see her mind spinning as she tried to remember if they had ever met.

"Few people know of our kingdom," she said. "Is it a ransom you want, then?"

He shook his head and chuckled. "First, Princess, I have no need to ransom you off. And second, I had no idea you were in the Amazon."

"You could be lying. You could have sent your friends to capture me."

"I could have. But I didn't."

She licked her lips and shifted on the bed. "Why was I taken?"

"I suppose they saw a pretty woman and thought I might like you as a prize."

Her lips pinched in agitation. "Then explain how you know who I am?"

"I visited Tulso on my travels. Four years ago, to be precise. It was during one of your sisters' weddings, I believe." Jensen didn't want to tell her any more than she needed to know lest she begin to wonder if the warriors had taken her on purpose and not on a whim.

"Teresa," she mumbled. "It was Teresa's wedding."

"The streets were lined with yellow flowers. The entire royal family was dressed in their finest, and your sister rode to the church in an open carriage pulled by four matching white horses. You and your family traveled in similar carriages behind her. It was a grand day in Tulso."

She lowered her eyes and nodded. "It was a long time ago. I was only fifteen at the time."

"Was your wedding as beautiful?" He wasn't sure what made him ask, but he couldn't believe that she was still unmarried, not a woman as beautiful and alluring as the one sitting before him.

Violet eyes rose to meet his. "My wedding is scheduled to take place six months hence."

A burst of hope flared in him. His cock throbbed, hungry to bury deep within her hot, slick sex. Jensen clenched his jaw as he fought to control his rising desire.

"Why am I still bound?"

He turned his head from her and took in a steadying breath. He had no answer for her, not when he wasn't sure if he could let her go. He knew he should, knew he didn't have any other choice, but for the life of him, he couldn't do it.

Whatever answer he was forming died on his tongue as the door to his hut was thrown open. Three women, each carrying a bowl, walked into his home. He stood, recognizing what the bowls were for. He opened his mouth to tell them to leave.

Only he didn't want them to go.

After all these years, the woman he had fantasized about and hungered for was in his bed. She was his to do with as he pleased. Only a saint would be able to let her go, and Jensen was far from a saint.

Without another word, he stalked from his hut.

3
_____

Arian felt her fear rush to the surface as Jensen left the hut. She wanted to call after him to stay, but a princess didn't beg. Not even one that was tied and at the mercy of a tribe of warriors.

The women situated themselves around her, setting aside bowls before they began to undress her. She clenched her hands to try to stop herself from shaking as her panic continued to mount.

She had thought for a moment that Jensen might let her go. To her surprise, his presence had calmed her. Their talk had given her a measure of hope despite the way his hazel eyes had roamed over her body as if she were a feast and he a starving man.

Many men had looked at her that way, but Jensen was the only one that didn't make the bile rise in her throat. The desire she had seen in his eyes had done strange things—exhilarating things—to her body. Even now, her stomach still quivered from his gentle caress of her cheek as he had taken the gag away.

His eyes met hers boldly as few dared to do because of her station. She liked his audacity. He treated her as a woman, not as a princess.

He had dark hair that reached his neck, and a strand that curled over his forehead, teasing his brow. He was handsome in a rugged sort of way, with an angular jaw and square chin, and his nose was bent as if it had been broken.

But it was his mouth that held her attention. He had a wide mouth and thin lips that she found herself wanting to kiss. Maybe it was the heat from the Amazon, but she had never felt so . . . wanton in her life.

While he had spoken to the two warriors that kidnapped her, she had noted his wide shoulders and how he towered over the others. She smiled as she recalled his strange accent. American mixed with British, and she loved the sound of it. She could listen to him talk all day and never grow tired of it.

He had sparked her interest, but it had soon faded when he left her with the three women. It was then she knew he had no intention of freeing her.

You wanted an adventure.

Yes, but not one that could cost her life. She took a steadying breath and tried to ignore the hands that took away her clothing.

Arian glanced into the bowls. Two held water, but one held dark oil. It didn't take her but a moment to realize she was either being prepared for a marriage . . . or a sacrifice.

She steeled herself to be sacrificed, for she refused to cry and let them see how frightened she truly was. She would stand tall and look them in the eye. They would know the true measure of de Busso royalty.

And Jensen. Him she would come back to haunt.

Her mind was jerked to the present when the women touched her. Arian gritted her teeth and looked at the far wall opposite her, thinking of anything other than the women's hands on her bare skin as they bathed her.

She found it more than peculiar that instead of her family or Tulso, she pictured Jensen's eyes, brown mixed with flecks of green. What was wrong with her that she thought of a man who would allow her to be killed?

Arian closed her eyes when the women touched her breasts. They washed her from head to foot, their soft voices filling the tiny hut as they spoke in a language she didn't understand. Once her bath was finished, one of the women combed her hair while the other two began to rub the oil slowly, meticulously into her skin.

Their fingers found muscles bunched in fear and tension and loosened them, gradually relaxing Arian until she felt herself begin to doze. She tried to keep her eyes open, but it grew more difficult with each heartbeat. She cursed herself for being ten kinds of a fool for trusting Jensen.

This could be a marriage.

Arian's eyes snapped open. A marriage? But to who?

Jensen. He did say the men brought you to him.

She swallowed, unsure of the joy that swept through her at the thought of being bound to him. He made her heart race, but he wasn't nobility. She couldn't marry him.

Or could she? She would much rather find herself married to Jensen than sacrificed. She had begged for an adventure, and she was certainly living one. If she kept her head, she might come out of it with tales she could tell her children and her grandchildren.

Arian could only imagine what her father and eldest brother would say to find her sighing in delight at the thought of being married to Jensen. She didn't know him any better than the man her parents had chosen for her, but there was something in Jensen's eyes, almost like a promise of pleasure.

She knew nothing of the pleasures of the flesh. Yet, with the fluttering of her stomach when Jensen was near, she wouldn't mind him instructing her. And if she returned to Tulso no longer a maiden, she wouldn't have to marry. She could convince her parents to send her to the country, where she could be herself instead of a princess.

Arian inwardly cheered at the thought and glanced at the women. Their gazes were appreciative as they looked over her body. One of the women smiled and leaned close. Arian thought she might whisper something in her ear, but a gasp tore from Arian's throat when the woman's fingers brushed over her nipple.

Her nipple sizzled with the contact and hardened before her eyes. No one had ever touched Arian so, and she was in such shock that all she could do was sit and watch as the women began to tease her nipples.

Arian couldn't tear her eyes away from her breasts as she watched the women. While one pinched a nipple, another ran her thumb back and forth until her nipples were hard, aching peaks.

A slow, burning sensation unfurled low in Arian's belly. Then there was the yearning. It called for something she didn't quite understand as it began to pump through her, heating her blood.

When the hands moved away from her, she didn't know whether to be relieved or angry. She closed her knees together when one of the women reached for her sex. Their hands were firm, insistent as they pried opened her legs. They spread her, exposing her sex to them.

Air washed over her flesh as shame consumed her. The women, unconcerned about her inner turmoil, bent and examined her most private place. Arian sucked in a breath and bit her lip to keep from crying out when one of them parted her women's lips and ran a finger slowly over her sensitive flesh.

All the breath left Arian's lungs as pleasure coursed through her. She was afraid to move for fear the woman would continue . . . or worse, stop. The woman grinned and tilted the bowl of oil to drizzle it over Arian's sex.

The warm oil began to heat her sex, creating an exquisite hunger inside her that she wanted to feel more of. Arian tried to ignore the desire and concentrate on freeing herself from her bonds, but it was useless.

Her sex throbbed, demanding more. She moaned when the fingers brushed over her again. Arian closed her eyes and turned her head away while the women began to rub the oil into her sex, teasing and caressing her flesh until Arian was panting, the need was so great.

The fingers were gentle, firm, as they shifted through Arian's curls and touched her, sending flames of desire shooting through her. Arian strained against her bonds, suddenly afraid of the sensations flooding her body.

The second woman began to tease Arian's nipples again. She ran her thumb over the peaks before circling the nubs until they were straining, begging for more. The third woman settled beside the first and dipped a finger inside Arian.

Arian lifted her hips, her mouth opened on a silent moan. The finger went deeper, stroking her until the woman spoke. Arian opened her eyes to see the woman remove her hand and say something to the other two. All three women turned to look at her with knowing smiles on their faces.

And as suddenly as they had come into the hut, they rose and departed. Arian was left with an unfamiliar and unrelenting longing pulsing deep inside her.

She arched her back and ground her hips into the bed seeking to ease some of the torment in her body, but it only made the hunger grow until it took over.

Jensen finished his bath in the hidden pool and walked back to the village. His cock had been hard since the first sight of Arian's dark nipples through her dress. As soon as he had realized he wouldn't let her leave before tasting her, he had wanted to take her right then.

It was by sheer will alone that he had made himself leave his hut and seek a bath. Every moment away from her was like an eternity. How many nights had he lain awake, his body shaking with need, as he pictured how he would kiss and stroke her until she screamed his name as she peaked?

Too damn many.

He stopped and leaned against a tree. He held control of his desire by a thread that was quickly unraveling. His mind told him to walk away from Arian, to forget she was there.

But every fiber of his being demanded he slake his hunger with the only woman who had ever haunted his dreams.

Jensen took a deep, steadying breath and straightened from the tree. That's when he spotted the women leaving his hut. His cock jumped. He knew what they had been doing, and he could well imagine what his beautiful Arian looked like with her skin glistening with oil.

Desire shot through him just thinking about his body gliding over hers, his cock burying deep inside her. His craving was too great to ignore. He had to have her.

His steps were slow, measured as he moved toward his hut. He didn't wish to frighten Arian with his desire, but the closer he got, the more his hunger grew.

He reached for the door when a hand touched his arm. He turned to find one of the village women beside him.

"She is a passionate one," the woman said. "Already, she is wet and waiting for you."

Jensen bit back a groan at the image of her words. He nodded to the woman before he walked inside his home. His gaze was riveted to the bed where Arian was still bound. Her naked body shimmered in the sunlight that spilled through a nearby window. Her midnight hair hung loose in thick waves around her shoulders to lay alongside her breasts.

He stepped closer and saw her eyes closed and her teeth biting her bottom lip. As his gaze moved down her beautiful body, he saw her hardened nipples and how her legs pressed together and her hips ground against the bed.

She was ready, just as he had been told. What had the women done to her? Not that he cared, as long as she was here and he could touch, kiss, and caress her as he had longed to do.

He wasted no time in removing his clothes and walking to the foot of the bed. Arian's hands gripped the bonds at her wrists, her head tilted to the side to expose her slim neck.

Jensen wanted to kiss down that neck to her full breasts, skim her narrow waist to the swell of her hips before parting the black curls at her sex and delving into her heat and wetness. When his gaze returned to her face, he found her beautiful violet eyes staring at him.

"What are you going to do to me?" Her voice was barely a whisper, as if it cost her greatly to speak.

He moved onto the bed and sat beside her. He saw her gaze go to his cock, and he found himself imagining her full lips closing over his rod to suck him deep in her mouth.

He inhaled. "You were given to me as a gift by the tribe. It is a gift I know I should refuse, but I cannot."

Unable to stay away another moment, Jensen reached up and cupped her breast. She sucked in a breath at his touch. The weight of her breast was mouthwatering and only made his desire soar. He moved his thumb back and forth over her nipple and heard her moan as her eyes drifted shut.

He leaned toward her and took the straining bud into his mouth, running his tongue over her nipple before suckling it. She moaned, louder this time.

It sent Jensen over the edge. His cock jumped, eager to be buried inside of her. Desire heated his blood, making his heart pound like a drum in his chest.

He had never hungered for a woman as he did Arian, never dreamed of all the ways he wanted to lick, taste, and suckle a woman other than the one in his arms. Her body was soft and curved just to his liking. She wasn't skin and bones, but all luscious, beautiful woman.

His mouth shifted to her other nipple. Her back arched, pushing her breasts against him while her breathing began to quicken.

"Oh, God," she whispered.

Jensen couldn't agree with her more. She tasted better than he could ever have imagined. He straightened and grasped her by the hips. He raised her up until he could move beneath her. When he opened her legs to have her straddle him, he felt her hesitate for just a moment before giving in.

He looked down at her damp curls and her sex that rested next to his cock. How easy it would be to slide into her, but he held back only because he knew she was a maiden. It was the only thing that stopped him.

She shifted her shoulders, and he knew she must be hurting, but he couldn't release her. Not yet, at least.

He once more cupped her breasts. He rolled her nipple between his fingers before he pinched it. Her eyes rolled back in her head and her lips parted on a sigh.

His cock rubbed against her damp sex as he leaned up to take her nipple in his mouth again. He couldn't hold back his groan of satisfaction, and when she moved her hips against him, he nearly spilled his seed.

It was pure torture touching her, but it would be like death if he turned away from her now. He flicked his tongue over her nipple before kissing up her neck. His hand moved to her sex, pushing his fingers through her curls.

She sighed when his fingers skimmed over her heated flesh. She was already wet and ready for him, but Jensen didn't want to take her yet. He wanted to savor the moment, for it would have to last him the rest of his life.

"What did the women do to you?" he asked.

She licked her lips and forced open her eyes. "They touched me."

"Where?"

"My . . . my breasts and between my legs."

He clenched his jaw just thinking of them caressing her. "Did you like it?"

Her lips parted as her brow furrowed. "I shouldn't have."

"But you did?"

"Oh, yes. I did."

He smiled at her confession. "Do you want more of it?"

"Yes."

"I've wanted you for so long that if I touch you, I may not be able to stop. I might end up taking you, Princess." It was honor that made him try one last time to walk away. "If you want me to leave, I'll go."

She shook her head. "Please. My body. It craves . . . something. I don't know what, but when you touch me, it feels wonderful."

Jensen shook from her words. He caressed her stomach until he came to her curls. Her gaze met his, her breasts rising and falling quickly. He shifted through her curls until he felt her heat and pushed a finger inside her. She moaned as her channel clenched around his finger. She was so very tight and hot, making his cock jump and thicken.

"Jensen," she whispered.

His name on her lips was the sweetest sound he had ever heard. He nuzzled her ear. "Relax, Princess, I'm not going to hurt you, only pleasure you."

At his words, she ground her hips against his hand. He pushed deeper into her before removing his finger and running it over her hidden pearl.

She let out a strangled cry and jerked her hips when he touched her. He pinched her nipple with his other hand and swirled his thumb around her pearl. Her lips parted on a silent moan as he continued to tease her body.

He knew she was close to peaking, but he wanted to draw it out as long as he could. He pushed a finger back inside her and began a slow and steady rhythm with his finger while his other hand rolled her nipple between his fingers.

Her hips began to move against him, soft cries coming from between her lips. He added another finger to the first, stroking her faster.

"Oh my God," she moaned and arched her back.

Jensen increased his tempo, pushing his fingers deep inside of her. He felt her begin to stiffen and gave her nipple a hard pinch. A soft cry tore from her lips and her body spasmed around him as her climax claimed her.

He closed his eyes and clenched his jaw as he fought himself on whether to take her or not. He sucked in a breath when her hips moved against his cock.

He was in heaven. He was in hell. To have Arian, who he wanted so desperately, in his arms was everything he had ever imagined it to be. But he knew it wouldn't be right to take her virginity. That was hers to give her husband.

Jensen knew he had to leave his hut or he would never have the strength to walk away from her.

Her voice was husky, soft, when she said, "Let me touch you."

4

Arian smiled into Jensen's startled gaze. She had shocked him, she knew, but she didn't care. She still wasn't sure what he had done to her, but it had been incredible. For a moment, she had thought she was dying, the bliss had been so intense, but as her body came back unto itself, she knew she wanted more.

Jensen lay back, his cock hard and hot as it rubbed against her sensitive flesh. She knew what it was for a man to take a woman, and she desperately wanted Jensen to take her. She yearned to feel his rod slide into her, filling her. She wanted to know what it meant to be a woman, and only he could give it to her.

Her sex clenched. She wanted to touch him, explore him as he had explored her, and she couldn't do that as long as she was tied. She had often wondered what it would be like to have a man touch her. Her sisters' opinions differed on the subject. Maria and Elizabeth claimed it to be the best experience of their lives, but Olivia and Georgina said it was so awful they often locked their doors against their husbands.

Now Arian knew what Maria and Elizabeth had meant. With

the difference of opinions it meant that a woman experienced such a wonderful outcome or not depending on how a man touched her.

"Untie me," she told him. "Untie me, and let me touch you."

He shook his head, his jaw clenched. "I cannot."

She tilted her head to the side and glanced down at his cock. "You want me."

"I do." His voice was gruff and low. "But if I untie you, I won't be able to keep my hands from you."

"If that were true, you would have already pushed your rod inside me."

His eyes closed at her words and his fingers dug into her hips. "Don't. Tempt. Me."

Arian was startled to find she did want to entice him. It was heady to see how much control her body had over him. The need for Jensen to thrust deep within her made her body shake with need.

"I am tempting you," she whispered. "You've touched me as no man has, shown me what it is like to experience a little slice of heaven. But I want more. I need more."

His hazel eyes snapped open. "You don't know what you're saying."

She ground her hips against his cock, loving the way it felt against her heated flesh. "I know exactly what I'm saying. I want to feel you."

"Princess, please. I'm hanging onto my control for you. I should never have let it go this far."

"Let go of your control. I'm asking you to take me. I'm begging."

He hesitated one heartbeat, two, before he reached up and untied her. Arian's arms screamed in pain as she lowered them, but she was free, free to touch the magnificent specimen of man beneath her.

Her hands ran over his wide shoulders. His skin was warm

and his body hard. With each caress of her hands, he moaned as if he never wanted it to end. Arian slid her hands over his muscled chest and rippled abdomen, enjoying the feel of his body beneath hers.

She licked her lips and glanced at his cock. She felt the heat of him against her leg, but she wanted to touch him. Just before her hand grasped his rod, he gripped her wrist.

"If you touch me now, I will spill."

She smiled. If there was ever a time for her to be herself, to say what was on her mind, it was now. "Ever since I saw you standing at the foot of the bed, I've wanted to touch you. I've never before touched a man like this. I've never even seen a man naked before you."

"Dear God," he said with a groan.

Arian didn't understand how her words could affect him so, but she found that once she began to tell him such secrets, she couldn't stop.

"One of my sisters told me how she took her husband in her mouth. She said he liked it very much. I think I would like to try that."

He cursed under his breath before he gripped her shoulders and pulled her against him. "You keep saying things like that, Princess, and there won't be anything left of me to explore."

Arian chuckled and touched his cheek. "You look at me like no one else has before. You actually see me, not the crown or my family."

"I've always seen you, Princess." His hand came up to push a strand of her hair behind her ear.

It was such an intimate gesture that for a moment she couldn't breathe. Her stomach flipped as his hazel eyes held hers, never wavering.

"Who are you really?"

His lips lifted in a slight grin. "I'm just a man who has spent the last four years dreaming of having you in my arms."

It wasn't pretty flattery that spilled from his lips but the truth. It showed in his eyes and in his actions. Nothing could have moved her out of his arms at that moment.

Her eyes drifted down to his lips. They had felt so wonderful on her skin that she wondered how they would feel on her mouth. She wanted to be kissed as only a lover could, but she wasn't brave enough to kiss him.

A kiss was erotic and personal. A man and woman could have sex and never kiss, because that kiss would take them to another level they might not want.

Arian licked her lips and regretfully looked away from his mouth as she wondered why he didn't kiss her. His cock nestled against her stomach, hard and hot, waiting to see what she would do.

Her sex clenched in anticipation, and her nipples, already sensitive from Jensen's attention, sizzled when she moved against his chest. A smile pulled at her lips when she heard him suck in a breath.

She leaned forward and began to kiss his neck, her hands caressing up and down his sides, learning the hard feel of him. When she could stand it no more, she began to kiss down his chest. She stopped at his nipples and flicked her tongue across the hardened nubs.

He groaned and dug his fingers into her arms, but he didn't hold her as she continued to lick and kiss down his chest. Her hair fell on either side of her face as she neared his rod. It jumped when her hair brushed across it, sending shivers of delight racing over her skin.

"Princess," he said with a moan.

Her mouth was breaths away from his eager cock. She wrapped a hand around his length and heard him hiss. She was amazed at how smooth he was, almost like the silk nightdress she had. And hot. Lord, he was so hot he nearly scorched her hand.

She moved her hand up and down his length, just as her sister had described. Jensen moaned, his hips rising to meet her. Her sex throbbed, hungry to feel that piece of him inside her. She brought the head of his cock against her lips and softly blew on him.

"My God." Jensen's hands fisted in the covers as a fine sheen of sweat broke over his skin.

Arian smiled before she ran her tongue over the tip of him, licking a drop of liquid that had formed in his small slit. He tasted salty, musky, and incredible. Without another thought, she parted her lips and wrapped them around him, slowly sucking his cock deep into her mouth as her sister had instructed.

He groaned, his body taut. But she wasn't ready to relent. She had discovered she liked touching him, tasting him. Arian angled her head and took him farther into her mouth, relaxing her throat. As she moved her mouth up and down his cock, her hands followed, bringing him as much pleasure as she could.

Nestled on her knees between his legs with her hair covering her face, Arian could only imagine how she looked. Desire began to hum through her as her body pulsed and her sex grew damp.

Her hand moved to his sacs and gently cupped his balls before rolling them in her hand. His moans grew louder, his body rigid, as if at any moment he would break.

She tasted more of his liquid, and she wondered if he was about to spill. She doubled her efforts, sucking him harder while her hand moved quicker.

"No." He lifted her and rolled her beneath him. "I want to feel you," he whispered.

Arian wrapped her arms around his neck and opened her legs so that he rested against her sex. "I'm yours. Take me."

It was all the encouragement he needed. He lifted his hips and guided his cock over her sex. Arian arched her back when he touched her pearl, sensations swimming through her. Her nipples ached for his mouth; her sex cried for his touch.

It was too much. Her body shook with need. "Jensen."

And then he pushed inside her.

Her breath lodged in her throat as his rod stretched and filled her. He eased out of her then pressed deeper. Again and again he pulled out only to thrust harder, deeper.

She knew the moment he met her maidenhead. Her sisters had warned her it would hurt, so Arian prepared herself for the pain. But as Jensen lifted his hips and plunged inside of her, she felt only a mild discomfort.

Her gaze lifted to meet his as he leaned over her. "Did I hurt you?" he asked.

"No." She wrapped her legs around his waist and shifted her hips.

He groaned and began to pump his hips harder, faster, their moans mingling. Arian loved the feel of him inside her. She couldn't believe how exquisite it was, and she never wanted it to end. The same wonderful sensation began to coil within her once again. With every thrust, it wound tighter and tighter.

She gasped when another climax tore through her, blinding her with its intensity. She held on to Jensen as he took her higher and higher.

Suddenly, Jensen pulled out of her, his cock landing on her stomach as his body jerked. Arian hugged him against her chest as his seed spilled onto her skin.

For long moments they lay together. She traced her finger over his back, content to lay as she was with his weight atop her. He kissed her neck and raised his head to smile down at her. Then, Jensen rose and walked in all his glorious nudity to a bowl where he dipped a rag in water and wrung it out.

Arian feasted her eyes on his beautiful body as he moved back to the bed. He gave her a wink and wiped away the blood on her thighs before he cleaned his seed from her stomach.

He tossed the cloth into the bowl and turned back to her. "I know I should apologize, but I cannot seem to find the words."

"I don't want your apology." Arian sat up and grabbed his

hand to pull him onto the bed. "I knew my trip to the Amazon would change my life, but I hadn't expected to find a man that would touch me so deeply."

"Your family will be furious at what you've done, not to mention your future husband."

She laughed and shrugged. "I don't care. I know I should, but I really don't. For so many years while sitting in the immaculate palace, I've longed for an adventure. It's why I chose the Amazon for my trip."

"An adventure, aye?"

"Yes. Don't think about apologizing, Jensen, when I should be thanking you."

"Princess."

She covered his lips with her finger. "You've given me something very special. No words can express how I feel about what you've given me."

5

———

Jensen blinked. He had known Arian enjoyed his touch, but he hadn't expected for her to feel as deeply as he. In all the years since his first time with a woman, not a single one of them had matched his passion or need.

Until Arian.

What made it even worse was that he knew he couldn't have her. He should never have touched her, but he hadn't been strong enough to turn away. When it came to Arian, Jensen wanted to give her all that he had.

Even now, all he wanted to do was lay her down and make love to her all over again. Her body was gorgeous, her taste delicious. He ran his tongue over her lips and tasted her. To be near her was to be scalded, but he would gladly burn to a cinder for one more touch.

"Were my men killed?" she asked.

Jensen blinked and focused on her face. "They are safe."

"My bodyguard, Vlad. There was blood."

"The warriors left all alive, Princess. Your man will be fine."

"What happens now?"

He shrugged. "I don't know. I've never had a woman given to me as a prize before."

She grinned and cocked her head to the side. "This is a first for me as well."

He chuckled at her teasing tone, but there was no doubt that he would have to release her soon. "I can take you to your men."

To his surprise, she leaned back on the bed, her breasts rolling to the side. "And if I'm not ready to return?"

"What do you want then?" He was proud of himself for sounding so calm when his heart raced at her words. He had dreaded the time she would leave, but it looked as though he would have a reprieve before he had to face it.

"You."

The word hung in the air between them.

Jensen looked away and raked a hand through his hair. As much as he would love to spend the day making love to her, the fact was, she was affianced to another. "When your betrothed finds out what you've done—"

"I don't care," she interrupted him. "For the first time in my life I'm doing something that I want to do without thinking of the consequences."

"But you must." He couldn't believe he was the voice of reason. Arian was here with him, wanting to stay, and he was trying to talk her out of it? Surely it was time for him to be admitted into Bedlam. "You have a responsibility as princess of Tulso."

She waved away his words and sat up. "I also have a responsibility to myself. Please, Jensen, let me have a few days with you. Let me forget about my duties and the future that awaits me. Let me be me."

He raised his head and looked at her. How could he deny her? If he was able, he would reach up to the sky and pluck the stars for her. "All right. If that is your wish."

She smiled and reached for his hand. "It's my greatest wish. Let's make the most of these precious moments we have."

Arian giggled as she listened to the story of Jensen's journey to Egypt. They faced each other from opposite ends of his bed, their legs tangled together.

"What was your favorite place?" she asked.

"Other than the Amazon, my favorite place has to be England or Greece."

"Greece?" she asked. "You've been there as well?"

He nodded. "Blinding white buildings against a bright blue sky, and the most beautiful turquoise waters you could imagine. I would love to return there one day."

"Hmm. Your description sounds lovely. I must make sure I see it for myself."

"If you go to Greece, you might as well venture into Italy. You would enjoy Rome."

"I'll put it on my list of things to see."

"Trust me," he said, "you'll enjoy Rome. There is so much history to experience."

She nodded, insanely curious about him. "Tell me of the treasure you found here."

"There isn't much to tell, really. Like all treasure, the stories of it have been passed through the ages, embellished each time. I heard the story of the treasure while I was in Budapest."

"Budapest?"

He chuckled. "Do you want to hear about Budapest or the treasure?"

"The treasure for now, but I definitely want to hear of Budapest as well."

"Another country I think you would enjoy. As I said, I heard of the treasure while in Budapest where the story said it was a vault full of gold buried deep in the Amazon River."

She leaned forward. "Was it?"

"Wait. Hear the story."

Arian blew out a breath and made herself lie back on the pillows. Jensen had such interesting tales. She could almost believe she had been with him as he spoke. "I'm waiting."

"Impatient are we?"

"I blame it on my upbringing."

He threw back his head and laughed. "Now, where was I? Oh, yes, the stories. I learned early on in my travels that as far-fetched as some legends may be, they began with a grain of truth somewhere. If you're patient enough, you can discover the origin of the stories."

"Is that what you did?"

"Yes. It took me longer than I anticipated, but it was well worth it. I've always wanted to come to the Amazon, and when I learned the stories circulating Europe began with the arrival of an explorer from the Amazon, I tracked him down."

"I'm surprised he hadn't found the treasure?"

Jensen scratched his chin. "Not for lack of trying. After I got him drunk, he told me the story he was told while in the Amazon. As soon as he finished, I knew it was something I wanted to look for myself."

"You actually got him intoxicated?"

"I do what I have to do."

"What happened next?"

"I started toward the Amazon. During my travels here, I stopped to do some research. The explorer had the wrong tribe. The treasure was stolen from the Yanomami."

"What kind of treasure?"

He grinned, a rakish smile that heated her blood. "It was a gold statue."

"Solid gold?"

"Of course," he replied. "It was a representation of one of their gods, the leader of their gods to be exact, much like Zeus was to the Greek gods."

She sat up and wrapped her arms around her legs. "How did you find it?"

"It had been a rival tribe that had stolen it. However, they feared keeping it, so they tossed it. Years later, a traveler was at the village when the leader grew sick. He recorded what he heard and saw, and one of the stories was that of the stolen god of the Yanomami."

"Amazing."

He shrugged. "The traveler's story went into great detail, but no one believed him. He told everyone he saw, which is how the tale of the treasure began to circulate the Amazon after so many years."

"But no one found it?"

"No. Despite the man telling everyone of the treasure, he had never told them how to find it."

Her brow furrowed. "Why not?"

"He wanted it for himself."

"Ah," she said and smiled. "He told everyone in the hopes that someone could give him information he didn't have. Did it work?"

"It did. He kept a journal with him and wrote down his finds as he trekked his way through the Amazon looking for the treasure."

"What happened to him?"

Jensen inhaled deeply. "He was so intent on the treasure that he forgot the first rule of the Amazon: Don't take her for granted. A jaguar attacked and killed him. The men with him found his journal and brought it back with them."

"And you found it?"

One side of his mouth lifted in a grin. "I did. I used the clues he had found with what I knew of the Amazon."

She scooted closer to him, eager to hear more of his tale. "How long did it take you? Did you have men with you? Did you know exactly where you were going?"

Jensen chuckled. "It took me nearly six months to find it, and, yes, I had men with me. No, I had no idea where I was going, or I would have found it much sooner."

"How did you discover it?"

"The jungle holds many secrets. Trees and plants and vines can cover an abandoned and forgotten city in record time. The man had said the statue was 'cast aside,' but what really happened was that the tribe had taken it to a lost city and plunged it deep within a hole in the ground that was used for sacrifices."

Arian shuddered at the thought. "You didn't go down it, did you?"

"I did. I didn't have any other choice. Even then, it took me nearly a week to find it. When I came out holding it in my hand, warriors from the Yanomami tribe were standing with my men."

"Did they demand it back?"

"Surprisingly, no. They had wanted to see if it could be found."

"So what made you return it to them?"

"It seemed the right thing to do. It had been stolen from them, and they hadn't demanded it back. They could have killed me and claimed it as their own, but they didn't. They simply turned around and left when they saw it in my arms."

She sighed, hating it when he paused in his story. "What happened then?"

"I cleaned the statue and found my way here where I presented it to their leader."

She pressed her lips together. To be a man and to travel as he did. How wonderful life could be. "What a grand adventure."

"Not for the faint of heart, I'll admit that," he said with a smile.

"What did the tribe do when you returned their treasure?"

He reached for her hand to thread his fingers with hers. "They gave me an honorary position as an elder. I found I enjoyed this forest, and since I wasn't yet ready to leave the Amazon, I made my home here."

Jensen glanced over at the small chest on a table near his bed. Inside housed the amazing emerald the Yanomami had insisted he take when he returned the statue of their god. The stone was as big as his fist and worth a fortune and would easily keep him and his children and his children's children in luxury.

"What is it?" Arian asked.

"Just thinking how life never turns out as I expect it to."

"What did you expect your life would be like?"

He watched as she moved onto her stomach, holding her chin with her hands. "I don't know, really. I left just looking to see the world. You don't realize how big it is until you begin to explore it."

"What did you learn from your travels?"

"That languages may separate people, but we're all fairly alike in many ways. I saw land so beautiful it hurt my eyes to stare at it, yet I couldn't look away. I saw people with nothing more than the clothes on their back, but they were smiling as if their life couldn't be better. They accepted their life and dealt with what was given them."

"Yet, still you continued to travel."

"I would stay a week or so in one spot, learning all I could about a culture. I wasn't a treasure hunter or a fame seeker. I just wanted to see what life was out there for me."

She smiled. "And have you been happy with what you've been given?"

"Most certainly," he answered without hesitation. "The lessons I've learned, the knowledge I've gained, and the friendships I've formed are irreplaceable."

The smiled died on her lips and her gaze lowered to the bed.

"What is it?" he asked.

She shrugged and lifted her eyes to him. "All my life I've been told how privileged I am to be a princess, how fortunate I am to have the world at my feet. Yet, the world isn't at my feet. It's at yours."

He didn't know what to say to her.

"A long time ago I heard a man tell my father that nobility and royalty weren't a birthright but characteristics defined by one's actions," she said. "I didn't realize what he meant then, but I do now."

Jensen reached out and ran his thumb over her lips. "Don't sell yourself short, Princess. You are traveling the world as well."

She snorted very unprincess-like. "I wanted one trip before my marriage. It took me nearly a year to convince my parents that I would be safe traveling with my bodyguard and the royal guards. One week in the Amazon is all I was given. Not so much a traveler, I'm afraid."

"Who says you can't travel later?" He'd almost said "after your marriage," but he hadn't wanted to remind her of the other man any more than he had to.

She lifted her brows as she considered his words. "You're right, of course. I'll make sure that I go to every city and country that is on my list."

"Good for you, Princess."

He stared into her violet eyes, eyes that saw straight into his soul, and yearned to pull her against him and taste her lips.

Somehow he had kept from kissing her when they had made love. At the time, he had been trying to keep his distance from her to keep his heart safe. But his heart knew then what he just now realized—his heart had never been safe from her. She had claimed him, heart and soul, the moment he had first seen her four years earlier.

Letting her go would be the hardest thing he had ever done. When she left the Amazon, so would he. He would never be able to look at the rain forest again without thinking of his time with her.

When she had asked to stay, he had told himself to keep a wall between his heart and her, but it had been useless. One beautiful smile from her and he had been lost, telling her things he had never told a soul before.

It was so easy to talk to her, to tell her of his fears when he'd been traveling and how difficult it was to leave some places behind. She had given him encouraging smiles and understanding nods as he spoke.

His heart clutched in his chest.

Dear God, he'd gone and fallen in love with his princess.

6

Arian opened her eyes to find it night outside. She must have fallen asleep after their supper. She recalled Jensen pulling her back against his chest and stroking her hair, and she must have dozed off after that.

Her first day with him had gone by as if on the wings of a bird. She wished she could stop time and stay with him for several weeks or months, but she had seen his hesitation in letting her stay at all.

She took a deep breath and felt something on her breast. She looked down to find his hand cupped her nipple between two of his fingers.

"I've been waiting for you to wake," he murmured in her ear just before his lips grazed the sensitive spot on her neck.

A chill raced across her skin. "I wouldn't have minded being woken in such a manner."

"You're giving me ideas, Princess," he said as he continued to kiss her neck.

Arian moaned when his fingers pinched her nipple, sending waves of pleasure down her body to pulse at her sex.

"I like when you have ideas."

He groaned, the movement vibrating against her skin. "You taste so good. I could lick you from head to toe."

"Sounds wonderful. Then I could lick you."

"You're tempting me again."

His finger circled her aching nipple, coming closer and closer to it each time he went around. Her breasts swelled, eager to feel his touch.

"See what you do to me?" He rubbed his hard rod against her bottom. "I don't think I'd ever get tired of touching your body."

Arian pressed her bottom against his cock as he flicked a finger over her straining nipple. She squeezed her legs together and felt a jolt as her sex throbbed.

"My body hungers for you," she confessed. "Don't keep me waiting."

In an instant, his hand was at her sex, parting her curls with his fingers. He sighed into her ear. "You're already wet."

"For you. I'm wet for you."

He groaned and slipped a finger inside her. He knew just where to touch, just how much pressure to apply to send her body spiraling into an abyss of desire.

Arian gripped the covers as pleasure swarmed her body, making her blood heat and her heart pound. He added a second finger to his first, stretching her more.

She moaned and arched into him. He began to move his fingers in and out of her, brushing against her pearl as he did. She gasped at the waves of bliss that ran through her.

Though she longed to touch him, he had her pinned, unable to do more than lay there as he pleasured her body with skilled hands and lips.

"Jensen," she whispered when his teeth grazed the skin at her neck.

"Shh, Princess. Let me love you."

She was more than willing to let him do what he wanted with her. That glorious feeling began to spread through her, letting her know she was close to peaking. She closed her eyes and gave her body to Jensen.

Her breath hitched as he moved his thumb over her pearl before thrusting his fingers deep inside her. And then suddenly, his hand was gone. A heartbeat later, he lifted her top leg and pushed the head of his cock inside her.

Arian moaned and shifted her hips to accept more of him. Her hand reached around to touch him, connecting with his hip. She felt him clench his buttocks as he pushed farther into her wetness.

Once he was fully sheathed, he lowered her leg and began to move with long, slow thrusts. The feel of him from behind was deliciously wicked and completely different from their first time.

He thumbed her nipple with one hand while he gripped her hip with his other hand to help hold her while he thrust. The pleasure was almost too much for Arian. She wanted to turn away, but couldn't. With each stroke of his cock, she felt herself rising higher.

"Come for me, Princess," he whispered in her ear as he found her pearl and gave it a gentle tug.

Arian screamed as her body convulsed with her orgasm. On and on her climax took her as Jensen continued to plunge into her until he, too, finally let out a shout and pulled out of her, his body jerking with his orgasm.

Little tremors racked her body, making her long to have him inside her once more. Was she becoming a harlot? It was never enough for her. She had to have more of Jensen.

She turned to face him. "Why do you pull out?"

He touched her face gently. "I don't want you to have to worry about carrying my child."

When you leave. He hadn't said it, but Arian knew that's what he meant.

He was thinking of her, but she wished she could feel him spend inside of her, to hold his seed against her womb. She swallowed nervously as she realized that she wanted very much to have his child. Children had never been something she wanted.

Until now.

Until Jensen.

"What is it?"

She shrugged and lowered her gaze from his. "It's odd how you think you know what you want, then something crosses your path that makes you rethink everything."

"What's made you rethink things?"

She lifted her eyes to his hazel ones. "You. The thought of your child growing inside me is something I would like very much."

His gaze filled with pain and regret. "You're only saying that because we've made love. A few days away from me and you'll regret ever saying that."

She didn't argue with him because she saw how painful her words had been, but she knew she would never regret saying such words to him. They had come from her heart, a place that she rarely let anyone see, and it was a place Jensen had wormed his way into easily.

He pulled her against him to rest her head on his chest as his arm encircled her. It wasn't long before his breathing evened into sleep, but Arian stared into the darkness for a long time as she considered her future.

She had promised her parents she would return from her trip. She hadn't understood then why they had extracted that vow from her, but now she knew. They had known the temptation the world offered, and they had known how she longed to get away from the palace.

But had they been worried she would never get tired of traveling or that she might find someone she wanted to be with?

Her hand caressed Jensen's muscled abdomen, and she listened to the steady beat of his heart. It seemed natural to be in his arms, almost as if they were destined to be together.

Yet he was right. She had obligations as a princess, obligations that couldn't be ignored. Still, she found herself contemplating doing just that if it meant she could stay with him. She would give up her title if she could spend her life by his side.

Jensen made her feel like a beautiful, erotic woman. She often found him staring at her as if he were trying to remember every detail of her face.

A tear slipped out of the corner of her eye. She was a princess, given anything she had ever wanted, but she wanted nothing more than the man in her arms—a man she could never have.

Jensen tossed his princess her clothes. She rolled over and rubbed her eyes. She glanced from her gown on the bed to him.

"If you want to see what surprise I have for you, you'll need to put on your gown."

She blinked into the morning sun and sat up. "You want me to get dressed?"

"I would be more than happy if you'd like to stay naked, but I don't think you will want to walk through the village without your gown on."

"I agree." She grinned as she scooted from the bed and reached for her clothes.

He watched her, trying to memorize her every action, her every word, so he could recall them years later. He had once thought to find himself a wife and have a few children, but after having loved his princess, he knew there would never be another woman that could touch his heart so.

"Why are you frowning?"

He looked up to find her standing before him. "Just thinking," he answered and took her hand as he led her from his hut.

His gaze scanned the village. He wondered how she saw it. Would she see the beauty in how the tribe lived off the land, how they made use of everything the Amazon could provide them? Would she see the grace and skill the warriors had, the kindness and acceptance the women offered?

He wanted to ask her what she thought, but decided against it. She was from royalty. He could only imagine how she liked living in a small hut with dirt as her floor.

Jensen cursed inwardly. He had been a fool to keep her in the village. He should have released her the instant he realized who she was. Now, he feared he might never be able to let her go. And she deserved so much better than him.

Sure he could get a fortune from his emerald, but money wasn't everything. It certainly wouldn't get him his princess. He was a commoner, far below her in status. No one would accept him as her husband, least of all his princess. She might give it a try because she enjoyed the way he made love to her, but it wouldn't be enough to last a lifetime.

Fingers threaded with his and he turned to look down at her. He smiled, surprised at her willingness to touch him when everyone could see.

"Keep to yourself whatever thoughts you're having that make you frown. I don't want anything to mar our time together."

He gave her hand a squeeze. "As you wish, Princess."

"Good." She gave a quick nod of her head and smiled. "Now, tell me where we're going."

"I would rather you see it."

He caught Yuso's gaze as they walked from the village. His friend's eyes held a note of concern. Did everyone know how strong a hold his princess had on his heart?

She raised a brow at him, and Jensen masked his frown with a smile. He tugged her behind him as he pushed through the thick rain forest. As they walked, he pointed out the many plants he had discovered, describing how each one affected the rain forest and the animals.

"Amazing," she said, a hint of awe in her voice.

Jensen grinned inwardly. He doubted there were many things he could tell her that would inspire such a voice, and he was glad he had shared it with her.

"I enjoy it," he admitted.

After a moment, he stopped in front of a plant with leaves as big around as he was tall. "Are you ready?"

She giggled, her violet eyes alight with excitement. "Yes. Please, Jensen. I can hardly stand it. I've never been good at surprises."

His heart clenched in his chest as emotion welled up inside him. How he wanted to drag her to his chest and slant his mouth over hers, tasting her sweetness. If only there was some way they could be together.

"Please," she begged and pulled on his hand.

Jensen let out a sigh and nodded. The kiss would have to wait. He pressed aside the leaves and gave her a slight push forward.

He heard her sharp intake of breath as he came to stand behind her. In front of them was a magnificent waterfall that cascaded down a high cliff to a pool in what amounted to utopia.

"I've never seen anything so breathtaking," she murmured.

He took her hand and started toward the waterfall. "I thought you might enjoy it."

They ran toward the water, her laughter filling his heart. Jensen could feel her enthusiasm, and he reveled in it. There wasn't much he could give a princess who had everything, but this was something no one else could offer.

She stood at the edge of the pool, looking into the clear blue water. She raised her skirts in her hand as she dipped her toe into the water and glanced over her shoulder at him.

Jensen leaned against the tree and captured the image of his beautiful princess with her mane of black hair loose about her shoulders, her violet eyes dancing, and her body framed against scenery so beautiful it almost didn't seem real.

"Is it safe?" she asked.

"Yes."

His cock began to thicken when he saw her kick off her boots and pull her gown over her head. He had meant to let her have some time to herself without his hands pawing at her, but as he looked at her delectable body, he found himself imagining what it would be like to take her in the water.

She stepped into the pool and glided out to the middle before she turned to look at him. "Aren't you going to join me?"

Only a fool would refuse such an offer, and Jensen was certainly no fool.

7

Arian licked her lips as Jensen swam toward her, her blood quickening by the desire she saw in his hazel eyes. After just one look at the paradise Jensen had brought her to, she knew there was no way she would swim in such an exquisite place and not share it with him.

She wrapped her arms around him as he came alongside her. Ever since she had woken that morning, she had seen a difference in him. It was almost as if he was distancing himself from her, and she didn't like it.

"You weren't going to swim with me, were you?"

He shook his head and placed his hands on her waist. "I thought you might want to have some time alone."

She pushed off his chest and went under water. She swam away from him before surfacing. "I spend all the time I want by myself when I'm in Tulso. I would rather spend what time I have with you. Unless there is someone who needs you."

His hazel eyes scolded her with their intensity as he slowly swam back to her. When he reached her, he brought her against his chest, one arm wrapped tight around her while the other cupped the side of her face.

"You are the only one I want to be with," he whispered.

She saw the truth of it in his eyes, and it made her heart ache. The more time she spent with him, the more she wanted to stay. Their gazes held as they searched each other's eyes. His head moved toward hers, and her breath lodged in her chest. She wanted him to kiss her, to give that part of him he had held back.

Her mother had once told her a kiss was like tasting a part of someone's soul. And Arian desperately wanted to taste Jensen's.

Her eyes drifted closed as his gaze moved to her mouth. Then he leaned down and kissed her.

Arian's heart skidded in her chest at the first contact of his lips. He slanted his mouth over hers, nibbling her lips until she parted them. Then he swept his tongue inside and swirled it around hers.

She melted against him as he deepened the kiss. She tasted his urgency, his need for her. It made her blood run hot in her veins and her sex clench in need.

Her nipples brushed his chest, sending ripples of pleasure down her body to center at her sex. She wrapped her arms around him, sinking into his kiss as if it were quicksand.

His mouth was hot and insistent as he stroked her tongue with his own, daring her to give as much as she received. Arian was quick to return the kiss and impatient to have more of them.

With each touch of his lips, he took part of her soul with him, but she gladly gave it in exchange for the pure unadulterated pleasure his mouth gave her.

His lips moved down her neck as the water swirled around them, teasing her breasts and her sex. She wrapped her legs around his waist and felt his cock, hot and thick against her stomach.

Her hands delved into his hair as his mouth scorched a trail to her chest. He lifted her so that her breasts were even with his face.

She looked down to find his eyes on her, a wicked gleam in his hazel depths, as he flicked out his tongue to lick her nipple. She moaned and held on to him as if her life depended on it.

His tongue teased her nipple until the tiny bud was hard and straining before he began to suckle it. Arian ground her hips against his chest as her need grew with each pull of his lips. His strong arms held her as he continued to pleasure first one nipple, then the other.

Arian dropped her head back and closed her eyes against the clear blue sky and sunlight. It was easy to pretend they were the only two people left on earth, their home the haven that surrounded them.

Her body was on fire. She wanted—needed—Jensen's touch. When his hand finally grazed her sex, she cried out his name. His fingers dipped inside her, stroking her as only he knew how.

"I need to feel you inside me." She cupped his face, afraid that he would see how much she hungered for him.

Jensen held her heart in his hands, and he didn't know it. Tears stung the backs of her eyes as she realized he had come to mean so much to her in so short a time. Somewhere . . . somehow . . . he had become her everything.

He lifted his head, his gaze catching hers. For one heartbeat, two, their gazes held before he shifted her so her sex hovered over his rod.

"Princess," he whispered and kissed her.

Slowly, he eased her down atop him until he was seated to the root. Arian let out a sigh. How she loved the feel of him inside her. "I cannot get enough of you," she confessed.

"You have me. Completely."

She felt her heart clutch as he began to move in and out of

her slowly, leisurely. Arian ground her hips against him and arched her back, taking him deeper.

"Bloody hell," he cursed against her neck. "Don't do that again or I'll spill."

"But you feel so good."

He leaned down and gently bit her nipple. Arian moaned, her breaths coming quicker as her body urged her onward. The pleasure coiled tighter, driving her toward the bliss that awaited her. His thrusts grew harder, faster.

Between one breath and the next, her body tightened as she climaxed. A scream lodged in her throat as she rode the waves of pleasure. Jensen gave a final thrust before he cried out her name and pulled from her, his seed spilling into the water.

She held him close as his body jerked with the power of his orgasm. When he stilled, she laid her head on his shoulder, their hearts beating together. He walked them to shore and sat her on one of the rocks.

Arian wasn't ready for their time at their paradise to end. She wound a lock of his dark hair around her finger and smiled as he placed a kiss on her nipple.

"Thank you for bringing me here," she said.

"It was my pleasure. I'm glad you wanted me to stay."

Arian wrapped her legs around him and brought him against her. It hurt to look into his eyes because she saw their time ending, just as he did.

"I wish I could stay here."

He chuckled and leaned back to look at her. "You can't mean that."

"I do so."

"Princess, you've been sleeping in a hut with dirt as your floor."

She raised a brow. "Have I complained?"

"No, but then again there hasn't been much time to complain, since I've spent every moment I could loving you."

She knew he meant making love to her, but hearing the words caused her heart to flutter. If there was a chance he felt for her what she did for him, she would stay with him forever in his hut with the dirt floors.

"I haven't complained about the loving either. Quite frankly, I've enjoyed it immensely."

He grinned and cupped her bottom. "I think I've turned you into a wanton."

"That you have. What are you going to do about it?"

"You mean besides make love to you for the rest of the day?"

"Oh," she said and reached down to take his cock in her hand. "I think that sounds scrumptious."

The corners of his lips turned up in a wicked grin. "Never let it be said I didn't give my princess what she wanted."

Arian giggled as he lifted her from the rock and back into the water. She tried to wrap her arms around his neck, but he captured her hands and shook his head.

"Jensen?"

"Trust me, Princess."

That was the problem. She did. She licked her lips, excitement running through her as he turned her to face the rocks. His hands ran over her back and her buttocks.

Her hands gripped the rocks, desire swimming in her blood once more. He trailed a finger from her neck down her back. His touch was feather light, seductive and enticing. She moaned as he paused at the small of her back before he continued on, dipping between her buttocks to tease her sex.

"What do you want, Princess?" he whispered in her ear.

"You. I always want you."

He suckled the lobe of her ear and bit down gently. "How do you want me?"

"I don't care." She looked over her shoulder at him. "Just touch me, Jensen. Make me yours."

Something flashed in his eyes before his lids lowered and he kissed her shoulder. His finger circled her pearl before he strummed it, sending a tidal wave of pleasure pouring through her.

"I want to hear you scream my name."

"Yes," she sobbed.

The water lapped at her nipples, adding to the sweet torment of her body. Her legs shook from the desire that pumped through her and made her sex throb. She bit her lip and moved her hips as she sought to move his finger inside her.

"Are you wet for me?"

She nodded, words eluding her.

He hissed as he pushed a finger inside her. "My God, you're so hot and wet."

Arian laid her forehead on her arm. She needed him inside her, to feel him thrusting so deep he touched her womb. Her sex clenched as his fingers stroked her. She shivered from the pleasure, unable to do more than hold still as he worked her body into a frenzy.

His lips skimmed her back while his other hand reached up to cup her breast and massage it. She moaned and pushed against him as he ground his cock into her bottom.

He pinched her nipple the same time he thumbed her pearl. Arian gasped at the sensations. When his lips moved across her neck, she turned to look at him over her shoulder. Their gazes met before he bent and took her lips in a searing kiss.

She tore her lips away and groaned as his fingers left her and he slipped his cock inside her. It was just what she wanted, all of him, as close to her as he could get.

When she would have started to move, he gripped her hips to hold her still. "Wait," he whispered.

Arian shook her head. "I can't. I need you too badly."

"Wait."

She bit her lip, determined to keep still while her body pulsed and throbbed with desire.

"There are many ways to take a woman," he said. "So many ways I would love to make you climax."

"Then do it."

"Oh, I will, Princess. I most certainly will."

It was a promise she intended to make sure he kept. He shifted, burying himself even deeper. She moaned, her breathing coarse even to her own ears.

"Don't move," he warned her.

Arian didn't know if she would be able to stay still, but she was determined to try. His hands released her hips and began to caress her. He cupped her breasts, rolling her nipples in his fingers until she was panting and shaking with the effort to keep motionless.

Her eyes drifted shut as he massaged her buttocks, his hands coming close to her sex. When his finger drifted in the crease of her bottom, she stopped breathing.

"I could take you there," he said as he caressed her hole.

She wasn't sure that was possible. "There?"

"Yes. You would enjoy it."

Arian enjoyed everything he did to her, so she didn't deny it. "Will you?"

"Hmm. I want to," he said as he nuzzled her neck. "I want to show you all the ways to enjoy sex."

"Then do it."

In response, he nipped her shoulder. Arian waited, but he continued to caress her hole. Just when she thought he wouldn't, he pushed a finger inside her. She gasped. He wiggled his finger, the sensation different and overwhelming . . . and wonderful.

"So damn tight," he ground out.

Arian wanted to move, to feel him thrusting, but he stayed frozen with only his hands teasing her. She clenched her sex and he moaned. His breathing was as ragged as hers, so she knew he wouldn't be able to hold out much longer.

His other hand moved to her stomach and through her curls

to find her pearl. The need to move was overwhelming, especially when he began to thumb her pearl.

"Jensen."

He whispered her name before he began to shift his hips with short, slow thrusts. No longer able to stand still, Arian met his thrusts with her own.

"Come for me," he said as he gave her pearl a gentle tug.

Arian screamed his name as she peaked. White lights burst behind her lids and her heart thundered in her chest. Jensen held her hips, thrusting deep before he threw back his head and pulled out of her.

She sagged against the rock, her body still pulsing from her orgasm. She felt the semen on her back, and wondered if any other man would have been as considerate of her as Jensen was. He wrapped his arms around her and laid his head on her shoulder.

"You screamed my name."

She smiled. "You asked me to."

"So I did."

Arian turned in his arms and moved a lock of his hair from his forehead. She opened her mouth to tell him how she felt about him when he placed a finger over her lips.

"Don't," he begged her.

She let him take her hand and lead her from the water. As they stepped onto dry land, Arian couldn't help but feel she had let her chance at a future with Jensen slip by her. For whatever reason, he hadn't wanted her to speak, and she had respected that.

But she was determined for him to know what was in her heart before she left.

8
───────────

The time at the waterfall had been blissful, and Arian knew she would never experience such joy and pleasure again for the rest of her days. All because of Jensen.

He gave her the world each time he touched her. There was no holding back, no worry over her being a princess. She was just a woman to him.

She smiled and ran the comb through her hair once again. They had returned to the village a short time ago, and an easy quiet had settled between them.

They were each lost in their own thoughts, and Arian had thought she might be able to think of a way to extend her visit. Yet, even as she thought it, she knew it would only hurt Jensen. He would never send her away, but to prolong their inevitable good-bye while bringing them closer together was not fair to either one of them.

"What are you thinking?" he asked.

She turned and looked at him. "I'm wondering what your future holds for you."

He grinned and sat forward in his chair. "I don't know really.

Anything is possible. I've stayed here longer than any other place."

"Does that mean you will move on soon?"

"I've been thinking about it."

She waited for him to say more, and when he didn't, she licked her lips and set the comb aside. The thought of him leaving the Amazon brought a sense of foreboding to her. Was he leaving because of her?

"How about you, Princess? What will you and your future husband do?"

She didn't want to think about her intended. He was a fine man, but he wasn't Jensen. "I would rather not talk about my future."

"Why?" He rose and walked to her. "I'm curious. I would like to think about you in a couple of years and know what you'll be doing."

Arian raised her head as he stopped in front of her. "My life will be just as my sisters' have been. I'll marry, and I'll either live in the palace or in a home of my husband's choosing in Tulso. I will be expected to have children almost immediately to ensure the line, of course."

"Of course," he agreed. "What about what you want to do? I thought you wanted to see the world?"

She shrugged. "It will depend on my husband. The man my parents chose for me is quite influential to our parliament. I doubt he will ever venture away from Tulso for very long."

"No honeymoon for you then?"

"A short one." She glanced away, hating to talk about a future that didn't include Jensen.

Jensen sat beside her, his face devoid of emotion. "Where will you go?"

"France maybe, or even Switzerland. It will be a small holiday, just over a week."

"Not long enough for your husband to enjoy you as I have."

She folded her hands in her lap. "No one will ever enjoy me as you have."

In the next instant, he gripped her by her arms and pulled her against him. His kiss was savage as he poured all of his frustration and anger into it.

Arian wrapped her arms around his neck and returned the kiss. A heartbeat later he softened his lips, deepening the kiss before he raised his head.

"Life without you will be very dull, Princess."

"We have time yet." She stood and began to undress. "I don't want to waste a moment of it."

He jerked off his clothes and sat her on the bed before falling to his knees between her legs. His hands caressed her, sending chills racing along her skin. His fingers skimmed her curls to tease but never touch her throbbing sex.

She sighed and closed her eyes as she laid back on the bed. He leaned down and licked her sex before coming to her pearl and swirling his tongue around the tiny nub.

Desire began to hum in her blood once more, making her sex pulse with need. Jensen's tongue laved her pearl, alternately licking and sucking until she writhed on the bed, her moans filling the tiny hut.

"You taste delicious," he murmured as he kissed her inner thigh. "I could feast on you all night."

Arian fisted her hands in the covers to try to control the violent hunger inside of her. She bit her lip to keep from begging him to return his mouth to her sex and give her the release she needed. He had always shown her exquisite pleasure, and she knew this time would be no different.

His hands moved to her sex, his fingers running through her curls before he dipped a finger inside of her.

"Your body was made for loving."

She whimpered and turned her head to the side when his fingers began to stroke her higher. While his finger was inside of her, he bent his head and licked her pearl again.

Arian screamed and arched her back as a jolt of desire quickened through her. She could feel her orgasm building, the insistent throbbing growing with each lick of his tongue and thrust of his finger.

And then he was gone.

She opened her eyes to find him standing between her legs. He leaned down and kissed her stomach, his tongue flicking her naval. Then he reached for her legs and grasped an ankle in each hand.

Arian's mouth went dry as she looked at his thick cock and the bead of liquid that formed on the tip. Her stomach quivered in anticipation of what he would do next.

He held his arms to the side, stretching her legs out and exposing her sex to his gaze.

"Beautiful," he whispered.

She tried to breathe but found her lungs refused to work. Her body shook from the desire swimming in her. "Please, Jensen."

He eased his cock to her sex and rubbed it against her flesh. "What do you want, Princess?"

"You," she cried. "I want you inside of me."

With one thrust he buried himself inside of her. Arian groaned at the glorious feel of him. Then he started to move. Slowly at first, rotating his hips, but then he began to plunge harder and faster inside of her. Sweat glistened on his skin as sunlight spilled over him.

He suddenly let go of her legs and leaned on his hands over her, his face inches from hers. Arian wrapped her arms and legs around him and leaned up to kiss him.

He began to thrust again, long, hard strokes that had her clinging to him as her climax built. All too soon, she shattered.

The room spun and her heart clenched as her body stiffened with the intense pleasure.

Dimly, she heard Jensen whisper her name before his body shuddered with his own orgasm. It was only a heartbeat later that she realized he hadn't pulled out of her. She closed her eyes as tears threatened, and though she shouldn't, she prayed his seed would give her his child.

Jensen tried to get his breathing back under control as he kissed the neck of the woman he had fallen head over heels for. Every time he loved her, he found his need for her doubled, until the thought of not being with her left him ill.

He rose up on his elbows and wiped away the hair that clung to her damp face. She was the most beautiful thing he had ever seen.

Her legs squeezed him and that's when he felt her sex clutch around his cock. His heart fell to his feet as he realized he hadn't pulled out of her. How could he have forgotten?

Because it felt bloody damn good!

But that wasn't an excuse. It was one thing to take her maidenhead, but quite another to make her worry that she carried a commoner's seed.

"What is it?"

He tried to swallow, but found all the spit gone from his mouth. "I'm sorry, Princess. I didn't pull out."

She smiled up at him, a smile full of contentment and happiness. "As sinful as it is to admit, I'm glad you didn't."

"And if you're now carrying my child?" Just saying the words aloud made his stomach quake with fear. And excitement.

Her hands brought his face down for a kiss. "Then I shall be the happiest woman in the world."

Jensen blinked, the joy spreading through him nearly too much to take. His mind raced with possibilities that they might be able to stay together, to make a life.

And then Magwi's voice reached him from outside his hut. "Jensen. You need to come outside. Her men have found the village."

All the elation and anticipation that had filled him just a moment before vanished at his friend's words.

Arian's head moved to look at the door before her gaze returned to him. "What is it? What did he say?"

Jensen gently pulled out of her and held out his hand. "Our time is up, Princess. Your men are here."

9

For a moment, Arian thought he might be joking, but the dead calm of his gaze showed her the truth.

"No," she whispered. "You must be mistaken. I'm not ready."

"It's for the best," he said and reached for her hand.

"No," she said again. "Tell them to go away."

Jensen brought her hand to his lips. He placed a kiss on her knuckles before turning her hand over and placing a kiss on her palm. "Let me help you dress, Princess."

Arian's mind was numb. She stood and woodenly began to dress, taking great care with each hook and clasp to prolong her departure. Much too soon she was finished. She turned to Jensen to find he had also dressed. He sat in his chair, his elbows on his knees and his hands clasped together in front of him as his head hung to his chest.

"I'm glad I was taken," she said.

He lifted his head and met her gaze. "Your men will not wait long, and I would rather there not be any bloodshed."

"I don't want to say good-bye." She took a step toward him, searching for some sign that he wanted her to stay. She would do anything to stay with him.

He rose to his feet with a sigh, his hazel eyes filled with pain and regret. "Don't make this harder than it already is. We both knew you only had a few days."

She opened her mouth to speak when Vlad's voice billowed throughout the village.

"Princess Arian? We've come to rescue you."

Arian heard the warriors begin to shout as they raced around the village. She squeezed her eyes shut and tried to think of a way to have her men leave. She didn't want bloodshed either, and she couldn't think of a reason to stay without her men.

She moved to the door of Jensen's hut and stepped through. Vlad and her men were being held back by the Yanomami warriors.

"I'm here, Vlad," she called. "All is well. Just give me a moment."

She hurried back into the hut to Jensen. "Come with me," she begged. "We can make a life together."

He smiled ruefully. "I cannot."

"You can."

"Princess, your family and your kingdom need you. Go to them."

She swallowed, determined not to cry in front of him. The pain in her heart took her breath away. She had never expected Jensen to refuse her. "I won't ever see you again, will I?"

He walked past her and through the door. She blinked rapidly, but her vision still swam with unshed tears. How could fate be so cruel as to give her the one thing that could make her happy only to take it away?

She had seen and felt the depth of Jensen's feelings. Surely she hadn't been mistaken. He cared for her.

Enough to leave his life and became chained to Tulso?

Arian cringed. Jensen was a wanderer. The blood in his veins demanded adventure and the horizon. She could only give him her heart, and she feared that might never be enough.

As much as she hated to admit it, Jensen was right. She had to go back to her family. She had given her parents her vow she would return. She owed them at least that. But the rest . . . that would require some thought.

She took a deep breath and took one last look at the hut Jensen called home and the place where she had found the love of a lifetime. She squared her shoulders and turned on her heel to walk outside.

Arian halted as she saw her men surrounding the village and the Yanomami warriors watching them warily. She found Jensen standing next to the two warriors who had taken her. They were his friends, his family. Without them, she would never have found Jensen, never have known what it meant to truly love.

She walked toward them. "Thank you," she told the warriors, hoping they understood. "I owe you a great debt for what you have done for me."

The warriors exchanged a glance before they nodded.

Arian turned to Jensen. She had never told him of her feelings, and by the pain in his eyes, it would only make things worse if she did. But her heart would forever carry the love she had for him.

His hand reached out and tucked a strand of her hair behind her ear. "No, Princess, you won't ever see me again," he finally answered her question.

"And if I carry your child? The babe will need a father." She knew she was grasping at straws, but she had to know that she could contact him.

He glanced at the ground. "You and the child would be better off with your intended husband."

"You don't even want to know if there is a child?"

"I'll know."

She shook her head, unable to fathom how he could possibly know such a thing if she didn't tell him. Before she could speak again, Vlad and the royal guards surrounded her.

"Come, Your Highness." Vlad's big form stepped between her and Jensen.

She looked around Vlad's shoulder to the man she had fallen in love with. Tears blinded her. She hadn't been able to say good-bye, hadn't gotten one last kiss, hadn't been able to feel his arms around her once more. She couldn't leave.

"She was taken by accident," Jensen told Vlad and the guards. "Guard her well on your return to Tulso."

Vlad gave him a nod. Jensen then turned and disappeared into the throng of warriors.

"Jensen, wait," she called, but he didn't return. "Jensen!"

"Come, Your Highness," Vlad urged her as he gently pulled her out of the village.

Jensen!

Arian let Vlad guide her, but she saw no more of the beauty of the Amazon. Her tears and the pain inside her were all she had.

Jensen heard her call his name. He gripped a tree with both hands and felt the skin on his palms split open on the rough bark as he fought with himself. He wanted to run to her, to scoop her up in his arms and run far away from her guards and anything that reminded her of who she really was.

But he was a realist. He knew she had no other choice but to leave.

Still, he hadn't expected to fall so deeply in love with her, nor had he anticipated feeling as if his heart had been ripped from his chest at her departure.

He rested his head against the tree and fought the urge to run after her.

"Jensen?"

He lifted his head when Yuso approached.

The warrior leaned a shoulder against the tree next to Jensen. "Will you be all right, my friend?"

"No."

"I didn't think so."

"I should have sent her away that first day."

Yuso straightened. "If you had, you wouldn't know how much you love her."

Jensen snorted, his throat clogged with emotion. "Better to have loved and lost than never to have loved at all, aye?"

"By loving her, you learned she is the one for you."

"She was never meant to be mine."

"I suppose this means you're leaving?"

Jensen released the tree and looked down at his cut hands. "Yes, I must leave. I'll suffocate here with her presence surrounding me. I see her everywhere, in everything."

"You'll see her everywhere no matter if you leave here or not. Your love for her is strong, and if she loves you in return, there will be a way for you to find each other again."

Jensen doubted it, but he cared too much for Yuso to say differently.

"Come," Yuso said. "Let us tend to those wounds before you leave."

Arian said not a word as she followed Vlad and Thomas through the rain forest. Vlad had asked her countless times if she had been injured or if the warriors had harmed her in any way. Each time she had answered no, until she couldn't take him asking one more time.

"Enough," she bellowed. Birds flew from the trees around them. Arian hated that she had snapped at Vlad, but she was only so strong. She wanted to wallow in her grief alone, not to be reminded with every step that she was leaving the man of her dreams behind.

"As you wish," Vlad replied woodenly.

She had hurt his feelings, but it was nothing compared to the anguish she carried now with her. She had only thought her life was awful before, but now, after a taste of Jensen and the joy they had together, her future looked bleak indeed.

Thomas tried to show her more of the Amazon, but Arian no longer cared. If she wasn't with Jensen, she didn't want to see it. He had shown her a part of the rain forest no guide could.

They walked in silence now, their footsteps the only sound as they moved through the dense foliage. Even the Amazon seemed to feel her melancholy, for the monkeys had stopped yelling and the birds no longer sang as they normally did.

With each step away from Jensen, she felt herself grow cold, isolated. Dead. Her view of the world had changed in a few short days, and it wasn't for the better.

She had come to the Amazon, spoiled and thinking herself above such things as love. Then she had been given to Jensen, and she had come to understand what it was to love someone, to see that there was more to being a princess than jewelry and pretty gowns. She had always hated the rules before, but now they seemed pointless and confining.

By the time they reached the port, Arian was numb.

"Here's your room, Your Highness," Vlad said as he opened her door to her hotel room.

She walked in and immediately went to the window that overlooked the rain forest. Jensen was out there somewhere. She wondered what he was doing and if he longed to come after her as much as she wanted to return to him.

"What happened, Princess?"

She closed her eyes and took a steadying breath. "Nothing, Vlad, and too much."

"You're different."

"Yes."

"Did the American harm you?"

She shook her head. "No. He loved me."

Vlad sighed. "There is a boat that leaves on the morrow at dawn. Maybe it's best if we are on it."

Arian let her tears fall unheeded. If she didn't leave tomorrow, she didn't know if she would ever have the strength to leave. "All right," she finally answered.

"I'll get the tickets right away."

Arian closed her eyes, the ache in her heart too great to bear.

Jensen took one last look at the hut. His gaze strayed to the bed. He could still see Arian bound, her body glistening with the oil.

He had wanted only a taste of her, but he had gotten so much more than that. Already his chest felt empty, as if she had taken his heart when she left. She had held his heart from that first look long ago in Tulso, he just hadn't realized until now how much he loved her.

Jensen walked from his hut to see the entire village stood waiting to say farewell. They had been his family, his friends. No other place had been more difficult to leave, but he had no other choice. Without Arian, the Amazon was no longer his paradise.

"Are you sure?" Magwi asked.

Jensen nodded. There was no way he could spend even one night in his bed without Arian. "I'm sure."

"You will be missed, brother."

He faced the warrior and tried to smile. "Thank you for bringing her to me."

"It was our pleasure," Yuso said. "If I had known how much it would pain you when she left, I might not have pointed her out to Magwi."

Jensen shook his head. "No. I'm glad you did."

"So she was worth the pain?"

"Without a doubt."

Magwi was the first to step forward. Jensen embraced him before moving to Yuso.

"Why don't we come with you to the port?" Magwi asked.

Jensen considered it. He was going to miss the two warriors who had welcomed him into the tribe. They were like brothers to him, but his pain was so intense, he felt the need for a solitary walk. "Not this time."

Yuso sighed. "Will you ever return to us?"

"One day."

"Where will you go?"

Jensen shrugged. Nothing held any appeal to him. "I don't know."

"Why not go after your princess?" Magwi suggested.

"She's not meant for me. She never was."

"Only time will tell. Be safe, my brother."

Jensen slung his satchel and bag over his shoulder. Magwi and Yuso fell in step behind him as he walked through the settlement. Jensen stopped at the edge of the village before the chief and forced a smile.

"We're sad to see you go, Jensen," the chief said.

"Thank you for your hospitality and for giving me a home with the Yanomami."

The chief bowed his head. "You will always be welcome with the Yanomami."

Jensen turned and lifted his hand in farewell. After one more nod to Magwi and Yuso, he faded into the forest.

The morning dawned bright and clear, a direct contrast to how Arian felt. She stood with Vlad on the dock watching the ship that would return her to Tulso. No sleep had found her last night, but she hadn't expected it to. Thoughts of Jensen—of his hazel eyes, wicked grin, and amazing body—filled her mind.

"Princess?"

She squeezed her eyes closed. Jensen had used her title as an endearment, his voice husky, sensual. Everything he did was sexual, and it had opened an entirely new world to her.

God, how she missed him. The anguish inside her was so huge, she knew it would never leave her.

She realized despite her intended marriage, despite her promise to her parents, she wasn't leaving the Amazon without the man she loved.

She whirled around to Vlad. "Get my bags off the ship. I'm not going home yet."

"But, Your Highness . . ."

She held up her hand for him to stop. "I'm only going to say this once, Vlad. I appreciate your loyalty to me and my family, but I refuse to get on that boat. Now, you can either find Thomas or some other guide that will take me back to the Yanomami tribe, or you can get on the ship and explain to my parents why you left me here."

Vlad's thick shoulders hunched in defeat. He ran a meaty hand down his face. "I knew something transpired between you and that American."

"Yes. Something did transpire between us. I love him." She smiled. It felt wonderful to say it out loud. "I refuse to live out my life without him in it."

"What of your intended?"

"I don't care."

Vlad crossed his arms over his chest. "Your parents went to a lot of trouble to find you a good match."

"But he's not a good match for me," she argued. "Jensen is. He's the one I want. He's the only one that could give me any happiness. Princess or not, don't I deserve that?"

Vlad nodded. "Of course, Your Highness. Everyone deserves that. I know you haven't been happy, but I didn't realize it was about the upcoming wedding."

"I didn't either." She laughed, the day suddenly looking bright and full of adventure. "But now that I do, I cannot go through with it. I know my parents will be furious."

"They'll likely disown you. It will cause a scandal."

"We are royalty, Vlad. Shouldn't we be able to do what we want without worrying what everyone else will think?"

The bodyguard pressed his lips together as he let out a breath. "I won't leave you here alone, you know that. I'll look for Thomas, but I have one question for you."

"What would that be?"

"What if your Jensen won't have you?"

Arian lifted one shoulder in a shrug. "I won't know until I ask him, and I have to ask again. He needs to know I love him. I won't forgive myself unless I do."

"All right, Your Highness. I'll take you to your Jensen."

Her Jensen. She liked the sound of that. He was hers. For the first time since leaving the village two days prior, Arian felt as if she was doing the right thing. She should have told Jensen about her feelings before she left, but she had been too hurt. And too scared of how he would respond.

Regardless of his answer, she had to try. Thank God she had realized her mistake before she boarded the boat. Even if Jensen refused to have her, she wouldn't marry the man her parents had chosen for her.

Though she had responsibilities to her family and kingdom, she also had a responsibility to her heart, and her heart belonged to Jensen.

What if you are carrying Jensen's child?

She put a hand to her stomach and smiled. Just thinking of her stomach growing with their baby made her giddy. After the desire she had seen in Jensen's face, she couldn't imagine him not wanting her. But if for some reason he didn't, she was determined to raise their child on her own.

Her gaze shifted to the rain forest. She knew he planned to leave. She had precious little time to find him. If only she had told him of her love before she left.

If only I had never left him.

10

"What do you mean, he's gone?" Arian felt sick to her stomach as she stared at the warrior called Yuso. He was one of the two that had taken her for Jensen, and, amazingly, he spoke English thanks to lessons from Jensen.

Yuso's brown eyes were full of sorrow as he looked at her. "I'm sorry, Princess. He left the same day as you."

Arian shook her head. "There must be some mistake." This couldn't be happening. She couldn't have lost him, not when she had been so close.

She scanned the rain forest. He could have gone in any direction. Jensen was a nomad, going wherever the tide or his heart took him.

Her gaze returned to Yuso. "Did he say where he was going?"

The warrior shook his head sadly.

Her head began to swim. The world spun around her, and she reached for something to hold on to.

"Easy, Your Highness," Vlad whispered as he steadied her.

She blinked through her tears. "He's gone. I've lost him, Vlad."

"I heard," he said softly. "There is nothing for you here now. Come. Let me take you home."

Arian looked at Yuso again. "If he returns, will you tell him I came back for him?"

"If he returns," Yuso agreed.

Arian nodded, her heart in pieces. Just a few hours earlier she had been smiling, eager to get on with the day. Now all she wanted to do was curl up on the ground and die.

She had never thought to fall in love, never thought to experience the joy and the pleasure that went with the emotion. But she also never expected to feel as though her heart had been torn from her chest.

Life wasn't worth living without Jensen. How could she face the long years of her life without him?

And did she even want to?

Jensen adjusted his bags on his shoulder as he stopped in front of a ship. It was the first one he found that was departing the Amazon that morning.

He turned and let his gaze scan the port. He knew he shouldn't have, but he found himself wandering here with a half hope that he would see Arian. It was the closest port to the tribe, and it was where he assumed she would go.

But she was nowhere to be found.

Jensen rubbed the back of his neck where a dull ache had begun. He had slept little during the night, and when he had, his dreams had been filled with Arian and her delicious body.

"Ye comin' aboard, lad?"

Jensen jerked and looked to the old sailor. Jensen nodded to the grizzled man and stepped onto the ship. He had no idea where it was headed, and he didn't care. As long as it took him far away from the Amazon.

But he knew deep in his heart that he could run forever and still Arian and her violet eyes would haunt him.

She had wanted to stay. He should have found a way so she could. But he had been too scared at the fierce emotions running through him. His need to keep her at his side and lock her away from everyone stopped him from doing something idiotic.

Like letting her go?

Jensen took another step then stopped and turned to the rain forest. The greatest pleasure, the greatest love he would ever know, was also his greatest find.

"Lad?"

"I'm coming," Jensen said and forced himself to face his future. "Where is this ship headed?"

"We'll be stopping in Africa. Ye can get off there or stay with us when we head to Spain."

Jensen pulled his ticket out for the man. He had no wish to see Africa or Spain again. In fact, there was nowhere he wanted to go. After all the tales of his explorations he had told to Arian, nothing sounded interesting without her by his side.

"Where's yer destination, son?" the sailor asked.

Jensen shrugged. "I have no idea. I lost my bearing yesterday."

"Maybe the ocean will help ye right yer heading."

"Maybe so," Jensen said as he moved past the sailor, but he doubted it.

He had always known where he wanted to go next, always had a heading. Until Arian stole his heart. Now he felt as if he were adrift in an ocean of nothingness.

Greece, six months later

"Your Highness, be careful," Vlad called as she walked down the flimsy gangplank.

Arian didn't bother to heed his words. She stood in awe at

the beauty of Greece. The water was just as bright turquoise as Jensen had described, and the buildings just as blindingly white.

"Princess Arian, please, don't get too far ahead of me." Vlad huffed out great breaths as he hurried to catch up with her.

She smiled. "I apologize, Vlad."

"No worries," he said with a wave of his hand. "I'm just happy to see you smile again."

She had returned to Tulso, but after just a few short moments in the palace, she found it impossible to stay. She had called a meeting with her parents and informed them she would be leaving the next morning.

Arian smiled as she recalled how her parents told her no and rose to leave as if that were the end of it. They hadn't expected her to refuse to accept their answer, but Arian had found independence in her adventure that she hadn't had before. And she found herself.

She loved her newfound freedom, though her parents were none too happy. When she had then informed them of Jensen and how she had fallen in love with him, her father had patted her head like a dog.

"You'll get over it," he had said.

It had been the last straw for Arian. She could still see her father's mottled face when she told him she wouldn't marry anyone but Jensen. When he had threatened to disown her, Arian hadn't even cared.

Her mother had pleaded with her to stay in Tulso, but Arian had to leave to see the world. She needed to see the places Jensen had told her about, to see their beauty herself. She might not be able to share it with him, but she could walk in his same footsteps.

"You're parents won't disown you," Vlad said in the silence.

Arian looked at her bodyguard. "They might. I think they still expect me to return and carry through with the wedding."

"No. Your father told me before we left he had already in-formed your intended that the wedding was off."

She blinked. "What?"

Vlad licked his lips and shrugged. "The king asked me not to tell you until after we had been traveling for a while, but I thought it would help ease your mind somewhat."

"I don't understand. I thought he was furious."

"He was, but apparently the queen had a long talk with him."

Arian should have known her mother would step in on her behalf. Her father always meant well, but sometimes he forgot he was a father and a king.

"Thank you, Vlad."

"My pleasure, Your Highness. I have to admit, Greece is as beautiful as you said it would be."

Her throat clogged with tears as she gazed at the city. This was Jensen's favorite place, so she had chosen it as her first stop. It had been quite a blow to learn she wasn't carrying Jensen's baby, but it steeled her resolve to travel the world until she found him. She wasn't giving up. He filled her life and her heart, making her whole when she hadn't even known she wasn't.

"Where to, Your Highness?"

Vlad's voice intruded on her thoughts. She turned to the beach and longed to have some time to herself. "Will you find us a place to stay while I take a walk?"

"You know I cannot leave you."

She sighed. "All right. Let the guards find us rooms then. I would like to stay at least a week if not longer."

While Vlad gave instructions to one of the two guards that accompanied them, she ventured to the beach. She hadn't got-ten far when Vlad caught up with her.

"Where shall we walk, Princess?"

She pointed to a group of rocks. "You can sit there while I

stroll down the beach. I promise I will stay in your line of sight, but I would like to be alone."

Vlad hesitated before he nodded. "As you wish. Just be careful."

"Of course."

She breathed in the sea air and shielded her eyes from the bright sun as she moved near the surf. She leaned down to kick off her shoes before she lifted her skirts in her hand and let the waves lap at her feet.

Greece was enchanting and stunning. Arian had gotten used to the warmer climate since the Amazon and had even contemplated making her home away from Tulso. After she toured the world, she would then decide where she wanted to live.

Her siblings hadn't understood her need to leave Tulso and the palace, but then again, they had not met Jensen and seen the excitement in his hazel eyes as he spoke of his travels.

"How long will you search for him," her mother had asked.

"Until I find him."

She smiled and closed her eyes, wishing with all her might Jensen would be in the one place he had said he wanted to return to.

11

Jensen stuffed his hands into his pockets and let the sea breeze blow his hair into his eyes. Not even the beauty of the Greek Isle could bring him out of the despair he had fallen into since Arian's departure.

After Africa and Spain, he had left the ship and found another. He had been surprised to find they were bound for Greece, but it seemed fitting. It was the one place that had always called to him, the one place he had always thought of returning to.

In a brief moment of insanity, he had contemplated going to Tulso and declaring his love for Arian in front of her family and the entire kingdom, if necessary. But the whiskey had worn off sooner than he would have liked and common sense prevailed.

Jensen kicked the sand at his feet as the tide rushed around his ankles. He didn't know what he was going to do with his life now. He could continue traveling, but it no longer held the same appeal it once had.

There was also the university. Maybe he should return to

America and begin teaching. There was nothing else for him to do.

He took a deep breath and looked over the turquoise waters. A ship had docked in the port, disrupting his quiet. He groaned at the noise and decided to move farther down the beach.

As he walked, he saw a big, hulking man atop some rocks grumbling to himself. Jensen passed him, dismissing him as he did everything else.

But the word "princess" made Jensen stop in his tracks. He jerked around and looked at the man again. Jensen blinked, unsure if the man was real or a figment of his imagination.

He walked to the man. The closer he drew to him, the more Jensen realized there was no mistaking the man to be Arian's bodyguard.

"Bloody hell," Vlad said as their gazes met.

Jensen's heart pounded so hard in his chest he thought it might explode. "Tell me she's here. Tell me she's with you."

"She is."

Jensen whirled around. "Where?"

His gaze searched for his princess with her midnight hair and violet eyes. Then he spotted her walking leisurely down the beach. He breathed in a shaky breath and started toward her. Each step he expected to wake from a dream, to have her jerked away from him as she was every morning when he woke.

It wasn't until he neared her that he realized he hadn't asked Vlad if she was alone or with her husband. Jensen cursed himself for being ten kinds of fool. He had been about to sweep her off her feet and kiss her.

Jensen stopped. He wasn't sure if he would be able to talk to her without touching her, kissing her. Yet, if she was married, he had no right to do either. He had never thought to see her again, and knowing she was just steps away from him but she might not be free was like a knife slicing his heart in two.

He had heard nothing of a wedding from Tulso, but then again, he hadn't wanted to know. The mere thought of her binding herself to another made him physically ill, but he had held out hope that she might swell with his child. At least then he would have some connection to her even though he never intended to see her again.

It was selfish, but, he had known it would be impossible to be near her and not touch her. He had only so much control, and around Arian he didn't seem to have any.

The very sight of her was like a ray of sunshine after an eternity of darkness. He started to turn away when she suddenly lifted her head and looked at him.

For several heartbeats they just stared at each other. When her lips broke into a smile and she ran toward him, Jensen knew he would fight to keep her now that he had another chance. Common or not, he loved her.

She flew into his arms, her laughter washing over him. He held her tightly against him, his heart bursting with joy. His eyes closed as he soaked in the feel of her wonderful, lush body.

"I don't believe it," she whispered.

He couldn't either. He was afraid to loosen his hold on her for fear she would disappear.

She leaned back and caressed his cheek. "Is it really you?"

"It's really me."

"I can't believe it," she said again as a tear slipped down her cheek. "I went back to the village for you the next day."

His stomach fell to his feet. "What? Why?"

"Because I love you, you silly man. I would have given up my title if I'd had to, but my parents relented and ended my engagement."

"You love me?" He had known she cared, but he had never dared to hope that she loved him.

She smiled. "I should have told you before I left the village, but I was afraid you would reject me. I don't care that you're a commoner, and it shouldn't matter to you. I just want you in my life. Always."

"I should have fought for you," he admitted. "I gave up."

She put a finger to his lips. "I don't want us to think about what we should have done. We've found each other again. Let us think of that."

"There's only one thing I want."

"What's that?" she asked as she kissed his neck.

"You. Will you be my wife, Princess Arian?"

She sighed against him. "I thought you would never ask."

He spun her around, their laughter mixing with the sea breeze. He looked down into her smiling face. "We'll get married immediately, unless you want something big and royal."

"I cannot wait that long. I've dreamed of all the ways I want to make love to you and I want to start right now."

"We need to find a church then."

Her violet eyes crinkled wickedly in the corners as she stepped out of his arms and took his hand. "I don't think I can wait for that."

Jensen glanced down the beach to find Vlad had left his station on the rocks. "There's a cove up ahead that is secluded."

"Sounds like just what I was looking for. Shall you take me in the water again?"

He groaned, his cock throbbing with need. "In the water, out of the water, on top, on bottom, behind you, and any other way. I just want you."

She reached down and cupped his rod. "Can I suck you again?"

"Bloody hell, Arian. Stop or I'll spill now."

She stilled. "That's the first time you've called me by my name."

He brought her hand to his mouth to kiss it. "That's because you're *my* princess. I love you."

"And I love you. Now what's this about being on top? Can I be on top?"

Jensen groaned as his cock jumped. His princess would certainly keep him sated and happy. He brought her against his chest, his hands just beneath her breasts. "Would you like to find out?" he asked as he ran his thumbs over her nipples.

She sucked in a breath and melted against him. "I want you to show me everything. As long as I'm with you, I'm happy."

"Then I don't want to keep you waiting a moment longer. Come."

Jensen took her hand and pulled her toward the cove. He had found it the first day he arrived, and he had pictured Arian naked in the turquoise waters.

She was breathless, her smile wide, when he slowed and drew her around the rocks. "It's stunning," she murmured. "And you can be sure Vlad won't let anyone disturb us."

"Just what I wanted to hear," Jensen said as he began to unlace her dress.

She pushed his hands away. "Let me."

He laughed and began to jerk off his clothes, his blood on fire for her. Naked, he stepped into the water and held out his hand for her. "Ready?"

"For you? Always."

She pushed against his chest and sent him falling back into the water. Jensen grabbed her hand and took her with him. They surfaced, their limbs entwined and their laughter filling the air.

"It seems an eternity since I last saw you."

He caressed her cheek. "I think it was at least two eternities."

"But we're together now."

Jensen hissed when her hand closed over his cock. "Bloody hell, Princess. I want you so bad I can hardly wait."

"Then don't." She wound her arms about his neck and smiled. "Take me."

Jensen reached between them and felt the wetness between her legs. He groaned and his balls tightened. "What do you want, Princess?"

"You, my love. Always you."

He lifted her and wrapped her legs around his waist. With a shift of his hips, his cock slid into her heat. He groaned at the exquisite feel of her.

Her hands threaded in his hair as he leaned down to suckle her nipple. He ran his tongue back and forth over the bud and heard her moan his name. She rotated her hips and caused him to hiss in a breath.

As desperately as he wanted her, he wouldn't last long. "Arian."

"I need you," she whispered in his ear before she bit down on his lobe.

Jensen's control snapped. He gripped her and began to move inside her slick heat with long, deep thrusts. She dropped her head back, her cries growing louder.

His orgasm was building too fast. He ran his finger between her bottom cheeks until he found her hole. With just a small amount of pressure, she screamed his name, her sex clenching around him. Jensen buried his head in her neck and let his seed spill inside her as he peaked.

With his body sated and weak, the next wave that crashed into them knocked him off his feet. He saw Arian's smile as he surfaced and moved them to the shore.

"I think I want a house by the beach or a lake. I quite like making love in the water," she said as she leaned up to kiss him.

"Tell me what you want, and I'll give it to you."

Her brows lifted. "What are you talking about?"

Jensen rose and moved to his discarded clothes where he fished out the emerald. He tossed it to her and smiled as she gaped at the size of the gem.

"Where did you get this?"

He sat beside her and tucked a strand of her hair behind her ear. "The Yanomami gave it to me for returning their god statue."

"You never said anything about this," she said as her gaze rose to his. "Do you know how much this is worth?"

"A fortune. It's all I have, Arian, but it's yours. I won't have you living on dirt floors in a hut as my wife."

Her lips curved into a smile as she moved into his arms. "For you, I would live anywhere. All that matters is that we are together. I don't need this stone or money to make me want to be your wife."

Jensen chuckled. "How did I get so lucky to get you?"

"I don't know, and it doesn't matter. Now," she said as she set aside the gem. "Didn't you mention making love to me while I'm on top?"

"I did." He laughed as she pushed him onto his back and straddled his hips. He groaned as she took his cock in her hand and began to stroke him.

"What do you want, love?" she asked him the question he always asked her.

Jensen smiled. "You. Always you."

THE REFUGEE SENTINEL

To my father.
A man lives until he's remembered; live so you'll never be forgotten, 09/11/1995.

pre prologue

The Last Human Age... that's what they called it.

When the world's population reached thirty-four billion and our ever-growing need for energy broke the capacity of the biosphere to renew itself.

When entire countries ran out of food.

When, for years, we battled overpopulation by castrating eighty percent of all newborn boys and sterilizing every woman after she gave birth.

When our numbers kept growing by a new billion every few months.

When civil wars out broke across the continents because people were dying of starvation.

When Greenland melted first, then Antarctica, and the oceans rose by two hundred and twenty feet.

When many of our coastal towns drowned.

When cities like Shanghai, New York and Rotterdam abandoned their flooded downtowns and covered the avenues with suspension bridges, tethered to the skyscrapers above.

When the world's independent governments fell, swept by the rioting of their own people.

When a new authoritarian regime, The United Lands of Earth, took over, born from the defunct United Nations.

When the ULE assumed military, legislative and executive powers over its former member nations, making Earth a single-country planet.

When our global capital moved to Mexico City, the metropolis with the highest elevation, and divided the world into eight autonomous Territories: US, Brazil, UK, Germany, Russia, China, Nigeria, and Australia.

When the ULE introduced a new voting law called "Defiance Day," meant to defy our lot and save us as a species.

When this law decreed that everyone had to earmark one other citizen to die, or take the place of an earmarked person by sacrificing his own life.

When we had three months to cast a vote with the results executed on December 19.

When the ULE tracked our voting status and whereabouts by mandatory chips, called "Digital Passports," implanted in everyone's right hand.

When ten million of the world's foremost scientists, artists, and politicians were exempt from voting to continue their contributions to the human race.

When the names of these High-Potentials were kept in utmost confidentiality and their physical well-being was guarded around the clock.

When rumors swirled that a third of them were American, a third Chinese, and the balance scattered across the other Territories.

When this took place... it was the year 2052.

4

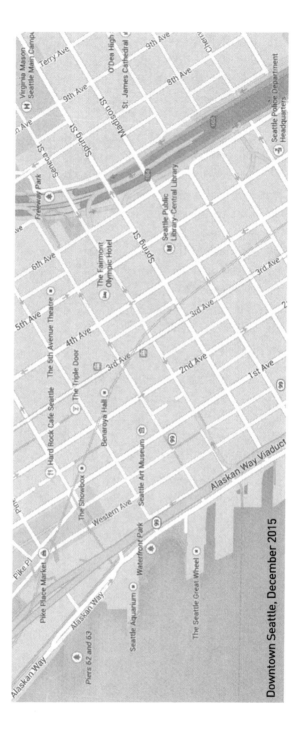

Downtown Seattle, December 2015

Downtown Seattle, December 2052

Flood Wall

Suspension Bridge

Dry Area

I-5 Protection Wall

Flooded Area

thirty six days till defiance day (prologue

It was a pity Gordon Vigna would die in the next two hours, because he was in a great hurry. The woman in the back of the cab didn't seem to mind Seattle's traffic despite what she had told him before, but Vigna kept cursing at it under a nose peppered with blackheads. Two minutes earlier and a mile to the south, he had dropped off his previous customer: a four-hundred-dollar grand-slam fare from downtown to SeaTac Airport.

Vigna pushed on the blinker to merge to I-5 and the city. His stiff neck cracked at the acceleration but he ignored the pain. Instead, he smiled and clicked his tongue – a sound full of hunger and saliva. He was going to Gregory's birthday party and the anticipation, honed by nine hours behind the wheel, was as good as the real thing.

It was the thirteenth of November and, defying the laws of probability, Vigna was ahead of his full month quota. At this rate, he could take a day off and take his genius boy to Greenlake. Vigna loved calling his grandson "his genius boy" because the boy was a genius. Who else hosted his directorial film debut at the Pacific Science Center on his sixteenth birthday? Vigna's own invitation had graced his bed stand for the last three months. He pointed the taxi's nose to the Science Center. Then he saw the woman.

She stood under the Alaska arrivals sign and waved a hand through the air when his "For Hire" hologram lit up. Vigna couldn't help it – his taxi was like a flame for the likes of her; moths in a hurry, too busy to notice their tiny moth lives ticking away. He glanced at the clock, six-thirty-pm. The massive chandeliers would stay on for another ninety minutes then the lights would die and Gregory's masterpiece would begin. And Gordon Vigna would be in Row WW, Seat 86, his chest bursting with pride and his eyes forgetting to blink.

His index finger would have greeted any other curb-waver with an exaggerated wag. His shoulders would have shrugged, as if to say, "Love to take you, hon, but I can't." But this woman was different. He slowed up, to hear what drop-dead gorgeous sounded like. The passenger side window went down.

"You should look for a white taxi, Ma'am," Vigna shouted at the noisy curbside. "I'm yellow and checkered, can't pick you from the airport." She ran two short steps and held on to the half-open taxi window as if that would have stopped Vigna from driving away.

"I'm running late to this business meeting," she said, "a firedrill."

"It always is."

"But I'm beyond late. I'm so late I might as well be dead."

"Where to?" he said, extending the conversation if only to accumulate visual material for use in the bathroom later.

"The Fairmont Olympic Hotel, 411 University Street." She smiled with the confidence of a woman who stayed in Seattle's best hotel.

He shook his head. "I can't even turn my meter on."

"You don't have to and I'll still pay you double fare," she said, "All cash. My boss will rip me a new one unless I get to this meeting on time. Please…"

He looked at the clock again. The Fairmont was six blocks away from the Science Center. Also, he'd be legal in the "Fast Pass" lane with two people in the car. Eighty-six minutes remained until Gregory's show.

"Five hundred fifty," he said. "Cash."

The woman squeezed inside the back seat and slammed the door shut.

Forty-five minutes later, Vigna could still see SeaTac's observation tower in his rearview mirror. In between every other song, the radio lamented a seven-car pileup on I-5. He cursed again. If he gunned it straight to the Science Center, cop stakeouts be damned, he might have stood a chance. But having to drop the woman at the Olympic meant failure. No amount of luck would rock-paper-scissors his way past this one. In his wishful thinking, he saw his hand pulling on the emergency brake, the taxi slurping to a stop in the breakdown lane. He imagined the rear door's child-proof bolt unlocking with the deceleration, then the woman stepping out and her leather shoes making acquaintance with the oily highway. He saw the cab's rear wheels spinning and hurling pebbles at her hands clutching a designer purse as he tried not to smirk much. If only...

In the real world, the cab's clock converted miles to minutes at the cruddy exchange rate of point five to five. On any other day, sitting in traffic would have been heaven and a gold mine too. Any other day, but the thirteenth. The beat-up Infinity seat bit into his lower back. More stiffness.

Vigna craned his neck through the driver-side window to confirm what he already knew. The cars in front, for as far as he could see stood as still as the last time he'd checked, their exhaust pipes belching on empty. He glared at the seat next to him that held a box wrapped in glossy paper. He had snatched the second-to-last PlayStation, at the mere price of one thousand five hundred dollars plus a six-hour wait at the Meridian Mall. By the time he walked out of the Sony store with the coveted square of glass and aluminum, he already hated it. But he remembered Gregory's pupils dilating each time a PlayStation ad popped up on his phone. And turning cloudy when some announcer on TV said the supplies of the damned thing were spoken for, for the next god-knows-how-many months.

His genius boy's happiness in exchange for a six-hour wait? Vigna would take the trade every time... without thinking. He peeked at the woman's reflection in the rearview mirror. A looker. Late twenties, shoulder-length Asian-black hair, no jewelry and no makeup. She wore a burgundy red suit, jacket and pants, showing no skin and covering two subdued lumps where other women would display cleavage. Yet, she had an allure. Like an Isotta Fraschini Roadster from the roaring '20s, whose components didn't shine when apart, but smoked the competition when you put them together on the track.

The skin on the woman's face glowed in the afternoon dusk. Her thin eyebrows described near ninety-degree arcs above coal-black pupils. Her lips were uncompromising, the lower one fuller and firm, like a foundation anchoring the rest of the face. Two muted shadows under her eyes were the sole whistleblowers that she must have arrived on a transoceanic flight from Asia. She sat straight despite the taxi's saggy back seat and hid her hands inside yellow leather gloves, lying in her lap like sleeping birds. Vigna was convinced she had come from someplace cold, or at least rainy, though the Big Melt had made the whole world wet.

He cleared his throat and turned a stiff neck. "Where are you from, Ma'am?" Her face graduated from a smudgy reflection in the mirror to a close-up, inches away from his nose. She stayed mum. "Hope you don't mind me asking. At this rate," he motioned towards the cars on the highway, "we'll be pitching a tent for the night."

"From Seattle," her steely voice filled the car, despite a million idle engines droning outside, "heading to a board meeting before going home."

"And where are you coming from?"

Her gaze traveled from some object outside to his rear-view mirror. "An overseas trip..."

"Right. You missed six days of straight November rain. As if we needed more water." He licked his chapped lips. "What do they call two days of rain in Seattle? The weekend..." Vigna snorted expecting her laughter to join his, as certain as a thunder following lightning. Instead, her eyes moved back to the road in silence.

"I like your taxi," she said. "Taxis are dependable and help people."

What a wacko, Vigna thought. This kind of beauty must come at the expense of the Department of the Brain. Dependable? The only dependable part about a taxi was the passengers' vomit and urine, not to bring up other unmentionables hugging her pretty behind right now. A taxi's back seat made a Seven Eleven toilet look like a NASA Clean Room. And the best way to clean up a taxi was to let other passengers wipe the grime. Do nothing and the stream of human butts, going in and out, would disinfect the seat clean. Vigna bet she wouldn't feel helped if she knew.

They had somehow reached the Olympic with eight minutes to spare. Lucky... Vigna turned around beaming. "How about I drop you on the Fourth Avenue suspension bridge and skip the main entrance roundabout?" A broader greasy smile. "I need to jet to the Science Center and it's a straight one-way shot from Fourth. If you don't mind, that is?"

"Sounds fine," she said and opened her purse.

"Thanks, hon. That's five hundred fifty flat." The taxi stopped and its hazards jumped into life. Vigna turned around for a second time. "You want a –?" The words froze in his throat because his forehead thumped against the muzzle of a semi-automatic Smith & Wesson. He then realized he hadn't seen the woman smile during the trip and for some reason the thought made him piss himself. The scent of warm urine took over the recycled car air.

"Listen to me, Gordon Vigna." How did she know my first name, his scattered mind flashed, "and do as I say if you want to live." Her ice-cold eyes drilled into his face.

"Your tongue. Stick it out, nice and big." Under a different circumstance, he would have flipped the finger to whoever said these words. In the present condition, his tongue came out as tears streamed down his face. The woman produced a syringe filled with semi-transparent brownish liquid and her knuckles, gloved by the yellow leather, brushed against his dry lips.

"A small prick," she said and pushed the plunger for what seemed like a full minute, like a worried nurse careful not to cause a swelling. Vigna's muscles locked and his jerking body wedged in the space between the front two seats. His head slammed against the woman's knee. She took his face in her lap and caressed the hair off his forehead.

"I'm sorry," she said, "for lying to you, Gordon." He snuggled his twitching face, as much as the spasms would let him, against her warm thigh. As the brown liquid took over his system, her next sentence was the last information Vigna's mind took away from the world.

"Almost there," she whispered to the man's departing soul, not to his already dead body. "Your grandson will inherit your life insurance, a much better birthday gift than a PlayStation. Chronic bradycardia will be the unwarranted cause of your death unless your insurance company runs blood tests for heroin." Her knuckles continued flirting with Vigna's forehead and her whisper, as rhythmic as a lullaby, treated the corpse with more respect than she had shown to the living person. "Rest, Gordon Vigna. I'll see you on the other side."

part one (colton parker

eighteen days till defiance day (1

The voice in the receiver shook like a live wire, but came across with perfect, brittle clarity. "Colton Parker? I want you to die. It is important to me that you die."

The man, who the voice had called Colton, squinted hard at the alarm clock. His eyes, semi-blind without contacts, somehow recognized the red outline of three-thirteen-am swimming in the darkness. He winced at the pain in his spine, as stiff as rusted metal, sat up on the bed and rested his head against the wall then shoved a hand inside his mouth, fishing out a chewed-up night-guard with a garland of drool clinging to the ground-down plastic.

"Who's this?" he mumbled with a swollen voice. The weightless space between sleep and waking up filled him with grimy disorientation that would linger until the piercing warmth of a morning shower. His brain was attempting to catch up to his reflex of picking the ringing cell-phone and holding it to his ear. Yes, he was sitting up in bed and the weight in his stomach was the Big Mac he had eaten around midnight. He rubbed his four-day-old stubble and cleared his throat. A steadier attempt, "Who's this?"

"This is Sarah."

"Sarah? Jesus..." The words came out moist and clammy, like the December night.

"You must Sacrifice yourself. For me and Yana. Most of all, for Yana." The voice broke, pushed away by a wet gulp, "Promise me, Colton."

He stumbled as he got out of bed. His mind was clearer now. Funny how cold words could replace a hot shower.

"Sarah, hi. I haven't heard from you in...too long... seven years?"

"Did you not hear me? Will you Sacrifice yourself for Yana?"

Another spasm shook his back. "Yana. How is she? Where are you, guys?"

"You almost killed her before." The voice gasped for air then grew into a scream dug from deep within the lungs. "You selfish man..." There was pain in her scream, interminable and unbounded pain.

"What is wrong, Sarah? What's wrong with Yana?"

Silence. When she spoke again, an invisible remote had wiped out the screaming. "They earmarked her last night. Who earmarks an eight-year old? Who does that, Colton?" More silence followed by the flat sound of the phone connection she had just killed.

thirty six days till defiance day (2

The woman shoved the body back into the front seat and left six one-hundred-dollar bills on top of the wrapped gift. The setting sun was peeking inside the taxi with voyeuristic curiosity.

She stepped out of the car and entered the hotel, her heels cracking against the Olympic's tiled floor and coming to a stop in front of the reception desk.

A pimple-ridden teenager in a purple uniform grinned at her. "Good afternoon and welcome to the Olympic Hotel, Ma'am."

"I have a reservation for six weeks," she said. "The President's Suite."

"Certainly, Ma'am. And what name is the reservation under?"

"My name is Li-Mei. Li-Mei Gao," she said and signed the check-in paperwork. She was annoyed by the rate of twenty thousand dollars per night but had no alternative if a room with running water was to be in the books. It was what it was and she chose to think about Vigna's glorious capture.

She hadn't assassinated him all by herself, Taxi's spirit had guided her even before she arrived to this wretched city. Her telemetry slate had lit up in unison with the plastic voice of the Alaska Airlines stewardess welcoming all Cincinnati passengers to Seattle and warning them to watch out for bags that may have shifted during the flight.

On the tablet, Vigna's holographic image had turned orange, an indication he was less than a mile away. The plane had shaken to a final standstill, she had gotten up and elbowed her way along the center aisle, ignoring the looks of frustration from the passengers she stomped past. She kept glancing at the slate's soothing orange as she squirmed by people and bags. She had turned her phone off at takeoff like the rest of the cattle in the main cabin, but was done following useless flight rules. Not when she sat in the deep plane guts, otherwise known as Seat 21E, with an orange-colored target blinking in her tablet's crosshairs.

She had researched Vigna like any other target. The man was average: a taxi driver, but also impressive – a grandfather of the youngest High-Potential in the world. Killing Vigna would be of average difficulty but she welcomed an average target. She had used the last nine months to assassinate fifty military officers across the former countries of Mongolia, Kyrgyzstan and Tajikistan. They were non-commissioned targets she killed off protocol because of a promise she had given to Taxi.

Going back to her Vigna target, the sole complication was that Seattle was going to close its airport in a day or two and remove the one reliable spot for her to locate a taxi-driver. After he had appeared as a marker on her tablet, his difficulty had gone down to one out of ten. And she had turned out to be right: Mr. Vigna had died on schedule and as expected.

She looked up at the receptionist. "I want to order hot spring water for a bath."

"I'm afraid, we don't offer spring water for bathing purposes, Ma'am."

"Then what I've heard, about the Olympic being Seattle's best hotel, is a lie."

"We pride ourselves on our reputation, but the nature of this request is," he stammered, "out of scope at the moment."

"Out of scope? Both sea-borders are dealing with the same floods."

"Ma'am, more than half of Seattle is flooded as I'm cert—"

"Spare me the drama. If you can't do this," she paused for effect, "I won't set foot in your one-star bungalow again."

"Let me check with my manager, please." He disappeared behind a wall divider and returned after a moment with her card key. She guessed the manager must have calculated her probability to survive Defiance Day and derived her customer lifetime value. "Good news. We can indeed accommodate your request, Ms. Gao. However, this resource comes with an unfortunate extra charge."

"Money is not a consideration."

"If I may, hot spring water delivery of this volume would cost five hundred thousand dollars."

"I'll give you another fifty thousand if you deliver in the next fifteen minutes." She headed for her room, done tolerating him.

Half an hour later, Li-Mei had undressed and slipped her hairless body in the tub. She shuddered with pleasure as the hot water covered her surprised skin. Her head dipped under the surface and the ceiling danced blurry in front of her water-filtered eyes. She exhaled, watching the bubbles race to the top, then sat up in the tub, stretching a dripping arm across the marble floor to pick up her tablet. She propped the tablet on her naked breasts. The screen greeted her with two horizontal sections – "Completed Targets" colored in green and "Outstanding Targets" colored in orange. A large, bold number "7" emerged in the middle of the "Completed Targets" section.

The orange section consisted of a table with three columns and four rows:

HI-PO	EARMARKED LOVED ONE	TARGET
Sarah Perkins	Yana Perkins (daughter)	Colton Parker (father)
Gregory Schwartz	Cecilia Schwartz (mother)	Gordon Vigna (grandfather)
Floyd Dubois	Lillie Dubois (wife)	Victor Saretto (ex-husband)
Eaton Wilkins	Chloe Gurloskey (mother)	Natt Gurloskey (stepfather)

Li-Mei read the names in the rightmost column, the only names she cared about, for what seemed to her the one-millionth time – Colton Parker, Gordon Vigna, Victor Saretto and Natt Gurloskey. She touched Vigna's name and smiled as the photos and profile data she'd seen countless times, inundated the screen. Once more, her fingertips flicked through Vigna's life, one page at a time, each detail and pointless fact, until she reached the bottom of the last screen. She selected an icon reading, "Confirm Target Deletion." First, the screen responded with, "Communicating with Mission Dizang," followed by, "Target Deletion Confirmed. Congratulations, Agent Taxi."

Other than the sweat trickling down her temples, Li-Mei's face remained as stiff as a wood carving. She returned to the tablet's home-screen - the rows in the orange table had decreased from four to three. For an imperceptible second, the corners of her mouth tilted into a smile then flattened again.

The top of the screen showed a large green "8."

eighteen days till defiance day (3

Colton's face looked like a melted candle. He grimaced, his pupils dilated and he dropped the toothbrush in the sink. He collapsed to his knees, slamming his forehead on the padded toilet seat. He closed his eyes.

The call had him disoriented. The person on the phone wasn't Sarah, couldn't have been. At least not the Sarah he had kept alive in his memories, who had made him marshmallows in bed on weekend mornings and sung him to sleep with lullabies on weekend nights. This phone woman was distant, a gone-bad version of Sarah.

He picked up his cell and dialed the office. Three-thirty in the morning was as good a time for a message, with his stupor still thick and the office still empty. He wasn't much of a faker but going to work today, after this call, was not going to happen.

"Hey Mike, this is Colton. Look... I won't be coming in today. Just crawled out of the bathroom vomiting a storm. I'll call you later today when I feel better."

He stopped in the kitchen with Sarah's words still ringing inside his skull. Had he forgotten about her? How could he? He missed her. He missed the lashy feel of her wet hair after a shower during those endless Seattle Sundays filled with rain and sex. He wasn't sure if this was how heartache felt or guilt, but he hadn't been whole since.

In the beginning, the sheer shock of their divorce had carried him through. As in, I'll show the bitch. How dare she run away with my baby? Her late work nights must have meant polishing the pole of some PhD who was supposed to take us to the Moon. He must have taken her somewhere all right, with her back against a lab fridge and her legs in the air. At the same time while Colton was changing Yana's diapers... The bitch. It was her fault. Had she come home that night, their lives would have turned out different... and normal.

In time, alcohol and the wet fear of being alone had declawed his accusations. He did miss her, the curve on her nose and the strands of hair she shed through the house. He missed how she snorted when she laughed and cocked her head sideways when she was in a good mood. When they had started going out in college, he dialed a radio station on Valentine's Day for two hours to request a song for her: "I Just Called To Say I Love You." In a way, she was always going to be the grace of his life. A morning of waking next to her was worth a million Defiance Days. Then smelling her hair and nuzzling in her morning breath, while she tried shielding it from him but in the end, capitulating to his full-on kisses. Then making love to her in the shower. She had given him countless mornings like that.

He had shared her with the algae for the first, and only, two years of their marriage. He had hoped Yana's arrival would bring them closer, but it hadn't. Sarah wasn't distant or tired or having an affair. She was crazy busy... all the time. And each time he complained about her absence, she would give him the same save-the-world bullcrap he'd grown to despise. "Don't you want your child to live in a world with snow caps and potable water? A world with wildlife other than ravens and sparrows. Don't you, Colton?" He had no antidote to her pitch. Not after the North Cap went, fueling a frenzied debate to replace countries with a central government structure the Australians had proposed calling The United Lands of Earth.

He had no antidote because he knew she was right but, most of all, because he loved her. He was a junior, a Finance major, about to flunk out of Northeastern University when they met. She was a year ahead and cruising, the future

Valedictorian of the College of Applied Biochemistry. She was spoken for with a post-graduation job offer from Amgen and a marriage proposal from Roger Maletta, the senior goalie who had strapped the Huskies on his back to two consecutive NCAA East Hockey titles.

One of the two offers had to cancel the other and, as luck would have it, Sarah chose Amgen in Seattle over staying put and being married to Maletta in Boston. It must have been a close call, because the combination of Maletta's orphan beginnings and chiseled abdomen had delivered three years of dating Sarah, despite him cheating on the side. She either put up with it or he satisfied her savior complex, which Colton got to appreciate later. Regardless, Maletta had drawn the short straw; Seattle - the long one, and she dove into her algae work, in the shadow of the Space Needle, with abandon she hadn't applied to anything else in life. Colton loved how happy she was as the Savior in Chief of an Earth that was dying a little bit more by the day.

During his senior year, he commuted between Seattle and Boston to see her on weekends, as if his academic work needed more obstacles. His life became a sleep-deprived series of shuffling in and out of classrooms and airports. He was broke and in the bottom ten percent in all his classes. But he spent time with Sarah, giving her the only gift he could – his time and thoughts. Seattle grew on him, all because of her, despite its ridiculous rain slugs, which Sarah called "my algae mustangs," a fixture in her lab work. In a few months, she let him stay at her one-room apartment, instead of at the Thunderbird on Aurora, the only place his budget could afford.

On Saturday nights, lying next to her, he'd been afraid to fall asleep, afraid to jinx the moment, as she slept in his arms snoring softly like a kitten. When he did fall asleep and awoke, he was happy to wake up next to her. When he proposed a year later, on one knee, looking up at her, during the seventh-inning stretch in a game where the Red Sox were crushing the Mariners and the cheesy "Marry Me, Sarah. Yours, Colton!" flashed on the main scoreboard, he thought he'd have a heart attack.

She blinked at him, her mouth frozen in the middle of chewing a hot dog. In his head, he heard a reverberating "No," but his eyes saw her stand up and nod in tears, her lips mouthing a "Yes," then smiling and adding, "I love you, Colton" with coleslaw drizzling down her cheek. If the world ended tomorrow, a thirty-percent likelihood event per the ULE Ministry of Science, he wouldn't care. Bliss was bliss, no matter if it lasted for a day or a decade. Later that night, the United Lands of Earth Senate passed the "Defiance Day" bill. Still, he didn't care. An atheist for life, on the night she had agreed to marry him, he was a born-again Christian and Mormon and Jew, all in one.

Now he was reduced to looking for her hairs around the house. He missed her with a bi-directional force that threatened to blow him up and, at the same time, crush him like a can of Coke. Sleep refused to come. Would the warmth of another woman's body do, if he imagined it was Sarah's?

The Déjà Vu Gentlemen's Club was bustling on a Friday night.

twenty days till defiance day (4

Mitko Benjamin liked the sound of mornings more than any other time of day. A morning felt right, his clock going off at six forty-seven sharp and filling the room with the cries of seagulls soaring above an ocean shore. Each time, he would wake a moment before the alarm and count down to the first piercing squawk.

Three, two, one... and take it away, Mr. Seagull. He'd leap out of bed and kill the alarm, until the birds came back to life twenty-four hours later, to face the same inexorable ending, all over again.

Snooze buttons were for spoiled Americans. As a child, Mitko had grown up in Estonia without snoozing – reporting to the kitchen every morning with clean hair, teeth and feet. Otherwise, he wasn't allowed to have breakfast.

He stood up and cracked his back. Not bad, not at all bad for a piano back. He took three steps forward, pivoted around the straw chair where he always folded his clothes before turning in, and opened the window. Its handles unlocked the sounds of the morning and comforted his palms with a mixture of smooth metal and worn-out paint. He inhaled through the nose. The November air rushed in the room as an icy-cold tease then warmed up as long as he had the courage to commit.

Mitko left the window open and, after a few more gulps, headed to Big Cold. The showerhead's ice water added to his appreciation of mornings, rushed his blood, and triggered dancing orbs in the temples of his eyes. Each night when he went to bed, he looked forward to seeing the dancing orbs. Ten minutes under Big Cold acted like a time machine, reminding him of his Estonian childhood when he raced against Grete across the frozen field behind their house, toward the well to pull out water for father and his work that day. His father would hug both Mitko and his sister. With a single hand he'd put the two pails they had dragged over the fire, then tussle the boy's hair. His father would smile. Mitko would smile in return... to this day.

He stepped out of the freezing shower and, with bluish but warming hands, brushed his hair. He opened the Wednesday drawer, its contents prepared two weeks prior: a pressed purple shirt, khaki pants, fresh socks and new underwear.

Mitko left home at seven-thirty-am even if his shift didn't start until noon. He slid his feet in the shoes he had polished the previous night and grabbed a coat. As the door locked behind him, he padded his left pocket for the assuring bump of the apartment keys and twisted the door handle several times. The door stayed shut and he stepped onto the wet Seattle pavement. For one impossible second, the morning song of chirping birds masked the smell of the flooding, the curfew and of no running water on weekends. Then the black mildew along Fourth Avenue bridge hit his nostrils. He kept walking.

The morning was warm with the natives grumbling at the forty consecutive days of rain during the always-mild Pacific Northwest winters. The Olympic would stay empty until spring seduced the tourists back to Mitko's adopted city. Then the peak season would begin and each day would copy the last. Each morning, a fresh score waited for him at the closed piano cover, in case he forgot he had played the same repertoire the prior day. He didn't mind. He molded each piece to the lobby's mood. His music channeled the intangible hum of conversations, ruffling shoes and arriving elevators, and flung it back at the world, in a way, giving life to the energy that had created it.

Mitko loved that "November Rain" was on the score for the month. The ancient ballad was the first complete piece he had learned to play as a child. Back then he had played for fun and with naïve nonchalance. Today the piano gig put bread on his table in a foreign land. Gratitude was a sign of nobility, so he thanked Guns 'N Roses for composing the song, as his fingers directed the keys.

Each day, he had a thirty-minute lunch break and two bathroom breaks, an inconvenience his aging metabolism spared him most of the time. The Lobby Manager would cut the shift at seven-thirty-pm and send all non-essential staff home. Mitko was non-essential but played on for free, because more than anything else he liked spending time with the piano. Afterhours also meant no score and less pandering to half-drunk patrons. It meant Guns, Ravel and Chopin. And Mitko loved that. Though he had stopped chasing progress and no longer did pieces like "The Flight of the Bumblebee" by Korsakov, he was going to play until he was good at it. He strived for containment and against the closure of his abilities. Despite his age, he was determined to not let it happen.

Life had mostly passed him by, but Mitko didn't feel bitter. On holidays, his chest would tighten some then he would go to bed early and squeeze his eyes shut, hoping sleep would fast-forward through his thoughts of what could have been – growing old with a family of his own, raising a daughter and a son, squinting at the sunsets through a bedroom window, before he fell asleep.

thirty six days till defiance day (5

Li-Mei didn't dry her body after the bath – she enjoyed how the tracksuit stuck to her back until the moisture lasted. She had been sitting or lying down since injecting heroin in Vigna's tongue a few hours ago and craved exercise. She took the stairs to the lobby.

Past eleven on a Thursday evening, the Olympic's lobby was semi-dark and deserted, other than a few salary men at the bar, wearing suits and buying stiff drinks on their corporate cards. She was in the main staircase when the music swallowed her – an elderly hotel employee was playing on a Grand Stein. The Stein sang wounded and alone, its music filling the mahogany lobby, hugging the hotel's Persian rugs and corporate art, then streaming through the rotating doors and ending over the rotting bridge-walk. In all, the music stretched from the piano to the outside, from birth to death, like a person's life but shortened and more intense.

She watched the man like a praying mantis studying a fly. The pianist was blind, a cripple... Defiance Day would do a favor to his kind, she thought. However, something in his music took her back to her childhood in Jenli, with Taxi. The pianist swayed in unison with the melody, his fingers creating music, the man and the instrument extensions of each other. His face told stories of the courage to do what's right even if the battle he waged was lost everywhere else, other than in the chords of his piano. Li-Mei liked to think she used to be similar – when her hair, bones and ear were whole... back when Taxi was still alive.

She approached the piano, one slow step after the other, buying time to recognize the man's melody. She had heard it somewhere before and within five feet of the Stein it clicked in place: Kreisleriana by Schumann.

"Do you play Schumann much?" she said.

"Schumann sounds the best when it rains," said the pianist.

"Must be Seattle's adopted composer, then." She laughed. "May I sit with you? I'm Li-Mei."

"Mitko."

"Are you working the night shift?"

"I've been off the clock since six."

"You're either overpaid or have an unusual idea of spending time off." He hadn't moved his head to acknowledge her presence and she wondered if a more self-conscious woman would have taken offense. "You're playing without a score?"

"Going by a score would be a waste. Schumann humbles you each time, with or without one. Like clockwork..."

"I can't be inspired by someone who checked into an asylum after failing at his own suicide."

"You choose to remember the asylum. I choose his music."

She nodded. "If Defiance Day is a smog, your music is like oxygen."

"Thank you, Ma'am," Mitko said as his fingers marched into the closing chords of the piece. "How long are you staying with us?"

"Through Defiance Day. Planning any further would be pointless."

"You wouldn't believe the rates we offer after." With the Kreisleriana finished, he popped his knuckles and rested hands on his knees. "Ten bucks a night. Fifty million of us, left in a world built for thirty-four billion. You do the supply and demand math. I'd love to see Stanford or Harvard fit this on their pricing curves."

"These fifty million will get to experience what the Soviets had described as Communism, in the twentieth century."

"Is today any different, you think? Our own government commands us to slaughter each other." Mitko waved a hand through the air. "Apologies... I'm sure you didn't come here to be lectured by an old croon."

"You're fine. I agree laws can't conceal that Defiance Day is about killing."

"On the other hand, maybe Defiance Day is how we save our unborn children." He rubbed his hands, getting ready to start a new piece, and spread them over the piano keys, as if warming his hands over a booming fireplace. "Your generation, Ma'am, must redeem all prior ones – from the Roman Empire to yesterday, when water capsules landed on the Moon. Could Defiance Day be overdue? I lose sleep thinking if the children of the fifty million survivors will remember history well enough not to repeat it. Or if another thousand years from now, when you and I have long become fossils, another old man will talk to another young woman in another hotel lobby, lamenting the coming of another Armageddon." The crevices of a smile fissured his face. "But what do I know?"

"May I ask a personal question?"

"Many years from now, when you get to be my age, you'll realize that Father Time, as he pushes us to the finish line, makes any question as impersonal as the other. What is it?"

"Will you vote on Defiance Day?"

Mitko dug into the piano, starting an etude by Chopin, and laughed. For a moment his laughter danced in sync with the music. "I have outlived love. Anyone I would care to Sacrifice for is gone. Therefore, spending my remaining years in prison, as they threaten the non-voters, is a better deal than becoming a murderer."

"Your company is a treat, but I should get going." Li-Mei slapped the lacquered Stein top. "Will I find you here tomorrow, if I get another lyrical urge?"

"I'll be here, for as long as my arthritis lets me."

"Like clockwork?"

"Good night, Ma'am." Mitko said and surrendered to the piano, as if the conversation with Li-Mei had not happened.

She walked outside and the rainy night changed her breath into vapor puffs. The trees along the Fourth Avenue suspension bridge were boxed with wooden planks from all sides, like tree prisons, or worse, tree coffins. The night was quiet, despite a dead Vigna still parked around the block and still sitting in his own urine. They hadn't even ticketed him yet. Way to serve and protect Seattle PD, Li-Mei thought. Their incompetence would likely help with her remaining targets. She couldn't imagine how accurate her hunch would turn out to be.

eighteen days till defiance day (6

Sarah's voice died along with the phone connection. Colton hadn't budged. Did she really expect he would? She slammed her fist on the desk. What was her winning good for, if it couldn't buy her daughter more than three weeks of life? She kicked the office chair and it swiveled in place. The fluorescent bulbs cast long neon tongues in contrast with the otherwise dark ULE embassy. It was just past six-am in Washington DC. She rubbed the bridge of her nose and headed to Avery's office to begin another conversation she could predict, blow by blow. At least she'd release some steam.

Maybe Colton had been right, all along. They were married and there were still birds in the sky; and he kept asking her to choose Yana. But she had chosen Earth. Saving Earth, to Sarah, meant saving her daughter. She knew the opposite wouldn't hold. Now she saw it more like he did – this world cared about surviving; it cared about restoring its atmosphere and establishing a colony on the Moon. Whether an eight-year-old lived another several days or not was of little consequence to Mother Earth.

Colton used to tell her how, underneath its mask of gracious benevolence, the world remained a strong animal that ate the weaker ones. And she had refused to acknowledge his theory as anything but ridiculous. How foolish of her. He hadn't become a three-time World Poker Champion by betting on the wrong hunches. And Sarah had not known what weak felt like, until tonight and this last phone call.

An oak door with no designation other than the number "1327" stood semi-open, shedding a triangle of pale light into the dark corridor.

"Avery?" Sarah said, a few steps before she knocked. She entered. Inside, a man with small glasses and a large forehead stared at the ceiling tiles. "Do I look stupid to you?" she said and closed the door behind her.

"You look as frayed as a live wire."

"Earlier I spoke with our Territory's Secretary of State. Mr. Secretary is as powerful as the janitor down the hall, after the dissolution of the US of goddamn A. Do you know what he told me?" She didn't wait for the answer. "He told me to show the world what American mothers are made of. And to steel myself."

"What do you want me to do, Sarah?" Avery said, arms stretched, palms facing down as if to convince a suicidal jumper not to jump.

"Last year, my work alone created a million kilojoules of energy for this sorry excuse of a Territory. God knows we're not a country anymore, because we've stopped acting like one."

"Did we not dispatch thousands of drones across the Milky Way to explore evacuating Earth?"

"I gave them more energy than New York City will consume in ten years, Avery. And in return?"

"Did we not castrate eighty percent of our boys at birth? Or sterilize any woman who gave birth? Did we not apply the death penalty for misdemeanors or worse?"

"Don't you preach to me. I'm called selfish for refusing to let my one daughter be murdered. Or for not celebrating being the definition of an American mother's strength in the Thesaurus."

"We did it all, Sarah, and nothing worked. The Defiance Day Protocol is our last chance."

"What a thankless bitch I must be, Avery," she said.

"You're a Hi-Po. And should act like one of the ten million highest-caliber humans in the world. But hell no," he stood up on the other side of the desk, keeping his distance, "you're the one Hi-Po in Hi-Po history to oppose

Defiance Day. And spit on her ULE-given right to be exempt from Earmarks or Sacrifice."

"Give Yana a Hi-Po status and I'll behave." She pointed her index finger at him and jabbed the air with each word. At the same time her heart sank an inch. Yana's life was slipping through her fingers and what had she, the mother, chosen to focus on instead? Lab reports and clinical research papers assuring the ULE that limitless algae energy was right around the corner. "Are you sure you're playing at the right table, baby?" Colton used to say. How she had hated his gambling analogies. "What's the point in saving the planet," he'd say, "when you haven't taken the time to get to know your daughter?" Hadn't Avery's defensiveness proven Colton's point, yet again?

She shook it off. It was too late to retreat. If she had played the wrong table, then so be it. Her scientific mind believed nature didn't tolerate imbalance. Somewhere else on this sinking Earth, it didn't matter how far away, another mother loved her daughter twice as much as Sarah loved Yana. And made up for Sarah's deficiencies, or as a religious person would put it, paid for her sins.

Avery voice came to her, as if from another dimension, "This isn't a library card, Sarah. High-Potentials are identified by the ULE as the finest human specimen."

"She's the daughter of a Hi-Po specimen, it must count for something."

"You're not listening. We've tested her multiple times upon your request. The results are conclusive: Yana is not a Hi-Po, even if she's the daughter of one. You're it... for hundreds of miles around. The US Territory likely has no more than three million of you. The rest could be in goddamn China for all I know. Even if I wanted to add a random eight-year-old to the list, I wouldn't know where to begin. Only the Congress of the United Lands of Earth could change that."

"I don't give a damn about The ULE Congress," she said, her voice both serene and furious. "There's got to be a way to save her."

"I've been trying for two months and have nothing."

"Did you try all your connections?" She was running out of words to ask the same question, over and over again. She already knew the answer.

"Favoring the populace over High-Potentials is treason, Sarah. You know that."

She took a deep breath. "She's my only child, Avery. The only one I was allowed to have before they burnt my ovaries. I won't lose her to a stupid law. Do you understand that?" Either room 1327 was full of dead people or their silence was a sign of consent.

two years and three hundred forty two days till defiance day (7

The scanning gun chilled Sylvya's palm with its steely weight. The infrared beam bit into Mr. Bormann's middle finger then marched north, over the knuckles and the rest of his palm: a textbook MRI. Once the scan reached the wrist, Mr. Bormann's identity flashed on the screen: seventy-two, colon cancer survivor, and a varsity discus athlete from the mid-seventies. The rest of the man's personal data – preferences, finances and affiliations – hid behind a digital ULE moat her nursing credentials couldn't access. She was only seeing his medical records.

Digging through a patient's medical past reminded Sylvya that everyone's information, hers included, was out there: naked, digital and in real-time. Mr. Bormann's fingers touched her hair. In thought, she had not noticed him waking up. "You remind me of a daughter I have back home," he said.

Sylvya pulled back and smiled at him, more out of courtesy than candor. He smiled back. People didn't smile as much, she thought. Not like her early years, when the Vegas Strip wasn't covered in mud and Earth still had a functioning South Pole. Back then, she taught herself to sleep on her feet, in ten-minute increments, and scoffed at concepts like weekends and time off. Saving lives came at the price of one's personal comfort and she wanted to be the best in the business. Wasn't that what nurses were supposed to do? Then the ice caps melted and even the workaholics like her had lost faith they could make a difference.

In the interim, Mr. Bormann had transitioned into a full attack. "My daughter tells me she can't find an eligible man her age. Not right, I tell you. Beautiful creatures like my daughter and you living alone. What's the world coming to, I say?"

Sylvya wished she could rewind time and go back to being that young nurse from Mountain View once again. When had she started hating her job? She sprung to her feet as soon as the scanner's ding announced that her patient's condition was within norm.

"Don't forget to finish your dinner tonight, Mr. Bormann," she said.

"You try finishing that goop."

"It's a nutritious meal designed to bring your cholesterol down." She had to go. "See you tomorrow."

She had one more patient left on her round before she could go home. Curfew had simplified her life into binary morsels. Run to your home station to scan your right palm. File an explanation with the local precinct if you scanned an hour late. Scan three hours late and pay a twenty-five-thousand-dollar fine. Scan later still, and spend the equivalent amount of time in jail. She couldn't afford any more curfew infractions. Truth be told, she couldn't afford a single one, the way her marriage stood with David.

Sylvya entered the room of her last patient for the day, two rooms down the hall from Mr. Bormann. An oxygen pump filled the cramped quarters with a faint hum. A thick bandage covered the patient's eyes. The machine hum reminded Sylvya of crickets singing in the yellowing grass of her childhood Septembers. She smiled at the thought then examined the patient's chart. His name was Colton Parker and he'd been going through bouts of wakefulness and stupor. She wondered how much alcohol it had taken to knock out his eyesight for this long. He seemed awake tonight and she decided to give it a go.

"Good evening, Mr. Parker. You came to us quite inebriated."

"Great, another genius deducing that vertigo, temporary blindness, and a migraine constitute a hangover," he said.

"You ought to stop drinking," she pressed on. "Another bout of this may kill you."

"You'll tell me Santa isn't real, next." He attempted to lift his head, but couldn't. "On the bright side, not being able to see isn't half as scary as I'd thought. There's always a bright side to things if you look hard enough, Doc. No matter how screwed up the original side looks."

"I'm Nurse Timmons, Mr. Parker, and you're in the Mountain View Hospital in Las Vegas. ER admitted you four days ago with alcohol poisoning and performed a minor abdomen surgery to stop internal bleeding before transferring you to us."

"In my condition, Mrs. Timmons, no surgery is a minor surgery and a minor one is a disaster. How did I get to the ER?"

"A West Summerlin sanitation worker found you unconscious on the street and drove you over in his dump truck. Without him, who knows if you'd be alive now."

"Good info. But I am alive and ready to check out." A coughing spasm ripped through his chest and Sylvya wiped his face with a moist towel. He sneezed. "Did I get you, nurse? They say tragedy plus time equals comedy, so if you're not laughing yet, you will be soon."

She wasn't laughing. "You're not in a comedy, Mr. Parker. You're diagnosed with a broken collarbone, two STDs, a Grade Three concussion, a laceration wound to the abdomen and failure of both kidneys." She sounded like a ref announcing a roughing-the-passer penalty. "Your right kidney is out of commission and your hemoglobin is fifty-three percent below normal due to the blood loss from your abdomen laceration."

"Are you impressed yet?"

"You can forget about discharge for another week. And you better have a good insurance policy."

Sylvya headed to the door but turned. "Your medical condition is not the only reason you're here. The circumstances of your check-in have made you a suspect in unreported crimes in the Summerlin area. A Las Vegas Police Officer is stationed outside your room. Not that it's any of my business, of course."

"So, whose supervision am I under, Nurse Timmons?" he said. "Yours or our armed friend outside?" Then in a more serious tone, "I hope my jokes don't offend you."

"Call me, Sylvya." She smiled.

"No flirting, nurse. I'm a criminal with a busted kidney and a bunch of pee-hole warts to boot."

"First, you don't sound like a criminal. Second, you don't have genital warts. Third, I'm married and fourth, you're not my type."

"You've got me all figured out, haven't you?" He raised his arms. "But I'll bet you rose oil to catheter fluid I'm not the good guy you think I am. Once upon a time, I might have been. It might have been the only thing I ever wanted to be."

Then he slumped his head into the deep pillow. "And Sylvya?" he said, "Please, call me Colton."

eighteen days till defiance day (8

Colton wandered in, alone and sober, past the frosted glass entrance. Then the human bark hit him. "Where to, chief?" A shaven head attached to an overweight torso, no neck in-between, unpacked itself from the check-in booth. "It's a hundred to get in."

"Didn't know about the cover," Colton said. "Sorry." Music blaring from the inside and around a corner drowned out his words before they had made it to the shaved head's ears. The ears would not have cared, regardless. "Here's an ID, too." Colton handed a one-hundred-dollar bill folded around his driver's license, like he was ashamed of how his DMV picture had come out.

"I just need the cash," the bouncer said, ripped a crumpled receipt from the cash register and shoved it in Colton's hand. "And, welcome to Déjà Vu."

A sanitizer smell with a sweet aftertaste hit Colton's face. The smell of sweat and semen hit him a second later. He stopped after taking a few steps in, as the dark corridor spilled into a large room. What was his plan for the night? Hire a stripper and have her read him Hemingway? The cheap sanitizer drilled deeper inside his nostrils. Colton exhaled, how could anything associated with this type of smell even begin to replace his Sarah?

"Move, dude," he was shoved to one side as a group of men poured inside the joint. He looked around the room – several rows of chairs, lined with librarian-like precision, faced a beige stage. A black female, wearing nothing but her skin was hurling herself at an aluminum pole. Countless neon dots, like butterflies, bathed her supple tattooed body.

Was it ten years? He couldn't place the last time he was at a place like this. The tattooed girl molesting the aluminum pole had to be in physical pain from the exertion, but she didn't look it. On the other hand, what did he know?

Maybe the current generation of strip-club goers required athleticism from their dancers or maybe he wasn't in the right frame of mind to appreciate tonight's performance and accompanying sweat. A waitress materialized, invisible until she got within inches of his nose. Her uninvited palm rested on his shoulder. "What would you like to drink, honey?"

"Do you have Sprite?"

"Yes, honey, we do." The palm caressed his cheek and twirled away.

"Hey, hey - come on fellas," a DJ's voice rose from beside the stage. The black dancer scurried off, arms cradling oversized breasts. Another stripper took over and struck a pose, expecting a cue to allow her to move. "It's three dances for the price of one, guys. Our lovely ladies will ride you senseless, if you know what I mean... here they come. On your right, you have the lovely Fiona..." The pole-bashing black dancer had returned, now wearing a white bikini. "...and on the left? Yes, the lovely Melody." Fiona and Melody waved with enthusiasm fitting for an Independence Day rally. "Come on, you, guys. Six hundred bucks gives you three songs with a gorgeous lovely lady." The women stepped down and two different dancers jumped onstage. "And the lovely Amber comes purring on your left then the lovely Summer is on your –" The humid line of female nudity filed on, with each pair taking stage for less than a minute, a quick break before returning to their next lap-dance. The DJ's barrage of "lovelies," the same word describing all girls, annoyed Colton. But he also smiled at the thought that in a room full of nudes, lazy grammar grabbed his attention the most.

A hand squeezed his shoulder, firm yet not too much. "Are you taking dances tonight, honey?"

A petite girl in her early twenties leaned on his chair. She wore a long wig and green contacts with black pupils that made her eyes seem as cold as alligator's. Nonetheless, her small bra and frail frame reminded him of Sarah. Underneath the makeup, the girl might have been pretty. He wasn't sure where to put his eyes.

"I charge four hundred, not three – that all right?" Through her alligator eyes, Colton saw how out of place he must look. A nube or not, he wasn't going to let a girl half his age take him for a fool.

"Sorry," he said with a short stammer, "I can only do three." The girl didn't flinch, maybe she didn't hear.

"But it's a three-for-one deal, honey." Each honey-ending sentence slapped Colton's face like a dead fish.

"Plenty of other folks here would take you up on this."

She rolled her eyes and moved to the next table – a rowdy group wearing orange hardhats. Colton stood straighter in the chair. His Sprite came back accompanied by another "honey," this time from the waitress. He held the paper cup with both hands, sipped on the diluted soda and looked in the eyes of the next dancer to come on stage, wishing she weren't naked. Why did he think strippers could replace Sarah? Another squeeze on his shoulder, same place and strength. He turned.

"What if I do it for three hundred, honey?" Alligator eyes must have struck out with the Home Depot crew.

"Wouldn't do that to you."

She grimaced. "Then how come you haven't taken a dance from anyone else?"

So Déjà Vu monitored his dance orders too? He wondered what analytics system they must have installed here. "You're the first one who asked."

"You want me to send another girl?"

His head shook. "No. I was leaving." Colton gulped the last of the Sprite from the sweaty paper cup and rose from the plastic chair. What would Sarah have said if she saw him here? What would she think? Yet another "honey" hit him within two steps.

"No refill," he said, "I'm leaving."

"I wasn't offering one and didn't mean to stop you."

Colton turned and saw a blonde with a pierced lower lip.

"Or I could talk like this if you prefer," she said with a fake British accent, then pulled two chairs and sat in one of them.

two years and three hundred twenty nine days till defiance day (9

Sylvya hung her scrubs and shut her locker for the day. She pressed the down button on the elevator and looked down the quiet row of patient rooms along the corridor. All doors closed, no clattering of heels or squeaking of equipment wheels. The fifth floor was dozing off like a senior taking a long nap.

David and the kids were waiting at home. Dallas was going to babble about how he was adjusting to the new grade at school and Sadie was going to pester her to knit together, before Sylvya had taken off her shoes, and cuddle at her side with eyes gobbling every turn of Sylvya's knitting hooks.

Sure, Sylvya would have to tolerate David's presence for five minutes and hide in her study, as if doing chores, until he left the apartment. But on a positive note, since moving out of their old house, both David and the past were loosening their grip on her, one day at a time. Sylvya had spent too much of her precious life in that house. The furniture dings, the colors when you walked in, or the fast food in the fridge had served as constant reminders of the years she would never get back. She hated that house, even with the kids, and would take them to Chuck E. Cheese or hunker down at the Starbucks across the street, after work. But she had started to heal in the new apartment.

As the hospital elevator buzzed open, she hesitated and didn't walk in. What if she checked on the patient in Room 34 one last time? Just a quick scan of his vitals. She could still catch the last Bunker Hill train, if she hustled. She liked spending time with the Room 34 patient. At first, she thought it was because his alcohol poisoning and the guard at the door tugged at her motherly instincts. Whatever... she didn't want to overthink it and she'd have plenty of time to narrow it down on the train tonight.

The cop was playing some video game on his smart watch. He glanced at her long enough to die on the level he was on then stretched his back and, with the level lost, gave Sylvya a short nod.

"Quiet shift, I hope?" she said.

"The best."

"I'll be a couple of minutes." She sailed past, her shoes playing cymbals against the quiet linoleum. Room 34 was heavy with dusk. The man's name was Colton, she recalled, and he was sound asleep. Sylvya walked up to his bed and stood over his pillow like the Tooth Fairy looming over a sleeping child. His breathing was firm and his vitals were solid. She cracked a pleased smile, the type that didn't show her teeth. She had salvaged this ship. The first day they had brought him in was like playing "Wheel of Fortune" with his life, where all spaces, except a couple, read "Certain Death." A goner. A creep too, if she looked at his charts: a broken body, busted internals and a few STDs for good measure.

Against these odds, she had nurtured him to life, like a mother. But unlike the kids, whom she shared with David and their grandparents, this Colton was her sole creation. Years after the floods had drowned her desire to give to others more than she gave herself, he had proven to her she was a capable nurse and a good woman, too. And she had birthed him, all on her own: her primal right. Sylvya's breasts felt tender and she locked the door. Still and quiet. His unshaven face swelled in her eyes and she unbuttoned her coat and rested a hand on her belt. She stretched her other hand over his sleeping face, an inch from the parted lips. His breath caressed her palm with billows of warmth. She stood erect and motionless by his bed but in her imagination she held him with unspeakable passion. The hand on her belt travelled lower. Sylvya closed her eyes.

eighteen days till defiance day (10

The Maharishi squinted at the near-perfect darkness inside the hut. He sat still until he made out the contours of a single room. Another step forward and he would have stepped in sheep feces on the dirt floor. The furniture consisted of hay bedding in one corner and a coal pit in the center. A part of him didn't mind reconnecting with places like this. Peasant rooms rekindled his love for mother China better than any historic reenactment or hologram at the Museum of History in Shanghai. He was one of the lucky ones crisscrossing China and helping the country folk earmark the loved ones of those in the West – a most noble calling.

Nonetheless, three months of dredging from one Chengdu village to another had taken their toll. He missed his wife and son, and he missed the glass condo in Jingqiao. He could go back to them in three weeks, if he were lucky. He closed his eyes and inhaled in a string of small breaths. He was a shadow of the Maharishi, or what the Westerners called the High-Potential, before his trip began. These days, it took him extra-long to summon meditation and replace the worries for his family with inner peace. At least he could be of service to China to the best of his insignificant abilities.

The hut smelled of fish soup. An old woman squatted by the dead coal-pit on the floor, stirring a pot blackened by many other soups before this one. The Maharishi spoke in Mandarin, the only language the woman understood.

"Good morning, tai Mother."

"Are you hungry for fish soup?"

He bowed to show respect, given he was about to decline the offer. "I am full, tai Mother. Thank you. The Party sent me to enlist you, if your name is Jie Ying."

"I've been expecting you."

The Maharishi produced a tablet from his suitcase. The device glowed in stark contrast with its non-digital surroundings. He knelt by the old woman and raised the tablet to her head. Blue laser lights scanned her face and a digital chirp confirmed her identity.

"May I guide your finger, tai Mother?" the Maharishi said and pressed the woman's index finger against the touch screen. The blue laser re-scanned her face, the tablet chirped again and this time its screen turned green.

"Now I need to hold another finger to the glass, tai Mother." The Maharishi scanned the woman's thumb and the tablet made one final sound. Then the blue laser flicked off and the screen dimmed.

The Maharishi stood up and bowed. Jie Ying bowed in return.

"Thank you, Dianxia," she said, "It's an honor to help our Motherland."

The Maharishi walked out of the hut and into the cold morning air about to be warmed by the early sun. He squinted at the light and reviewed the screen one last time before shutting down the tablet. First, he double-checked his next destination: a voter Meng Fa, seventy-nine years old, living in a village thirty miles down the river. Then, he re-read the confirmation of what Jie Ying had done: "Voting Event: Defiance Day || Citizenship: US Territory || Social Security Number: 231-010-8760 || Name: Yana Perkins || Date of Birth: December 25, 2044 || Status: Successfully Earmarked."

seventeen days till defiance day (11

"Maggie. Good to meet you," the blonde dancer said.

"I'm Colton."

"You a regular here, Colton?"

He hesitated. "First-timer."

"Yes, you are," she said. "I would have remembered you otherwise. I'm good with faces. And you are how old?" She sounded like a primary care provider during his initial patient visit.

"Forty-three." He should have left this place by now. The smell was making him sick. "You?"

"I'm twenty-four."

Colton followed with the most banal question a customer could ask his stripper. "Have you been doing this long?"

"Five years. Got into it somehow."

"You've got another three weeks left until we all vote and go to hell."

"Way to murder the mood."

"Sorry, I was –"

"Relax, Colton. I was giving you a hard time."

"Have you voted yet?"

"Are you a Defiance Day cop or something? Like you said, I have three weeks left to earmark someone."

Colton sighed. "Earmark. Sacrifice. What does that even mean?"

"You're kidding, right?" Maggie put hands on his shoulders. "I get it. You must have just got up from a coma or you've travelled here from the past."

His laughter joined hers. "I know what Defiance Day is."

"No," her exaggerated denial. "Prove it, Mr. Teleportation."

"I do. I'm just floored by how these words have crept into the language, to help us to send each other to the slaughterhouse." He raised both arms in the air. "But who am I to question ULE's finest decree."

The waitress reappeared. "Hi, sexies." Now that he was almost a paying customer, he had graduated from a "honey" to a "sexy." "Would you like to buy this lovely lady a drink, sir?"

Before he could reply, Maggie leaned on his shoulder. "I'd like a small Red Bull." Her right breast nudged against his hand.

"Sure," Colton handed over a crisp fifty-dollar bill, "one small Red Bull for her." The waitress snatched the money like a vending machine and dashed away.

Maggie kept leaning on him. "And what do you do?"

"I work for a casino. I tweak their betting algorithms and design new gaming products for their clientele." He didn't expect her to understand, but she did.

"Are you trying to impress me with fifty-dollar words?"

"Am I?"

"You're a programmer who codes the software in roulettes to make the odds worse for gamblers like me."

He should have checked his prejudice at the door. "You got it; that's what I do."

"The next time I'm at the Sno and lose at roulette, I'll know who to blame."

"And you?" he said. "Did you pick up your British accent in London?"

The waitress reappeared with a Red Bull for Maggie and no change for Colton. The end of the world did a number on inflation, he thought.

Maggie smiled under the coat of makeup meant to give her face a mysterious look. "Never been to London," she said. "Can't imagine I'll be going. Not anymore. Not with Earth being a single-country planet."

"You still can if you want to."

"The government of the United Lands of Earth and its high-as-a-kite capital in Mexico City doesn't care about giving London papers to a girl like me. I can't travel with a young son at home, anyway. This joint gives me all the fun a single mom needs."

Colton glanced at her breasts. Under the bra they looked as small as they had felt against his palm. If she were telling the truth, her son must be older.

"You know what a pain traveling can be," she said. "I'm lucky I like Seattle. And I wonder how the poor bastards from say, Lincoln, Nebraska must feel like, stuck in their corn-hole." Maggie threw her head back and laughed, her neck vein pulsating with each breath and her breasts ballooning closer to his face, exposing both nipples. She fanned her fluttering eyelids with a hand. "The short of it is, I've never been much of a traveler, even before they closed the West Coast airports." She wiped the corners of her eyes with a pinkie, careful not to smear the mascara. "But enough about me, Mister. You married?"

"I used to be. But she left me."

"Good riddance. You wouldn't be here otherwise, I take it."

"Maybe I shouldn't have come anyway."

"On the contrary. When's the last time you had sex?"

"Not sure. Maybe a year."

She looked at him with raised eyebrows. "You're the only male I know who doesn't rush to Screwville, with Armageddon around the corner."

"Maybe no one's offering."

"I'm sure it could be arranged." Maggie emptied the last of the Red Bull and slapped her naked knee. "Should we do what you came here to do, Colton?"

"I didn't bring a condom."

Maggie laughed. "I meant a lap-dance, tiger."

"For three hundred?"

"Three hundred." Her eyelids opened and closed, instead of a head nod. "I heard you're hard to move on that one." Maggie took Colton's hand and headed for the VIP booths in the back. She adjusted him into the deep plush of a purple sofa. By the third song, she had unbuttoned his shirt and was rubbing her oiled body against his chest. Colton's senses focused on Maggie's warmth as the booming music receded in the background. And he let her rock him, like a doomed Titanic in the middle of a lifeless ocean. His missing Sarah didn't go away. But he did doze off and given the circumstances, that was a win. At some point, he realized the gyrations had stopped and opened his eyes to see Maggie's petulant smile an inch from his face. Her teeth glistened in the neon lights with almost menacing whiteness.

"I hope I didn't put you to sleep," she said and laughed as her fingers twisted his bare nipples. "Go on, say yes and break my heart." Colton's eyes paused on hers then moved to the surroundings. He stifled a groan at the realization he was still in Déjà Vu, instead of in a bad dream he could leave by waking. He lifted Maggie by the waist.

"How much?"

"How about fifteen hundred," she said, "I danced five times and felt super comfortable with you. You had a good time too, no?"

"Is there a cash machine around?" Colton's face was losing color by the minute.

"You don't think I'd lie to you, right? It was five dances." Maggie sounded almost apologetic. "I'll show you the cash machine." She took him by the hand and, with an unbuttoned shirt he followed. She rubbed his shoulders while he waited for the ATM to dispense money. "By the way, clients usually don't tell me their real names," she said, "Why did you?"

"Didn't think not to, I guess."

"You know," she said. "How about you meet me after I finish work in an hour? Would be nice to spend time, like normal people."

"Don't take this the wrong way, but I think that having sex would be a bad idea."

"How about a conversation and a single malt at my place?"

"Your house?" He blinked. "Isn't it illegal to meet with clients?"

"You'll tell on me?" Her bleached teeth winked at him again. The ATM shoved the cash against his palm and he passed the bills to Maggie without bothering to count them. She had earned it. After all, she had him fooled into forgetting Sarah, if for a moment.

"Are you really sure that's a good idea?"

"You're acting cute and coy. You'd almost think I'm the customer here."

"Maggie," he spoke her fake name for the first time. "I'm dealing with this problem that —"

"Defiance Day is a bitch, no?" she said with a tired smile. The booming music changed from a ballad to reggae. "I got to go. I'll be done in an hour." She sniffed and pulled on her bra. "See you outside?" She kissed him on the cheek and walked toward Déjà Vu's main stage and neon lit up the tattoos on her back.

She met him as promised, an hour later, her stilettos rattling against the parking lot pavement like a machine gun. "Here I am." She smiled and her teeth didn't look menacing in the moonlight. Her face looked ten years younger without the mascara. "You ready?"

"You're a different person with clothes on." Colton meant it as a joke but she shot him a tired gaze and a sigh. He led her to his car and she sat in the passenger seat, palms tucked between her knees, like an interrogated person wanting to show she had nothing to hide.

He started the engine and wondered how she felt after work. Sweaty? Victorious? In the seat next to him, she punched her address in the car's GPS. If he didn't want sex, as he had said, why was he driving a stripper to her apartment, instead of sleeping in his own bed... alone? He remembered how Sarah insisted on always saying what was on their minds. She was a scientist and subtleties didn't fly. In their old world, saying no to sex would have meant having no sex. How low he had fallen without her.

"You can park in any spot without a number on it," Maggie said. The tidy residential building glistened on the outside. Colton nestled the car in an opening between two high-end Volkswagens and killed the engine. He looked at Maggie and wanted to say something supportive but the metamorphosis of the girl, since exiting Déjà Vu had left him speechless. If he hadn't felt her naked body on his, he wouldn't have guessed the semi-asleep young woman burrowed in his passenger seat was a dancer. Even her tattoos were hidden under jeans and a tee. On the other hand, why was he so eager to stereotype her? What right did a killer of daughters have to judge a stripper?

He followed her into the apartment and ended in a small kitchen decorated with bunches of dried lavender and colorful clay pots strung on a line over a gas stove. She invited him to sit at a table inside a wall nook and emptied the last of a dusty Johnny Walker bottle between two glasses.

"So what do you for fun?" he said.

"I like to study old paintings to find out what the painter had in mind when he created the piece."

"Do you paint too?"

She waved a dismissive hand. "Strippers don't paint. I just enjoy watching paintings of mayhem. The larger the devastation, the more it draws me in."

He smiled. "You should just tune to the news if you want devastation."

"Our devastation is boring. Theirs was poetic."

Colton scratched his nose. "Are you sure?"

She nodded. "Let's take "The Battle of Waterloo," for example. I could study it for hours, like a giant Where's Waldo puzzle. The dying horses, the men impaled by bayonets in isolated skirmishes, the pockets where the hopeless French fight on despite Wellington having already won." She twirled the shot glass on the table. "Napoleon's remaining men were like French lavender tossed across an angry British sea, surviving one wave, maybe two, but due to succumb by nightfall."

"You have an appreciation for history."

"With human history as crazy as is, how could you not?"

"The fight to save the polar caps today feels like one of your devastation paintings," he said. "With us being the French, of course."

Maggie's hand massaged the back of her neck. "Look who's the poet now."

"If you don't mind me saying, you don't sound like what you do."

"No kidding. I realized I was a good dancer when I was seventeen. My way of being creative, you see." She took a sip and grimaced at the whiskey's potency. "And now you'll ask me how many people I've slept with."

"I don't judge you, Maggie."

"Yes, you do." Her quiet words cut off his next sentence. "The only reason you're here is screw me for a couple of hundred bucks and jerk off in my face, before the door hits your judgmental ass on the way out."

"I'm sorry I came." Colton stood up, unsure where to put his hands. She took them in hers.

"If I ask you not to judge me, the least I can do is offer the same in return. And stop being so serious, you wouldn't be here unless I wanted you to be." She slurped at the last of her whiskey and looked at him. For the first time, Colton didn't avert her gaze. "Answer me a question, Mr. I-Know-Defiance-Day-Cold."

"Who's making fun of who now?"

"When everyone votes for someone else to die, wouldn't everyone die?"

"Wouldn't that be a snag," he said. "And you'd be right, but for the Sacrifice votes."

"So what?"

"So those who receive a Sacrifice will survive Defiance Day. And the future will be populated by silver-spooners. Other than the children, of course. I'm sure you'll sacrifice for your son."

"Lying about being a mom is a part of my gig in the club."

Colton smiled. "You'll make a great mom one day. When you get around to it." He squeezed her hand, which still held his. She didn't squeeze back. "This stripper gig you do," he said. "You're better than that. If I were fifteen years younger, I wouldn't need a lap-dance to ask you out."

"You're asking me out?"

"Sure I am. Let's do lunch, sometime. You know... as if I were your old and funny uncle or an even older friend."

Her hand pulled away. "What if your niece has had four abortions and more failed relationships than she cared to remember?"

"We've all messed up. But we do carry on."

"Do me a favor?"

"What is it?"

She exhaled. "I want you to kiss me. On the mouth. Like you kissed your ex-wife."

"It's been ages since I kissed anyone. Sarah and I stopped –"

"On the mouth," she repeated.

Colton met her halfway around the kitchen table. He pulled at the tiny waist and kissed her with eyes closed, once. Like he'd kissed Sarah countless times. In this moment, he could swear Sarah's breath hit his face and his tongue nudged between the gap of her front teeth. Then he opened his eyes and saw Maggie.

The twenty-four-year-old ran a tongue over the trail of their kiss on her lips. "I should have been born a hundred years earlier..." she said, half to Colton, half to the empty room, "when people had a future to look forward to, instead of this..." Her eyes smiled at him and her hand caressed his hair. "Give me a moment," she said, turned around and slid out of the room.

He returned to the table, counting the color pots over the stove. One blue, one green, two yellow... The sound of shattered glass jolted him erect and he rushed out of the kitchen and into the bedroom but Maggie wasn't there. He went for the only other room in the apartment. He opened the bathroom door and clammy thighs slapped his face. The smell hit him too. Her bleeding knees dangled at chin level, her toes sparkled with orange nail polish she must have put on at Déjà Vu earlier in the night. The sliding shower door, thrashed by her convulsing knees, sprinkled the tiled floor with shards of broken glass. A leather belt looped around the ceiling fan and her neck. Her body spun around. The lips that had kissed him a moment earlier were smattered with blood. Her teeth were ground shut by the unconscious pressure she had applied in her final moment. A bitten-off piece of her tongue, like discarded chewing gum, sat in the pile of glass on the floor. Colton turned to one side and wept.

two years and one hundred ninety one days till defiance day (12

It had been months since his hospital discharge, yet Sylvya missed Colton more than she dared imagine. She looked up his Mountain View passport records and was paralyzed to discover he had left Las Vegas. It took calling his former casino employer and role-playing as his personal physician to find out he had moved to Seattle. Seattle made no sense – it was cold and distant and, most of all, flooded. And where did this leave her? Was she going to let him walk? And if she did, how long would it take for her dream to come back to life with another patient? Assuming it could come back, at all. Then her decision formed: all cities needed nurses, most of all the coastal ones. She would peruse the Seattle job boards, get hired by a hospital there and move to the upper-left corner of the continent... for the sake of the dream he had rekindled in her.

Virginia Mason offered her a nursing position after a single phone interview. She flew with the kids from Las Vegas to SeaTac, the last functional northwest airport handling traffic from Boise in the east to San Francisco in the south and every other town in between. Sadie and Dallas were sleeping next to her. It was fortunate that Dallas was asleep on both beverage runs. His new gig was to fill his cheeks with soda and squeal at the bite of the bubbles against the inside of his mouth. The cheeks would stretch, with saliva and pop drooling from his puckered lips, until everything from the inside squirted out.

She caressed their small heads. What mother would relocate her children to the other side of the continent with weeks to go until Defiance Day? A batch of turbulence shook the cabin and Sylvya let out an unconscious cry drowned by the roar of the engines. She tried to imagine Colton's reaction to seeing her in Seattle for the first time.

Would he lift her off the ground and plant a hot and dry kiss on her lips? Would his unshaven stubble grind her lips into a mush? Would he kiss her forehead and hug her, but not too long, before squatting down to embrace Sadie and Dallas, and with a big smile melt their discomfort that a stranger had kissed their mom in public.

Another turbulence bump. Sylvya rubbed her bloodshot eyes, squishing a contact lens under her lid, upper or lower – she couldn't tell. The world became a fuzzy mess on the right but she didn't care. She was headed to him and that was all that mattered. The thought of him set fire through her veins as powerful as the maternal love for her children. He made her feel the way cancer cells felt about chemotherapy. Bones with cancer lit up the scanners in bright yellow and red; the brighter the colors, the further along the tumors. But several Zometa treatments later, the red would turn into hollow black, filled with dead cells. He was her Zometa. Without him, the desire, unfettered and red, to take care of someone would chew through her until she either died or lost sanity.

The plane's wheels thudded on the SeaTac tarmac. Dallas and Sadie woke and started playing slapsies. Sylvya gathered their toys from the faded seats, nostalgic for her own childhood. She would love to play a game of waking up in Colton's arms and smelling peanuts on his breath.

She cleared the airport checkpoint without a hiccup thanks to the Virginia Mason nurse-permit. As luck would have it, others from her flight weren't as prepared. A middle-aged couple with two teenage sons were detained for traveling with forged relocation permits and dispatched to confinement cells until the day of their voting executions. Because of the delay, Sylvya's group arrived in Seattle after curfew and were forced to spend the night at a ULE detention center until their city permits could be processed the following morning.

The curfew horn woke Sylvya at eight-thirty-am and she held her breath, despite the sleep deprivation, at the view of Seattle's majestic skyline flanked by the Cascades against the morning sun. The Puget Sound waters had devoured the city, but the mountains rose proud in the back, impervious to the human hubbub underneath. At noon, their paperwork cleared and the Timmonses were allowed in town. After an hour of navigating through suspension bridges and submerged neighborhoods, they reached the Virginia Mason. Defiance Day had so drained the city of nurses that, in addition to the employment permit, the hospital accommodated the three Timmonses in a rent-free condo downtown.

The quiet evening found mother and children in a new two-bedroom home with working lights and running water. Soon, the kids' rhythmic breathing filled the bedroom with calming frequency. Sylvya, too, lay down feeling full. They had a safe home – dare she dream for more? Would it be greedy to wish Colton fell asleep beside her too, for months on end, and years, together with the kids? She knew he'd embrace her the moment they saw each other. Seattle was her American Dream, where she would reinvent herself for him.

The smell of rot didn't feel repulsive anymore, the sights of desolated bridges felt temporary, and the ticking bomb of Defiance Day felt like another calendar date to come and go. She felt hopeful. She would claim the person who was hers and help him see life as she did. Sylvya Timmons fell asleep a happy woman.

seventeen days till defiance day (13

Natt Gurloskey scanned Seattle's downtown from the precinct's twentieth-floor windows and his heart wept. Drowning in the rain, the city had given out and the lives of the fifteen million Seattleites have become barrack lives. This defeat lay in the years before. In the decisions that weren't made and the visions that weren't there. But it was also his fault. This was his city, after all, and it had gone out for good, like a flare at the onslaught of a permanent night. Not the night that gave way to the morning after, but an incurable virus demanding capitulation. Once this virus had moved in, it refused to leave. It turned buildings into mildewy rubble. It took away the oxygen and sunlight, and demanded hope as a hostage, shipping it away somewhere far, never to return again. The night grew thicker with each new inch it captured. First, it took over one street corner, then a second one, then sprawled over to all adjacent alleys. The parts of town that fell under its control forgot what living felt like. The other parts bid their time until its inescapable arrival, assuring themselves they had lived well and that any life, no matter how good, had to end sometime. These were the depths to which Natt's city had fallen. Except there was no night, but it felt like there was.

Yet again, Natt hadn't slept. The three espresso cups he had downed earlier gurgled in his stomach, good for no more than inflaming his gastritis. He had to see the mayor today, sometime before the five-pm curfew, which his police department had imposed on this once vibrant, but now besieged, city. Natt walked on the beaten down linoleum and into the elevator hoping no one else would jump in with him. He disliked strangers. He disliked them even more in proximity. The elevator doors closed in unison with another gastric salute from his stomach. Someone had scratched a hasty star, to designate where the new lobby was, next to the plastic button for the twelfth floor: vandalism with a pinch of dark humor. Six months ago, the star would have sat next to the tenth-floor button. Six months from now, Gurloskey and whoever else was dumb enough to still live in this dead city would have to move the star higher. The elevator ding startled him. It wasn't noon yet but he couldn't keep his eyes open and gave himself a solemn promise to turn in by nine tonight.

He followed the handmade "Exit" arrows scratched on the walls and ended at what had once been a solid sidewall, now cut out and replaced with the gaping entry of a jet bridge leading to the main suspension bridge outside.

The rot hit his nostrils as soon as he stepped into the open. Fourth Avenue looked like a Venice canal, only more run-down. The water lapped at awnings and sidewalls, hundreds of feet above the submerged street level. High-rises jutted at crooked angles, like scattered concrete dominos, sunk partway in the sloshing waves. Barnacles covered the walls as high as a foot above the water and soiled sea-foam cuddled along once-functioning windows, now boarded by steel plates. Mayor Mullins had learned from New York's U-shaped berm and Rotterdam's seven-hundred-foot floodgates. As a result, Seattle was prepared when Greenland melted. But when the flood stayed, the city started its three-year-long suffering. The outer ocean wall bought some time for Mullins and Gurloskey to erect suspension bridges above the major downtown avenues. But when the wall bowed head to the persistent tidal pressure, whatever lay behind stood no chance. Furniture and computers, carpets and wiring were gone in less than a week. Entire city blocks were submerged to their third floors. The cars parked in the streets drifted in the water, like bobbing apples, and Seattle turned into a ghost town, without electricity, heat or human compassion. The smell of death filled the air as the waters corroded the buildings from within. The city's seaport, once a proud gateway to Asia's largest economies, became an oversized and lifeless aquarium.

This was the flood Gurloskey fought against, set to reclaim his tattered town even if it meant strapping Seattle on his back and pulling it away from the waters of the Puget Sound. He imposed a night curfew, growing in perimeter and time with each passing week. He dispersed the crowds of protesters that had been picketing for months. He converted banks into prisons and filled them with looters. Without search warrants, he barreled into residences within ten miles of the flooded downtown, confiscating any firearms his cops could lay hands on. He slept in his office for months without going home, regardless of how tempting it felt to flee to the high suburbs of Woodinville. He hadn't seen Eaton and Chloe and missed them, but a part of him didn't mind, because they weren't supposed to know him like this.

In time, one slow week after the next, the riots subsided, the night patrols uncovered fewer and fewer dead bodies at dawn, running water was restored to the municipal buildings and several downtown shelters opened for those without a place to call home. People were pulling together, seeing that togetherness was the ticket for survival. Mullins featured his Police Chief in a growing number of video calls with other mayors, dishing proven advice on how Seattle was coping. By the end of the sixth month, to Natt's exhausted astonishment, it felt like he'd turned the tide on Mother Nature by a creaky inch. By less than an inch. But it wouldn't be unreasonable to imagine life in his city returning to relative normalcy. A new normalcy by any account, but a normalcy anyway. He felt good and more in love with his family and the Seattle he had begun to save.

Then Antarctica fell and raised the oceans by another two hundred feet.

sixteen days till defiance day (14

"Good to hear your voice when I know who I'm hearing," Colton said and moved the phone from one ear to the other.

"We're divorced, Colton."

Through the phone line, he wanted to crawl to her, to the woman he'd be drawn to forever because of guilt and adoration, in equal parts. "How have you been, Sarah?"

"I shouldn't have called that night…" she cleared her throat. "The ULE Ministry of Science gave me your number and I didn't know what else to do."

"I was relieved to hear from you."

"I was in a poor condition."

"I didn't mind."

"How have you been? Still in Vegas?" she said.

Underneath her question, Colton sensed impatience. She'd always been lousy at pleasantries. "Vegas was the closet for too many skeletons. I'm in back in Seattle now. For a couple of years of what I call my post-Sarah era."

"Took you a while."

"You see, I kept one of your old voicemails on my cell. The time you asked me to get formula on my way home. Yana had turned red from crying while you were taking a shower and you called because it couldn't wait. Then you dropped the phone in the water." He chuckled. "The message died midsentence, before you could ask for the formula, but I figured it out. I could finish your sentences back then." He coughed to steady his voice. "I copied this message from phone to phone, for more than three years. But holding on to it felt like a monument to my sins. I deleted your voice and moved to Seattle, starting a life of starting to forget you. But your call the other night…"

"Always the poet who chooses the bigger good, over the lesser evil," she said. "Are you married now?"

"No more marriages for me, Sarah. Not after you."

"Don't..."

"You asked." He closed his eyes.

"I have no room for distractions. Living with Yana and without you has been good, until this tragedy. Which is why I called last week. Should have handled it better, but I still need your answer."

"First you call me a distraction then you say you should have asked me to die in a more thoughtful way."

"Don't fight me on this, unless you've already voted."

"Only for me to know," he said, wondering when was the last time they had a conversation without fighting.

"I need to know too." He could hear her teeth clench. "If there was a way to avoid knowing, I would have."

"You find the best words to convince a man, Dr. Parker. Or are you back to Dr. Perkins?"

"My surname is irrelevant."

"I haven't voted yet," he said, "or sacrificed."

"Then I have to."

"You have to what?"

"Ask my question from the other night. But I don't need an immediate answer. You still have a couple of weeks to decide."

"Until Defiance Day?" Colton's hand that wasn't holding the phone, rubbed his eyes. A headache was tiptoeing underneath his temples, not at full strength yet, but coming.

"It would mean Yana lives."

"You're doing it again."

"How about I re-marry you?" she said.

"Is remarriage the going rate for my life?"

"If there was another way, I'd have found it."

"Which only makes you a High-Potential, prohibited from Sacrifice or earmark," he said.

"Focus on what matters, Colton."

"What does? As a Hi-Po, maybe you can explain it to me."

"Voting matters."

"Is that what you call forcing a person to choose another person for extermination?"

"It's a legal earmark vote."

He laughed. "So if the extermination is legal, then it's good extermination."

"Think of how lucky she would be. To survive Defiance Day with the other Sacrifice recipients."

"You know people call them Silver-Spooners, right?"

"I don't care about people's high-minded bullshit. Defiance Day will solve Earth's population problem with one sweep that's legal and efficient."

"And barbaric..." he said.

"There'll be no more castrations afterwards, Colton. No more curfews and no more disappearing species."

"Just a few million Silver-Spooners with an irrevocable sense of entitlement, tasked to rebuild our world."

"Stop being such a child. Vote Sacrifice if you hate voting earmark so much."

"Which is what you'd have me do."

"Law requires you to vote one way or the other," she said.

"If Defiance Day is this humane process, why do you need my Sacrifice to save your daughter?"

"She's your daughter too. Whom you almost killed before her first birthday."

"I can always count on you to remind me."

A noisy breath through the nose. "You win. OK?" she said. "I'm begging you. I'm not telling, I'm begging. Do you realize how hard this is for me?"

He did. The Sarah Perkins he used to know was the one on top. Always. An oversized painting of "La Niña," the sole

Columbus ship to survive the journey to the New World, hung in her lab. The words of the Great Explorer were etched on it, "All my life, I've been chasing the Sun. Now I'm going to catch it." She was born a Sun-chaser. He suspected she married him to have a child and keep colonizing the unknown, through Yana, long after her own death. Now Columbus was begging him and he hated having pushed her so far.

"I'll think this over. How do I get a hold of you?"

"The number I'm calling from should be on your Caller ID. I'll make sure I call you too."

The phone went dead. She was getting good at hanging up without giving him the chance to say goodbye.

two years and forty nine days till defiance day (15

Wet hands covered Colton's face and closed his eyelids, forcing the high-noon sun to dip into darkness. A giggle tweeted from behind and made him jump in the chair. "Guess who?"

He turned his head, but the wet fingers stayed on. With purpose, he grabbed the foreign hands, their skin smooth and supple against his grip, pushed them away and saw her. The motley eyes, the tear-shaped bob like a blonde Afro, the dimpled smile stretching from side to side. He stitched the parts together and gasped at the full picture.

"Sylvya?"

The snickering exploded into laughter. "Hello, my love." She stood before him, in the Seattle downtown library, with wet hands, which he had forgotten to let go. She leaned in and kissed his mouth, making a noise and prompting several library patrons to look their way. Colton shook his head, as if she had slapped his face instead of kissing it. He set her hands free and she hugged him hard.

"I've missed you," she said in his ear. "Don't run away anymore." She held him for another second before letting go.

"Could we sit for a moment?" he said. "Better yet, let's go to the lobby. This is the quiet floor."

"A boy scout as always. But who'll take care of you, Mister?"

He left the question unanswered, grabbed her hand and led her out, under an increasing hail of disapproving glances. In the library café, they sat at a corner table, him holding her hand all along, as if she were a child.

"You're visiting Seattle, of all places?" His eyebrows formed an arch with a tip in the middle of his forehead.

"I'm not visiting, silly. I am relocating." She yodeled the last word with Christmas-like cheer. "The kids and I arrived from Las Vegas, last week. The one-hour bus ride from the airport took almost a day because this city has one highway left that's not under water. And don't get me started on the curfew checkpoints. Why are you guys so anal up here? The bus made five checkpoint stops." Her smile pushed through the annoyance. "But that's not important. Seeing you makes it all worth it, in the end."

Colton's mouth twisted. "You decided to take the kids and just leave Vegas?"

"I didn't just leave," she said, slapping his shoulder with a hand. "I'm not such an airhead. After evaluating my life options, I chose to move to Seattle and start fresh. Plus, there's so much crime in Las Vegas now and no jobs." She uncrossed her legs and crossed them again in different order. "Aren't you glad to see me?"

"I'm... surprised. Did you know I lived in Seattle before you moved here?"

"I did." She looked away with the quiet pride of a student expecting praise from her math teacher. "But in case you want to know, you're looking at the new Chief of Nursing at Virginia Mason Oncology. Can you imagine?" She clapped hands in the air. "I started last week."

"I'm... happy for you."

"Well..." her lips puffed air. "It's not all glory and unicorns. Their staff is so overworked they are sleepwalking with exhaustion. I've worked my share of night shifts in Las Vegas, but didn't realize how much worse the coasts had it. It's like a different way of life here... the highlands versus the coast."

Colton stared at a passerby outside, then ventured a smile. "How did you find me in the library?"

"Pure fate, dear."

He had to admire the benevolent energy of a woman who could love with a full heart. Why couldn't he respond? Why was he so stuck on Sarah who, chances were, hated him still? Humans were born screwed up and, in that department, he was a model human.

"I was out, strolling along these burly suspension bridges you call downtown here. I'm drinking my frozen beverage..." She waved an empty Starbucks cup, as if presenting important evidence to a jury. "And who do I see as I walk by the library's windows?"

"I... I have to run home," he stammered.

"Wait," she tapped a finger on his nose. "You can't leave without giving me your number."

"I live in... that direction." His thumb jabbed at the air behind his back.

"That was clear... Not." She gave a pout after the deliberate pause. "I live and work there." She pointed a finger in a random direction. "But that didn't give you my contact information, did it? So let's get rid of the guesswork and have dinner at my place tonight? You'll see how much the kiddos have grown."

He stood up. "I have to leave," his voice full of ice. "Virginia Mason is lucky to have you."

Sylvya's face turned red. "I can imagine how busy you are, but we must make plans to see each other." She held to his green suede jacket as he was beginning to leave.

"I need to go, Sylvya." He ran outside, among the Seattle pedestrians whose purpose, together with everyone else on Earth, was to kill time until the day of their deaths. Sylvya ran after him, jostling bodies out of the way.

"Wait... wait for me," she said.

He kept walking, the back of his head bobbing up and down among the sea of others. Then he dove into the Starbucks at the corner of Denny and Fourth.

She stormed behind and slammed the door shut. "I only saved your life," she screamed.

He turned around. She was right. He would have died without her.

"And now you're running away from me," her face twisted; mascara, dark and splotchy, invading her cheeks. "How can you be so selfish?"

He took a step away from the entrance, pulling her with him. "I admire you for saving my life," his head hung as he spoke, "and won't forget that. But you see... I don't feel about you the way you feel about me. And should never have led you on."

She reached inside her purse and dabbed her eyes with a crumpled tissue.

He raised a hand. "Let me, at least, get you a latte," he said and headed for the counter before getting an answer. He returned with two paper cups, a latte for her and some other brown liquid for him. They sat down and he took the lid off her cup. "It will cool down faster this way," he said. Heart-shaped foam swam like a melting iceberg in the middle of the hot coffee.

"Am I not attractive to you?" she said. "Is there someone else?"

He gulped whatever his cup held, bottoms-up, and clenched it with both fists, careful not to shred the paper to bits. His love and allegiance would always belong to Sarah, even if Sarah hated his guts. "You are a looker. And no, I'm not dating anyone else. It's just that... you should deal with your life first, before you get to me."

"Deal with my life?" Her moist voice gave way to a harsh undertone and Colton shuddered, unsure if this other voice was a permanent part of her, lurking under the tears when she didn't get what was hers.

"Let me be," he said. "You can have any other man you wish." A smile hung on his face like a coat on a tin hanger. "Your kids. Your husband, if you are still married. They are the most important. Your new career in Seattle. I don't come before any of these."

"Grow a pair and spare me the bullshit." She stood up, walked away and came back to the table, swift and threatening. "I'm smart and I deserve respect, and you... you are pathetic."

"Why don't you –"

"I haven't been myself these days but I am a good person, Colton. If you don't want to be with me, have the decency to tell me why. Don't tell me I'm attractive and you're grateful while you're acting the opposite. The truth is you despise me –"

"Look, I –"

"And you're rude and selfish. And you want to keep me around for free hospital access." Her body shook with sobs. "I thought you were different. I admired the way you spoke about life. Now, I know you're a coward." Her shoulder-length hair tossed, as if blown by invisible wind.

"I'm sorry."

"I'm a good person, Colton," a fresh avalanche of sobs, "I've never done this. Doctors ask me out all the time and I always say no. With you... I don't know. Maybe it was how we met, you in a hospital bed within an inch of your life."

"I'd be dead without you, Sylvya, but we can only be friends."

"But you do understand my feelings?"

Colton had heard enough. Expecting her to understand logic was like hoping the sun would rise at midnight. He wiped off a coffee stain on his chair and leaned back, prepared to wait her out in silence until she was done or until the place closed.

As if she had seen through his intentions, Sylvya buried her face in a napkin and soaked the recycled paper with fresh tears.

fifteen days till defiance day (16

The day's grime and politics were behind Natt, but family dinner wasn't; a task laden with as many traps as he had navigated during his nine-to-five. He pulled his chair closer to the table. On his right, Eaton and Chloe sat next to each other, chewing in silence. Eating dinner wasn't a time of many words in the Gurloskey household – it was sitting together for a meal, the old-fashioned way. Natt insisted on this forty-five-minute ritual every night because the streets of downtown Seattle weren't the only casualties to the rising waters. Notions like family time and finding out about each other's day were also falling prey to the floods.

Soup didn't precede tonight's dinner and coffee wouldn't follow it. It was a single-meal, main-course-plus-salad affair. Macaroni and chicken flanked a lonesome bowl filled with broccoli and lettuce. Natt never much cared for vegetables, so the salad was the same as last night's and as from the night before.

He chewed several times before swallowing each mouthful. Chloe and Eaton, too, spent the forty-five minutes stuffing food in their mouths, one deliberate forkful after the other. Natt saw through their conspiracy but didn't want to push his luck; boring wordless dinners plus on-time curfew sign-ins worked fine to keep his family safe, thank you very much. And family was Natt's most prized achievement.

Eaton was eight and full of life. After dinner, he would dash to his room to resume charting flight patterns, designing apps, and obsessing over whatever other boys his age obsessed with. Natt loved his stepson with intensity reserved for loving your own. He couldn't explain why. He hadn't been present at Eaton's birth to develop fatherly hormones. The ULE Population Fairness Act hadn't forced him to report to a ULE Decision Room within seconds of

Eaton's cord being severed. He hadn't pressed the button new dads pressed that delivered the message "Castration Aborted" twenty percent of the time or, for the other eighty percent, the message "Castration Authorized."

Natt hadn't lived through any of that, yet loved Eaton as if he had. Eaton was his ticket to heaven and the proof that no matter how screwed up the rest of life got, Natt would get this one thing right... without excuses. He loved the boy even if the boy's abilities scared him and sometimes even made him jealous.

Chloe was a different story. He couldn't recall when and how he'd fallen out of love with Eaton's mother. Courting, surprise sex and dinner dates had ended as soon as they got married. The city flooded when they moved in together and she stood no chance competing with the rotting Seattle downtown. Once in a while, despite his better judgment, Natt would drop by Déjà Vu, to take the edge off, before going home to his wife. As the months passed, the strip-club trips grew longer, the drinks multiplied and the lap-dances finished with happy endings. He wasn't proud of himself, far from it. He still believed he was a good person but knew he had become a cheater. Chloe knew it too... women had a sixth sense about these things.

One weekday, they stopped having sex. Fatigue and busy schedules were a logical excuse, at first. Then touching her became unpleasant, compared to how Déjà Vu made him feel. In time, she stopped pushing for it and he was happy to oblige. Chloe's birthday, three years ago, was the last time they had been intimate. Natt had surprised her by coming home earlier, sneaking behind her in the kitchen, squeezing her breasts from behind, and whispering "Happy Birthday" in her ear.

Since then she had been his in their marriage certificate only and the Seattle Chief of Police was too weak to end it – either his marriage or his infidelity.

fourteen days till defiance day (17

"Last call, Colton..." Sarah sounded like a bartender but, in a way, had described her daughter's fate as well.

"When can I see you?" Colton asked.

"Maybe after Defiance Day," she said. "Maybe never," and he wondered how many hours she was sleeping these days, assuming she slept at all. He had time to sleep and that made him feel guilty.

"How is she?"

"Struggling with algebra. We'll work on her homework when I get home tonight."

"They get algebra homework in third grade?"

"There's nothing like crunching numbers while waiting for someone to vote you dead."

"You haven't told her she was earmarked?" His voice was matter-of-fact.

"I haven't. And if you choose well, I won't have to."

"I love you, Sarah... but sometimes –"

"Just hit me with it."

He thought she already knew the answer but the scientist in her wanted the final proof point, for the sake of closure. "I'm not sure I can do it, Sarah. I'll never forgive myself for what I did to her but I don't think I'm ready to die yet."

Silence. If Colton didn't know her better he would have sworn she was crying. Crying silent tears in Washington, DC, with a cell phone pressed against her ear. Then her steely voice broke the illusion. "I'd pay a thousand dollars for each day I could subtract from your life span, Colton Parker." She breathed in-between words, like she was climbing stairs. "I've never understood people's obsession with religion. But now I wish God did exist, to judge you after you died. As far as I go, or your daughter, you're dead already, or better yet, you never really happened."

The line went dead. It was raining in Seattle.

**one year and three hundred twenty one days till
defiance day (18**

The phone rang again for what, to Colton, felt like the
thirtieth time. He had lost count. This time he picked up, to
prevent his sanity from blowing through his ears, and
almost burst into laughter after hearing the voice he had
expected. How else could he react to her tenacity? Or
should he be laughing at himself: a middle-aged man with a
potbelly, a history of STDs and no family? Not quite your
top-shelf dating material, yet this beautiful woman with
great breasts, great education and two wonderful kids was
stalking him. And he wanted none of her. He remembered
the first year without Sarah, when he would have proposed
to a stripper if she had as much as kissed his cheek in the
middle of a lap-dance... of course, none of them had. Back
then he would have killed for a stalker like Sylvya. But here
he was today, allergic to her insistence. What was wrong
with him? He waited for her to speak and bit into his lower
lip to ward off a wave of cackles.

"Colton," Sylvya's voice was in rags. She sounded like
hatred and yearning, at the same time; like a zombie
attacking a human while hoping he'd kill it to rid it of its
misery. "How could you be so selfish?"

He'd heard this drill before. His smile went away. "I
think you should seek medical help."

"Medical help? I am medical help, you bastard. How
dare –"

"We've had this conversation, Sylvya. You tell me you
love me and I tell you I don't. What else is there?"

"I'm calling from outside your apartment."

"You what?" He ran to the door, fumbling his keys for a
moment then pushing it open. She was leaning against the
wall, cell phone pinched between her shoulder and cheek,
eyes locked on him.

"Jesus... How did you find my place?"

"I looked up your medical records at Virginia Mason." She held her purse with both hands, like a shield. "It's not something I'm not proud of, Colton."

"Security downstairs should have stopped you... past curfew, no less."

"I told the guard you were my husband. Did I lie?"

"Did you not?"

"Today... is my birthday. And I wanted no other gift," her hands made a nervous circle in the air, "but to spend time with you. I'm sorry I caught you off-guard, but we had to talk about us."

He groaned behind his teeth.

"Don't," she said. Her hand, palm-first, shot toward his face, to hush whatever words were due next. "You can't deny a birthday wish, can you? It's a yes-or-no answer, Colton."

He stepped aside with a hung head.

She didn't need another invitation and sat by a coffee table, the largest piece of furniture in the room other than a mattress and a small electric range. "What a lovely place you have. This must be a living room and a kitchen in one."

Sitting across from her, he stared at her legs – waxed and glowing. He picked a ballpoint pen from the table, clicked and unclicked, then exhaled through trumpet cheeks. "All I can afford is this studio."

"Does this mean we're sitting in your bedroom?" Her eyebrows wiggled up and down.

He ignored the question. "What did you want to talk about?"

"Nothing, with this kind of tone."

Colton looked up from her legs. She was acting coy, as if wild horses had dragged her to his coffee table. Maybe that's what groupies did around their music idols. They looked forward to it but felt out of place when it happened. Not that he took himself this serious. If there was a celebrity at the table, it was her. She had saved his life and as much as he hated letting her inside on her birthday, anything less would have been an amateur act.

Sylvya buried her face in her palms. "I had lost respect for you," she whispered behind her fingers.

"I'm sorry."

"Let's go to my place. I'd love to introduce you to my kids."

"I don't think we should see each other again."

Her shoulders hunched over the table and her eyes reflected the studio's recessed lights like fresh-water wells. "Never? Not until the day I die?"

"I'd want to see you the day before."

The joke lit up her face and despite her visible efforts to the opposite, she smiled. "Funny."

How smitten I would have been with you, had we met at a different time, Colton thought.

"Should I tell you what's on my mind?" she said.

"No."

"Well... Since I'm the birthday girl, I don't need your permission."

His smile went away. "I'll be honest, Sylvya. Your love blinds you. My kindness to you doesn't mean I love you back."

"What do you mean?"

Colton had to hurt this woman. Hurt her enough so she wouldn't come back. He shuddered and wished they could trade places after what he was about to say. "I don't want to see you ever again."

"Why not?"

His voice rose, its pitch broke before it steadied again. "Because you'll never be my lover and you'll make a lousy friend."

Her lips shook. "Where is the man I fell in love with?"

"He's dead other than in your imagination."

She squeezed her head then wrapped her hair in a ponytail. "What have I done to make you detest me?"

"You should go." Colton was out of strength to argue. His mouth opened and closed and nothing came out. How had he ever found her funny?

"I don't think so." Tears burnt pink trails down her cheeks. "Not after we bonded during the darkest days of your life, dear. With a bond stronger than the theatrics our society calls marriage." She tightened the ponytail with both hands and swatted a non-existent strand of hair from her eyes. "Didn't we? If a marriage is sacred, what we have is even better... it's cathartic. Merging into a single being during our Mountain View days, in emotion, spirit and sex."

He stood up and walked to the window, like a caged animal, and tossed her a glance without breaking stride.

"Do you realize what you're doing? You lied to the guard that you're my wife. And you claim we share a bond stronger than marriage." His chest heaved up and down. "While I'm in your debt for saving my life, I don't owe you the rest of it as a repayment. And to check that my ears still work, did you say you screwed me in the Mountain View hospital, while I was in coma?" His face felt like the face of someone going insane. "Do you know what rape means, Sylvya? It means jail and forfeiting your nursing license and never getting it back."

"That's what people do, when in love."

Too dizzy to stand, he leaned against the window and sagged. "Leave now." He had bought grapes earlier, from the grocery store around the corner. A half-pound, the maximum allowed, and had imagined eating them for dinner, their juice filling his mouth and trickling down his throat. He'd close his eyes and travel back to Cancun, his last vacation with Sarah, with Yana in her belly. Cancun was the last time he had eaten grapes. Ever. He'd been avoiding them since. Until today, when he was going to convince himself Earth was not a foregone conclusion. And he would toast life and mock Defiance Day. But Sylvya and her rape story had killed the grapes' magic and he wanted the fruit out of his apartment. He wanted her out too.

"Leave. Now..." screaming this time, "or I'm calling the police." His head hung between his knees. "I don't want to see you. Do you understand?" Silence followed, with neither of them daring to break it. "Get out of my life. You damn –" Colton looked up ready for another drawn-out battle. He was sitting alone on the floor. She had left and he was shouting to the empty room.

thirteen days till defiance day (19

Li-Mei found him alone, in the Big Daddy bar in the suburb of Woodinville. The GPS tracker on her tablet guided her north, past the drenched Seattle skyline and along the potholes littering what once was the I-5 highway. Li-Mei had never set foot in Woodinville before – the Napa of Washington, now – a Marine outpost conscripted by the ULE in case the Mayor and his police force lost control of the Emerald City. She wouldn't have guessed Colton would be drawn to such a place. His behavioral records showed a thirst for strip clubs, hookah bars and pot joints, none of them available in your typical military base.

She parked outside the Big Daddy – a bar that an optimist would call gritty and a realist a dive. The muggy evening begged the skies for a rainy relief. She hated sweating, but welcomed the meteorological assistance, given she was about to jump into the role of a clingy Asian woman on a weekday suburban night. Li-Mei unbuttoned her plaid shirt and took it off, together with the tee underneath. Her white bra glowed in the late evening, moist flesh transmitting a dining invitation to all mosquitos within fifty yards. On her chest, she glued a fake dragon tattoo that started between her breasts, extended around the neck, and peaked next to her left earlobe. She put the tee back on, and the plaid shirt, refreshed her lips with a coat of raspberry red lipstick and walked in the bar.

Big Daddy felt cavernous and empty. A rectangular bar dominated the middle, with a dozen keg hoses dangling above the marble top, ready to deliver more alcohol than any human liver could process. An unshaved bartender sat on a beat-up stool, propping his face on his elbow and twirling a set of matches next to a half-drunk glass of beer. The place housed fewer than a dozen souls and she spotted Colton at a table in the back of the room. His hair was shorter than in the profile photos she had, but otherwise he looked identical, down to the suede jacket she recalled having seen in one of his digital folders. A crowded room would have helped conceal her approach and their ensuing conversation. An empty room was a nuisance, but something she could handle.

She sat at the bar, across from the bartender who kept twirling the matches. His stare followed her in a lazy arc and rested on her tattoo.

"What can I do you for, Missie?" His front teeth were missing but he flashed a broad grin, as if unaware of their absence.

"Make it rum and coke," Li-Mei said with the raspiest voice she could muster. He squeezed and rattled the drink from the dangling hoses and slid it toward her across the marble top. The glass left a sweaty trail, sloshing some of its contents along the way and coming to a stop within inches of Li-Mei's hand. She swallowed the shot, exhaled with a cough and tossed a toothy grimace at the man.

"Keep 'em coming, till I say not to," she said. She didn't need to look over her shoulder to sense men ogling her from the minute she had walked in. Colton was the one guy who hadn't bitten and kept staring at his beer. Li-Mei whistled at the bartender and tilted head in Colton's direction. "What's his deal?"

Mr. No-Front-Teeth didn't hesitate. "Him? Not a regular."

"You think he's stationed at the base?"

"Nah. I know the local boys." Then he winked at Li-Mei. "You one of them TV people, snitching on our boys for breaking curfew and smuggling shit?"

"What if I was?"

His face twisted. "I hope you ain't. I spit on them TV folks."

"I'm not with the TV. I'm just a woman looking for handsome guys."

"Don't know about him," his tongue licked his chapped lips, "but you can make do with me." A yellow smile seconded his words.

"Maybe I'll come back after he and I are done. If you can handle me, that is."

The bartender's nostrils flared. "I'm off at two," he said. "And I live close."

"I'll be back soon, lover." Li-Mei swallowed her second shot and headed to the back of the bar.

Colton was picking at a scratch that ran from the edge of his table to his half-full beer glass. Li-Mei sat across from him with a theatric thump. Four other empty glasses flanked the half-full one.

"Excuse me, sir," she said, "is this seat taken?"

A shade ran over his face, as his eyes lingered on her hair. "Be my guest," he said, with less slurring than she had hoped. Then he went back to fixing the groove.

So much for the tattoo, she thought. "How about you buy me a full one of these?" she said and flicked an empty stein with her index finger.

His eyes didn't move. "I'm sure other men in this room would be glad to oblige."

"That's why I am asking you."

Colton turned to the bartender, "Two more beers, Charlie," then back to Li-Mei. "I'm Colton."

"Li-Mei." She rested her face on her cupped palms and started blinking with the flirtatious frequency she had seen in a black-and-white film in Jenli. "What brings you around these parts?"

"It's my first time here. Looking for a change of pace, I guess."

She leaned back, flaunting a white smile and a red tattoo. "If a military outpost is your idea of change, you must be a party animal on schooldays."

"And you?" he said.

"And me?"

"Who are you? A colonel-major who mingles with the platoon folk?"

"Points for a vivid imagination." She laughed with a head thrown back and a tattoo glaring at him in the husky light. "I could turn into a colonel-major for the right audience. Maybe you could bring it out in me?"

"Who knows?" he said and looked at her with an empty stare that forced Li-Mei to revisit her basics. The man loved easy women, an assertion built on the empirical data he spent his weekends in strip clubs. But he hadn't bitten so far and she decided to change her approach. She covered her mouth.

"You're right. What am I doing?" she said and buttoned her shirt with shaky fingers. "I find a decent guy…" still stuttering, "and I don't recognize myself. Ever since my dad was… you know, chosen, my life has become undone, like a kite without a string." She squeezed the back of her neck to soothe some pain there, or stiffness. "A colonel-major? I can't even score a cashier's gig. Instead, I book rooms in hotels to meet guys with my tits hanging out, as if…" She shook her head and turned for the door.

"Stay." His voice stopped her. "You should stay." He couldn't see the smile rising on her face.

She turned around, smile gone and lips quivering. "You sure?"

Outside, crickets sang in the evening. "Were you and your father close?" he said.

By the time she returned to his table, the promiscuous Li-Mei had died. A new one, as fragile as a nun, sat down.

Whatever it took for Parker to change from an orange dot to a green one by the morning.

"What brings you here?" he said, coherent still, but getting slurry. "The Seattle glitz is to the south of Woodinville."

She glanced at the time. Eleven-thirty-pm. If she were lucky, he might be dead by one-thirty. Guaranteed dead by two.

"Since when is rot a synonym for glitz?"

"You're right." He smiled for the first time.

"I'm here looking for…" she stopped. "Here I go again, spilling my guts to a stranger."

"Carry on." He stretched a hand, brushing her knuckles by accident then pulling back, as if her flesh were on fire.

She exhaled through puckered lips. "I'm lonely. I was looking for… you know, men in uniform who are strong and principled… sort of like knights."

"We all look for heroes without realizing we are the ones we've been waiting for."

"Maybe… But what kind of hero am I? Here? In this… place." Li-Mei swept a hand at the empty bar then buried face in her palms, muffling a whimper.

"It's OK falling apart sometimes. As long as you pick yourself up in time…"

"Are you falling apart?" She shot a teary smile designed to go straight at his savior complex. "I'm tough to compete with in the falling-apart department." The fallen angel was proving more effective than the tattooed slut.

A self-pitying grin distorted Colton's face. "If it makes you feel better, I've been struggling too… for years." He took a sip of his beer. "Made a mistake when I was younger that wrecked my past. Now I'm fighting to prevent it from wrecking my future."

"Defiance Day will take care of the future."

"True. Yet we must be prepared for what happens after."

"You're a planner, aren't you? You must not be from around here."

"I used to live in Nevada."

Li-Mei nodded, realizing she knew everything he told her, yet not in the same way he was telling it. For the first time she saw the man beyond his digital profile, valuable knowledge for eliminating a target. On the outside, she clasped hands against her chest. "Tell me more. It's remarkable to meet someone who thinks further than two weeks from now. The rest of the world hunkers down, but you are like: no, no, no." With each "no," she waved a finger in front of her face then stretched a hand above her head, tracing an invisible newspaper headline. "Mr. Colton meets Defiance Day. Lives On."

"I would have died in a Vegas hospital," he said, "if not for a nurse who arm-wrestled Death for my life, for weeks, and won. I moved to Seattle after, to start fresh and stop the nightmares," the sorrow on his face gave way to anguish, "and when I thought I had pulled it off, this ghost crawled out of my past, dragging me back to the beginning."

"The way you talk, you could pass for a knight."

"And you could pass for a comedian. Or a world-class flatterer." He drank the last of the beer and wiped his mouth. "This knight will drink until Defiance Day and then... we'll see."

Li-Mei gave him a smile that belonged to her younger self, the girl from Jenli, before the training and the growing up. "How about you drive me to my hotel? I don't feel safe by myself, after curfew."

"Is this the itchy woman speaking again?" He started to apologize, but she spoke first.

"Sorry for bringing this up, I–"

"I acted like a jerk. Of course, I'll drive you."

On the outside, Li-Mei thanked him and smiled to stay in character, the corners of her mouth continuing their marathon workout. On the inside, this man's kindness made her sick. He gave himself, piece by piece to anyone who'd bother asking. None of her other targets deserved to die as much as this man did. The closest she came to understanding his mindset was comparing his daughter to Taxi. Only, Li-Mei wouldn't have died for Taxi. Did this mean she was less devoted to her mission than he was to his? Should she fear him? She hadn't felt fear since the day Taxi had died on a gray morning twenty-one years ago. She shook the thought; today was different.

"Shall we?" She rose and he followed. She took his hand, her fingers prying his fingers apart. He squeezed back in return. A smile bloomed on her lips, but the skin-to-skin contact made her feel uncomfortable inside. Not that she was a virgin. She had slept with twelve people during her twenty-seven years, including different ethnicities, a girl and a threesome. She didn't mind sex, but didn't appreciate it either. The sloppy mess that followed was too much to bear and after repeated disasters, she demanded all her partners wear condoms. Tonight, her tally wasn't going to go to thirteen but her target didn't need to know that.

He opened the door for her. A shout came from behind, "Better use protection, tiger," and laughter from drunken mouths. She closed the door and silenced them.

"I'm in the white Camaro," he said pointing to the back of the parking lot. They reached the car and he shut the passenger door after she got in, careful not to slam it against the car's frame. He turned on the ignition and switched into drive.

Once and again she glanced at him and planned his death as they flew toward Seattle, under the I-5 curfew sensors scanning their passports. The China Territory's non-negotiable requirement was that the deaths of her targets appear natural or self-inflicted. Li-Mei didn't mind. Throat slicing was what she had in mind for Colton – her favorite suicide setup because it gave her the tools to show appreciation for the victim. She would force high-quality cognac into her victims' stomachs then drag them to a bathroom and induce vomiting until they regained their wits. Then she would slice their throats and watch them flap in an inch-deep pool of their own blood. As they died, she felt as close to them as siblings. Li-Mei had never felt such a bond with a living person.

Forty-five minutes later, Colton, with Li-Mei in the passenger seat, parked at The Fairmont Olympic Hotel.

twelve days till defiance day (20

An Olympic bellboy with a plastic smile tapped on the driver's window, as Colton killed the Camaro's engine.

"I'll leave in a moment," Colton said, stuffed a dollar bill in the plastic boy's front pocket and waved him off.

"Ma'am," he turned to Li-Mei, "I had a good time. And I thank you for it."

"Who says the good time is over?" she said and stretched in the leather seat. "I scored a cute room here, the Presidential Suite. Business must be slow if girls like me get suites." Her fingertips hovered along the contours of her seated body as if showcasing a prize. "It would mean a lot if you came up. How about a cup of tea to clear your hangover for the trip back?"

He looked at her with eyes reddened by lack of sleep. "I'm fine. I live just around the corner."

"Why are you punishing yourself? I'll never see you after tonight. And after Defiance Day, I won't see anyone."

Colton snorted at the joke. "I don't know why you're so persistent."

"So you're coming up for some tea?"

"Are you one hundred percent sure you want to do this? The last time I went alone with a woman to her place, a horrible tragedy happened. Tonight doesn't feel right either."

"Do I have to strip naked here to convince you to come upstairs?" She froze in place with raised eyebrows. "Look. If I didn't want you in my room, then you wouldn't be here, so shut up and let's have some fun." The two of them got out of the car.

"Welcome back, Ms. Gao." Another bellboy greeted her by the elevator doors then saluted Colton. "Good evening, sir."

Running into the second bellboy wasn't good news, she thought. The more people saw Colton come in, the messier her pending operation. The elevator proclaimed arrival with a muted ring. She stepped in, pulled Colton with a firm tug, and kissed his cheek as the closing doors hid them from sight. At floor twenty-six, he stretched an arm. "After you."

"We're going that way." She pointed to the left, down a row of numbered mahogany doors. "The last suite on the left." He walked ahead, his shoes leaving imprints on the feathery carpet. Behind him, her pupils dilated.

"I understand you have a daughter," she said. She had worked hard for this moment and was going to enjoy it.

"Yes, an eight-year-old. How do you know about Yana?"

"I'm sure her mother has called you asking for help even if she still hates your guts."

"Who are you?"

Like a tigress who couldn't purr, Li-Mei closed her eyes to show happiness because losing vision lowered defenses and tigers only did so when feeling happy. "I can't let you save that girl. I can't let you Sacrifice for her. My mission doesn't allow it." She opened her eyes and looked at her target, alone and filled with the ridiculous desire to save her. She gave Colton one final smile, colder than the melted Antarctic.

Afterward, she struck.

twelve days till defiance day (21

With a screech, Colton's world stopped for a second or two. He wondered if he had acquired some special power to stop time, but a corner inside his mind sounded an alarm that stopping time wasn't good news. Cold sweat covered his face and the sound of sandpaper scraping over matted glass filled his body. Time stopped; for how long, he couldn't tell. Then the stillness cracked and Earth resumed its rotation at the slow-motion pace of a Seattle slug. Specks of dust, usually too small for the naked eye to see, danced as large as snowflakes in the lazy glow of the hotel wall-lights. Then the sandpaper feeling gave way to weightlessness. He realized his head was smashed into the wall but he sensed nothing. No pain, as if the dust snowflakes had muted his senses. His brain gave a standing slow-clap ovation – he could get used to this. Or was he sure?

He should have stayed away from her in the pub. He should have fled after their first flirtation. He should have refused to drive her to Seattle. These "should haves" made him sad. How the rest of life could have unfolded, forever impacted by not meeting this woman. The dust snowflakes whirred on, a sign he was still alive but déjà vu hit him. He recalled the same sense of irreversible loss after the Yana accident. That night, he swore, his eyes unseeing with tears, he would never be on the wrong side again. Never on the unfixable side. Yet, a mere seven years later, the exact same bone-crushing desperation had swallowed him whole. He had run out of excuses. His brain registered his hands pushing against the hallway carpet, likely in an attempt to stand up. Too late… Would people, at his funeral, notice his unclipped fingernails in the coffin? He smiled in his head, because his face had lost the physical capacity to do so.

Next, the dust snowflakes bid him adieu and the world sped back up to normal, ending his sensory anesthesia.

Blood, gushing out of his broken nose, pooled red in his cupped hands, as the unmuted world re-entered his ears.

Colton felt a steel blade bite into his neck and his pulse accelerated against the cold metal. Was this how death felt? He wasn't rebellious or sad. At times, while driving on the WA-520 bridge above Lake Washington, he had imagined swerving into the concrete highway divider. In his mind, his knuckles firmed and his hands turned the wheel, inch by inch. Then in this War of Curiosities, Good Curiosity of what old age felt like would win out over Morbid Curiosity of crashing into the divider at ninety miles-per-hour. Good Curiosity had won by a photo finish, the last few times. Tonight, no photo finish was needed; the ugly stepsister, Ms. Morbid Curiosity, was the clear favorite.

He felt the knife break the skin of his neck. In a moment, the blade would meet his carotid artery and unleash the rivers of blood coursing through it. Any moment... Colton had never been more certain of anything else in life. He felt special like all other creatures faced with their passing. How many others, around the world, were dying together with him in this moment? He lay still under the crushing knee of the woman whom he had wanted to help earlier and looked at her with the dread of a good man hurt beyond repair. Gasping a flickering breath, he spoke without expecting an answer. "How many others will you kill today?"

The question seemed to stunt her. The blade stopped its march and she looked him in the eye.

"Why does this matter to you?" she said.

"They'll catch you," Colton said, hoping she wouldn't delay killing him much. Being alone with this woman scared him more than death. He didn't imagine dying was fun, but had thought he could do better than being sliced like a turkey in a dim hotel hallway. He missed the slow dance of the dust snowflakes and wanted them back. He also missed Sarah.

His ex-date pulled him up and his head swam with vertigo. The lights went from bright to muted to full dark. He thought he saw the restroom door on the twenty-sixth floor open. At two-am? Fat chance. But a man's silhouette did appear, clutching a cane and coming straight at them.

Colton opened his mouth to have it crammed shut by a sweaty tee. The man didn't move. What was wrong? Colton must have made a sound, a whimper – for sure. Even if this person were drunk, it would be hard to miss two bodies playing a life-and-death game of Twister. Then Colton saw it, more in his mind than with his eyes: the restroom man was blind.

twelve days till defiance day (22

Li-Mei lay on top, crushing Colton in perfect stillness and staring at the man coming out of the restroom. She blinked. Was it two-am already?

She had only herself to blame for taking this long. Each time she had deviated from the script: first with Taxi then with the Purple Servant and now with Parker, she had invited chance into her plans. She hated breaking her plans. She was expected to assassinate Parker, not gloat or become his psychiatrist. Later, she would punish herself for the stupidity by gashing her heels as a future reminder with each step she took. Now was not the time though; this was crisis and she had to focus.

She removed her tee and thrust it down Colton's throat, her knuckles feeling the pressure of the screams she had stifled. Good... amateur hour was over. She squeezed Colton's ribcage with both knees and sensed a pop – she must have crushed a rib. Not a deal breaker, but life would get harder if she gave him additional detectable damage. Her thighs eased on his ribcage by a hair but she grabbed his testicles and twisted clockwise with strength she didn't expect to produce at such awkward angle. He jerked once more and passed out.

Li-Mei focused on the intruder next. She had seen him somewhere. Rummaging through the last few days of memories, the answer rushed in, accompanied by a sense of relief. He was the blind pianist from the hotel lobby. She sized his physique: an average torso, with average strength, that moved with agility uncommon to a person without sight.

"Anyone there?" the blind man said. He blinked hard and didn't wear shades, a sign he wasn't ashamed of his dead eyes, which Li-Mei could respect. She pressed closer to the carpet, brushing lips against Colton's left eye as if nuzzling with a lover. No more stupid risks. Parker's destiny was to commit a suicide by cutting his throat and the piano man was to live. She had to let the blind guy walk.

The pianist lingered and took another step forward, his cane tapping a foot away from Colton's unmoving knees. So close that Li-Mei smelled hand-sanitizer on the hand holding the cane. Each fiber of her body pushed her to incapacitate the old man with a strike to the abdomen followed by a-hundred-and-eighty-degree snap of the neck. Yet she stayed pinned. Like a dolphin, sending UV waves into the darkness, the blind pianist stared at the location where her knee was crushing Colton's ribcage.

At last, the man's head shook; he scratched his chin and muttered, "Serves me right for getting just four hours of sleep," then turned around for the elevator. The cane's tapping along the wall came back with increasing distance. Li-Mei exhaled and lowered her head. Parker's suicide would be complete in fifteen minutes max. In another thirty, she would soak in the Presidential Suite bathtub, down the hall, and submit his status update on her tablet. All was well that ended well... until a swooshing sound ripped her from her thoughts.

She looked up. The blind man loomed above, somehow having flown the distance from where her eyes remembered him last. What's worse, his swinging cane was heading toward her head. A bang and, for a moment, her world brightened into a canvas of white light. He lifted her body then threw it face-first into the wall. She chuckled through bleeding teeth – she had lived to witness such infamy. He went for her head next and pressed his hands against the sides of her face. She closed her eyes expecting the inevitable snap of her neck. But then for some reason he let go. He wasn't much of a fighter. And Li-Mei opened her eyes.

Her feet pushed against the wall, buying room and oxygen for her crushed face. He held her skull in his palms, making the two of them look like a pair of Olympic gymnasts: the one cradling the other's head and spooning her body, in preparation for the Gold-Medal sequence.

She curled her body upwards, by the sheer strength in her abdomen, and flipped like a soccer forward hitting an overhead kick. At the end of the rotation, she sat piggyback on the man's shoulders and squeezed her thighs around his neck. He staggered back, looking to hold on to the wall. He was late. His unconscious body collapsed to the ground like a bag of bones.

part two (li-mei gao

twenty-one years and two hundred eighty days till defiance day (23

The forests, surrounding Jenli from three sides, and the river, from the fourth, were all Li-Mei remembered, no matter how far back she went. She had just materialized in this village but come to think of it, any regular child became aware of conscious life after the eureka moment of her mind awaking for the first time. From that moment on, children learned how to form recollections and memories. Li-Mei was the same. The difference was she couldn't remember her parents.

She didn't know her age either, but had a hunch she couldn't be that young. She could count to one billion, wrote in Mandarin, English, Spanish and Korean, played the piano and was a jujitsu green belt. She guessed she was at least six – you didn't learn four languages and the piano in less time.

Sometimes, certain smells or images would tickle associations of a different place, but she couldn't be sure. She loved Jenli and her routine. Mondays were reserved for language training. A random instructor would show, which meant she had to be prepared in all her languages. In time, the preparations became a non-issue, as her improving multilingual skills would resolve any assignment they threw at her. Then the Servants would add a new language to the mix.

Tuesdays meant complete physical training. Any weekday morning started with a mandatory five-mile run, but Tuesdays were in a league all their own. She ran laps, did crunches and pull ups and competed against the Servants. She lost a lot, almost always, but kept going, because it was expected of her. Swimming and rock-climbing followed in the afternoons, capped by jujitsu training in the evenings. She would crash for the night squeezed like a grape, which made Tuesday nights a near-lock for a surprise drill. On average, she had three night drills per week. The Servants shoved her out of bed in the middle of the night and made her run, climb or swim past obstacle routes that seldom, if ever, stayed the same.

She loved Thursday afternoons the best. The Servants would take her to the second floor of the tall brown building at the village square where she had to watch a new film each week. She liked the alternate worlds she learned about, ranging from barbaric European battles to colorful Chinese tea ceremonies, or the beautiful music in "The Godfather," her absolute favorite. All Thursday movies were dubbed in one of her four languages and subtitled in another. After the viewing, she had to submit written reports, one in each language, describing the protagonist character's development and struggles. If she scored less than a "B" on each report, she wouldn't receive dinner for the week, until the following Thursday. On one occasion, she couldn't attend two consecutive viewings because she had the flu, followed by cracking her tibia at jujitsu practice. She didn't mind not eating for fourteen straight days, but no dinner meant no food for Taxi and she took exception to that. Taxi was her only friend, and friends didn't let friends starve.

Unlike her love for movies, live TV annoyed her. She was tired of watching self-proclaimed messiahs trumpeting the end of the world from their flooded cities. What did she care? Jenli was safe. Granted, she wanted to see new people other than the Servants, but that seemed like worrying about a zit on the chin when others were dying of lung cancer. The only TV she liked watching were the ULE Senate debates when they debated issues like overpopulation and melting polar caps, in a way that left hope alive or, at least, didn't outright kill it. She sucked these discussions in like a sponge and sometimes, as far as she knew, invented more eloquent ways to debate than the ULE senators'. The surreal comparison of the TV world to her life in Jenli left her puzzled, but also reinforced the urgency to study and train. What if, as an outside chance, the TV was right and the world was drowning? She was going to be prepared.

In a recent broadcast, the Australian ULE senators advocated a resolution that would force each citizen to vote for one other citizen to die, with the catch that a voter could choose to sacrifice himself instead, and take the spot of an earmarked person. Li-Mei understood the argument; she had studied Plato's theories, contrasting a life of burden versus a sacrifice with purity. However, she opposed the Australians' proposal and questioned their population-control ethics, much like the rest of the ULE Senate.

Li-Mei spent her days with a purpose, but if someone asked her if she were happy, she wouldn't know what to say. She wanted to uncover the secrets of her past and share her present with people other than the Servants, but otherwise, she wasn't unhappy. She had Jenli, her classes, her jet-black hair, which she loved to comb before going to bed, and for a few weeks now, she had Taxi.

twelve days till defiance day (24

Mitko's unconscious body fell like a bag of bones and Li-Mei rested her hands on her knees. She panted, more with rage than exhaustion. The two unconscious men at her feet had given her excruciating amounts of resistance and sabotaged the deletion of a target. And that was plain inexcusable. She closed her eyes to let the rage trickle out. The piano man would stay out for at least a few minutes. Parker's eyes fluttered under the closed eyelids, but the one-two punch of her assault and Big Daddy's alcohol would keep him innocuous for another hour. She exhaled through her nose, opened her eyes and considered her options.

She had two accidental deaths to stage, on the same floor of the same hotel. The news would spread through Seattle like fire, then coast to coast, and put Mission Dizang at risk. Or... she gritted her teeth. She could walk away and allow Parker to survive their encounter. The only other target to survive her was a Korean man who, years ago had lived through a "suicidal" leap from a sixty-story building, only to die several days later of internal bleeding at the hospital. Tonight was worse... far worse.

Li-Mei thought of Taxi on the day when the Purple Servant had almost crushed her young life out of existence. Taxi had saved her then, despite the odds. He had overcome his fear, their assailant and death itself. In this clammy and overpriced joke of a hotel, she was in need of a similar miracle. But Taxi was dead and she had to do it on her own. With a sluggish mind, she went through the pockets of the two men, collecting wallets and keys. Could she kill them... a robbery that cost the victims their lives in addition to their wallets? No, she couldn't. Not when the scene was polluted with her footprints on the wall and Parker's blood all over the carpet. A robbery would have to do: a late-night mugging of two upstanding citizens. For now... so she could live to fight another day. And boy, was she going to fight.

Li-Mei walked toward the staircase exit and the floor swayed under her feet. She looked back one last time. The two unmoving men, dark silhouettes against the wall, were taunting her retreat.

twenty-one years and three hundred eight days till defiance day (25

The village was without children, other than her, of course. There were no grown-ups either, unless you counted the Servants, which Li-Mei didn't. Sometimes she wondered if they had built the village just for her or relocated everyone before she showed up. She hoped they hadn't moved the people. Where would they move them to anyway? And why would they?

One evening, she heard a whimper, as she limped home on a swollen knee from a jujitsu practice where a sparring partner had crashed into her leg a second before the closing whistle. The whimper came from around the corner while she was shutting her front door for the night. Li-Mei exhaled with the resignation of a boxer summoned for a new fight at the end of a long day. This was looking like another challenge: the Servant challenges never ended, no matter how late or how tired she felt. She stepped out and saw a shaking ball of fur, small enough to fit in her palm, then waited for the pop drill to start. The ball of fur shivered on, without an obvious agenda, other than being cold. After some hesitation, she brought the Shiba puppy inside. He shook so much that she gave him a fifty-fifty chance of making it through the night. Dead or alive, she would turn him over to the Servants the following morning. She dipped her pinkie in leftover milk she had picked up from the cafeteria at dinner and let him lick it. Forty or so licks later he stopped shaking and fell asleep in one of her shoes.

That night, she woke as something poked on her shoulder. She let him crawl under the covers but remained awake until dawn, waiting for drill sirens. On the contrary, a quiet morning marked the longest time Li-Mei had spent this close to another being.

She marched into the cafeteria, dog in hand, his head bobbing in unison with her steps.

"Here... take your dog back," she walked up to the nearest Servant.

He stood silent and unwilling to accept whatever it was she wanted to give.

Li-Mei left the Shiba on the floor. The ball of fur commenced to whimper as soon as it lost touch with the girl's palm. She headed for the door, but turned at the noise from behind. The puppy was zigzagging, with the clear intent of following her, but too young to do so at a steady pace. Li-Mei stomped her foot. She knew the dog was an exercise but didn't know to what purpose. Her life was a chain of drills choreographed by the Servants to always elicit a consequence: either punishment or reward. But last night had felt different. Not because of the sleepless hours or her stiff back from making room in her bed, but because of the conscious stance she had taken. Li-Mei decided to keep the Shiba, as her first act of free will.

She walked back and picked him from the floor and patted his semi-blind face. The whimpers stopped on cue. In her most recent Sociology class, she had studied the world's public transportation systems. The mayors of Boston and London had gone as far as prohibiting all methods of city transport other than the subway: no buses, no cars, and no bicycles. Taxis remained the only exception. And here she stood, in the middle of the Jenli cafeteria, with a little Shiba dog who was worlds apart from the Servants. So if the Servants were like subway trains: frequent and invisible, as if moving underground and the dog was the exception on the surface, then he must be a taxi.

So Taxi he was, she decided.

twelve days till defiance day (26

Each heartbeat shook Colton's head like a platoon of marines marching against the pavement of his brain. He opened his eyes for the first time and winced. Greedy green lights flooded his retinas then turned to purple and then to white. Bright white. Lessening the marauding glare, the shape of a head crept into slow focus, like a picture downloaded at a dial-up connection speed. Colton would have said, "Thank you," if he could speak. The head belonged to an old man. He stuck a hand in front of Colton's nose and held it there, as if to coax a skittish deer he meant no harm. His long fingers rested on Colton's face, traversed the cheeks and chin then froze mid-crawl above Colton's fluttering eyelashes. The man was indeed blind.

"You OK, son?" The words were as warm as the touch. "I'll get an ambulance."

Colton raised a hand despite the marching marines. "Don't," he said with a whisper that bordered on lip-syncing.

"Come again." The blind man's face came closer.

"Don't." Colton pushed out the words and gritted his teeth, as the exertion to speak triggered a fresh coat of pain. He hoped the old man wouldn't ask for a lengthy explanation. "I beg you." The headache had graduated into a migraine, which meant he had suffered a concussion. "I need your help." Colton took a breath. "They want to kill my eight-year-old daughter."

The humming hotel elevators, ferrying their human cargo late into the night, seemed to beckon the old man to go seek assistance. "Tell you what," he cleared his throat, "you seem banged up, but not as bad as fixing you myself. Let's go to my place."

Colton nodded, forgetting his savior couldn't see. The old man ducked his head under Colton's right arm and the two rose together, in a series of spurts.

"Thanks," Colton said. "For saving my life."

"Mitko. I play the piano here and it's good to meet you, though not at this price."

"I'm Colton and though I don't look it, my specialty is not getting mugged in five-star hotels."

A room-service employee walked past, trying not to look at the two men leaning on each other. She hastened her step and Mitko stood still until the elevator ring announced she had departed.

"We should get going," he said, "I'm sure she wasn't amused by us spooning outside the men's room at this fine hour."

Colton cracked a pained smile.

Mitko propelled both of them forward, wobbling at first then firming their collective gait. "We should take the stairs," he said, "if you want to stay out of people's way."

"What floor is this?" Colton wiped his mouth and checked for broken teeth.

"Twenty-sixth."

"And you live how far?"

"About a ten-minute walk. Just what the doctor ordered when a girl beats you up."

"You mean both of us?" Colton said and opened the exit door. The two hugging men disappeared down the stairs.

twelve days till defiance day (27

A blue kitchen. Colton wondered if Mitko didn't know or didn't care. Who had time to color-coordinate their cooking rooms anymore? The world was going to the slaughterhouse and blind men lived in blue kitchens.

Colton watched Mitko navigate the room, hands detecting their way from one point to the next: left, right and left again. Then backtracking to the starting position in reverse order. He'd be better than me at night, Colton thought, because the place seemed to have no working lights.

"You sure you don't want to go to the hospital?" Mitko said.

"No hospital. We should Google some treatments, though."

"You can't download stitches to the face, kid."

"But I can get on the Defiance Day site."

"Can't this wait until I patch you? I don't need eyes to tell your face is beat up."

"Help me vote, please," Colton said. Four words. Followed by silence.

Mitko touched a holographic panel above the table. The holograph scanned his right hand and logged him on. "Knock yourself out," he said, "I'll be in the other room to give you some privacy."

The Defiance Day site was simple and fast, built to handle votes in the billions. Colton took his time to read the instructions on each screen before moving through the following steps.

"Are you earmarking or sacrificing yourself, kid?" Mitko's voice came from a thousand miles away.

"I'm saving myself." Colton closed eyes and saw Yana's face. Better yet, he saw what he imagined her face would look like seven years after he'd seen it last. His baby. Whose life he had almost taken away. She was going to live this time. The death of a forty-three-year-old, even if a former poker champion, would be, at best, collateral damage. Defiance Day was going to erase his biggest mistake. And it took fate, disguised as a female killer, to wake him from his stupor.

Colton scrolled to a section captioned "Sacrifice Vote." At his fingertips, the holographic screen felt like an ice lake. He typed "Yana Perkins" in the name box and a positive match lit up the display. The destiny of his eight-year-old was packed neatly on the screen, like a bento box at the whims of a crazed Earth. But no more, because he would watch out for her. I'm coming, patte, he thought, I promise. He wanted to stretch this moment, of Yana needing him and him being her sentinel. The years of alcoholism and odd casino jobs melted away like a forgotten rounding error. He was her father and he was saving her life, even if it had taken him this long to get it right.

"Whoever you were, who earmarked her..." Colton whispered to himself, his whisper full of gravel, "not on my watch." He touched "Proceed" and the screen asked him to confirm the identity of the "Vote Recipient" then his own identity. He held his right palm, five fingers stretched over the holographic ice lake. After another scan and a reconfirmation, DefianceDay.com thanked him: "Mr. Parker. You have successfully cast your Sacrifice Vote for Yana Perkins (SSN 231-010-8760.) The confirmation of your voting transaction is below:

Voting Event: Defiance Day || Citizenship: US Territory || Social Security Number: 760-902-2587 || Name: Colton Parker || Date of Birth: August 27, 2009 || Status: Successfully Sacrificed.

Yours, ULE Defiance Day Committee."

Colton shut off the screen and looked at the Seattle skyline outside, glowing like an army of fireflies through the evening mist. One of these lights came from the ULE embassy.

How tempting was it to walk there and announce to the cameras at the gate he was the ex-husband of Sarah Perkins. The security lasers would scan his retinas and right-hand passport and he'd be asked to wait, then the steel gates, crackling with electricity, would yawn open and he would amble through the embassy's yard, not too fast and as dignified as he could. The lock on the mahogany front doors would buzz green, inviting him to push through. Once inside, he'd ask them for shelter. They'd push back at first, like they were supposed to – an average civilian occupying a ULE embassy for longer than an hour would violate all kinds of Earth-salvation protocols. But he'd insist and fall to his knees. And if he had to, he'd play his trump card with the words "Saving Yana's Life" written on top. He was the ex-husband of the scientist on whom the world had bet its energy chips. He was the only person willing to die to save this scientist's only daughter and, by extension, the scientist's sanity and the energy chips the world had bet. All he had to do was ask for shelter... until Defiance Day.

Otherwise... the descending fog in his mind grew thicker. He had no idea what "otherwise" would even mean. He was alone, an odds-on favorite to be assassinated, in a city that was too desensitized to care. So, his road to survival was to seek refuge, with the people who, several days later, would murder him in full compliance with the law. Like a sacrificial lamb eating at the hand of its butcher until the slaughter bell rang. And some day, many years from now, when his bones had long turned to dust, they would ask his daughter how she remembered her Dad. And she would tell them he had hidden under her mother's lab coat, then died, like good cattle should.

Colton sniffed. Not on his watch. A ship in a port was safe but that's not what ships were built for. He was going to fight for Yana's life, and if Ms. Red Tattoo turned the screws on too tight, he could always run back to his future killers. Mitko pulled him out of his thoughts. "Is she your daughter?"

Colton looked up, blinking. "Yes, my eight-year-old."

"Tell me about her."

"Her name's Yana. She likes sharks and sometimes I call her the most special girl in the world."

"She'll be proud of you. Maybe already is."

"The odds are she's wondering why her old man tried to kill her when she was a baby."

"I doubt you ever came close."

"For all she knows, I did and almost succeeded."

"Shall we go to the hospital or will you yell at me again for mentioning it?"

"No hospital," Colton said, his broken nose producing a scarlet trickle over his lips. "What you witnessed in the hotel," he walked up to Mitko and placed hands on his shoulders. "This woman wants to stop me from sacrificing myself. She wants to kill me, so Yana would die too... and I... can't let this happen."

"God help you if you're telling the truth," Mitko said and sat at the kitchen table.

It must be good living in the dark, Colton thought. It must be healthy and real. He walked to the magnetic strip above the oven, where all kitchen knives were stuck, from the smallest one to the largest. With his left hand, he took a fourteen-inch-blade cleaver. Before he'd allow himself time to reconsider, he raised and brought it down full force, cutting off his right hand at the wrist: cleanly and with one sweep. The smell of blood – cottonweed with sweet aftertaste – filled the blue kitchen. Colton was screaming. Mitko jumped to his feet. "What did you do?"

Colton stared at his severed hand, palm facing up, on the hardwood floor and the soup pots he had prepared on top of the oven – one full with blood and another one halfway there. "Tourniquet..." he said with a cloud of spit accompanying the word.

Mitko flew through the kitchen – left, right and left again. He grabbed a set of spare piano strings and a wooden spoon from a kitchen drawer, placed both next to Colton and took a step back.

With his left hand, Colton threw three coils of string around the geysering stump, plunged the spoon underneath and turned it several times. He covered the stump with a towel, which turned bloody in an instant, and spoke for only the second time as a one-handed person.

"I cut off my hand and I'll pass out in a minute. So, you must listen to me, because the lives of others will depend on what you do." Colton's words turned into grunts. "First, no hospital. Cut me to pieces if you will, but don't send me to a hospital. Second, the police will come looking for me because my passport has gone dark. Third, put my cut-off hand on ice. It's important you –"

Colton Parker collapsed on the kitchen floor before he could finish the sentence.

twenty-one years and two hundred forty nine days till defiance day (28

A regular student would have disliked having to do homework every night, but Li-Mei was not a regular student. If she finished her assignments early, she went on walks around Jenli and walked and read until it got so dark she couldn't see the tops of her shoes. Then she would sit and enjoy the silence until summoned by a random pop drill or the time came to turn in. Li-Mei liked almost all non-fiction and went through biographies and guides, looking for the books' practical lessons.

The Janissaries were her favorite topic, speaking to her with more clarity and force than anything else she had studied. They came alive in her history books, warrior-poets of the fourteenth-century Ottoman Empire that sprawled between Damascus to the east and Vienna to the west. Fifty thousand Muslim men marching as one. They were non-Muslim infants once, so many moons and training drills ago that their childhood memories had disappeared like a dream. They were Janissaries with shaven heads and glistening moustaches. A muddy flashflood of human minds and bodies, disciplined yet drunken with their immeasurable power. Along their unflawed battle formations, Li-Mei looked into these men's eyes, strained by days of marching, yet hungry for their next clash with the infidels. In the front, two hundred of them played on mahtars and cymbals, as if beckoning death with childish rapture.

Li-Mei held her breath at their warfare domination, honed by two centuries of endless battles. In the book, they had demolished yet another group of Christian rebels in the far-flung regions of the Ottoman Empire. Ever gallant in their victory, the Janissaries took the infant sons of the defeated population, to raise as future servants of the

Sultan. Often a Janissary would return to the same home from where he was taken as a child and take away new infants, like they had done to him before.

Li-Mei powered down the tablet. A cacophony of crickets made the night too loud to think. How could a parent give her child away and replace it with a new baby, like a defective egg in a grocery carton? Or maybe a mother let go of her infant sons to grant them a new beginning in the capital of the Empire: a re-birth and an act of love. Li-Mei, too, wished she could ask her parents why they had let her go.

Every so often, fiction popped on her radar, but fiction was flawed and frustrating because it didn't follow logic. "The Long Road," a book she had read, about a father and his son in a post-apocalyptic world, had pleased her with its factual description of a nuclear apocalypse. But the rest of it was worthless. Why would a father sacrifice himself for a six-year-old son who was weak and offered no value in return? On each page, the father sabotaged Li-Mei's reasoning by taking on additional hardships and, in the end, giving his life to save his son. She made a list of the ways in which she exceeded the boy, and stopped counting after forty-six. But in one aspect he was stronger: he had a father who had sacrificed, and Li-Mei did not.

For the next few weeks, the images of the dying father and his son followed her. She re-read the ending several times – each striking an ear-ringing slap on the face of her logic. Nobody would ever sacrifice for her, other than Taxi, of course, but he was an animal and didn't count.

After "The Long Road," Li-Mei refused to read fiction unless her courses demanded it.

twelve days till defiance day (29

Li-Mei had been sitting on a street bench at the intersection of Galer and Boston for two hours. Maybe three. The smell of mildew from downtown reached even here, in the high hills of Queen Anne, but she didn't notice. She didn't notice that her hair was hanging in wet clumps around her face. For the last two hours, maybe three, she had even forgotten about the three remaining orange names on her tablet.

She stood up, wet clothes sloshing on top of goosed flesh, and walked toward the building with a crumbling yellow façade. The occasional pedestrians outside were as unknown to her as those on any other street. It would have made sense, except this address was 1227 West Galer Street. Her fingertips hovered over the unremarkable panel of intercom buttons, as if cracking a braille code and stopped on one of them, no different from the rest. She took a breath and pressed it.

"May I help you?" an intercom voice cackled.

"I'd like to have a word with Connie or Albert Stone, please?"

"This is Connie. Who's asking?"

"Mrs. Stone," why the goddamn lump in her throat? "I'm Li-Mei Gao, with the Seattle Genealogy Institute and would like to rectify some gaps in your family lineage records before Defiance Day." Li-Mei laughed for good measure. "Wouldn't take longer than five minutes."

"Come on up, then," the intercom voice turned cheerful. "We're the only non-metal door on the fourth floor."

The front gate let Li-Mei in with a buzz. She ignored the elevator and went for the stairs. Emotions weren't supposed to interfere with Mission Dizang, nothing was, yet why was she here, visiting these people? She reached the fourth floor, knocked on the wooden door and a smallish woman in her late fifties opened.

"Li-Mei?" A question, but the hostess disappeared inside the apartment before collecting the answer, her voice trailing. "I'm cooking something yummy in the oven. Let yourself in."

The strong smell of cinnamon filled Li-Mei's face. Either Connie had dropped a bucket of cinnamon in her cooking or she decorated the house with the smell.

"Albert, we have a guest," Connie shouted with a faint Mandarin accent. She reappeared before Li-Mei had made a second step. "Come on in, young lady. Let's join Albert in the living room. He'd be the perfect husband, you see, if he didn't spend twenty hours a day on that bloody couch, watching TV. But what can you do? Only one perfect spouse is allowed per household." Connie giggled. "Would you care for some green tea?"

"No need. I'm here to ask my questions and leave."

They entered a dark living room that would have come across as well kept in daylight. Albert was a balding Chinese man with large brown eyes sparkling with a youth uncustomary for the rest of his seventy-plus-year-old body. He sat in a plush sofa, his head blocking the view in the square window behind.

"I'll have to greet you from my throne here," he said. Several lines cut across his forehead, deepening as he spoke. "My knees turn into arthritic nests whenever it rains."

Li-Mei gave a polite hand-wave and sat in a chair under a wall-mounted brass clock – an antique more than a functioning appliance, judging by the silence.

"It's good to see a new face, Miss...?" Albert's voice rose, the way the British asked questions: with their tone, not with their grammar.

"My name is Li-Mei Gao."

"With such pretty name, you must come to us from China."

"I was born in Seattle."

"I was off by a generation then," Albert smiled. "Did your parents immigrate here?"

"They passed when I was a child."

"A shame," he puffed full cheeks. "The time God lets us, parents, spend with our children is too short sometimes."

Connie walked in with a tray of piping cinnamon rolls. "I had a hunch to start these an hour ago," she beamed, "right on cue for our guest." She placed the tray on a coffee table jutting above a carpet with a pattern of blooming roses then hurried away for something else.

"Dig in," Albert said, reaching from the sofa and biting into one of the rolls. "So," he spoke in spurts, around the hot dough inside his mouth, "what brings you here? Other than the good fortune of stumbling onto Seattle's best cinnamon rolls."

"I'm here for a short survey."

"A survey of how low our lives have fallen?"

"A genealogy survey, Mr. Stone."

"What's this world coming to?" Albert sighed and swallowed a cinnamon bite. "Someone earmarked my Connie this morning. I mean, look at her... We've been married for thirty-six years and I couldn't figure out why she chose me... until today." He rubbed his eyes. "Now I know she married me because I won't ever let a government or a stranger take her away. Defiance Day be damned."

Connie reappeared, this time balancing three cups of tea on the tray. "Albert, dear," she said midstride, turning her head back and forth between her husband and their guest, "Li-Mei wants to ask you about our family genealogy. How fun? She wouldn't find a bigger ancestry buff in Seattle if she tried." The tray landed safe on the table. "If not for the rain, Albert and I were planning to go to Kerry Park. To think, we would have missed you..." Connie's shoulders rose and shuddered. "Like I always say, I'm happy to be lucky."

Li-Mei felt her face flush in the growing dusk. She didn't know what to make of these people, of their small lives and sick obsession with each other. The roses on the carpet, the steaming rolls, the darkness in which they sat by choice, closed on her like a vise. She'd give them another minute, five at most – she had wasted too much time on them anyway.

"A recent power outage wiped the last thirty-five years of data for some of our citizens, including you." She paused as if looking through the drawers of her memory. "Meaning we have lost your civic records since you immigrated to the US Territory."

"Back then, there was a USA," Albert said. Connie put a crooked index finger on his lips. "Let me go first, dear," she said. "We came to this country in 2017, thirty-five years ago. We had married the previous night, right before boarding our plane. I was twenty-five and had known Albert for a month. He was a hugger and the first man to give me flowers – tells you about my romantic life before him. He said he wanted to share the new world with me. And I said I would follow him anywhere. Our early years here were like the terrible-twos of a newborn. He delivered pizza and I did baby-sitting. But we were the happiest we've ever been."

Albert glanced at Connie then hugged her shoulders with his arm, as if to confirm her story with this simple gesture.

"How about any offspring?" Li-Mei said. "Did you have children?"

Albert let go of his wife's shoulders and handed Li-Mei a picture frame she hadn't noticed in the dark room.

"Jeremy Stone," he said, "our pride and joy and a doctor at the Cleveland Clinic. It's a Top Five Hospital in the world." The words "Top Five Hospital" came capitalized and bolded out of his smiling mouth.

In the photo, a straw-haired Caucasian male in his mid-thirties laughed in the embrace of an older black woman, who drank him with her eyes. To their left, a boy, no older than ten, held onto a stroller with newborn twins inside. Everyone sat in a grassy park and squinted at the bright sun.

"Forgive my bluntness, but did you adopt Jeremy," Li-Mei said, "or was he your biological son?"

"Li-Mei, dear," Connie said, her face darkening some, in concert with the rest of the room. "Jeremy's biology, which I'm sure you can guess from his looks, is moot to Albert and me."

"I'm here to gather data with zero assumptive guesswork." Li-Mei was through with the theater. "Have you birthed any children?"

Albert left the sofa and turned on the lights. In the sudden brightness, the Stones shielded their faces, blinking a storm. "We have nothing more to tell you, Ms. Gao," Albert said. "Jeremy is our only child."

"I should warn you it's a crime to enter Defiance Day with incomplete genealogy."

"I have already answered your question. Unless you want another cinnamon roll, now would be a good time to leave."

"Do you have any children who died?"

For a moment, Albert's grief surfaced on his face then submerged again. Connie shifted next to her husband, as if the conversation was squishing her against the couch. The roll lay untouched in Connie's plate; the tea undrunk and cold in her cup.

"You look like a respectable woman," Albert said, then paused. "Please, honor my request and leave our home."

"Jessica Stone," Li-Mei said. The oxygen in the room evaporated. "Who is Jessica Stone?"

Albert winced. "Who are you?" he said.

Li-Mei reached for a cinnamon roll and chewed, one crushing bite at a time, as if the dough was made of nails. She didn't blink, her jaws the only part of her body that moved. She recalled an African proverb that an enemy was someone whose story we didn't know. Bullshit. She had given these two a chance and they had blown it. Asking them for an explanation was as useless as forgiving them for what they had done. Enough was enough.

Li-Mei leapt over the coffee table and struck Albert's throat with a cupped palm. She lifted Connie, still wearing an apron, and threw her on the floor with a move fit for a martial arts cage, not a living room with a gaudy carpet. Connie's body bounced off the ground. On the other side of the table, Albert was clutching his throat.

"Once again... Who is Jessica Stone?"

Albert raised a hand like a coach calling a timeout. "Jessica was –" a ragged cough sliced the sentence, then tears rolled down his cheeks – either in a physical reaction to the asphyxiation or an emotional one to the violence, "our daughter, who was taken from us at the age of two and a half."

Li-Mei's hands folded into fists and unfolded. She tried to inhale but failed, as if she was the one with the crushed windpipe. She closed her eyes and begged Taxi to come soothe her thoughts.

Albert crawled by his wife's side and caressed her hair. Connie sat up, leaning against his body. "Jessie?"

"Why me?" As much a question as a labored breath. "Why me, instead of him?"

Albert wept. His hands kept stroking his wife hair. "We searched for you for years," he said. "I still do sometimes, wondering how –"

"But you gave up your own daughter and kept someone you adopted."

Connie stretched arms towards Li-Mei. "Jessie – dearest, I can't believe –"

"Shut up." Li-Mei's voice was colder than the Seattle rain outside.

"Don't you talk to your mother like this," Albert's face turned red. "We welcomed you to our home and in return you... broke our hearts. If you are the woman who used to be our daughter, you'll understand." Li-Mei approached within an inch from his face and felt his troubled breathing on her skin. "What did they do to you, Jessica?" he said.

"You killed Jessica when you gave her away. My name is Li-Mei Gao, the pride of Jenli. I was curious about you two," she looked at Connie first then at Albert. "That's all. I have not loved you. I loved a dog, who was better than either of you. He never abandoned me. Unlike..." she breathed in and out. "Why not my brother? Was he the better one?"

"We love you more than words can express," Connie said. "They kidnapped you, love. We would have given our lives to prevent that. But now God has guided you back home."

"I thank you," the woman once called Jessica said, "because by giving me away, you made me the opposite of you."

"Why do you say such...?" Connie stretched an arm toward Li-Mei then froze. Albert crumpled by his wife's side and held her head in his lap. Tears rolled down his cheeks, some falling on her face.

She couldn't feel them. Connie Stone had died of a heart attack.

twenty-one years and two hundred fourteen days till defiance day (30

Li-Mei had learned to avoid the Servants. Early on, she used to ask for their names or if their day was going well, but each conversation would end with a stinging face slap, which in time taught her they were just guards, who monitored progress and enforced order.

He was a Servant like the others, except for the purple birthmark covering half of his face. A tall and quiet man, he practiced Jenli's dress code of a grey top and black bottoms and if not for the birthmark, Li-Mei wouldn't have recognized him in a police lineup. Until the Friday when she went home to check on Taxi during a class break. She was sitting in a bamboo chair, with the Shiba in her lap and the awning at the entrance of her building giving them shelter from the stop-and-go rain. She was rubbing Taxi's back to keep him warm and when she saw the Servant, approaching with a straw bag on his shoulder, thought Taxi had gotten in trouble.

Li-Mei cleared her throat, as the man came within a few feet, and addressed him in Mandarin. "This is my dog, Taxi. I'm sorry if he chewed on something you own," she shouted as if her voice could erect a sound wall to block the man from advancing, "or if he's peed inside your house. He likes people and means no harm."

Those were her first words to the Purple Servant, as she would call him from then on, and the most words she had traded with anyone other than Taxi or outside of class.

The man reached Li-Mei's chair, the invisible sound wall unable to stop him. "The Shiba Inu is another matter," he said. "I take issue with your hair."

"My hair?" Hair trouble was preferable to Taxi trouble. "I take issue with it too. It takes an hour to comb each morning." She pulled at a black curl to demonstrate. "I bet short hair like yours is easier. What's your –"

The Purple Servant hit her left cheek with a fist, triggering the wail of an air-raid siren in her ear. Her teeth clanged shut, biting into her tongue. She hiccupped.

"I want you to cut it," he said.

He grabbed Taxi by the neck and threw him inside Li-Mei's room, closed the door and turned toward the girl. In a moment, the Shiba reappeared at the window, pushing against the glass but unable to break through.

Li-Mei stood up, chin pressed against her chest. "Who are you?" she said. Her left eye brimmed with post-impact tears, which she wiped away with a fist. He struck her again, with an open palm in the same spot. She howled – a mixture between a cry and a curse – covered her head with both arms and leapt forth, like a heat-seeking missile. His lungs emptied with a surprised gasp as she crashed head-on against his abdomen. He fell over backward then scrambled to his feet. Li-Mei rose with him, the left side of her face crimson-red and her eye swollen into a purple crater. He went for a third strike, but this time she was ready. She bent away from him, at the waist, and did an overhead backflip. As her body turned mid-air, her extended foot hit his face, as hard as a six-year-old foot could. The sound, more damaging than the impact, felt like sweet music to her ears, especially the swollen one.

She fell into a defensive stance, wishing her Jujitsu training was further along. Taxi kept bouncing off the window pane. The Purple Servant took a fishing-net and a kinjal out of his bag. He threw the kinjal at her. Li-Mei dove to the ground. Her face buried in the squishy mud and the knife screamed through the air where she had stood, failing to connect. As soon as she fell down, she realized she had made a mistake; the kinjal was a decoy. The fishing net, her real enemy, was flying toward her now. She rolled to one side but stood no chance on a ground so thick with rain. The steel net blanketed the girl, the ends falling first, followed by the mesh.

Li-Mei looked up at a sky perforated by steel wire. Her mind raced. This must be an exercise, she thought, Jenli was home. Jenli had a higher calling for her and a better destiny. Better than being slaughtered under a steel trap like an animal.

The Purple Servant squatted by her head. As hurt as she was, she couldn't hide a smile, seeing the bruise where her foot had kicked his face. Go ahead and explain that to your buddies tonight, she thought. How a six-year-old kicked your butt... and your face. The Purple Servant grabbed her hair through the wire and lifted. She closed her eyes as the net sunk into her neck then his kinjal flew at her again. This was it, she thought, but his blade cut the net surrounding her head. When the knife was done cutting, Li-Mei was wearing a gown made of steel wire. She had been right – they weren't planning to kill her in Jenli. But then she looked at the Purple Servant's eyes, as lifeless as roadkill, and her hope sank. And the first haircut in her life began.

The long black hair fell around her, severing the last link to a life she would never remember. Tears followed then rage and she shook like a racing horse that had galloped to exhaustion and her heart would have burst and killed her on the spot, if she were fifty years older. If loving fathers, she thought, like the one from the book existed, then why didn't they help? Instead, her severed hair fell in the mud and the Purple Servant's feet stomped on it as he circled around, again and again, careful not to miss a spot. With eyes brimming with rain, Li-Mei looked at the window of her room. Taxi was still trying to break through.

In a parallel universe, the Purple Servant had stopped cutting. He wiped his kinjal on her shoulder and helped her untangle from the net. The sky above had turned as black as the girl's murdered hair on the ground below.

eleven days till defiance day (31

Natt's mouth gaped in a silent scream for oxygen. No sound, despite the effort of every cell in his body. His lungs craved air, both to breathe and scream, and dark stains of sweat pooled around his neck and armpits. For some reason, he felt self-conscious about the stains, as he watched his reflection, in front of the reflection of the woman, in the wall-to-wall mirror. He could swear the mirror somehow magnified his sweat.

The woman's hands crushed his throat like roots of a blackberry forest, ripping his trachea away from the esophagus. Natt swung as far behind as he could reach, but only peddled air. His jaw opened and closed, and his nostrils bloomed, seeking oxygen that wasn't there.

"Stick your tongue out," she said with the same tone as one would order a latte, "it will help you breathe." Natt obliged, but no oxygen followed. His face turned purple and he felt freezing cold despite the sweat raining from his pores. The woman must have lied. She wasn't interested in helping him, she was waiting for the end.

When she had attacked him at first, in the men's restroom of the Seattle Public Library, he was certain he could overpower someone with her physique. He had just finished taking a leak, and was washing his hands along a row of sinks in front of the restroom mirror, and thought she was a downtown prostitute looking for work in all the right places. Protocol mandated he wait until the last second before issuing the arrest, for the solicitation charge would stick. And Natt had waited until she touched his back, to offer a blowjob or whatever her repertoire was. An attractive guy like him had been propositioned before, what could he do?

Instead, the woman grabbed his throat with both hands, her steel-cage abdomen refusing to budge against Natt's elbow punches. She absorbed his prepared blows then returned the favor with rapid undercuts to his kidneys. Always a step or two ahead, she chop-blocked his hand reaching for his holstered gun. Then she spun around and clung onto him, like a child playing piggyback with her father. Natt's fists flailed above his head then he lunged back, at the opposing wall, to shed her from him, but she remained out of reach. In the interim, her fingers were unpeeling Natt's life, one breath at a time. With the last spark of his fading consciousness, the cop mouthed a plea – his final Hail Mary, and a poor one at that.

His brain entered a shutdown mode, sending spams along his body... then the woman's fingers parted. Air ushered down his mangled throat with the noise of a freight train whistle. She dismounted from him.

The Chief of the Seattle PD fell to his knees, his face pouring tears.

"I'm the Seattle PD Chief and my Police Department will do anything you wish," he said again, this time with audio.

She stared at him for a moment, going over some unknown options in her mind. She tossed an old Nokia phone at him and he caught it before it hit his face. "We'll meet twice a week," she said. "You'll receive texts with the location and the time before each meeting."

Natt sensed an impending inevitability about this woman, as if he was thrust into a Discovery Channel special where a tiger was licking the forehead of a captured gazelle in the African savannah, the two looking like best friends. Then, without warning, the tiger's jaws mangled the gazelle's neck and she accepted her death with everyday banality. If this woman wanted him dead then Natt guessed dying would work. And in the interim, he would play with her for as long as she wanted.

"Deliver me Victor Saretto and Colton Parker. Alive," she said. "Otherwise, I'll finish what I started."

Natt's head nodded like a metronome. She walked out of the men's restroom. Not a single other library patron had walked in.

ten days till defiance day (32

Colton's mind swam up, underneath the surface of reality and the blue walls around him. Then the agony of torn up flesh, as if his hand was caught inside a meat-grinder, pulled him down again. His brain took several tries to start and grasp the good news: there was no meat-grinder; then the bad news: he didn't have a right hand.

Colton didn't know why, but the blue walls gave him comfort. They were a sign that the world was still going on and he was fighting, with the final bell at least a few rounds away. "Where am I?" he said.

Mitko leaned over. "You tell me, kid. You've been out for a day." Unlike the meat-grinder pain, Mitko's voice was a welcome chaperone into reality.

"Have they been looking for me?" Colton said and bit his tongue to muffle a groan.

"Were you expecting anyone?"

"My passport is no longer connected. Give them another day and they'll come knocking." Colton attempted a smile, until the pain in his right stump wiped it from his face. "You've done more for me than anyone else but my mother. It says a lot about the quality of my other relationships, I guess."

"You judge yourself harsh, kid."

Colton ran a dry tongue over his chapped lips. "My cut-off hand. Did you save it like I asked?"

"Next to the beef tongue and the chicken hearts, in my freezer." Mitko laughed.

"When the scans from my dead passport lead them to you, tell them I forced you to keep it."

"And why should I do that?"

"I don't know… because you didn't save my life to throw it away with a "Return to Sender" sticker on top. And because you'll go to Heaven as—" Colton grunted and kicked the wall at the fresh onslaught of pain in his severed limb. If this was a boxing match, pain was ahead in technical points and he was running out of rounds to catch up. Now he had to tell Sarah, too, and somehow, telling her he had voted Sacrifice, made him feel more uncomfortable than taking on her rage that he wouldn't. He sat up, despite the blue walls pirouetting in front of his eyes then called her number.

"Colton," Sarah sounded like a rattlesnake, "now is not a good time. Work's in the toilet." The algae were refusing to lie down without a fight. "I'm restarting Project Atlas, but I'm sure you don't care. You only want to talk about Yana without wanting to save her. What about her, Yana-boy? This morning, she threw a fit over some purple jeans I destroyed in the laundry. And she has the mumps. So, whatever you called to fight about, can you call later, or better yet, next year?"

"I did it," he said.

"You did what, Colton? Jacked off in the shower this morning? Hired a prostitute? Let me guess, you got your unemployed ass off welfare?" Sarah's screams echoed like she had put him on speakerphone. "Why the hell should I care about what you did?"

He imagined she had been swimming in an ocean of pain for years, alone and without a lifeline, his Sarah, who had served him marshmallows in bed and given birth to the most special girl in the world.

"I did it, baby." He wondered how she must feel having achieved her innermost wish. What would he do in her shoes? If his most sincere dream had come true? What would he do if Yana gave him a hug and called him Dad? Would he take her to the Point Defiance Zoo and get her chocolate ice cream? Would they laugh at the penguins until their faces hurt and ice cream came out of her nose? Colton smiled... it felt good being alive.

Sarah's voice pulled him back into the blue kitchen. "I don't know what to say. Is there..." a pause, "anything I can do for you?"

"As a matter of fact there is," he said. "I'm asking you for it after I've given you what you wanted, which makes me a terrible negotiator, but I'd like both of you to visit me in Seattle... before Defiance Day. It would mean a lot."

"I don't know." She seemed incapable of saying more than a couple of words at a go. She was also hyperventilating. He had shut her up, for once. "The ULE Ministry of Science is collapsing," she said, "the project, too. But I'll see if we can come see you."

Colton looked outside. The city was falling asleep under cloud-infested skies. "I should go," he said.

"We'll talk soon, yes?"

He had to tell her now or he never would. "And, Sarah..."

"Yes?"

"Sorry it took me this long."

"You're fine, Colton," she said then added, "Goodbye," before hanging up.

"Goodbye... my love," he said to the disconnected cell phone.

During the call, Mitko had been scrubbing the kitchen of Colton's blood from a day earlier. "Being around you is an education, son," Mitko said. "Life is a sketch drawn with a stick in the wet sand. But it's all we have anyway. Go hide. I'll help you how I can. Saving lunatics like you beats playing the hotel piano."

"Wherever heaven may be, old man, I hope I see you there, before the devil knows I'm dead."

"You'll be dead in a couple of days, unless I take you to a hospital," Mitko said. "I've cauterized your wound, but you'll need stitches and professional treatment."

"I didn't plan this cutting business as well as I should have, did I?" Colton said. "If you could have seen her face you'd understand." He rose like a drunken man, his feet somehow absorbing the weight of his body. "You've done enough. Hide my passport and I will deal with the rest of me." He put a foot forward then the other, waddled towards the blind man, and gave him a one-arm embrace. Then he left the apartment without saying goodbye, ashamed he had nothing else to give to Mitko other than more empty words of gratitude. Outside, it was about to rain.

twenty-one years and two hundred seven days till defiance day (33

It was a late Monday. The setting sun warmed Li-Mei's face, adding to her satisfaction of feeling tired after a day of solid progress. She had spent the last ten hours conjugating grammar drills in Korean, her worst language, but had done well.

Jenli's young night felt clingy and humid. Carrying her reading tablet and Taxi's leash, Li-Mei headed to the river. Ever since she had discovered the river two years ago, she loved spending time there. She had followed the currents and run upstream, along the bank, until reaching the electricity wall and the Servant guard-tower marking the brink of Jenli. That was it, as far as she could go, but it also meant the river kept going, which made her happy. She had read about rivers starting as fountainheads, growing stronger along the way, and joining the ocean in the end. But the textbooks failed to capture the liquid rush and the sounds and smells, and the force she hadn't seen anywhere else. She could stare at the rapids for hours, chin planted on the grassy banks, eyes low and as close to the water as possible.

Minutes of sunshine still remained, plenty of time to read and walk. After Korean, she needed a good change-of-pace book: "The Ultimate Guide to Professional Poker" would do. She ran for the river and into the surrounding forest. Taxi ran in front, turning for an occasional glance, to check if she kept up. He was growing strong. She wouldn't have it otherwise, not on nights like tonight. And, in return, he had become her proud Shiba Inu, the color of cocoa and with a face stretching in a grin whenever she was around.

The forest glowed in a jacket of dimming yellow light. Li-Mei heard the water rumble in the distance and picked up her step, with Taxi happy to oblige. She hummed a song,

"Live and Learn," in rhythm with her running footsteps. "Live and Learn" felt like her middle name these days: first getting a dog, then the Servant cutting her hair, though she had to admit a boy's cut felt more comfortable. She had read in a meditation book, once, that the best way to deal with change was let go of the past. Maybe she would meditate for the first time tonight... after it got too dark to read.

She had forty pages left in the poker book, bobbing in front of her eyes as she walked. Her nose, planted in the tablet, joined the earlier counsel of her ears and smelled the river drawing near. At last, the water emerged like flowing glass, cutting the Jenli forest from end to end and as far as the eyes could see. Li-Mei let the misty spray greet her face then turned for the hollowed trunk of a Japanese Red Oak she had been using as an observation spot for a while. The departing day squeezed the light out of the air making it almost impossible to read. She focused on the last few sentences, as the white space at the bottom of the page where the chapter ended, beckoned her peripheral vision.

Taxi was out of sight again but guaranteed to reappear soon. The poker chapter clung to its last sentence of life in unison with the dying Monday sun. Her nostrils tickled with the expectation of putting the tablet away, crawling inside the oak's embrace and meditating while stroking Taxi's ears. Just a few more steps and she would have Monday beat, like she always did.

She finished the chapter and pressed the tablet's power down button. Her body went into a free-fall and her ankle exploded with the pain of being turned or broken. She realized she had forgotten to change from sneakers in Jenli to hiking boots for the forest. Left unattended by a brain too busy reading, she must have stepped on a pinecone or the mossy riverbank. Li-Mei lost her balance, her face hit the ground, and she skidded down the slope. Stones, dirt and branches threw punches at her body. Couldn't be that bad, she thought, she'd plop in the water then swim back to shore; a pity the sneakers would be ruined. Then blinding pain tore up her left foot.

A passerby would have witnessed the six-year-old tumble down the riverbank in a pile of arms and legs and flashing white sneakers. He would have winced, seeing the girl's foot catch on a tree root jutting out of the ground, like the arthritic fingers of a buried giant. The root refused to let go and, for a moment, the girl's body hung in mid-air. Then gravity took over and broke Li-Mei's left leg.

She fell through the humid air then hit the river, frigid despite the month of June. Pain, more consuming than Li-Mei had experienced before, arrested her breathing and hammered at her brain while water rushed into her throat. All she could think of was that somewhere above, Taxi would look for her. And that as much as she'd want to respond to him, she wouldn't.

ten days till defiance day (34

Eaton lay on the floor, slaying holographic aliens on his PlayStation portable. On the couch, Natt was relaxing with a fresh glass of scotch. Funny how progress had a way of crushing even the most ambitious. No matter how strong Natt felt, someone stronger, younger and hungrier was bound to come along. His stepson was the future and Natt was thrilled as a parent, but as a man, he was jealous. Eaton, at eight years old, was already smarter than his stepfather and the realization bothered Natt like a stone in the shoe. Of course, he would never admit to it, at a confessional or on his deathbed. He shuddered at the unstoppable force of the kid's future. What heights would Eaton achieve at twenty? How about thirty? And Natt... He'd drool, head bobbing up and down, in front of a retirement home TV, with his dentures soaking in a mouthwash by his bedside.

Eaton looked up at his stepdad and smiled with his whole face. The sheer presence of this smile assured Natt that everything would end well: Seattle would survive the floods and Defiance Day wouldn't be as bad as everyone thought. Natt had a hunch other fathers loved their sons with similar intensity, but also knew Eaton was different. Eaton's math and programming skills were untouched. Last month, he was invited to the ULE Presidential Palace in Mexico City to consult on how humankind could colonize other planets in the Milky Way. Eaton had made it through several rounds for the privilege and crushed at each stage to the point of demoralizing his opponents. Eaton's method of pulse combustion was both brilliant and simple. While the rest of the field fell over each other researching solar and renewables, he looked to the past, reverse-engineering the twenty-first century NASA shuttles. He replaced their primitive fuel-thrust sequences with nanotech algorithms and their steel engines with quantum alloys. The stunning aircraft, called "The Razgrad," could, in theory, cover light-years worth of distance at acceptable velocity and unparalleled fuel efficiency. President Sanchez had made time to meet Eaton and commissioned a North Dakota ULE lab of four thousand engineers to translate the boy's approach into a working prototype.

On the floor next to Natt's couch, Eaton gave out a high-pitched, "Yes," his thumbs mashing the controller, tongue sticking out of his mouth. As easy as it was to forget, he was still just eight. Natt put the glass down and scooted on the floor, next to his stepson.

"What have you got here?" On the holographic screen, a busty brunette mauled through space aliens with a plasma machete.

"Oh, Dad... you wouldn't like Lara Croft," Eaton shook his head. "I have another two levels until I beat the game. Depending on how bad I suck." Natt moved closer, until his knee touched Eaton's, and hugged the boy's tense body. Why did life have to be this rotten? How could he keep his family alive through Defiance Day? None of them had been earmarked yet, but what if they were? What if Eaton was? Natt hung his head. He loved the boy, but he loved himself too. Death by Sacrifice was too final a verdict at forty-nine. As airplane safety instructions read, when the oxygen masks fell you helped yourself before helping those next to you. Even if Eaton were earmarked, Natt couldn't give up life. What else then? He could make a newer version of Eaton: a new son to lessen the sting of the lost original. Assuming everything else failed, of course... And Natt did mean everything. Otherwise, such thoughts would be despicable. Next to Natt, Lara Croft's hologram completed the second to last level.

ten days till defiance day (35

The Prius bounced along the high ground route stitched with barricades and detours. This First Hill neighborhood of Seattle was still dry but who knew for how long before it, too, succumbed to the rising waters. Natt twirled a glass of Johnnie Walker between his thumb and forefinger, his other hand on the steering wheel. As he drove, ice cubes chimed against the heavy crystal. The Police Department had given him this set on his twentieth anniversary with the force.

The cop gulped the last of the whiskey then threw the glass against the windshield. Who, the hell, did she think she was? Waltzing around, killing his people and screwing up his town, which Mother Nature had already screwed up plenty. As if he had nothing better to worry about, with the city decomposing at the seams, or Eaton and Chloe growing more distant by the day. His pallid reflection stared at him from the rearview mirror. Screw her. He was the Chief of the Seattle PD after all.

He checked on the Ruger for the fourth time: in place, loaded and ready to spew. Natt went through the motions in his head again: point at her face and pull the trigger. Mopping up afterward would be a nuisance but not new. He would convince the department he had murdered the woman in self-defense and that would be that. Not that it mattered, but if he played it cool he might get a medal out of it too. Natt brushed off broken crystal from the seat.

If his plan was so picture-perfect, then why was he so nervous? He was scared of her, that's why. He had considered calling for backup but what if she escaped or, worse, surrendered? And what if, after the arrest, his vaunted SPD couldn't deliver the evidence to keep her locked away? Natt could hear the defense's arguments, "a terrified Chinese tourist wrongfully accused of being an assassin." The most she'd get would be a week in county jail, followed by a forced extradition to the China Territory. Then she'd come back and make him pay. No, he couldn't take the risk. She was too dangerous alive and only he could render her dead.

The Prius's tires screeched to a stop on the suspension bridge outside of Macrina Bakery. Natt stepped out of the car and didn't bother to lock it. If he succeeded, the place would be crawling with cops. If he failed, he'd have bigger problems than a stolen Prius. From around the corner he peeked inside the bakery. She was sitting at a table, alone.

"You idiot," Natt muttered to himself. Had he arrived first, he could have camped in a corner booth with the Ruger tucked under the tablecloth, while munching on a bagel. He could have risen up and shot her in the face when she arrived. Then he would have bought another bagel.

But she had come first. He paused at the door. Don't hesitate, he thought. Walk in and pull the trigger. He gripped the gun in his pocket, pushed on the door handle and entered the bakery. Li-Mei was the shop's only customer. Natt waved with an innocuous left hand but she didn't acknowledge. He walked to the cash register. A semi-asleep teenage girl was leaning on the counter.

"Welcome to Macrina. What may I get you?"

"A medium drip. Black with no room." Natt looked over his shoulder while fishing for money from his gun-less pocket. She hadn't moved.

"Would you like a receipt, sir?" In addition to being sleepy, the teenager had a stuffed nose.

"I'm good." Natt took the coffee, turned around, and headed for the table. Five feet away... He scanned the floor between them. Clear. He would pull the Ruger in another three feet, then she'd be impossible to miss. Impossible not to blow her brains out.

He took a step. The Chinese woman remained as motionless as when he'd entered the bakery. He took a second step. As much as he wanted to hurry, he felt like he was running in a tar pit. The air turned into cotton candy, viscous and sticky. He took a third step. His right hand squeezed the gun. No more steps left. This was it, his moment. In slow motion, his hand left its pocket hideaway. The Ruger, wearing the turtleneck of Natt's clenched fingers, pointed at Li-Mei.

He functioned in a dream, or was it a nightmare? The Ruger's muzzle now stared at the space her head had occupied a second earlier. Li-Mei was no longer there. He saw her empty chair bounce off the floor. She dove into him, like a base runner sliding home to beat a high-tag. Her elbows cut into his ankles and the Ruger went off, more by accident than intent. Natt's knees buckled forward. His face, sucked by gravity and momentum, banged on the ceramic floor tiles and his nose exploded. He felt her climbing on top of him, taking the handcuffs from his pocket and restraining him in his own equipment. She picked up the Ruger, lying in a puddle of spilled coffee, and shoved it in the pocket where the handcuffs used to be. She pulled him to his feet then headed to the door, her entire repertoire performed in silence.

As she passed the cashier, whose fatigue had been wiped clean by the last twenty-five seconds, Li-Mei uttered three words, "Armed robbery attempt." Then added two more, "You're welcome."

The teenager blinked, closed a gaping mouth and clapped twice... with hesitation.

Li-Mei shoved Natt forward, his nose dripping a blotchy trail of liquid crimson. On the bridge-walk outside, she opened the Prius door and he sat in the front passenger seat while seeking approval through constant eye contact. She sat behind the wheel and addressed him for the first time.

"I will kill you in the next five minutes but want to ask a question first. On the off chance you give me a correct answer, I will postpone your death." She faced forward. "Why haven't I killed you yet?"

Natt swallowed. Li-Mei turned and spat in his face. He felt her saliva descend down his skin, like a slow glacier from a mountaintop.

"Silence is the wrong answer," she said.

"You haven't killed me, Ms. Gao," his voice shook, "because you haven't felt like it. And because you're graceful."

"Always remember that." Her eyes were as cold as a Himalayan blizzard. "Attempt what you did in the café again and no answer will spare your life."

She left the car. Natt exhaled, as her figure dissipated in the misty Seattle morning. Her saliva splashed down on his pants. And made it look like he had wet himself.

twenty-one years and two hundred seven days till defiance day (36

Li-Mei kept sinking. The liquid frost had swallowed her whole and she couldn't feel her legs. Not much of a loss, considering one of them was turned and the other one broken. What a relief that Taxi was the only witness to her embarrassing fall, she thought. The two of them would laugh about it later. It served her right for forgetting her boots.

Then an inside voice questioned if concepts like "later" and "serve right" would exist in her future. She had to see to it that they did. Li-Mei's brain S.O.S.-ed a paddling command to her legs but she couldn't tell if they had picked up the transmission. Her logic tried to convince her panicking thoughts that at least it felt like she had stopped sinking, but she wasn't surfacing, either. Was it possible to surface in a river this cold? Of course, it was; she just had to keep churning her legs even if she couldn't tell if she did.

In what felt like a year of paddling, she broke through the surface for the first time. Water gushed out of her face then she sucked air into lungs shrunken to the size of thimbles. Here's to baby-steps, she thought. First, to no longer sinking and second, to surfacing. Now she had to focus on breathing, and last, on getting out of her beloved river. She floated for a moment to collect some strength, inhaling a cocktail of oxygen and water with hoarse breaths. The problem was she couldn't afford to float. The river was taking its toll, a million microscopic knives slicing at her skin from all angles. How long until she fell into a hypothermic shock? Another minute? Another three, at best? Li-Mei wished she hadn't studied about hypothermia. What you didn't know couldn't hurt you.

The watery frost tightened its embrace by the second, refusing to let her lungs unfold and the currents accelerated, a sign that the river was shrinking. There went knowledge again, she thought, ever the mathematician, even when drowning. A boulder the size of a small horse floated past her. Time to add a new baby step: stay clear of rocks. Getting to either bank in this current was wishful thinking. Her best bet would be to stay clear of rocks and reach for tree branches close to the water. The river had a different plan.

A vortex caught Li-Mei and threw her toward a submerged granite rock. Her face hit the stone and her nose shattered, along with four of her teeth. Again the frost pulled her mouth apart and rushed inside, like a snake. This time, her jaws felt like rubber, too weak to bite off the snake's entry. Instead, she swallowed, again and again, to get rid of the searing cold. Her legs, blue from toe to thigh, stopped paddling and shivered in defeat. Her eyelids flung open. The frost burrowed inside her body, pushing out the last remaining ounces of warmth. The six-year-old went limp. It was only her ears that still worked and Li-Mei thanked them. The ears were her warriors who hadn't quit unlike the feet or throat or lungs, or worst, the white sneakers, that had started it all.

Then, when she couldn't imagine how the frost could get any more crippling, it relinquished for a moment. Blood gushed from her broken nose and her undefeated ears heard sloppy barking. Li-Mei didn't know that Shibas could bark. A switch turned her pupils on and they registered trees and a dark sky jotted with stars. She lay in a net, above the roaring waters, that dragged her away from the current and toward the barking. Spasms tore up her throat and she retched the frost out of her body, again and again, unable to stop. Then her skin hit against something solid: gravel and dirt. The barks swallowed her whole and his tongue did too. Li-Mei lay on her stomach and coughed harsh and wet for what felt like forever. Then she breathed in and looked at them. The two Servants with their fishing net, and him.

As loud as a typewriter, her teeth took over her body. Despite their scary clutter, Taxi didn't run when she leaned over to hug him. He nuzzled his nose against her cheek, his version of a kiss - the only one she didn't mind. Li-Mei turned, attempting to kiss him back. Her lips touched the rubbery nose then her forehead bumped on it, as she shook too hard to hold steady. "Thank you for saving my life," she squeezed past her lips despite the clattering teeth, the shaking, and the rising frostbite pain.

The Shiba didn't seem to hear, but he seemed to understand.

ten days till defiance day (37

Victor's memory with names was as precise as an elephant with a fiddle. The sender's name on his home terminal looked hopeless and unfamiliar. He read the email again:

"Dear Victor Saretto,

You committed a sign-in curfew infraction at 10:32 pm on June 3, 2052. This infraction pushes your cumulative violation balance into a penile status. Therefore, you must appear in-person at 1332 Fourth Avenue, Seattle, WA 98109, within 24 hours of receipt of this notice. The City of Seattle reserves the right to commence criminal proceedings against you, including arrest and incarceration, should you fail to act in compliance with these instructions.

Respectfully,

Natt Gurloskey

Chief of Police, City of Seattle"

Victor couldn't imagine how he had broken curfew. Like religion, he signed-in at his home station an hour, sometimes an hour and a half, before the five-pm cutoff. Scanning early was his bulletproof method to beating a system known to chug every night, as billions hustled to scan the Digital Passports in their right palms. June had happened more than six months ago and a sign-in violation made no sense. Could he have been a few minutes late that day? Conceivable... But five hours late meant the system had crashed. The darn mildew must have seeped inside the city's mainframe.

Victor read the mail for the third time. He had no dispute option available, but to show in person – in stinky, rotten downtown Seattle. He shut the terminal off and cracked his neck to relieve the stress piling on his joints. Few other lunacies could poison the mood as well as government bureaucracy did. Victor ironed his favorite striped suit and hung it on a chair by his bed. He set the alarm for five-am the following morning, the police headquarters opened at eight, but it was always better to show early. As he lay in bed, struggling to fall asleep, the name of Natt Gurloskey flew inside his head. He couldn't place the name and couldn't help not being able to place it...

Victor suffered from memory lapses since Robert's death. And his performances at the Benaroya had taken a tumble. Each time the cello nestled between Victor's thighs and the conductor's baton tapped the podium to start the evening's performance, Robert's image would flood his mind. Victor survived on a few occasions by the mercy of other instruments drowning out his mistakes. However, Maestro Ludovic Geoff begged to differ. Victor semi-expected a trashing when the conductor scheduled him for a one-on-one weekend meeting.

Lack of focus, sloppy hands, graceless apathy – all accusations Geoff hurled at him, like darts at a dartboard. Victor's smartest move was to stifle a chuckle, "Sloppy-hands" would have been a fitting nickname for Robert. The thought ushered memories, then grief, then Victor's tears, but not enough to burlap Geoff's guillotine. Victor was terminated on the spot and walked out of the conductor's office in reverse, bowing once and again.

When he went back, a week later, to collect his final paycheck, he found out it had taken Geoff a day to update the "Who We Are" symphony portraits in the Benaroya lobby with the face of a new cellist.

nine days till defiance day (38

If Natt were a hundred pounds lighter, he would have killed it in Hollywood. "Too damn easy," the caption under his beaming face would have read if he were on a movie set. He leaned back, hands clasped over his head, with fingers drumming Beethoven's "Ode to Joy" on the top of his skull. It wasn't even eight in the morning and the day had started like a whopper. A hunched-over Victor Saretto, who looked like a man who made his own bed when he stayed at hotels, sat across from Natt's desk.

"Mr. Saretto," Natt's balding head shook, "I'm concerned with how long you've waited to ameliorate your situation."

Saretto squirmed in his chair and exhaled a response. "This is the first time I –"

"You failed to get back home on time, did you?" Natt cut him off. "Was it car trouble? What do you drive?"

"I don't have a car."

The cop picked at a set of matches while his gaze jumped between Saretto and Saretto's reflection in the polished top of the office desk. His index finger held the matches straight and his thumb spun it around with a whirring sound.

"So you don't have a car yet. But one day... when you get your own set of wheels." Natt smiled showing two rows of uneven teeth. "You should turn off the radio and the AC. Tell the girlfriend in the passenger seat to shut it. And drive. Listen to the engine. Close your eyes for a few and feel the kinetic push inside your gut. Sense how soft the brake pedal feels under your foot. Push on the gas. Get closer to the car in front. So close he's thinking you're that goddamn bastard who's pushing the slow drivers out of the carpool lane. Sense the hum of the pistons. Open your eyes. If you don't have a huge-ass grin on your face, I don't want to know you. To me, you might as well be dead meat."

"Excuse me, but how is my car ownership relevant to the case?"

Natt pushed back in his swivel chair. "If you had a car, you wouldn't be in this mess. But let's get on topic. I was saying I hate to think how long you'd have waited without our notice."

"The notice was issued in error."

"Don't blame us for enforcing curfew. I can arrest you right here in the office."

"I'd like to see the official records proving my curfew infraction."

"Look, son." Natt leaned over, hands planted on the desk like arched pillars. "If you rubbed the legs of a grasshopper for four hours, it will trigger its brain to swarm and become locust. Don't do it. Don't force me to swarm."

"You must be doing this on purpose for some reason..." Saretto trailed off.

"Are you accusing the Seattle PD? I'd step careful in your flippers, son. It's either..." Natt thumbed through a stack of papers with a licked finger, "six hours of jail to get your violation balance in line, or nine months in ULE prison for libeling a police officer. You understand the difference between Seattle jail and ULE prison, right?"

Natt had taken the cellist for the type who'd capitulate at that point, but Saretto pressed on, "In this case, I'd like to request access to a state-appointed —"

The cop walked around the desk and pulled the front two legs of Saretto's chair. The cellist fell backward, hitting his head against the floor. Standing above the crumpled body, the cop's foot crashed into Saretto's ribs. "How about I give you access to my boot? Convincing enough? Time to get you to our Capitol Hill detention center, son."

Unannounced, Saretto's tears gushed. "What you're doing to me belongs at a prison," he said, "not the Seattle Police Headquarters."

Natt lifted the man by the collar and spun him. Cold handcuff steel clawed into Saretto's wrists.

"Victor Saretto, I charge you with breaking the curfew provisions of Seattle City proper and with besmirching a police officer." Natt pushed the cellist out of the office and past a row of cop cubicles, "You have the right to remain silent. Anything you say —"

The two men walked through the building. Another cop arresting another curfew dodger on another day in the Pacific Northwest. Natt stuffed Saretto in the back of a police prowler and sped into the gray morning, heading toward a Capitol Hill detention center that didn't exist.

nine days till defiance day (39

Sarah's tone left no room for negotiations. "One hundred percent unacceptable."

"What do you want me to say?" Colton coughed like he was suffering from an asthma attack. Something fell and broke on his side of the line.

"The ULE would rather mummify me than let me out of their sight."

"I only took her spot, Sarah."

"Unless you've discovered teleportation, getting us to Seattle is not going to happen." Then she laughed in the receiver. "It would be a stretch even with teleportation."

"Soon you'll be the only one left, Sarah. But now, I have as much right to be her parent as you do."

"Do you really think your melodramatic lines are helping the situation?"

"I may have been the drunk who scarred Yana for life, but I'm still her father."

"Then you should act like one and stop being selfish."

"And you should, for once, put her before your work. The next nine days won't obliterate the world any more than it already is."

Sarah knew he was right. On any given day, her schedule spanned from four-am to midnight. She had to give him that, even if being wrong was not Dr. Sarah Perkins's forte. She was the world's foremost molecular biophysicist, and humanity's last hope of squeezing more energy out of the dog-tired Earth. The team of forty-five under her, and the management above, had gotten used to doing as she asked. Not because they were yes-men but because Sarah was always right. The ULE Ministry of Science had endorsed her inclusion in the High-Potential program and the US Territory Governor had filed the motion with the ULE Congress. Whether her Hi-Po candidacy was approved would always remain classified information, but everyone knew that Earth would be screwed if Sarah weren't on the list.

She knew Colton was right – only a small person would deny a father the right to see his daughter for the first time in seven years... and maybe the last time. Sarah rummaged through the dependencies on how to get this done. It was an outrageous decision tree and it also wouldn't be her call. A committee of ULE politicians and military strategists had full control over the Hi-Pos' itineraries and whereabouts. She paced around her desk, eyes jogging back and forth between the speakerphone and a coffee stain on the wall.

"Shake those lab rats off your tail." Colton interrupted her thoughts. "Move to the ULE embassy in Seattle, if you have to. When a father's dying wish is to see his daughter, the world, and I mean the whole damn world, makes way. Least of all, this Bunsen-burner project you're working on." He hung up in the middle of another coughing fit.

Sarah had to guess he was fighting a cold or perhaps coughing because of the fear that even sacrificing his life wouldn't be enough to see Yana again.

nine days till defiance day (40

"Mom?" Yana's voice hung in disbelief. "You want to go to Seattle? After what he did to us?"

"What I said about him..." Sarah paused, her hand on her forehead. "Some of it I said when I was emotional, and —"

"But you said he almost killed me," Yana couldn't believe her Mom had allowed the rebellion to last this long. "And that he could never redeem himself." Each time they argued, Sarah would lecture with stern and complicated words Yana didn't always understand. And that would settle it. But tonight Sarah shrunk back further, as if her daughter's argument was pushing her out of the room. Yana knew her Mom was hiding something. Like she hid Defiance Day. And Yana was pretending not to notice. But she did notice, because everyone at school talked about how you would die unless your Mom and Dad took your spot and died instead of you. Yana also knew, though she wasn't supposed to, that her Mom was one of the special people prohibited to Sacrifice herself. It didn't matter, because she knew Mom would find a way to save her, in the end.

"He did almost kill you." Sarah's voice started slow then grew in size. "That's why I divorced him. But he used to be a better man, once. And he was my college sweetheart." Yana knew her parents' college story by heart, but didn't interrupt. She liked hearing about the time when Mom was young, before Yana was born and before Mom's work became more important than anything else in the world. "His love made me believe the world wouldn't end, even if I failed to perform a scientific miracle. But then he developed a gambling addiction. And allowed gambling to take over our lives, including you and I." Sarah pulled a graying strand of hair away from her face. "But now, he's trying to turn the page. Why don't you spend an hour with him in

Seattle and show him what a great daughter he's missed out on. Haven't you wondered what he's like?" She crossed her arms like a protective barrier. "Look... you have the right to be upset, but seeing him is important to me, too. You and I could go to Seattle together. It's less cold there than DC this time of year." She nodded, maybe expecting Yana to follow. "You'll have fun, OK?"

Yana tried to smile. "OK, Mom," she said. "Let's go to Seattle, if you want. But, we're seeing Dad because you're asking me, not because he is."

Sarah hugged her daughter with arms smelling of lab cultures and Yana wished she could fast forward time, until Defiance Day were finished and done with already.

twenty-one years and one hundred sixteen days till defiance day (41

This time he hadn't come for the hair. Li-Mei saw it in his lifeless grin, like a notary stamp on a license to do to her the unspeakable. Today, to break her would be to spare her. The Purple Servant had come to annihilate what was decent in her, as homage to something she didn't quite understand. Maybe that's why they had brought her to Jenli. Six years to prepare for this... and turn her into a monument to humanity's sins. Li-Mei's past no longer mattered, her future was irrelevant, even death had gone into hiding. The Purple Servant was the only one here. Other than Taxi, of course.

"Do you remember me?" the Purple Servant said.

"I don't, because you are forgettable."

"Cherish this moment, for you will never be the same after."

Li-Mei knew she had to be strong but around her the air was like a hot and sludgy soup. She was sweating and guessed it was what fear felt like. Her eyes asked him for mercy, then for an explanation. He gave none and she understood she'd remain eight forever. Then Taxi bumped a wet nose against her left calf, the one that the river had broken. The Shiba hadn't checked out like the rest of Jenli. He was with her and his muzzle shook with a guttural growl. If her dog could growl at this man, why couldn't she?

The Purple Servant shifted weight from one foot to the other. She knelt and tickled Taxi's ear. His growl deepened. He walked from behind her and bared his teeth. Li-Mei laughed.

The Purple Servant responded by unsheathing the kinjal from their last encounter. The blade reflected the setting sun in a golden stripe across her face. He ran a thick tongue over his lips and thrust hips back and forth, then screamed, draining all air from his lungs.

Li-Mei took the screams in, standing straight. She wouldn't repeat the mistakes of their last faceoff; she would be the aggressor this time. The girl ran toward the Purple Servant, Taxi in tow. A step away from the man, she jumped with both feet, above his head. He turned around before she could land behind him. His hand, clutching the hungry kinjal, flew forward, aiming for her limbs. He smiled with the anticipation of the blade sinking in her thigh, just above the knee. Then canine teeth shredded the back of his neck.

The Purple Servant spun around but the teeth remained locked in his nape. He let the girl land on her feet and directed his attention to the dog. Blood poured over his shoulder from the wound. He swiped at the air behind his neck and on the second try, snatched the dog's tail then pushed the animal closer. Behind the two, Li-Mei jumped on the Servant's ankle with both feet. It snapped with a muffled pop. The man screamed in pain then sunk the kinjal into Taxi's body. She couldn't see where the knife had hit but that didn't seem to matter. He held the dog in place as an offering, twisting the blade then taking it out and hitting again, this time in a different spot. Taxi's teeth unclenched and the Shiba fell to the ground. The Purple Servant roared, turning to sink a third and final blow, but after a step, fell to his knees, as the broken ankle collapsed under his weight.

"How do you like my dog now?" Li-Mei shouted. "His name is Taxi in case you forgot." She stomped her foot on the ground, as if that settled it.

The Servant hit his forehead with a fist to refocus. With stuttered bounces, he rose up on his good leg, torn ankle dangling at one side and the purple birthmark glowing against the rest of his lilac-white face. He wiped the kinjal on his sleeve then knelt down again, all the way, until it looked like he was sitting on the ground. Then the leg uncoiled and the man flipped on his arms, two points of support instead of one, in a cartwheel. He rotated into a full-blown somersault that smashed into the girl, his thighs hitting her chest and clamping her body like an iron vise. His fists tore into her face. Left, right then left again; he kept hitting until she couldn't feel his knuckles on her skin.

The Purple Servant raised the kinjal above his head and plunged it into Li-Mei's right thigh. Her flesh swallowed the steel to the hilt but she didn't move. Another hit, in her left leg. This time she whimpered, the pain ungluing her from the unconsciousness. The Servant limped around his prey; with two gashed legs, she wasn't going anywhere. He took in her every cut and bloodied bruise. She was the prize and the encouragement. And she was broken.

He sat on her chest and under his knee, twisted her left arm until it broke with a soggy snap, followed by Li-Mei's gargled screams. He took her right arm next, twisted and broke it. He turned her head to one side then grabbed her right ear and rested the kinjal's blade at the part she would have pierced one day, as a teenager, with an earring. With a sharp tug, he cut her ear clean and threw it at the whimpering dog, injured but still alive. "Have a snack," he said, "you'll need the protein to recover."

Li-Mei widened her eyes as blood trickled out of her skull in spurts. The Purple Servant swayed like a drunk, dragged his broken ankle to a nearby bell and rung it to summon medical help. The sun was setting above the single-floor Jenli rooftops.

nine days till defiance day (42

Avery sat at his desk in room 1327 and held a crumpled paper between his thumb and index finger. His head was glistening bald. Ink stains spotted his military shirt and half a dozen scuffs dented his collar. His bloodshot gaze, buried behind glasses that sat too low on his nose, darted between Sarah and the paper. He took off his glasses.

"Should I shred this request or are you going to, Sarah?" Avery leaned back and covered his face with both palms, thumbs massaging his temples in opposite circles. "A two-day vacation is out of the question. Anything else?"

"I do insist you reconsider."

"The Atlas synthesis can't afford an hour of downtime while we're staging billions of mutation clusters." The palms over the face distorted Avery's voice into a mutter.

"But even if I were to derive the correct sequence, at once," Sarah's fingers snapped to illustrate her words, "I'd still need to test the formula in the field, unless we figured out how to bring the ocean to DC. It could happen if the damn waters don't stop rising, but what I'm saying is, we'll need to perform full-scale oceanic tests in one of our coastal labs soon."

The man shook his head without looking up, either too exhausted or too annoyed to speak. "You're skipping way ahead. The Atlas sequence is not ready and I can't afford the downtime of you not being here. Field tests mean squat if the sequence continues to fail. Get it working first and frolic anywhere the hell you want."

"We can do both scientific and field work in Seattle, Avery. You know that. Our oceanic facilities there are the best we've got. The hydraulic energy of that town lights up the entire West Coast. Let's swing for the fences on this one." Avery's thumbs stopped making laps around the temples but his face stayed put behind the palms. "How about I set up shop in Seattle and onboard the field to start production in the next few days? By the time we extract the sequence, their Pacific Northwest pipeline will be ready for prime time. We can just flip the switch and light up the whole continent. In another week, the world's energy will run on algae. You know we need this, Avery. You know we're dead without a functional production environment."

Avery's hands let go of his face. His small, naked eyes blinked at the sudden torrent of light. "You want to see him that bad, huh?"

"I do." She leaned on the desk. "And saving Atlas happens to take place in the same city where Parker lives. That's all."

"Did you know our childbirth mortality rate is at forty-eight percent?"

"How is that relevant?"

"One of two kids, in this Territory, dies at birth, not because of a protocol failure or a disease. Some doctors are... you know, envious of newborns." Avery put his glasses back on. "Some earmarked doctors like dragging their patients down with them. Best case, they don't want to help create new life. It's like, babies get born by themselves these days."

"These are hateful —"

"Are they, Sarah?" He jumped to his feet, pointing a gun at her face. Sarah remained motionless. "Are they?" The fatigue had left his mauve face. "Like them, I will die in a few days... But you won't. You don't know how many times I've wanted to blow your goddamn Hi-Po brains out." He panted as if in the middle of a marathon. "Give me one reason I shouldn't shoot you right here."

Her face eked out a smile. "Your grandson," she said. "You're dying in a few days, but will he?" The metallic muzzle remained fixed on her forehead. "Will you Sacrifice for him? So he can have a better life than you did? Shoot me, Avery. But who else could pick up Atlas from where I left off? And will they produce more energy for your boy than I will?"

The gun slithered off his hand and fell on the floor. "I'm tired, Sarah." His eyes locked with hers, as if seeking assurance that Project Atlas was going to work. He collapsed in the chair. "Damn you... Go, but be careful in Seattle and remain in the ULE embassy, at all times. It's an order. Will you be contacting outsiders, other than Parker?"

She thought for a moment. "I'll need to find a replacement piano teacher for Yana. That's it."

"Pick someone who clears the ULE background checks and stick to the visitation protocol... Do they have blind piano teachers in Seattle?" Avery's shoulders shook with either laughter or sobbing. Sarah preferred not to have to guess.

nine days till defiance day (43

Seattle bathed in the evening dusk. Natt woke with a snap, the back of his head hitting against the car seat. He rubbed a palm over his face and smacked his mouth, thick with unflossed breath. He recognized the inside of his work car, exhaled and turned around. He recognized Saretto there too, awake but quiet in the back seat.

"Mr. Gurloskey... sir?" Saretto's shaky voice travelled through the divider mesh. "There's been a terrible mistake. I'm sure I can explain."

Again, Natt smacked his mouth and opened the glove compartment with a grunt. Damn, no chewing gum left. He was tired, too tired to cut Saretto off. Waking up in the prowler drained Natt every time. The car seemed to have changed Saretto too. In fewer than four hours, the cellist had gone from thrashing, to being quiet, to groveling. Natt was about ready to grovel too. How much longer was she going to be? Her text had said to meet her at the flooded Walmart in the SoDo area. But that was four long hours ago.

Fresh whining interrupted Natt's thoughts. "Sir? It's getting dark. I'll miss my mandatory sign-in, tonight." Then a car engine growl, followed by brakes prompted him to glance outside. Piercing headlights stopped a foot from the prowler's front tires and the newcomer's car shut down. Acres of empty parking and an evening with the color of ink engulfed the two vehicles.

Saretto broke into muffled cries. Natt pumped the air with a fist. High damn time, darling, he thought and unbuckled his seat belt, then turned to Saretto. "Don't worry, pumpkin. We'll check your records and have you off in a jiff. Not even jail, you lucky dog." Natt patted the steel mesh with a reassuring palm and jumped out. He crouched by the door of the other car with his palms on his bent knees.

"Who's in the prowler with you?" Li-Mei said.

"You'll be pleased, my lady."

"Quit the Alexander Dumas bullshit and answer the question."

"Come find out." Natt wouldn't have dreamed of such fraternization with Li-Mei, but the cellist inside the prowler made for a great icebreaker.

"Saretto or Parker?"

"What have we got on today's menu? A cellist or a gambling man?" Natt spun around like a ballerina and opened the prowler's back door. Saretto's head poked from the inside.

Li-Mei got out of the car and walked to the cellist, who was trembling – either with fear or with the evening chill. "I owe you an apology, sir, for how you've been treated. And I'm here to rectify your situation," she said, maybe to stunt her victim's resistance by offering him normalcy for the remaining few minutes of his life.

"An outrage." Saretto tumbled out of the prowler in a bundle of rediscovered energy. "I hope you realize the severity of your actions, Officer Gurloskey. I'm a US Territory citizen and a performer at the world-famous Seattle Symphony." Li-Mei folded her arms as Saretto fished a phone from his pocket and started dialing a number. "Not only do I refuse to spend a minute in curfew jail, but I will sue you for this travesty. You don't know who you're dealing with."

"No need for a call, sir," Li-Mei said. "It's past curfew and the cell towers have switched off their civilian traffic if you haven't signed-in. How about I drive you to any destination you –"

"The King5 TV headquarters," Saretto said. "My story will anchor the seven o'clock news tomorrow."

"I can do that. Please, take a seat in my vehicle."

Saretto looked at Li-Mei's green Mustang. "I want to call a cab."

"Curfew docks all cabs by law, sir. King5 wouldn't dispatch a car to pick you at this hour. And you couldn't walk there either because you'd be arrested in minutes. Your safest bet is to let me to drive you."

Saretto shivered. "Fine, but he can't come with us." He pointed a finger at Natt.

"Of course not. Officer Gurloskey has no authority over you anymore."

Saretto glowered at the cop while squeezing into the Mustang's passenger seat. He buckled and tugged on the belt to ensure it worked. Once comfortable, he blinked several times, looking straight ahead and broadcasting relief at having survived the night without even a citation.

While following the green Mustang, Natt couldn't shake the sense of dread. He thanked providence he wasn't the one riding shotgun next to Li-Mei, on route to God-knew-where. Both cars crept through the suspension bridges of the curfewed city, the prowler's flashing lights granting them a safe passage.

The Mustang came to a halt in a walled-off alleyway behind the Seattle Public Library. The massive edifice – once, one of the finest buildings in North America – didn't have a single light turned on and wore the same taint as the rest of downtown. Li-Mei stepped out of the car and Saretto followed.

"I said King5 TV, not the library." His protests filled the night, as Natt walked up to the pair.

"Isn't the library is as much of a bastion of free speech as the TV?"

"But I asked –"

"Unless you do as I say, I will ... kill you." Li-Mei paused before the last two words and Saretto winced, as if they were needles thrust in his flesh. She led the cellist to a shaft protruding from a septic tank at the back of the library. Natt recognized the tank - a product of the Sanitation Revival Program he had proposed with the Mayor to condemn Seattle's flooded sewers and install individual septic tanks at all large public buildings.

"You have a nice suit, Mr. Saretto," Li-Mei said. "Do you like it?"

Saretto's voice was small, "It's my favorite."

"I love it too... but you'll have to soil it some tonight."

Li-Mei jumped on top of the tank and smashed the padlock on the circular entry shaft. As soon as her back turned, Saretto dashed for Fourth Avenue, large and bright at the library's main entrance. Gurloskey cut the fleeing man off with unusual agility for the cop's two-hundred-plus-pound frame. Then following a scuffle with a predetermined end, Saretto lay face down on the pavement with Natt on his back.

"I apologize if our company has bored you, Mr. Saretto." Li Mei approached the two heaped men. "Or are you that fond of your suit? I would be, too, if I had a suit like yours. Stripes are always in style, aren't they?" She produced an oxygen mask and handed it to the Chief of Police. "Put this on and bring our guest back to the tank." She put a second mask on her head and pulled the septic hatch open, hinges creaking in rusted protest. A column of steel steps descended into the tank's gut, the top few rungs gleaming in the pale moonlight.

"God. The smell..." Saretto wept as Natt shoved him forward.

"Rotten eggs, if you're wondering," Li-Mei said. "Fear not, it shall pass. You may enter the tank via this ladder, otherwise, Mr. Gurloskey will have to deposit you inside." Saretto's watery eyes scanned the two oxygen masks staring at him.

"And by the way, don't forget to tie yourself to the steps inside. You wouldn't want to fall." Li-Mei handed Saretto a nylon rope, which he took with both hands like a precious offering.

"Please, don't do this," he said.

"We need you in that tank, dear. Go down but do continue to believe in miracles. The sinking of the Titanic must have been a miracle to the lobsters in the kitchen."

Victor Saretto stared at Li-Mei's amber face for another moment, turned away from the pit and inhaled a last gasp of semi-unpolluted air. He held his breath and climbed down one slow step at a time, the septic tank hiding his body from sight. "Oh, I almost forgot..." Li-Mei's mask covered the patch of sky, cut off by the hatch opening.

Victor's head reemerged from the darkness. He was still holding his breath.

"Don't speak," she said, "nod, instead. The crestfallen Mrs. Dubois divorced you when she found out you were gay four years ago, correct?" Victor nodded, his face wet with tears. "If the two of you loved each other as much as I'm told you did, you should look at tonight as doing her a favor. The first female President of the ULE Patent Bureau makes a great catch for a second marriage, don't you think? Four years is long enough to mourn someone who isn't even dead. Us women could get too sentimental for our own good sometimes. And in your case, you never know... death might bring her closure. Of course, I'm not saying you're going to die tonight."

Saretto nodded again.

"What a good boy, Mr. Saretto. Don't forget to strap yourself to the steps." Li-Mei sounded maternal. "We'll come get you in a few. We can even get food on our way to King5. You shouldn't go on national TV on an empty stomach, no?" Saretto kept nodding. "I'll close this now to give you some privacy."

The hatch creaked shut over the cellist's face.

"We'll come get you..." Natt said on the fresh-air side of the tank and slow-clapped.

"Check on him in twenty," Li-Mei said. "With a little luck, he will have tied himself to the steps before the hydrogen sulfide kills him. Leave his body by the open tank somewhere. The story will write itself."

"Our septic tanks claim another innocent victim." Natt imitated the booming voice of a news anchor. "But why would Saretto break into a padlocked septic tank in the middle of the night? At the Seattle Library, no less?"

"You're the cop, you figure out a motive before people find his corpse while returning their books tomorrow morning. If there are any readers left in this goddamn city, that is."

Li-Mei opened the Mustang's door. "And Gurloskey – don't forget to put your oxygen mask back on when you go in. Even a monkey could take care of business from here."

Natt laughed, agreeable and sweaty.

"Parker's the last one left. Get him to me and I'll let you live." The Mustang's window shot up. The night was getting colder.

eight days till defiance day (44

The black coffee scalded the top row of Natt's taste buds into numb white dots but he was too groggy to notice. Light, born at five-am, seeped into Macrina Bakery. He sat alone, at the same table where Li-Mei had locked him in his own handcuffs last week. She had texted him earlier, demanding a morning meeting. More like a middle-of-the-night one, it felt to Natt.

She marched into the bakery, her appearance affected by the early morning no more than a late afternoon. Her hair was lush and shiny and her movements deliberate. She pulled out a chair and sat across from Natt.

"Parker's status with eight days left?" Only she could fit so much in so few words without a single verb.

Natt's palms encircled the ceramic "For Here" mug, eking out warmth, and maybe shelter from what was to follow. He took another swallow of the steaming coffee and spoke with the servile tone he had developed in Li-Mei's presence. "I've flooded the ULE Most Wanted wires with his info. We have enough for a criminal charge: he has severed his passport. That's at least ten years for desertion."

"He cut off his own hand?"

"At the wrist. The curfew database confirmed his vitals stopped refreshing four days ago... your classic case of Defiance Day desertion. The bad news is, without a digital passport, our systems can't track the guy."

She sighed. "You're on my list and, if you can't find him, you've seen what I do to people on my list."

His voice was thick with insomnia. "But I took care of the cellist last night. The Seattle PD found his body this morning... no issues."

She pushed her plastic chair and stood up. "Find Parker."

Natt stepped in front of her while avoiding her eyes. "I should also mention," he stammered, "to convince you of my intentions —"

"Get out of my way."

"— that I voted last night."

"Sacrificing yourself for your son does not solve my Parker problem."

"I earmarked someone else."

She shot him a tilted look. "You voted for someone else?"

"Laura - our babysitter who looks after Eaton." Natt's palms kept hugging the cup, white knuckles on blue ceramic. "I wanted to show you I can't Sacrifice for him and I'm not a threat anymore and you shouldn't... Meaning, if you continue with what you want to do to me. You know... it will be tragic for Eaton to lose his Dad..." Natt breathed in and out. "Also...I wanted to prove to you I'm not a threat."

"Eaton can't be earmarked. Ever." Li-Mei scanned the Police Chief from head to toe.

"But even if they did earmark him," Natt followed her outside, "I can't undo it anymore. Not after I voted last night. This is convincing you right? What I did?"

Li-Mei stopped on the bridge-walk, her back to him. "Chloe, your wife, will be earmarked a few hours before the deadline. And you are right, you wouldn't be able to undo it — one way or another." She disappeared within the swirl of the waking city as morning delivery trucks and salary men rushed to early meetings. Natt Gurloskey did not attempt to follow.

eight days till defiance day (45

Moving to this other Washington had made Yana feel like a scattered picture puzzle. She wasn't supposed to like change at eight years old, least of all when forced to leave home. The smell was her very first introduction to Seattle, right after she had jumped on the yellow helipad of the ULE Seattle embassy the previous morning and ran up to her mother. "This place smells bad, Mom," she had said.

"We'll stay here no longer than we have to. I promise," had been her Mom's reply, but unconvinced Yana had clung to the hand. Her Mom had called Yana's father over the chopper's blades whirring through the air, "We've arrived and will see you in the embassy when you get there." Then her Mom had hung up.

They had reached Seattle the hard way. With SeaTac Airport decommissioned because of the floods, Mom had convinced a ULE Coast Guard General to give them a lift to Cheyenne on a ULE topography mission. Afterward, they had made the final leg to Seattle on a food-supply chopper run.

That's when Yana had taken her first breath after disembarking and had cringed. The morning breeze had lost to the rotting smell and, like a waking person who wanted to stay in bed, despite a burning bladder, Seattle had woken one block at a time, dark windows turning into lighted ones.

To be fair, the ULE embassy's yard here was covered with grass, which she penciled as the only plus of moving to Seattle. But the rest were mammoth-sized minuses like rain, rot and pedestrians roaming the suspension bridge-walks without a purpose or umbrellas. She had seen a woman in hair-curls, a man wearing shaving cream on his face then another man, starting a gas grill at a corner.

She felt strapped to a rollercoaster ride she was afraid to finish because of what waited at the end of the tracks: a first-time meeting with her father. She used to have nightmares about him growing up and she wetted her bed. Her Mom insisted such accidents were normal then rocked her, until Yana would fall back asleep. Yana never told her Mom or the special doctor her Mom had hired, that dreaming of her father was what caused the nightmares. She stayed mum because she wanted to get rid of him on her own. At times, she succeeded and woke dry in her jammies the following day. These mornings meant absolute happiness and, in time, started outnumbering the wet ones. Until her Mom told her they had to go see him.

"I owe you an explanation," her Mom had said on their first night in Seattle.

Yana didn't want explanations, she wanted to wake in her dry DC bed without feeling guilty her father had left or being afraid that nobody but her Mom would ever love her again.

"I know he's been on your mind a lot." Her Mom kept beating the topic like a woodpecker. "And I also know the thought of seeing him upsets you."

Yana was chasing a fugitive pea with the tip of her fork and, despite her Mom's long stare, wouldn't look back. "A mother's job, you'll find one day, is to protect her child without regard to the cost. A good mother, it may seem to you now, would do the opposite of what I'm asking. She wouldn't uproot you from your home or force a piano competition on you. She wouldn't bring back the days when you wet your bed."

"Mom... You're embarrassing me," Yana said, her fork disemboweling the pea. The Pacific Northwest rain was pounding against the windows like a drumroll that would sound cozy in in inland city. In Seattle, the sound of rain spelled doom.

"If I could wave a wand to take your worries away and store them inside me, I would," her Mom said snapping her fingers, "like that."

"You don't have to explain, Mom."

"There's something good about your father you don't know yet, but you will find out one day. Until then..." Her Mom stammered, "You should know he regrets his mistake and wants to convince you of it, too. That's why he asked to see you and I agreed. Does any of this help you, Sweetie?"

The word "sweetie" caught her unprepared. Other mothers used pet words to call their daughters, not her mother. It gave Yana a glimpse of her mother's true burden. Her Mom would absorb her fears and wetting of beds, if she could. It didn't matter that she couldn't... wanting to was more important than the act.

Yana reached out and held her Mom's hand. "You're doing great, Mom. I'll meet my father. It's OK." She pushed her chair back and jumped on the tiled floor, her bare feet making a suction noise against the cold marble. "And thank you for dinner." She turned around and headed upstairs to check her room in their new embassy home, for the first time.

eight days till defiance day (46

Li-Mei watched as the merry-go-round turned, slow and creaky. Yana stood next to the churning axis, the backbone of the whole steely operation. Someone had shut off the music and the customers had disappeared too, but the carousel moved on: bright electric bulbs illuminating the wooden horses from multiple angles. Some of the horses' manes floated like frozen waves, some horses pulled on invisible loads with necks turned sideways. All animals, without exception, had open mouths and bared teeth, and sported fresh coats of paint on top of chips and scratches that excited little customers had inflicted, without meaning to in the slightest.

Yana stood in the middle, where a machinist would. Nine times out of ten, the machinists were high school dropouts with the job of pressing a green button then ten minutes later, pressing a red one. Today, Yana did the honors.

Li-Mei got closer. As the carousel turned, a bucking bronco hid her from the girl's sight then Li-Mei was visible for a moment before disappearing again behind a royal carriage with a tall steel spike.

"Who are you?" Yana said, squinting around the moving figures.

"I can't tell you, but I'm glad I found you."

"Are you Chinese?" Yana said.

"Most Caucasians can't tell the difference. But that doesn't apply to you, I see." Li-Mei smiled. "How did you get in the middle of these spinning horses with open, painted mouths? And do you need help getting out?"

"I'm good. If I press here," Yana pointed to a red button with the word "Stop" etched on top, "the wheel will stop and let me get out."

"Why don't you do it, then?"

Yana thumbtacked a smile on her face and pressed the button. In another half rotation, the merry-go-round ground to a halt. She took a step forward then another. Her shoes rattled against the carousel's metallic floor. As soon as she came within reaching distance, Li-Mei's fingers bit into Yana's hand and Li-Mei's smile melted into a leer.

"You're hurting me," Yana said.

"That's my intent, little one."

"Are you going to kill me?"

Li-Mei's low whisper rippled through the air, "Drama is anticipation, mingled with uncertainty, but you're a smart little girl, aren't you? You knew why I had come the moment you saw me."

"I guessed... Now I know."

"Killing you will save the lives of many others."

"In what way?"

"My role coming here, to this..." Li-Mei paused while her free hand swept around, in a gesture showing what words couldn't, "Territory... was to take the lives of those who may Sacrifice themselves for you. Then earmark you and make sure you to sleep after Defiance Day."

"Why would you do this to me?"

"To make your Mom sad. So sad she wouldn't want to work after your death. And that would give a chance to other scientists in a different Territory, our Territory, to catch up with her inventions."

"So you are going to kill me either today or on Defiance Day. But if I died now, I will save the lives of the people who love me?" Yana said.

"Your death will save them, yes. It's something they would have done for you, without hesitation."

"And you promise my father is one of these people?"

"I promise."

Broken clouds hung above, completing the carousel's transformation into an execution alley. Li-Mei lifted Yana by the armpits and walked toward the royal carriage with the steel spike, fewer than ten feet away.

"I won't forget you, Yana Perkins," Li-Mei said and impaled the little girl's head on the spike. Yana's feet twitched once. Her eyes filled with blood and her teeth, as they ground themselves to pieces, carved up the inside of her cheeks. Under its own weight, the body slid down until it hit the carriage's top, then rested there, as if taking a breather.

Li-Mei stepped back and exhaled; killing children was never easy. She started walking away but a squeak prompted her to turn for a second look. Yana's eyes, previously open and filling up with blood, were now shut. Li-Mei returned to the carousel and stared at the girl's dead face. On cue, Yana's lips curled into a slow smile and her eyelids opened to reveal lucid eye-whites without a single bloodied vessel.

"Have you forgotten me yet?" Yana said "or have you kept your promise?" As she spoke, the spike inside her mouth glistened like an oversized tongue stud.

Li-Mei sighed. "I should have cut your head off, little one. Let's hear you ask questions without a head." She plunged a kinjal into Yana's white neck, made whiter still by death, but the blade bounced off with a thud.

Before Li-Mei's mind could reject the absurdity of what had happened, she woke drenched and mumbled with a sleepy tongue, as if pierced by a rusted stud. "I hope meeting you in person would be as memorable as meeting you in my dreams, little one." Then she turned and fell asleep until the morning.

seven days till defiance day (47

Above Yana's head, a bird chirped. She had run outside to look for it, in the embassy's fenced lawn, and chased the chirp with her eyes but only found the yellow sun, stamping her vision with round blotches. Like that bird, for the most part, Yana felt alone and invisible. She had watched films about birds and seen a stuffed sea hawk in her biology class once, but never the real thing. It was a robin, based on its song, and an impossible one to spot, no matter how she twisted her neck and shielded her eyes with a palm. In another couple of minutes, Yana cut her losses with a sigh and moved on to playing hopscotch. In her mind, she could see imaginary squares drawn over the Seattle grass. Barefoot, she tossed a pebble on the nearest one and hopped forth. The grass, brushing her bare feet, and the invisible robin had somehow led her thoughts to her father. "He's irresponsible and doesn't love you," Mom had said a long time ago in DC and Yana had decided to become the best daughter in the world at doing something important, to prove to him he was wrong to leave. She had thrown herself with equal abandon at homework, house chores and playing the piano Mom gave her for her fifth birthday.

Time and growing up would, once and again, silence the thoughts of her father. He hibernated in a dark corner of her mind where she didn't dare go and even forgot it existed. But he never went away; life wouldn't let him. At school, Yana learned that children often had two parents and that her Mom disliked talking about why Yana was different. So Yana became an expert at reading her Mom's moods and at filing away scraps of information, on a scavenger hunt for missing memories. She transformed these bits into imaginary stories about her father. Whether he was a pirate or a rich sea merchant, he was always unavailable and always placing other projects above his daughter.

After a recent sleepover at Gabriella's, Yana had come home burning with new questions. The Guzmans, unlike Yana and her Mom, ate dinner at a living room table and talked about their day. And though Mr. Guzman had a whiskey smell on his breath, Yana liked the thought of having dinners together every night, as a family. The following evening, before her Mom could take her coat off at the door, Yana attacked with questions.

"Could we have dinner at our table, Mom?"

Sarah stretched her lower back. "I thought you had a bite already."

"I waited for you to come home."

"I'll fix you something quick then."

"I already started something." Yana spun around. "And I made the table."

Her mother had smiled back, but her knuckles whitened as she was hanging her coat. She threw a glance at the kitchen; Yana had chosen a festive tablecloth - lavender blue with yellow dots along the edges. A large salad bowl in the center of the high square table pulled at the eye first with sliced tomatoes, cucumbers and onion circles. Two plates, with silverware flanking each side, and two crystal glasses, filled with what looked like water, completed the ensemble.

Sarah's eyes moved from the table to Yana. "Well done, young lady."

"I fixed us some scrambled eggs. Left them in the oven, to keep warm."

"Thanks for remembering to cook my favorite food."

The girl sat, feet dangling at the table and beckoned with a wave. "Sit down, Mom."

"What's the occasion?"

"I told you. I wanted us to eat at a table. Like Gabriella and her parents do."

Sarah scooped some tomatoes on her plate.

Yana threw the first punch. "Why can't we have dinner like this, every night?"

Sarah put a tomato slice in her mouth. "Great idea. We could have gourmet food delivered. How fun would that be? A surprise meal every night and –"

"I don't want take-home. I want you to do it." Yana bit her lip then went nuclear. "I want Dad to come home too. I want the three of us to have dinner, every night."

Sarah laid down her fork with care, as if it were a loaded gun. So that's what the table and eggs and Yana's sweet smile were about. "Is there something you'd like to tell me?"

Yana jumped in without a second prompt. "Where's Dad? Why do we never talk about him?"

"We've covered this before."

"We've covered nothing." Yana's lips stitched shut between sentences. "You've told me he didn't love me and that we're better off without him. But I want to see him before I die."

"Before you die? Silly, you're eight years old."

Yana's face turned white. She reached for the salad, her hand wrapped around the fork. "I am his daughter and I have the right to know him."

"You want to know him?" Sarah wiped her mouth, stood and walked to the window, away from her daughter. "What do you want to know?"

"Everything."

"Everything?"

"Everything," Yana said. "I want to know him, not your opinion of him."

Sarah hung her head and stomped out of the kitchen. She returned with an envelope in her hand and chucked it at the table with an underhand motion, like a softball pitcher. The envelope landed between the salad bowl and Yana's untouched plate.

Sarah's voice was as hard and sharp as a diamond. "If that's what you want, then that's what you're going to get. It's all inside. Your father was a certified poker addict who, on a certain August night, seven years ago, while I was at work, came within minutes of murdering you."

Yana's eyes glowed without blinking.

"He had been grocery shopping, earlier that day, and left a plastic bag next to your crib. I mean, who does that?" Sarah's fingers stretched and curved, like bird talons. "You were suffocating while he played online poker, in the other room... for fewer than a couple of minutes, he claims, until I called. Maybe it was a couple of minutes, maybe it wasn't. The single reason, my dear truth-seeker, that you're sitting in this room with me, hearing my story, and breathing air, is because I called him on that August night. You're alive because of my premonition or just dumb luck – you choose." Sarah bit into a chapped fingernail. "He was sweet, telling me on the phone, while walking to your room, how much he loved me. Whispering it, not to wake you up, what a full day you two had, as his hand was pressing on the door handle and his phone teetered, pinched between ear and shoulder. Pausing a ranked poker game meant he might as well quit, he said, but that's how much he loved me.

"I remember hearing the door open, then his screams. Then nothing. His cell must have fallen to the floor." Sarah covered her face and inhaled through her palms, as if demonstrating what suffocation looked like. "The ER took an hour to restore your pulse. You were in a coma for a month. We didn't know how your brain would work when you woke. We didn't know if you'd wake at all." Sarah sat back down in front of the salad bowl. "I divorced him as soon as you regained consciousness. A week later, the courts issued a restraining order and I haven't seen him since." Her voice faltered, its million icicles melting away. "Excuse me, but I lost my appetite. I should get back to the lab, too."

Yana was staring at the salad bowl. Her balled fist kept clutching the fork.

seven days till defiance day (48

The day had arrived, at last. Waiting in the embassy's conference room, Colton shoved his stump in the front of his pants, hoping Sarah wouldn't notice the pocket didn't bulge where his hand should have been. The wound was infected and the surrounding flesh had started to ooze, but he gritted his teeth and wiped the cold sweat off his face. He didn't want her to see him in pain when she saw him for the first time in seven years.

"How have you been?" Sarah said, her eyes glassy with the lack of sleep.

"I'm good... for someone who has, so far, survived a manhunt by Mrs. Death Star." His self-deprecating smile fell unreturned. His ex wasn't in the mood.

"Look. For what I said... I'm sorry," she wiped the corners of her mouth mid-sentence. "And for what you did, I —"

"I've forgotten how pretty you were."

"Colton..."

His lips squeezed a smile. "Thanks for coming to Seattle, Sarah. Was she OK to meet me?"

"She knows you want it and she'll honor your request."

"Did you tell her about me taking her place?"

"I haven't, but I'm sure she'll figure it out."

"That's fine. After Defiance Day she can do whatever she likes."

"Why did you agree to go through with the Sacrifice?"

"Because of you asking me to take her place. And because anyone else in my place would have done it."

"Bullshit." She rolled her shoulders to release tension in her upper back. Her motion reminded Colton, with painful clarity, about the late nights when she would come home, her body liquid with exhaustion and her back shivering with muscle spasms. Sitting at the edge of their bed was the most she could muster. He would massage her back with lavender oil, starting by touching the skin with two fingers then moving up and down the spine, more of a caress than a massage. His fingertips were magical Zen sticks, he would say, sucking out her backache. And he'd go for hours, telling her about his day with Yana and how much or how little the two of them had done. "If you save the world," he would ask, "who's going to save you?" and knew they both agreed on the answer, until the accident.

Today, he would give anything to sit closer to her, in this gray ULE conference room, and massage her sore back again, without a word, as homage to their lives back then.

"Bullshit," Sarah said again. "No one else would. I also hope you didn't do this out of guilt." She lifted a hand to stop his reply. "So... What do you think... fifteen minutes?"

Colton's face twisted. "Just fifteen?"

The curfew sirens blared outside. "I'd take fifteen, if I were you," she said.

"I don't want to fight, Sarah. The Chinese woman has a monopoly on my fights, these days. I'll see my daughter for fifteen minutes, but I want to see her at least once more after today."

"We're in Seattle, you might as well. She can meet you this Thursday too, for an hour. But I wouldn't push for more time or more meetings." Sarah stood up, putting an end to the argument before it had started. "She'll be in soon," she said and left the room.

Colton shifted in his seat, heart thrashing in his chest, as noisy as the sirens outside. After seven years, he felt like someone who was about to find his lost religion. His good hand hovered over the chair, where Sarah had sat. He felt tired and part of him wondered about walking into the nearest precinct and letting the Asian woman take care of the rest.

He punched his shoulder with his stump and winced. "Enough... You are Colton Parker," he spoke out loud. "You give people hope, you don't destroy it." Then the door opened and jolted him up. Yana walked in. She took two steps and sat in a chair by the wall, as far as possible from him. He scraped his tongue with his front teeth to freshen his breath and ran his good hand through his hair. He didn't have a comb; five fingers would have to do.

seven days till defiance day (49

Colton rose from his chair, as if Yana were royalty then tumbled back when he saw her face. She was beautiful, more than he knew. If there were a graceful way to pile hundreds of freckles on a human face, it would have been hers. In the same room together, he realized how much he had missed her, and how the years had flown. The eight-year-old smiled at him.

"Mr. Parker."

"Yana. Hi." He struggled to remember the last time any two words had required this much effort.

She stared at his eyes with the intensity of an optometrist examining a patient. "We don't look alike much, do we?" she said and fiddled with a loose lace on her sneaker.

Each time he had rehearsed their first meeting, he'd sworn he wouldn't let silence set in. Silence was bad news for men who almost killed their daughters before the daughters were old enough to start teething. Silence made him feel aware of his crumpled face and his teeth chipped at the base and turning yellow in the front. He rubbed his graying short hair with his good hand to conceal a receding hairline. And he hid his right hand in a pocket, thinking she wouldn't notice. He smiled back but his armpits were swimming with nervous sweat.

"Your Mom tells me you like sharks," he said.

Yana sat, in a far-away chair, with palms tucked under her legs. "Sharks are fine."

"Which one is your favorite?"

"The great white one. Its teeth are a hundred times sharper than razor blades."

The toes of her sneakers bounced against one another, dangling in the air. Colton felt like reaching over and caressing her golden hair to test if their years apart had made it softer or pointier.

"Mom told me you hurt me when I was a baby," she said, "but I don't like holding grudges."

"This is the best sentence… I've heard in a while." Colton paused at every word as if speaking a foreign language for the first time. "I've been a stranger to you." He tucked a frayed edge on the seat of his chair and patted the smooth bundle with a palm. "But I'd like to change that, if it's OK."

"I'd like that, too."

"Do you know what I called you while watching you sleep in your crib?"

"Tell me." Her toes kept bouncing against each other.

Taking his eyes off her felt like passing a kidney stone but on the other hand he didn't want to stare. "I called you patte."

"What does it mean?"

"In college, I lost a bet to your Mom, where the loser had to enroll in the most obscure course the winner could find. She chose Intermediary Bulgarian. "Patte" means duckling in Bulgarian."

Yana wrinkled her nose and looked up from her shoes. "I should get going."

"So soon?" Colton said, his face crumpling more.

"I have to. Plus, Mom said you would see me again tomorrow or the day after."

"Of course." He covered his eyes and when they reappeared, his face was smiling. Not a beamer, but a smile anyway, even if surrounded by sadness. "Don't give Mom a reason to worry, OK? And also… tell her how happy I was to see you." He raised a finger for emphasis. "One last question before you go – have you been to a wishing fountain in DC?"

"What's a wishing fountain?"

"It's a place where you can wish for anything then toss a coin in the water for your wish to come true." Yana tilted her head. She didn't interrupt. "Many years from now, when this madness is over and you have become a beautiful young lady, you should go to Italy, where so many wishes are made that, from time to time, the authorities have to remove the coins from the fountains and deposit the money in the bank. What I'm trying to say..." he swallowed, "is that the wishing fountain of my life is you."

"What do you mean?" Yana's brows furrowed. "You mean I'm like a water fountain and you're throwing money at me?"

"One day you'll understand."

At the door, she waved goodbye and slid out. Colton waved back, spreading his fingers in the air, then walked around the beige table in the middle of the room. A lap later, he sat in a different chair from where he'd started and wished Thursday could come sooner.

seven days till defiance day (50

Mitko leaned back from the piano and cracked his knuckles to keep the arthritis at bay. He stood up and with his hands on his hip, took laps around the Stein: right, right then right again; marble floor switched to carpet at each turn.

A voice flew in from his left. "Your evening workout, I take it?"

"Ma'am." Mitko grinned at the air where her voice had come from. She sounded like the patron who disliked Schumann, from almost a month ago. He recalled her name was Li-Mei. "How have you enjoyed your stay with us?"

"Seattle grows on you, if you let it. Stench and curfew aside, this place must have been beautiful once."

"Without eyes, I'm no longer the foremost authority on beauty. But I hear other people feel the same."

"I'll be leaving your hotel soon and wanted to thank you for the music. And also ask a question." Her voice grew thinner like wood whittled into a spear. "Do you know a man named Colton Parker?"

Mitko cracked his knuckles again; stubborn arthritis. "Can't be sure. In my line of work, I meet a lot of people. Maybe one of them was this... Colton person." Then without warning, his hands shot up and clasped her head. He didn't squeeze or inflict pain, but cradled her sides like a father would when sending his daughter away on her wedding day.

She froze then pushed his wrists away with a swoop. A groan died in her throat then she stood still.

"It was you," he said, "all along." His fingers rested tranquil on the piano keys. "The person who attacked Colton in this hotel last week had a missing right ear and so do you. Who did this to you?" He tried to imagine how the two of them must look: a thankful Olympic customer chatting up the lobby pianist during his break.

"The better question is if you want to end the day in a body bag. Which is what I'll do if you don't tell me where Parker is."

"As a younger man," he said, "I lived in a far-away country, where I was involved with people who wanted better lives, for themselves and for their children. You may say I was their leader. We were optimistic and hopeful. We met and grumbled like young people do when you take away their freedom. In the beginning, we were about a dozen, then the squares couldn't hold us, in time. The government sent soldiers with guns and live ammo. I remember how afraid I was the first time I heard them approach. I felt this fear, yellow in color, of what they were going to do to us. Being a blind man, you see, I think of emotions as colors.

"One evening, at nightfall, the soldiers attacked and beat us. They beat me too, but, a funny thing, the first blow of their batons on my body shattered my fear and it hasn't come back since." His tongue wet his lips. "Look at me again, Ma'am. Do you think your body bag scares me?" He turned away from her, starting a new Schumann. His break was over.

"Parker's passport signature beams from inside your apartment. I know you're helping him."

"Then come over and put us both in body bags."

"Do I look like I need a dinner invitation? Where...is...he?"

"Every few years, enough crazies believe Rapture is coming. This year's flavor is Defiance Day. I see you as one of them, Ma'am. Make my day and become my personal Rapture. See how much it moves −"

Before he could finish, Mitko felt six of his fingers shatter like saltines. She had slammed the fallboard on top of his playing hands. Somehow, the next thought in his head was whether anyone would notice, in the loud lobby, that the music had stopped or he had doubled over his Grand Stein.

"Do you believe me now?" she said. "I will crush you... like a worm."

"You couldn't kill him... because I stopped you," he said. "But if you dropped by the next couple of days, I'll fix you a cake to celebrate you crushing me... like a worm."

He smiled despite the pain then heard her footfalls depart toward the Olympic's revolving doors, as if his smile was a powerful projectile that had driven her away.

seven days till defiance day (51

Natt pounded his desk with a fist, his fingers groaning and the wood underneath groaning louder. The son of a bitch had him beat, as much as Natt hated to admit it. The Police Chief had tagged the ULE Interpol wires with a screaming urgency uncustomary for your standard passport deserter. He had turned Parker into an AMBER-Alert pariah, incapable of buying groceries or eating at a restaurant for the rest of his life. Parker's biotelemetry was plastered all over the apartment of the blind pianist, with the lab concluding the man's right hand had to be stashed inside. But that was that. Two of Natt's squads had kept the apartment under surveillance and had discovered no leads.

Natt slammed the desk again, this time with the other fist. With every passing hour, Parker made him look like a bigger idiot. None of his staff cared for passport deserters – "Defiance Day junkies," as cops called them – but the damn Chinese woman did. He had to do something. The Police Chief stormed out of the makeshift City Hall lobby. Covert surveillance had exhausted its course; it was time to pay Mr. Benjamin a visit.

The old man's apartment looked dark from the outside. Natt knocked heavy on the door, his fist still hurting.

"Who's there?"

"Police Chief Gurloskey from the Seattle PD. Open up, please."

The door squeaked ajar and Mitko's unwashed head filled the crack.

"How may I help you?"

Natt flashed his badge by habit, as if the pianist could see. "I need to ask you a few questions about a certain Colton Parker, Mr. Benjamin."

"Come in, please." The pianist disappeared inside. Natt stopped to let his eyes adjust. All the lights were off and for some reason he thought he'd love to have this place's electric bill. He found Mitko waiting in a kitchen with blue walls, where, judging by the number and variety of items, the pianist spent a lot of his time when home.

"Apologies for the darkness, Officer. I don't have much use for the light and have shut off my electric service. It makes me feel good knowing I'm helping Puget Sound Energy."

"I appreciate your social sacrifice given your limited condition, sir," Natt said. "Time is of the essence here, so I should jump straight to it. Do you know Colton Parker?"

"Never heard of him, I'm afraid."

"How about anything unusual happen to you the last few days? You'll be surprised how telling even small details could be." Natt's eyes narrowed then relaxed. He wouldn't need his poker face today. He was interrogating a blind man.

Mitko shook head from side to side. "Nothing unusual, Officer. Just surviving like everyone else."

"Nothing at all?" Natt's smile remained stitched to his face. Behind it, he wondered where Parker's passport was hidden. Anywhere in this apartment would be madness, of course. He dared the blind fool to keep lying in the face of an evidentiary DNA lab report. "You bumped into no one and no one bumped into you?"

"Remember the good old days, Officer? Before the waters took over our lives? People were different then." Mitko sighed. "Now that you mention it... say an unusual fellow did contact me. What is it you want from him?"

"He's an illegal combatant."

"Terrible."

"And a Defiance Day passport deserter–"

"What is our world coming to?"

"–who'll face the full extent of the law. We may live in a flooded city, Mr. Benjamin, but not in a lawless one. Say, you've seen..." Natt started then stopped... that was the wrong question. "Sorry... Say, Mr. Parker has contacted you. Would you happen to know where he went?"

Mitko took a step toward the Police Chief, the men's faces no more than inches apart. "Come to think of it, I do remember this boy."

"If you helped him by as much as an ounce, I'll make your life hell, sir."

"He robbed me at gun point and left. I would never help such a senseless brigand, Chief Gurloskey."

"Listen well, old man. You two could be butt buddies for all I care. Unless you start telling me where he went, I'll deport you back to whatever overseas armpit village you call home." Natt's perma-smile made him sound like a background vocal to a love-song. "And I'll see you go there a broken man, the way we found you when you crawled onto these sacred shores."

"You listen, too," Mitko's voice carried despite the sirens outside announcing the start of curfew. "You'll never catch him. He wants what he's after too much to let himself be caught." The pianist stepped back, as if sizing up Gurloskey, who shivered at the thought of a blind man scanning him like a page. "I wish you could see yourself like I can..." The sirens stopped, followed by the lapping sounds of water in the streets. "It's time you left now."

"Insult me one more time and I will break your blind face in the middle of your mole rat apartment." Natt's upper lip was sweating. "Do we understand each other?"

Mitko raised both hands to his face. Six of his fingers were in splints. "More than the person who did this? She was asking about Parker too. Or will you break my toes next, because I refuse to be bullied?"

Natt's neck vein stood out like a swollen leech on his skin. "You are a dead man. A blind and useless dead man."

"Don't threaten me in my own home. And don't you dare come back without a warrant."

"You should have lived the life of a blind dog overseas. It beats being blind, dead meat."

The Police Chief left Mitko's apartment. After him the sounds of lapping water in the streets grew louder with the oncoming night wind.

seven days till defiance day (52

Mitko entered the lobby of the Seattle ULE embassy. His hands swam through traffic like live dolphins and his head, cocked at an angle, seemed to examine something peculiar on the ceiling that no one else could see.

Sarah met him at security and escorted him to a private conference room. "Take a seat, Mr. Benjamin," she said.

"I imagine the table is a foot ahead, Dr. Perkins." Without her confirmation, he swiped at the space in front, his palm grabbing the empty chair and sat, facing her, as confident as a seeing person.

"You're quite the pianist, I hear," she said.

"I've played some in my past."

"Forty-four years behind the piano qualifies as more than some, in my book."

"You flatter me, Doctor. How may I help?"

"My good manners compel me to ask if you'd like a drink, first."

"A glass of water, please."

Sarah walked away to a room corner then returned. "The paper cup is a few inches away from your left hand," she said. "Straight ahead."

"You're a fast learner."

"Speaking of your hands, who did this to you?"

"I had a minor accident at work. I'd rather we focus about why you called me here."

"OK... My eight-year-old will compete in the ULE Classical Prodigy next month."

He puckered his lips, inhaling a whistle. "The Prodigy. You must be proud."

"I am and I'd like you to train her."

"A month is not enough to prepare."

"She's played since four and a half —"

"You realize they'll blow her away," he said. "No disrespect."

"—under the supervision of a certified Prodigy tutor in DC."

"You two have travelled a long way from DC. And I'm sure you realized, your move would disrupt your daughter's preparations."

"Us moving to Seattle couldn't be helped," she said, "and isn't as fatal as you make it sound. Yana is a gifted young pianist in need of a replacement tutor."

"Did you move here because of Defiance Day?"

"Are you in, or are you out?"

"Sorry. I was trying to get context."

"You and sixteen other applicants we're interviewing..."

"Where will I tutor her?"

"In this embassy... every single day. A car will shuttle you from here to downtown and back."

"Will my condition impact your final decision?"

"Your condition?"

"I'm blind and six of my fingers are broken."

"No. But your fee will. How much are you charging per hour?"

"If I do this, Dr. Perkins, I'll do it for your daughter, not for money. May I meet her, please?"

"I'll get her from the other room and have you two meet one-on-one," she said. "You should start getting used to each other's company." Sarah left and in a minute a little voice flew to Mitko like a verse from a lullaby. "Good afternoon, Mr. Benjamin."

He waved without standing up. "Don't be frightened, dear, but you should know that my eyes can't see."

"That must be difficult."

"It's not so bad. I can see with my heart, instead."

"You can? Will you teach me how?"

"Only if you promise you'll keep it a secret. Then I'll teach you the piano too."

The girl sounded like a pout on a face. "I already know how to play the piano."

"You're right, I misspoke." He smiled. "I can help you prepare for your piano competition while I teach you to see with your heart."

"And I promise I won't tell anyone. Deal?"

"Eight years old and already a negotiator. If I didn't know better, I'd guess you didn't like playing much."

"I like playing for fun; I don't like competitions."

"Your preparation will be fun, I promise. Please, go get your Mom, now."

Yana skipped toward the door. It closed and when it opened again, Mitko heard Sarah standing in it. "Do we have a deal?" she said.

"We can start with an assessment of how she'll do at the event. A couple of favorite pieces, followed by her competitive composition."

"We're beyond assessments, Mr. Benjamin. I want her to win the Prodigy."

"I'll give your daughter my best, Doctor."

"Pleasure to meet you, Mr. Benjamin. We'll see you tomorrow for your initial class with her."

For the first time in a long while, Mitko meant it when he replied, "The pleasure was mine."

six days till defiance day (53

"Not bad," Mitko whispered after a moment of contemplation. Yana had just finished Nocturne.

"It's the first one I ever learned." She clapped hands. "I'm glad you liked it."

"I did. And you? Why do you like the Nocturne?"

"I imagine spending time with my family when I play it."

"Tell me about it, please."

"Mom and Dad are together and I have a brother, too. Dad's teaching us to ski and Mom's fixing dinner in a lodge at the base of the hill. A foot of snow covers the ground. I walk in the middle. My brother pokes me with a stick and asks me to pass it forward, but I don't poke Dad because I love him. It gets dark by the time we get back to the lodge. Before we enter, Mom gives us each a cup of hot chocolate to warm our hands." Yana sounded like she was smiling. "Then we go inside and throw our frozen clothes in the laundry and bundle up in thick blankets in our jammies. Mom has started a fire. I sit close, my head on her lap, because I've missed her during the day. Dad plays Nocturne on his guitar. Then we eat and Dad stops playing from time to time to take a bite. We're all safe and we talk and we're together."

"Have you seen snow before?"

"I haven't," she said. "I imagine it's beautiful."

"I don't remember how it looked anymore, but it felt warm to the tongue. When you see snow for the first time you should try to catch a snowflake with your tongue. I'll be with you then."

"Deal," she sounded like a cat about to pounce on a sparrow. "But how do you mean you'll be with me? Will we catch the snowflakes together?"

Mitko pinched Yana's nose as if he could see it where it was, all along. "You're a natural at seeing with the heart, kid. Tell your Mom I want you to play Nocturne at The Prodigy."

"You're the best teacher I've ever had," she said then, as loud as a fireworks show, she left to give her mother the news.

Alone, Mitko walked to the water fountain in the corner of the room and drank. For some reason, Yana's company had prompted him to think of Colton. The eight-year-old student's joy next to the agony of Colton's severed sacrifice – two polar opposites that emerged side by side in his mind. Colton's daughter was called Yana, too. Could the two girls be the same person? Mitko would never forget touching Colton's tears, warm and vast and born by despair so unbeatable, it forced self-mutilation, when nothing else would do.

Then the girl... hidden behind a guarded gate. He had met her protective mother, but never the Dad. Wasn't it in the job description of fathers to look after their daughters? And if Colton were linked to the girl, as crazy as it sounded, why wasn't he with them? Why cripple himself and play hide-and-seek with a one-eared assassin, rather than hide in the ULE safe haven? What kind of man gave his hand for his daughter but refused basic help?

Mitko took a drink from the paper cup, his forehead coated with sweat. A connection between Colton and his student bordered on lunacy, but as much as logic mocked at his speculation, the inkling refused to go away. Who else could know? No one, that much was certain. Not that he'd share his intuition with either of the two or anyone else. He just wanted to help soothe their anguish, if he could.

The table shook and his paper cup fell over. The water inside spilled on the lacquered surface, Sarah had walked in. "Chopin?" she said. "Do you know how many contestants do Chopin each year? Every kid not inflicted by cerebral palsy will play the Nocturne."

"That's where her heart is," he said. Under his fingers, the spilled puddles merged in a larger one.

"Then teach her heart to be in Boulez's Second Sonata. She's practiced it for eight months."

"Yana's Nocturne technique is peculiar in ways I haven't heard in other pianists. And I mean peculiar in a good way."

"Look, Boulez is a whale to play and my daughter's performance is imperfect, I get it. But changing the piece is... unthinkable."

"I agree that if she does a half-decent job on Boulez at her age, she'll impress the judges. She might even win the Prodigy. But –"

"What else is there?"

"If you love a flower, Sarah, you don't pick it up. It will die and cease to be what you love. If you love a flower, you let it be. Love is not about possession."

She applauded, one palm clapping the other. "Spare me the poetry. I'm a bit tied up fighting off Armageddon."

"What I'm saying is –"

"If you won't teach her Boulez, we will find someone else who will, Mr. Benjamin."

"Ask her what she –"

"And that is that."

With a short nod, Mitko went to the door, fumbled for the handle and left the room.

six days till defiance day (54

Wednesday night, before meeting Yana for the second time, Colton had slept for no more than three hours. He boarded the six-am bus the next morning and sat on two seats in a single motion. Today, he wasn't interested in sitting next to anyone else other than Yana.

The daughter of his past had been an abstract image, evoking in him a ferocious amount of guilt. She'd been an icon he prayed to each night before falling asleep. Then they met and the encounter grounded his love in reality. Yana was real and seeing her, for the first time in seven years, had wiped away the doubt if his Sacrifice vote had been worth it. The bus driver announced the ULE embassy stop and Colton stood and hugged a rail to keep steady. With his good hand, he straightened the front and back of his pants and as the doors sighed open, ran toward the meeting he couldn't stop thinking about since their last time together.

By the time he made it to the conference meeting room she had beaten him there. She was wearing a green backpack. He paused to catch his breath; she didn't need to know he had run up the stairs because the elevator looked too slow.

"Did you sleep well?" he said.

"Mom says I give Sleeping Beauty a run for her crown. You need a naval battle to wake me, she says." Yana adjusted her backpack. "Why do you ask?"

"I remember otherwise when you were little." He noticed the fingers of his good hand drumming against the table's ledge like unconscious living drum sticks and stuffed them in his pocket. "You were, by far, the worst sleeper in the neighborhood."

"How do you know what I was like? I don't remember you."

"It's the biggest mistake of my life. The one mistake beyond redemption." Colton's eyes held remembrance, not reproach.

"What does that word mean?"

"It means to correct your mistake or make it right some other way."

Yana's face cleared. She was wearing blue jeans and a shirt with a neon red mushroom from an old Mario Brothers game. She took an orange from her backpack and unpeeled the skin in a continuous strip, with care uncustomary for an eight-year-old. "I spilled milk on my bed sheets once, which upset Mom. The next morning, I brought her breakfast in bed, while she slept."

"That was redemption," he said.

"Orange?" She handed him a slice. "Please, tell me more about when I was little."

He put the orange in his mouth and sucked on it, without chewing. "It was you and me, for the first eleven months of your life. Your Mom worked a lot, same as she always does. She shot you out of her body and gave you to me with one hand, while mixing an algae tube, with the other." Colton finished the slice and collected its seeds. He wanted to remember he had had an orange with Yana. "You and me. We did all right, despite the endless nights or the diapers I had no idea how to put on. One July evening, I even ran to the ER – two miles from our house – with you burning up in my arms and me wearing boxers, stubble and the weight of the world in my hands... But we did all right."

Yana wrapped her arms around her knees. "Why did I forget you, then?"

"I had to leave, so I wouldn't hurt you again."

"Fathers should protect their daughters, not hurt them."

"I wasn't a very good father."

"Am I safe with you, now?"

He waved a hand and shook his head. "When you were six months old, you cried so much, your face would turn purple. We had a coloring book at home, with ducklings. I'd show you a finished duckling first, colored in yellow then trace over a black-and-white one with my finger, as if my finger were a brush. Your eyes would blink, tiny coffee beans, and you would stop crying and take deep sighs. And you'd watch me trace the ducklings with my finger."

"Did you keep the book?"

"I lost it the night I carried you to the ER. I took it with me, so you wouldn't be scared in the hospital. I didn't take my eyes off you, but I forgot the book. And I paid the price the following months. You refused to fall asleep without the ducklings. I would pace inside our apartment with you in my hands – we'd go for miles."

"I have a piano competition in two weeks. Will you come watch me?"

Across from her, Colton breathed through the nose to collect himself. "I wouldn't miss it, patte." Then he found the courage to ask about her and Yana shared with generosity. How she always wanted to have a pony she'd call Nicholas. How she postponed pulling out her loose tooth for an extra day because she wanted to give the Tooth Fairy a full day's notice. And how she planned to marry Bobby Tober, the only boy in her class she didn't feel yucky about. He took her in, remembering the words verbatim, as if to last him another seven years. Then the door opened, "Mr. Parker," a face peeked in the frame, "two more minutes," then disappeared.

He reached over the table and caressed Yana's cheek with the outside of his hand. She didn't pull back. So this was how happiness felt like, he thought, and swallowed to unclog his throat. "Today's the last time I'll see you in a while," he said.

"That's OK. I won't be much fun until my competition is over anyway."

"I'll come to your concert wearing a bright red hat so you can spot my head in the crowd – like the mushroom on your shirt." He gave her a grin.

"What happened to your hand?" she said.

"This guy?" He raised his stump, looking at it as if it were a foreign object. "Tsk, tsk... I must have dipped my hand in invisible ink."

Yana slapped her forehead. "Invisible ink doesn't exist."

"Of course, it does. I can dip you in it sometime, holding you by the nose, so the only part of Yana you'll ever see again is this nose floating around..."

The door behind them opened again. This time the head walked in with a body attached. "Time's up, Mr. Parker."

Yana looked at the clock on the wall. "I need to go to my piano class." She headed for the door then turned. "I think you might be a good person, I will prove it to my Mom and to you."

"Eight-year-olds aren't supposed to talk like you."

"Eight-year-olds aren't supposed to grow up without their fathers, either." She waved goodbye and disappeared.

six days till defiance day (55

Colton collapsed on the mossy bridge-walk then squatted against the wall to keep out of sight. Walking through the main entrance of a hospital with a missing passport was a no-go, so he kept waiting and hiding in the shadows. As elated as he was from seeing Yana earlier in the day, the pulsating wrist had become impossible to ignore. Mitko had been right: cauterizing the stump had been a patch-up job, never meant to replace surgery. And six days later, in full capitulation to the infection, Colton saw it the same way too.

He had come to the Virginia Mason seeking the help of a certain someone he hadn't seen for more than a year. And was going to find out how she'd respond... unless Sylvya wasn't at work or had already gone home for the day. She had to be here. Otherwise, it was game over. He'd be forced to camp on this bridge for the night until the curfew crews arrested him by the morning. Then... his mind gave up, planning this far out was pointless and painful.

The winter evening was about to save Seattle from itself. The dusk embraced the city's empty bridges and their rotted foundations. It masked the air too, upgrading its smell from offensive to somewhat tolerable until the following morning. In the dark, Colton struggled making out the silhouettes leaving the Oncology ward. He dozed off then snapped awake. What if he'd missed her? The thought carried sweet resignation bordering on relief, as the stump kept throbbing in pain.

That's when he saw Sylvya step out of the revolving doors. So far, so good; he had to catch up with her, say hi and convince her to save his life, as she always had. But he couldn't move. He sat up and breathed in, once at first then twice to collect more strength, and shouted her name, "Sylvya..." Vertigo shook the world and his palm grabbed his forehead. She hadn't heard him. He sighed. Back when he was married to Sarah, he used to mock bad TV standup with a similar sigh. Tonight the joke was on him. He had to try again before she had walked out of sight... for Yana's sake.

Colton leaned on one elbow, bracing himself, in case he passed out. This was it, ladies and gentlemen, he thought, the final card-reveal at the final table. He took a breath and let out what, to him, sounded like a scream, "Help me, Sylvya..." He keeled forward and fell, unable to soften the drop. Sorry for letting you down, patte, he thought, face on the steel bridge. He tried to push up but his arms felt as strong as boiled macaroni. It was OK, he would catch his breath first then get up and find Sylvya at the metro station; even if he'd have to crawl like a two-year-old.

His body then lifted, either by the power of persuasion or by the power of God – if God hadn't packed his bags yet from this sinking planet – and Colton saw the person who did the lifting and recognized her face. He'd never seen anything more beautiful.

"What are you doing here?" Sylvya hugged him and sobbed then hugged him again.

He tried to respond but words were more work than he could afford. He tried again and this time she understood. "Don't call the cops? I won't."

She kissed his lips, washing them in tears. "I'll take care of you. But you're not allowed to pass out on me anymore. Not until I get you inside." She draped his arm over her body and stood up. Like a marionette, Colton stood up with her. He smiled.

"I will return in a minute." Sylvya looked for an acknowledgement, until his head nodded; either that or he had blacked out. With her tongue sticking out and sweat budding on her face, she steadied his body against the wall, let go and took a hesitant step back, her arms the last ones to lose contact. She touched his lips with hers, one last time, and ran toward the hospital's main entrance. Then came running back, pushing a gurney without breaking her stride. His figure was still there, where she'd left it. She collected him, as one would a child, placing his torso on the gurney first, then his legs.

Colton was breathing and, as a bonus, looked like a regular patient. She pushed her cargo toward the main entrance, the gurney's wheels rolling without a rattle. Without checking him in, she headed to a treatment room and latched a dozen IV bags into his veins.

Seattle felt like Mountain View again, and the night rain felt like a blessing.

five days till defiance day (56

The piano wept under Yana's hands. Then, without warning, a couple of notes hiccupped, tripping the follow-up ones like a domino line. Boulez's Second Sonata teetered from side to side and collapsed into a cacophony of noises. Yana hung her head. "I keep slipping up in the same spot."

"The Second is a difficult piece, kid," Mitko said. "But the good news is, you'll live longer if you learn it well."

"You're making it up."

"When our brains do something new, it takes us longer to recount what happened. It's the reason why childhood feels so long. Do something new every day and you'll slow down time."

"This is not new. I've been playing it for the last eight months."

"Tell you what: let's get you some reinforcements for this fight." Mitko brought chocolate ice cream from a conference room fridge and placed two cups with two spoons on top of the Steinway.

"About your slip... don't press, let the music come to you – it has nowhere else to go. Hold the keys firm, pause and don't let up until, one-two-three," his hand waved in the air, "the next bridge takes you over the sequence. It's about the nuance and the length of your silence...The judges might notice if you skip a few notes, but what matters is how you transition to the next D-minor and they won't score you down much if you do it well."

Yana's head dipped up and down. She sighed. Next to her, Mitko pulled a chair up and flicked off invisible dust specks from the Steinway's polished top. He put an arm around her shoulders.

"And how about a story before we move on?" By instinct, she leaned into his embrace.

"But... do we have time?" she looked at the wall-clock. "Eighteen minutes until the hour is through."

His fingers patted her shoulder. "Remember what I promised you? The bit about teaching you to see with your heart?"

She nodded again, this time with more conviction. "So in eighteen... seventeen minutes," she corrected herself after another glance at the wall, "I'll learn how to see with my heart?" Her eyes were like two lakes, one filled with excitement and one with doubt.

Mitko put a finger over his lips and leaned closer. "A promise is a promise. But only if you keep your end of the bargain."

"I won't tell a soul," she whispered, the conspiracy in her voice, as earnest as if they were discussing the disposal of a body. "I swear on Stumpy's life."

He pulled back. "Who's Stumpy?"

"My plush robot. Sometimes I take him to bed if I've had a bad day or if there's a thunderstorm outside. But I try to leave him alone at night because robots are nocturnal." She pressed her knees to her chest. "Go ahead... tell me your story."

"Once, in a country called Estonia, lived an eight-year-old boy..."

Yana interrupted. "I'm eight too."

"Yes, he was as old as you."

"I like that."

"The boy, who was as old as you, liked playing the piano as much as you do. It didn't matter if he had schoolwork to do or run chores for his Mom, he looked forward to the evenings, because that's when his teacher taught him piano." Yana shook off a yawn and tucked her hair behind her ears. "One evening, as the boy came to his teacher's apartment for a lesson, he heard loud noises. Worried, he rushed in, and in the teacher's living room, he saw a scary sight: a thief had tied the teacher and held a knife to his throat. The boy froze, not knowing what to do. Should he fight or follow the thief's orders to save the teacher's life?

"Free my teacher at once, the boy said and stomped the ground with a foot. If you let him go, I'll give you all my money. The boy emptied his pockets and a total of three dollars in coins fell on the floor between him and the thief."

"Three dollars is not a lot of money," Yana whispered.

Mitko took a bite of ice cream before continuing the story. "The thief laughed. I don't want your pitiful coins. I want your teacher's Steinway piano, there are no others like it in our town. Step away or I will slice your teacher's throat.

"The boy had to think of a solution. If I play a song, on the piano, will you let my teacher go, the boy said.

"Why would I let your teacher go because of one song, the thief said.

"Because it will be the most beautiful melody you've ever heard, the boy replied. And it will melt your heart and convince you to let my teacher keep his piano.

"The thief laughed until tears ran from his eyes. Go ahead and play, you foolish boy, he said.

"The boy sat at the Steinway and rested his fingers on the keys. He didn't know what to play. He had lied about a special melody his teacher had taught him – he knew no such thing. He closed his eyes and decided to follow his heart. The music came to him and poured out of the Steinway. The months he had spent with his teacher flashed in front of his eyes. And as he played, he decided he didn't want to impress the thief but give a gift to the teacher, a gift of thank you and goodbye. After the boy finished the thief dropped his knife and ran out of the apartment in shame. He had indeed heard the most beautiful melody in life."

Mitko cracked his back. "So, there you have it. Each time you sit at a piano, think of the boy whose music defeated a thief and play from your heart, at the piano and in life."

Yana hugged the pianist with both arms.

two days till defiance day (57

The bridge-walks swam in water because of the tears in Sylvya's eyes. Recounting the injustices of her past felt like a punch to the gut and she had to hold to a lamppost to keep steady. She was a good person – always had been. Since the age of seven, she wanted to become Cinderella when she grew up, or Sheryl Sandberg at least. But day-after-day, she had fast-forwarded to two children and a failed marriage.

Still, she held on to hope, squeezing her eyes shut each night and imagining the life the seven-year-old had planned. Sometimes the make-believe helped and the following mornings didn't feel as bad. On such days, the showers felt more refreshing and her children more precious. If only she had the courage to live this different life she imagined. And leave behind her work and the snooty boss and David's voicemails about splitting time with the kids. But she didn't and kept on living as she was. Often she hid in the hospital storage room, gasping for air, like her pulmonary patients would. The difference was the patients would recover while her affliction would remain for life.

Then Colton came, impossible to spot at first – a wreck of his own making. He seemed beaten up beyond repair but, in time, she realized he hid even deeper scars beneath the physical bruises. Her natural empathy and professional training were the first to kick in then other emotions joined. He treated her different and she loved his company though she couldn't explain why. His jokes were borderline inappropriate, but she attributed it to his bad luck and to whatever emotional saddle weighed him down. After a week, she wondered if he was the man she had dreamed of as a seven-year-old girl.

She ended up following him to Seattle and the city waltzed into her life with more grace than she thought

possible. Like a fairy Godmother, Seattle heaped on her the
Virginia Mason job and a free apartment and she often
pinched herself making sure she wasn't dreaming. One day
she walked into the Starbucks on the Fourth Avenue bridge
and Seneca, her smile clashing against the baristas' gloom,
and asked for the sweetest frozen drink on the menu. She
walked out, sucking on ice and mocha through a fat straw
and saw him, the one person among the millions she had
come here to find. Colton was sitting in the Seattle Public
Library, framed by a bay window.

At first she figured he was a ghost inside her over-
stimulated mind and kept walking. But it was Colton,
leafing through a book, at a library table. As she tiptoed
behind him, careful not to be spotted, she feared God would
hit a pause button and wake her. But God stayed put and
the world remained as she wanted. She was incapable of
defining how she felt. The closest was wishing that this
moment stretched forever without caring to miss anything
else in life. Then she saw the tremor and the veiled
annoyance in his eyes. Maybe attacking him with wet hands
was to blame – he never much cared for surprises.

Shattered... with mascara running down her cheeks,
Sylvya somehow staggered home then hid in the bathroom
for an hour. She managed to join the kids for dinner,
hurrying them to bed so she could fall apart on her own.
The following morning brought relief and a new
perspective. He must have been shocked to see the past he
had travelled so far to leave behind, catch up with him
again. Hope told her a second meeting would be different
and magical. She would show up at his apartment and he'd
invite her in. They would make sweet, passionate love
throughout the night and she'd wake in his arms the next
morning. They would go to a local bakery for a late
breakfast. He would pay the bill and insist on spending the

weekend together. Then he'd take her to the movies or rollerblading or to an ice cream spot.

But their second meeting wasn't magical. He looked so handsome but when he opened his mouth, his words thrust a dagger in her, cutting out any room for wishful interpretation. Colton didn't love her. And that was that.

Getting home was a blur. She came to her senses still dressed under the steaming shower, drowning out the pain that was devouring her whole. She didn't speak afterward – not to Dallas and Sadie, not to colleagues or patients – and her eyes kept leaking with anguish that only complete silence could befit. For a while, nothing mattered. Reviving her career didn't matter. Dallas falling in love with Seattle and asking, "Could we stay here for good, Mom, or for as long as we could stretch it?" didn't matter. Sadie being asked out by a curly-haired boy from her YMCA swimming class and skipping around the house the day he kissed her cheek didn't matter.

At the end of the week, the Chief Nursing Officer ordered Sylvya to take time off. Virginia Mason Oncology had blossomed into a higher-quality ward in the one week since she had joined and the Chief wanted the goose that laid the golden-eggs back in tip-top shape. Work could wait until her emotions unsnarled, he said, from the knots they had become. Sylvya was too tired to argue. She spent the following week in bed, with a wet ball turning inside her rib cage and stretching it end-to-end. Over time, the ball grew until Sylvya couldn't breathe. She went back to work with it spinning inside and shuffled from day to night and back to day, and learned to breathe in spurts, like an animal in heat. Then, almost two years later, when she least expected it, she saw him again...

She had heard her name come from somewhere she couldn't see. She had turned several times. Then, as she headed for the commuter station, a splash of red caught her eye. She saw a crimson bandage where a man's passport should be. Her gaze followed the arm to the torso to the face: Colton's face. He must have cut his hand to desert Defiance Day. Sylvya shook. She had never thought of him as a deserter. The man she loved was selfless. She walked to him and he grunted a sound she couldn't understand but his eyes spoke plenty.

In this moment, the wet ball inside her burst and she patted a shocked hand on her chest, as if checking for wine stains on her lab coat. She breathed in for what felt like a minute until her lungs stopped expanding, still no pain. She smiled and looked at him and saw a different person; someone whose magic over her was gone. She did kiss him, to make sure she wasn't imagining it and the ball wouldn't come back. She wasn't imagining. He was no more but another patient with a male anatomy. She ran back for a gurney, drunken by this new sense of being pain-free.

Of course, she sheltered him. He was a patient and she was a nurse with an attached Hippocratic Oath. An abandoned supply room became his recovery quarters. Brooms, paint buckets and a broken refrigerator gave way to a coil-mattress coupled with an IV stand. She stitched his stump, nerve clusters and shattered bones, then pumped him full of antibiotics and two IV bags at a time, one for each arm. When he woke, gaunt and ravenous but inflammation-free, she fed him with medicine and food. On the second day, his condition improved to patched-but-stable and he told her about an Asian woman on a mission to kill him. Sylvya listened with a smile, the wet ball inside her gone and replaced by clarity.

His story wasn't bad, but after honoring Hippocrates, she had to do her civic duty. Seattle, along with the rest of the US Territory, was bursting at the seams with deserters who cut their own hands to survive Defiance Day. These lost souls branded themselves as fugitives – refugees in their own Territory – until their inevitable capture. Police protocol called for their immediate arrest, but with jail space more scarce than beachfront property, the cops deferred the information until after the nineteenth of December when the jails throughout the Territory were guaranteed to unclog.

Sylvya punched 911 on her cell phone. An Officer Grant, with a well-trained voice, logged her report of a felon who had self-severed his passport.

two days till defiance day (58

"Mrs. Timmons," a booming voice stretched her ear, "this is the Seattle PD Chief, Natt Gurloskey."

Sylvya shifted her cellphone from one hand to the other. "How... may I help you?" Her mouth threw roadblocks between words to buy time. In her brain, she thumbed through any outstanding hiccups she had had with the law. Could it be some ancient scuffle from her Vegas days, or a permit glitch at the SeaTac airport transfer? Then Sylvya gasped... the kids, something was wrong with them.

"Are Sadie and Dallas, OK?"

On the other end, the man laughed. "This doesn't concern your children, dear. They're safe in their St. Francis School classrooms, being the good students they are."

This cop knew where Dallas and Sadie went to school. The premonition of something rotten under his laughter made Sylvya sit down. At least the kids were safe. She could handle whatever else they threw at her.

"I'm calling in response to your report about Mr. Parker's felony and current whereabouts."

A second wave of relief, "I reported his crime a few minutes ago."

"We owe the world to citizens like you." A rich cough rearranged pieces of saliva along Gurloskey's throat. "You just moved to Seattle and are contributing already. If I may say so, I love you, Mrs. Timmons." The rotten smell grew thicker. "Anyway, I need to let you know what's expected from you for the success of operation Jailbird."

"You've given this arrest a codename?" she said. The Seattle PD had too much free time.

"Affirmative. I've also commissioned two prowlers with Special Ops personnel to depart to Virginia Mason as we speak. I will accompany them, too." The cop sounded like a six-year-old discovering a coveted gift on Christmas morning. Such glee, hiding in severity's clothing, was out of place in the voice of a cop about to capture a fugitive. "My personnel are authorized to apprehend Mr. Parker dead or alive. Your task is to keep the target at the current premises at all costs. Otherwise, our mission would face incalculable risks."

"I understand," she said and closed her eyes.

"If the target is not at the current location when we arrive, we'll presume you've become his accomplice. But if we bundle this cat you'll get all the recognition you deserve." The cop snorted like an animal about to be fed. "Questions?"

She shook her head in silence.

"Mrs. Timmons?"

"No questions."

"Keep him nice and tight for us, then." He hung up.

Fresh ice heaped on top of the old ice inside of Sylvya's chest, like a freezer overdue for service. She had fulfilled her duty and saved his life for the second time, when the rest of the world wouldn't offer him as much as a handshake. And the world had been right. His cowardice had killed her love for him, along with a part of her identity. The Mountain View Sylvya – who had fallen in love with Colton and fought round-the-clock for his life and preempted his every condition before it happened – had died. Duty and a smattering of repulsion had taken over. She hated Defiance Day deserters – end of story.

On the bright side, she only had about an hour left to endure. The Johnny-on-the-spot cops would purge him from her life and she'd go back to building a home in her beautiful new city.

She felt like she had lost fifty pounds of heartaches. Deep inside, she felt satisfaction, too.

part three (sarah perkins

two days till defiance day (59

With each twist of the road, Colton's head hit against the prowler's window. He sat in his own waste, his arms cuffed at the elbows. He had expected they'd get him; they did in his nightmares. But reality had turned out worse.

He had just sat down in the bathroom and let loose when the first gas canister had hit. His eyes had switched off and he had reeled sideways, slapping the floor with his one hand to avoid falling down. His stump, by instinct, had shielded his burnt eyes. A second canister had rolled in. His muscles had locked. Then the armored men had stormed in and a kick to the abdomen had depleted whatever oxygen was left in his lungs. Invisible arms, more than two, had held him down and cuffed his elbows behind his back.

Natt's voice from the front of the prowler brought him back to the present. "Are you there, Ms. Gao?" The cop was on the phone. "I have delicious news... I have him... The one-handed freak... Yes... He's been in Virginia goddamn Mason, all along..." Natt was cackling. "How about we do one better? There's a condemned warehouse on South Lander and Utah in a tiptop shape. You can take your sweet time there, with a warm roof over your head... Yes... You bet... See you there in two hours." He hung up and turned to Colton.

"At last, Mr. Parker. We have some time to bond on the way to your final destination. And I do mean – final destination..." Natt's booming chuckle drowned the end of the sentence. "You comfortable back there?" The Seattle PD Chief wrinkled his nose. "You've developed a bit of an odor, friend," he said and raised the acrylic divider between the front and back seats. Then he turned on the intercom, his voice arm-wrestling with the static. "Better... Did my boys catch you in the act? I apologize for them goofs, we'll clean you up. Not to worry."

Colton's head kept bouncing against the window.

"Tell me..." Natt kept on, "how does it feel, to survive us this close to the end? You proud? Disappointed?" More laughter filled the intercom, followed by the clapping of a hand against a leg. "Got to level with you, I thought you might pull it off. But look ... I thank God, or whoever else is running the show up there, that I got you. I'd drink to it if I weren't driving."

"Why..." Colton slurred the words, his tongue, thick and foreign. "Why did you do it?"

"Come again, sunshine?" Natt said.

"Did she promise to spare your life?" Colton swallowed.

"What do you care?" Natt's face kept smiling, but his voice had grown thinner. Colton coughed, discharging a fresh column of drool from his face. "She told you she'd let you live, did she?"

"It's none of your business."

"I'd turn this car around if I were you and drive in the opposite direction until you run out of gas. And when you do, I'd get out of the car and run." Colton stared at Natt's face in the rearview mirror. "Granted, fleeing will buy you a few extra hours of life, tops. Not much of an improvement, really but..." Another coughing fit swallowed Colton's words.

"If your hash-brown brain doesn't work too well because of the shit fumes, let me break it down for you." Natt rubbed the bridge of his nose. "Eat, drink and be merry, Colton Parker. For in two hours, you die." The intercom clicked off, taking with it the static and the conversation.

two days till defiance day (60

Purple dusk waited inside the warehouse on South Lander. With elbows cuffed behind his back, Colton entered first, stumbling over the threshold. He teetered from side to side then stood straight. His eyes, still defective from the tear gas, tried to cut through the surroundings and focused on a solitary column of light framed by the open door and the setting sun outside. The rest of the warehouse was steady black. Natt's pushing from behind had stopped. The cop, too, was busy learning to see in the dark.

The large warehouse was bone dry. A wide ledge rose ten feet from the ground to form a complete loop along the interior walls. Scattered hay and insulation gave proof that someone had filled the cracks on walls and windows to keep out the moisture and any prying eyes. A box, as tall as an airport x-ray scanner, hulked a dark silhouette in the center of the room. The rest of the space seemed empty, other than a floor lamp and a couple of folding chairs. Colton wasn't done examining the porta potty, but his peripheral vision registered movement and he recognized her in an instant — despite the sting of the teargas and having seen her just once before.

"Mrs. Gao," the cop boomed from behind. "Look who the cat dragged in." He slid the front door almost shut, reducing the column of outside light to the size of a two-by-two, then shoved Colton forward with rediscovered vigor.

"Welcome to my humble abode, Mr. Parker." Li-Mei's voice echoed in the open hall, bouncing off walls. "I've missed you since we saw each other last."

"You've changed some," Colton said. "No longer the frail orphan from that Woodinville bar."

"That frail woman had the lifespan of a gnat: she was born, served and died," Li-Mei said. "Like the rest of us are bound to do. Only she did it all in a day." She switched on the floor lamp, illuminating the two chairs and the three people, as if on a theatric stage inside a dark performance hall. Natt pushed Colton into one of the chairs then plopped in the other one. The cop exhaled like a train-whistle and lifted his hand in a high-five invitation for the Chinese woman. She ignored him without looking.

Colton blinked at the light. "You're the best at what you do, Gao. I'm surprised I lasted this long."

"Then why did you even resist?"

"I already know what giving up feels like – I wanted to see what happened if I didn't." He spat on the dusty floor. "I also thought you'd do your own bidding without relying on the likes of him." Colton gestured toward the cop. "I'm sorry I couldn't protect Yana from both of you."

"She's such a worthy child, isn't she?" Li-Mei said and through the dusk, Colton heard a smile in her reply. Outside, the sun was tumbling behind the horizon.

"I should thank you for helping me realize how much she means to me," Colton said. He looked ready to keel over. "Protecting her from you felt good. I should have done it ages ago. You gave me hope – a purpose – unlike before, when I was wading through each hopeless day and falling asleep at night, for no other reason but self-preservation. In other words, life's been all right since you showed up, even if you've made it unbearable."

"I wish we'd met earlier, Parker," she said. A draft of air squeezed through the open front door, picked up her jet-black hair and, after toying with it for a moment, dove into some insulation on the floor. "Maybe things would have ended different then. Maybe you would have been on my side of the river... For some time to come."

"Call me crazy," Colton blinked off the sweat trickling over his eyebrows, "but I think you're hitting on me." He coughed what was meant to sound as laughter on a better day. "A hit woman, who's hitting on me. Sorry to burst your bubble, and grant you, not my smartest move given the circumstances, but you're not my type."

"You're about to die, you realize that?"

"Too flat-chested, I'm afraid. Which reminds me, I've been wondering when's the last time you got laid?"

"My intimate life is of no concern to you."

"Killing me won't slay your demons, Gao. It might slow them up for a day. Two, if you killed the cop. What then?"

"I'm so sick of you," Gurloskey jumped in, "and your monkey face." He cocked his gun and shoved it against Colton's right temple. "Say another word and I'll splatter your brain on the floor."

"Stay out of this." Li-Mei's words froze the cop in place then he shriveled back in his chair. She turned to Colton. "Twice you've caught me unprepared, Parker. First you survived our encounter then cut off your passport. Fewer targets than you could ever imagine have earned the right to see me twice. You have... and to reward your tenacity, I'll let you choose how you want to die."

"Should I send you a thank you card for the privilege?"

"Choosing your death is the finest compliment I could give you. So your two options are living less and dying without pain or living a few hours longer and dying in agony. It's the same coin really, with opposite sides. Option one puts you inside this portable sauna room." She pointed at the box in the middle of the warehouse. "We'll click the heat dial to two-hundred degrees and, ten minutes later, we'll take you out dead. Or option two," she raised two fingers like a victory sign, "will pump enough Ricin in your veins to kill you in twelve hours."

She started a lap around Colton's chair. "These are tonight's menu specials. Given how bad I am at small talk, I should warn you that spending twelve hours in my company is the main problem with option two. Plus, you strike me as someone who prioritizes quality of life over quantity. But... I've given you my word and will grant you either choice."

"Why not shoot my face, like fatty here suggested?"

Li-Mei leapt in the air, kicking Colton's chest with both feet, a move he would have failed to dodge even with healthy eyes and untied arms. His chair crashed backward and threw him to the ground. When he opened his eyes, he saw her towering above. She stepped on his ribcage, on the same place she had kicked, and leaned in so he could see her face.

"Wasting time is useless, you see. No one's coming to save you." She caressed his face and parted his hair down the middle then nodded her approval at the result. "If shooting you was an option, I would have paid money to do it... You have ten seconds. Unless the next words out of your mouth give me a preference, you'll get the sauna room. Now..." she paused, "I'm listening."

Lying on his back, Colton coughed away pepper spray. "Sauna room," he said, "and I'll see you in hell real soon."

"Despite the color commentary, I will focus on your guidance." Li-Mei grabbed Colton by the leg and dragged the bundle of man and chair toward the large box. "You'll be sitting inside. Asking you to burn while standing up would be barbaric; there could only be one Joan of Arc, after all."

A trail of splintered wood, like a brown chalk line, left by the chair dragging against the floor was the last image Colton remembered before passing out.

fourteen years and one hundred forty four days till defiance day (61

It was Li-Mei's last day in Jenli, the type of day you'd read about years later. The rain pelted the submissive ground for hours and the air hung heavy with retribution.

She stood at the smudged mirror and funneled her arms through the sleeve holes. The black and green tunic – as narrow as a bowtie at the neck – cascaded from her collarbone to her ankles. She put a bamboo belt on, then washed her face, the water hugging the peach fuzz of her cheeks. Li-Mei had grown up. Taxi had come to her several times today, his head nudging her feet, until she whipped him with a look, both long and impatient. Distractions and cuddling were moot. Today, Jenli was cowering under the weight of something dark.

She walked into the square, bustling with Servants in tight foot traffic, like a human version of a busy anthill. Were they drawn by the heavy rain or was it something else? Her presence brought about an instant hush that swallowed the crowd like a glove. The branches of an old oak tree in the square creaked, as if in conversation with the falling raindrops. Her tunic billowed, impregnated by the wind, as she stood unmoving under the cutting sheets of rain and scanned the crowd, one face after another. Without breathing, they looked away, as if the girl were a young Medusa.

Li-Mei was about to turn a page. But first came this last trial on this last day. Then Jenli would let her go. She was lucky to have made it this far. Her butchered scalp, broken arms and amputated ear stood silent witnesses to the price the six-year-old had paid to reach age thirteen.

He appeared in the crowd and, in an instant, she knew he was it. Her final challenge: the price to pay to continue living beyond Jenli. The crowd withdrew from the center of the square and he stumbled forward in the open space, like a rock left behind by the departing tide.

"Do you remember me?" Li-Mei said. "I'm the girl whose soul you crushed."

The Purple Servant smiled. The last time his grin held terror. Today, she thought she saw a flash of cowardice in it. His voice shook in the wet wind. "I did what I had to do. And now I will finish it."

"No," she said and her face twisted. "Today, I'll become a part of you, Servant, as big as you have been of me." She caressed the right side of her head, where her ear once was and spread arms through the rain, like two waterfalls. Then she soaked the downpour, motionless, as the water gushed in her eyes and clobbered her skin. "I never lose, Servant," she shouted. "No matter what you throw at me. You hear?"

She ran toward him and he waited, with legs deep in the boiling rainwater and knees bent. He swung hard for her, with the kinjal, but she slid between his planted legs, at the same time as a flash of thunder tore through the sky. Her fists shot up, two pistons cloaked in skin, smashing against the Servant's groin. He collapsed to his knees, chin tucked in, as if praying to the gods of pain to let go. He shuffled around on his knees to protect his back. Too late... Like a shadow she rose behind him and struck his torso twice more, breaking two of his ribs. The Purple Servant keeled, gasping for air and clutching where she had hit.

Li-Mei put a foot on his back and pushed, sending him splashing into the mud then jumped in the air and landed on the back of his ankles, where the fibulas connected with the heels. Both sets of bones shattered, the left one broken by her for the second time.

"Get me a rope," she shouted. The crowd stood stunned by her efficiency. A moment earlier, these two had risen against each other and now the battle seemed done. The rope appeared and Li-Mei tied it into a hangman's noose that she secured to a branch of the oak in the square. The rain was letting up and turning to a mist, and the silent crowd watched, pregnant with morbid fascination. She dragged him to the tree, then hit his throat with a karate chop and slid the noose around his neck. The Purple Servant left the ground and burrowed fingers under the noose in a desperate barrier between neck and rope. Li-Mei kept pulling, hand over hand, and the rope, heavy with rain, swayed like a line swallowed by a wounded marlin. His breaths whistled in and out: hard air dotted by gurgling. She held on and waited. He waited too, looking at her, his palms under the noose, precious breaths inching into his throat.

Then she let go. The Servant fell down in a heap of coughs and again, she kicked his back. "You've taught me well," she said from behind and put her foot on his shoulder blade. The sound of his shoulder breaking filled the square. She broke his other shoulder next.

Li-Mei took the rope and pulled again. This time, he offered no resistance and rose with arms dangling like empty laundry. He looked at his executioner and whispered "Vaya Con Dios, young one." Then the rope ran out of coil and Li-Mei's next pull propelled the man upwards, disconnecting him from Jenli's muddy square. He kicked three times, lost control of his bowels and died. When he touched the ground next, the Purple Servant was a lifeless body.

two days till defiance day (62

Sylvya laid face down on Colton's makeshift mattress and inhaled. Mixed with his scent were the foreign smells of the mute commandos and their Police Chief. She hadn't said a word when they had cuffed him or when he had screamed they'd kill him because he had sacrificed for his daughter or when he had gone limp, his rage breaking in sputtering wails.

If they had come and dragged him out of her life, like she wanted, why did justice feel so hollow? She massaged her temples in a useless attempt to shake the feeling she had done a low deed. Was she going through a letdown after achieving her goal? And was it true he was trying to save the life of his daughter instead of deserting Defiance Day?

Her gut felt full of lead and her ears buzzed. She looked around the empty room, like a general surveying a battlefield littered with the corpses of the men she had sent to die. What had she done? Had she betrayed and killed him? She did love Dallas and Sadie, what mother wouldn't, but a life without Colton wasn't worth it. She had tried living that way for years and was not going to go back. On autopilot, she took a fistful of Ketamine syringes from the controlled-substance lockbox and rushed out of Virginia Mason.

She was flying through downtown at forty over the speed limit. The cops, by a miracle, had not yet arrested her for reckless driving, as she barreled toward the building, which should have done the arresting. She saw no other choice but to undo this. Please, God, she was praying without knowing why. As a nurse, she had witnessed too many deaths of people who didn't deserve to die and was convinced that if God existed, he had the ethics of an alley cat. She prayed anyway, to arrive safe to the Seattle Police Headquarters and it looked like God was answering by getting rid of the cops along the way.

As she got closer, Sylvya downshifted and headed for the back entrance – not even God could eliminate all cops in the front of a cop station. In the backstreet, two prowlers idled with their stoplights bathing the night in red. She held her face while her lips whispered to her unhearing ears, "Focus. Focus. Focus."

The prowlers took off before she could park and she jerked forward to keep up. She didn't ask herself why or how a green Jetta would look following two police cars or what distance to keep to remain unnoticed. There was no time for such details. She had minutes to go until curfew, when invisible choppers with thermal sensors would crisscross the sky and arrest her on the spot if they felt like it. She bet that Colton was inside one of the two cars and clung onto that bet as the only information with substance. The prowlers merged on the Fourth Avenue suspension bridge and kept driving until Seattle's downtown bridges turned into suburban streets and then a two-lane road.

At a red light, the cars stopped. Then at the following green, one took a left and the other drove forward. The Jetta stood motionless, Sylvya's muscles were paralyzed by the irreversible present. She had to choose... She stepped on the gas pedal. Nothing. Then took a breath and pushed again. The Jetta winked forward, then stopped. In day traffic, this kind of driving would have gotten her rear-ended. Instead, the night took it in with patience. She had to choose... And standing still was the wrong answer. Sylvya's foot went for the pedal again and her hands steered to the left. This was it, she had made a choice and collected her random-pick lottery ticket.

Empty streets stretched ahead. She drove and cried, quiet sobs at first then loud, almost screaming, in chorus with the revving engine. How long had she stayed at that light? Half a minute or a full one? The sweat on her back pushed through her shirt and her legs shivered, frozen with the tension of facing the truth. The prowler was lost and no amount of driving would help her catch up. By taking that left at the light she had pointed back to the city, while the other car, with Colton inside was well on its way to some far-away detention center.

Sylvya was driving through streets and suspension bridges at ninety miles per hour, the buildings flying by, blurred like in a racing video game. This was the moment preceding a calamity, which afterwards people would replay in their minds, with the realization their lives had changed forever. Pull over and live, her common sense told her, stop tempting the thermal sensors and a future of unending what-ifs. Yet she kept driving because even if the physical catastrophe of plunging into a building or being shot down by a chopper hadn't yet happened, she had already crossed the mental point of no return. She had lost, without a mulligan to save her. Why worry about a carnal disaster when the bigger one had already struck? Her head rested on the steering wheel and her shoulders rose and fell, like pistons of an engine propelled by sorrow beyond description. She floored the gas pedal.

"Please, help me God," Sylvya whispered, lifted her head and saw the oncoming side of a high-rise at a fast-approaching T-section. In self-preservation, she took a sharp turn then regretted it the next instant. Did she seek salvation or not? Her face firmed and, with a made up mind, she guided the bulleting Jetta. No more swerving... the next T-section would be her last. She saw a "Dead End" sign and turned. No more mistakes. Death grinned at her then extended a bony handshake, as Sylvya closed eyes again and leapt off the ledge of the world. But in that moment, as her toes separated from the edge, she saw the prowler. It was parked on the sidewalk of an intersection, the last one before the dead end.

Sylvya slammed on the breaks and turned the steering wheel. To think she could avoid impact was to laugh in the face of at least twenty different laws of physics. The Jetta tumbled sideways, like a clumsy drunk, four tires going airborne prior to impact, and smashed into a boarded-up beige building.

Sylvya clasped Death's expecting hand with both palms and commenced introductions. She swore she could see the airbag deploy, millions of talcum particles exploding everywhere. They danced, like liberated snowflakes in a December nor'easter, as she had once seen in a TV documentary recorded before she was born. Then for some reason, Death pulled out of the handshake.

The outside noise poured into Sylvya's ears and her old life, the one from before the crash, snapped into place. She surveyed the damage. The front of the Jetta had collapsed like a giant ice-cream cone with her, a vanilla scoop, sitting in the middle. She attempted to move, starting with her toes. As far as her brain told her, they wiggled fine.

The prowler's hazard lights blinked a hundred feet up the street. Hope, the most stubborn of all emotional weeds, pushed roots inside her heart. If the cop car was here, maybe Colton was too. Maybe he was alive. But first she had to get out of the scrap pile. She pushed against the driver's door, but it would not budge. She tried a second time and a third – it refused to open. She looked around the car again. Option two was to exit through the windshield, which was no longer there. Sylvya could march a squad of cheerleaders through that hole, as long as she could free her legs. She tucked them and, thanking a God she had converted to in the last ten minutes, she twisted.

Each pull bit into her flesh with teeth of glass and jagged metal. She felt something above her left knee tear, followed by pain and the sticky trickle of warm blood. Her legs had to make it, at least until she found Colton. Afterward, she could collapse legless and bloodless for all she cared. She turned in the driver's seat, first to one side then the other then lying on her stomach, and pulled an inch with each rotation.

Ten minutes later, she had broken free. She pressed her bloody knees to her chin. Bleeding gashes, the largest one on her left thigh, and swollen bruises covered her legs. She patted them down, from ankle to hip and thanked her new celestial friend once again. In her professional estimate, she had suffered no broken bones and could cope with the pain for the next hour, driven by adrenaline alone. Then all bets were off. She crawled through the shattered windshield, bloody feet negotiating the carpet of broken glass until she stood on the sidewalk.

She ran toward the prowler's blinking lights, reached the car and stuck to it, palms and wild-eyed face pressed against the glass, looking inside and remembering to breathe. No luck – the one-way windows showed the reflection of her face and nothing more. She went for the passenger door and it swung open with a muted whoosh, revealing the car's interior. The smell of leather greeted her, mixed with the smell of human waste and blood. She placed both knees on the back seat and leaned in. The prowler, reminiscent of a soccer-mom-mobile, swallowed her up to the bare ankles. There was no one inside, yet she wanted out in an instant, maybe because of what she imagined they must have done to him there. Then she saw it and took a step back: Colton's suede jacket was in the front seat.

Sylvya fell to her knees. She had chosen the right car and had found him.

fourteen years and one hundred forty three days till defiance day (63

Li-Mei tilted the alarm clock to see the time better. The morning flooded her room with messy light, reflecting off the puddles yesterday's downpour had left outside. Her head hummed with the remote murmur that would blossom, nine times out of ten, into a pounding headache. Through the night she had checked the time every few minutes. It was six-am at last and she had pushed through.

A notice had appeared under the door last night. At first, she refused to believe it. What hadn't she done? For all she knew, the Purple Servant was still hanging in the square: the end to all tests and all battles. She was supposed to report back the following morning with packed bags. But last night, as she was heading for the shower – she had never killed a person before and her body hurt to the bone – she saw the paper slip.

She took her time turning around and covering the distance between the bathroom's tiled floor and the front door. It made no sense to rush. No matter how fast she opened the door, the carrier of slips always disappeared without a trace. In the beginning, she would check behind corners, run around the building and waited for him by the door, but had never caught a glimpse. For a short while, she thought the slips were a game of hide-and-seek. It wasn't a game. Some slips were explicit: "Battle against seven Servants at nine-am tomorrow in the square." She'd show up and they would beat her teeth in, then she'd crawl home, hoping the next slip would wait until she had the chance to heal some. As she grew stronger and refined her combat style, the losing slowed and stopped altogether. Consequent groups of Servants would find themselves knocked out with concussions and sprains. On principle, she stayed away from spilling blood or breaking limbs. Sometimes, she would defy the slips and skip the encounter to test the system but without exception, her opponents would find her, always more numerous and always carrying weapons. So it paid to do as she was told.

But the slips weren't always appointments. Sometimes they would lecture her: "Be true to your courage," or "Remain vigilant and pure." Nothing happened on days following such brainteasers... with two big exceptions. Two slips announcing: "Prepare for tomorrow's reckoning," had preceded both encounters with the Purple Servant. Last night's slip read "Save Taxi."

Under the hot shower she hoped it was a lecture slip... it had to be. Throughout the years, the Jenli system of drills and classes and slips had been blind to Taxi's existence... until last night. She considered locking him in her room, checking out alone and coming back for him before leaving. But how could she, after this slip? She'd never let anything bad happen to him. "You're coming with me," she said and opened the door. Enticed, he bolted out.

Li-Mei locked her room one last time and turned around. The world was wet and shiny from yesterday's rain, with the morning sun ricocheting from the pavement and the grass. By sheer solidarity, such days were meant to keep harm at bay. Or was it a decoy? She held the door handle to steady herself.

Taxi was hard to find because of the glare but she heard him shuffling ahead through the grass. His barometer would sense danger long before she could, so his enthusiasm helped ease her nerves. Maybe the paranoia was in her head? She doubted it, but who was she to question hope.

She headed for the square, the destination of whatever was in store. Taxi, still giddy with the morning, paused at every puddle and shiny smell along the way. She inhaled the wet air and the wind filled her nostrils with pinpricks. She was thankful to be alive. A glorious feeling that didn't discriminate between a gifted athlete or a legless cripple. Or a thirteen-year-old girl and her dog, excited to start the rest of their lives. Then the wind threw in her face the scent of sweat and leather. She saw them surrounding the square from all sides, in no apparent hurry. They wore purple overcoats, as if paying homage to their comrade she had killed. Li-Mei hadn't seen these men in Jenli – dark men with the rugged skin that only the sun of open horizons could forge. They formed three lines around her. She counted fifty of them.

"This village is Jenli," she said. "You may stay if you come in peace."

One of them stepped forward. "We come in peace to everyone but you, Li-Mei Gao."

Taxi arrived by her side, his rapture with the beautiful morning forgotten. "You've come here in error," she said. "The Purple Servant was the final test."

Without a reply, ten of the men attacked. The others fell back, in the absurd scenario that she survived the initial assault. With an elbow sweep, Li-Mei broke the nose of a six-foot tall Mongol whose face was covered with tattoos. Then, with a sidekick, she crushed the jugular of a turban-wearing mulatto. The other eight attackers flanked her, pummeling her feet with long bamboo sticks. She evaded the first dozen hits with high jumps but as they kept coming, both the hits and the men, she fell down, her heels littered with cuts. The rest was a travesty. Four men, each holding an arm or a leg, pinned her to the ground. The end. Her earlier pledges of unending resistance seemed like a lifetime ago. So be it. She owed it to herself to regroup and collect her wits. She sought Taxi with her eyes. He was dazed, too, entangled in a mesh and trying to chew his way to freedom. The heavy rope damaged his gums more than his teeth damaged the rope, but he pressed on, and would have broken free if the men had left him unattended. Their intentions were different. One of them threw him in a sack and tied it to the branch where the Purple Servant had hung the previous day.

Li-Mei looked at the sun, so inviting before, yet unwarming now. Two birds chasing each other scuffled in the air above and danced on, discussing something important. Her ribcage rang with pain. Someone had just stabbed her right side, above the kidney. "Are you prepared to die?" said the man who had addressed her before. A blade, dripping with her blood, hovered an inch from her chin.

"You don't scare me." She thumped the ground with a fist in the most movement afforded by the men holding her down. This new Purple Servant – she realized there would always be a new one, no matter how many she killed – leaned over her head. A mask hid his nose and mouth. His eyebrows formed furry upside-down grins and the mask over his month puffed and fell with each breath. She cracked a thin smile. If this was the view that preceded death then the act itself couldn't be that bad.

"This is the sword that will take your life," he said, "a weapon superior to your entire being." The blade swung above her face. "Observe its unremarkable steel." His eyes moved from her to the sword, and back. "All your hopes, all the roads you've taken, will end with this blade. You've marched toward its steel since the day you were born. Take a moment and welcome it."

Li-Mei sensed the sword split her stomach apart, the shearing of muscles and nerves. White snowflakes exploded above her eyes but didn't fall because it wasn't snowing. Blood gathered, hot and sticky, in her belly button then spilled over her sides. She closed her eyes. Keeping them open was useless because the snowflakes had blanketed her vision white. In a way, this new Purple Servant was right: she was thankful to know the blade that would kill her. Humans were hard to kill – their deaths took time. It was right they understood what was going on. The searing pain burned on as the blade sunk deeper in her stomach, pausing its slow descent once and again then resuming.

The voice of the new Purple Servant came in waves. "Welcome it and claim your place among the souls who fell to this steel. Unless..." he paused and she knew she didn't want to hear him again. She didn't want to hear anything. Please, push the blade in and cut the theatrics, she thought, but he continued. "Unless you think I should give you a chance."

Her eyelids rose halfway. The sky seemed brighter and with a resolution several times sharper than what she remembered. "Take your chance and shove it..." she wanted to say. Instead of words, blood trickled out of her mouth.

"I know." His voice sounded like the voice of a smiling man but the eyes above the mask remained cold. "Isn't hope wonderful? We can't quit it, even if it quits us. Even with a sword stuck in our gut, we cling to it. I'll give you one chance to live."

Someone thrust a kinjal in her hand and the man who sat on that arm pressed her fist against the ground with doubled strength.

For a moment, Li-Mei considered fighting through the fifty men, but dismissed the thought. Instead, her head fell to one side. A sack sat a foot away from her face. A Servant cracked it open and inside she saw Taxi, his front legs tied together. He lay on his side too and his eyes blinked to adjust to the bleached morning. Then he saw her and barked once, with unmissable joy. His voice filled the air and made everything OK for a moment.

The new Purple Servant crouched between her and the dog. "How does it feel to have a second shot at life?" he said. "Wait... Don't answer or I might reconsider. The sword that's tearing your abdomen is in my hand, but the knife that could save your life is in yours."

Taxi had drawn closer, his hind legs paddling inside the bag. She raised her neck to see him better - the tarp over his torso lay flat. He had covered about a foot, leaving a bloody trail in his wake, bright against the gray square pavement. She closed her eyes and when they opened, Li-Mei was crying for the first time in her life. Her neck swung around looking for the new Purple Servant and her hand squeezed the kinjal until her fingernails bled. "What did you do to him? I'll kill you and everyone else you brought along; one by one. I promise."

"Honesty is the purest gift I have for you," he said. "Maybe the second purest after death. Your abdomen is pouring blood. And at this rate, you'll die in minutes." Then he looked at the Shiba and shook his head with concern that almost seemed genuine. "Poor Taxi – broken pelvis and a cut-off tail. I guarantee he won't survive the blood loss." The new Purple Servant leaned and caressed her hair. She pulled away from his hand. "Your dog is gone, but if you kill him before he dies, I'll spare your life. Look at my men, if it helps you, study their faces and, years from now, come after us to claim revenge. Or leave them out of it and come after me. Break my pelvis to get even and watch me bleed to death. But first, you'll have to kill your dog to save him from his pain."

Li-Mei's tears spilled down the sides of her head. She turned away from the Servant and looked at the sky. Taxi's nose had almost reached the fingers of her hand. She screamed at the clouds and wished for death. She strained, as if giving birth and emptied every breath from her lungs then raised her stomach against the blade, begging the steel to sink deeper. Another inch should be enough. More men fell upon her, pushing her torso to the ground.

She inhaled through clenched teeth then sobs ruptured her breathing into hiccups. She felt like a rebellious mare who had run to the ends of the earth, only to find out that the saddle remained on her back. The sensation of defeat poured into her chest with pain that made her minced abdomen feel like a paper cut in comparison.

She had fought against Jenli and landed her punches as hard as she could for longer than she could remember. But Jenli had come back stronger after each blow she gave it, claiming her with a bond she couldn't break. In return, the least she could do was be its loyal daughter.

Her brain registered Taxi's tongue licking her fingers. He had reached her palm, at last. How long ago, she couldn't be certain. She squeezed the kinjal and lifted her hand and sunk the blade in Taxi's neck. He didn't have time to react. His tongue licked her fingers one more time, in a mechanic sequence that took his brain a second longer to process. His eyes stayed fixed on her face.

The Servants loosened their grip, the blade exited her stomach and pungent oils took its place. The last thing Li-Mei saw before the blood loss extinguished her consciousness was Taxi's eyes. They had on them his last sentiment before death took his soul from his body: his eyes were full of love for her.

two days till defiance day (64

Sylvya had almost found him and it was time to tune in to the Get-a-Grip channel. She counted to a long thirty. On the job, she had seen how doctors who panicked in the face of urgency lost every time. She breathed in and out through her nose, closed her eyes and as much as she itched to rush into whatever came next, forced another thirty out of her.

The first item on the agenda had to be to find her bearings. She opened her eyes and located the Jetta, a folded green accordion in the distance, then looked around. She had to be in Seattle's SoDo district somewhere - at a higher elevation than the flood line. Sylvya catalogued the string of buildings up and down the street to decide which one would make a good holding cell for a felon. She had no clue. Nursing school hadn't taught her how to deal with cops and Special Ops teams, unless they were bed-ridden and in a coma.

Across the prowler, a two-floor structure with its front door cracked open, beckoned her to take a peek. Her hands hugged her sides and she took two steps forward and shivered in the night breeze. What if someone stood on guard behind that door? Could she take them on? She became aware of how unfit she was for a physical confrontation in her scrubs. She had to go for stealth over brute force, which meant getting in through a side entry.

Sylvya walked around to the back of the building where the shadows were darker and undisturbed by the blinking orange from the street side. She stretched a hand and rested her fingertips on the porous back wall then walked in a straight line. Her hand traced the wall, until bouncing against something wet and metallic: an evacuation ladder. She looked up, but the black sky hid how high the ladder rose. It didn't really matter. She grabbed the steel with both hands and climbed, placing a foot on each rung then bringing her other foot level. As she went up, she examined the surrounding wall and came across what felt like a window. Sylvya flicked the glass with a finger to check for cracks; it was solid and large enough for her to squeeze through, but after several minutes she hadn't figured out how to get it open.

She climbed two more rungs and, with a swing of her right foot, kicked through the glass. The window broke with a noise that, to her, sounded as deafening as a fire alarm. She waited for a reaction from inside but other than warm air billowing from the broken opening, the black silence continued to hold the world like a cocoon. Sylvya pried the frame clean of loose shards, which she placed in the side pockets of her nurse gown – she'd rather swallow the glass than make more noise by throwing the pieces away – then poked her head through the frame and heard muffled voices from inside.

She swung her right leg over the windowsill. Smaller leftover shards bit into her thigh as she shifted weight. She inhaled and lurched forward, hoping the glass wouldn't cut too deep. She touched a ledge on the other side and padded around on what felt like a metallic plate. She tumbled over the windowsill and the plate accepted her full weight without a creak. An orb of feeble light coming from below grabbed her attention. She peeked over the ledge and pressed palms against her face to suppress a scream. Colton sat in a chair. Alive. The cop sat next to him and a woman paced about in a way that left no confusion she was in charge.

Lying as low as she could manage, Sylvya shrunk behind the metal ledge. None of the three people below seemed aware of her presence. Colton and the woman were talking, and the policeman was listening. The words "quantity of life" and "fast death" reached Sylvya. A loud crack, something wooden against something concrete, shot up and she heard the woman's metal falsetto: "You have ten seconds. Unless the next words out of your mouth give me a preference..." She had heard enough. Colton was right – she had delivered him to people bent on taking his life, unless she could do something to stop them.

Sylvya patted over the Ketamine syringes nestled in the front pocket of her scrubs. There were four of them. She took a syringe in each hand and pushed their plungers until two wisps of liquid shot into the air. Cocked and ready. She crept along the metal ledge, stopping above a large insulation clump next to the three people below. The woman was dragging Colton by the leg and the cop was sitting sideways. He turned and saw Sylvya, his mouth forming a circle. It was time.

She jumped with a syringe in each hand, like a surgeon entering a life-saving procedure. She landed hard, the insulation underneath her too shallow to cushion the fall. Pain inside her right leg bleached the surroundings for a moment and her body rolled over the floor, grinding one of the syringes in her hands and the two in her pocket into glass and tranquilizer fluid. Sylvya stood up, reeling with the pain in her leg and hobbled forward. A few yards separated her from the cop, the woman, and the love of her life, who she would never let go again. The woman turned, bewilderment painted on her face. The cop, a polar opposite, observed the attack frozen in his chair. Sylvya got to him first, the flesh of his neck gobbling the needle of her only remaining syringe. She pushed the plunger, screaming like a gladiator who had felled an enemy to gain her life, then pulled the spent syringe, its needle dripping cop blood, and turned to the woman.

Sylvya tomahawked her hand forward, gripping the syringe with a full fist. The Asian parried the attack then grabbed Sylvya's hand and broke it at the wrist. She kept kicking Sylvya's doubled-over body until the nurse stopped moving.

two days till defiance day (65

For the second time Li-Mei had let stupidity get the best of her. She turned to Natt, still sound asleep, then to Colton. In the lamp's forty-watt glow, an empty chair stood where Colton had lain before the nurse's grand entrance. The front door swung on its hinges, revealing the street with a yawn. Li-Mei sprinted outside and up and down the street – nothing but the blinking hazards of the prowler. She went back inside and closed the door. She locked it too, just in case, then walked to the center of the warehouse, closed her eyes and attempted to meditate. Useless… Instead, her rage flowed at the two unmoving bodies. And of course, most of all, it flowed at herself.

On the floor, Sylvya twitched. Her battered body oozed blood and her broken wrist had bloated like unnatural origami. Li-Mei looked at the nurse, this creature who had foiled the mission, when everything else was wrapped. With black spots dancing in front of her eyes, Li-Mei hit the woman's face with a fist. The woman's nose caved like a ripe fruit and her lips muttered a sequence of tangled sounds. Why bother, Li-Mei thought, the nurse couldn't feel the payback.

She headed for the cop next, his half-open mouth snoring at uneven intervals. Li-Mei unholstered his gun, unbelted his uniform and pulled his pants down to his ankles, like a hammock connecting two hairy tree trunks. The Seattle PD Chief slept on, with the type of naked erection only the deepest slumber could sculpt.

Li-Mei dragged the nurse's unconscious body to an open pipe on the wall, turned the valve, and let the cold water run over Sylvya's head. At first, Sylvya didn't register that she was drowning then a glimmer lit up inside her retinas followed by full-on sloshing underneath the rushing water.

Li-Mei returned the coughing woman to the policeman and pressed the cop's gun against the nurse's forehead.

"Suck on him," Li-Mei said.

A string of coughs bracketed Sylvya's reply, "No."

Li-Mei fired the gun at the ceiling, the warehouse groaning with a reverberating echo, then pressed the smoking muzzle against the nurse's forehead, burning the skin with a perfect twenty-two-millimeter circle.

"I will not ask again. Suck on him."

Sylvya wiped her broken nose with her broken wrist. "I hope you die," she said.

"Death comes to us all, darling... starting with you unless you put him in your mouth."

In her good hand, Sylvya continued holding the cop. He was harder than before.

Li-Mei moved the gun to the nurse's temple. "Now bite it off," she said.

Sylvya shook her head no.

"You see how easy I pull the trigger. Don't make me do it again."

With eyes of a caged animal, Sylvya withdrew her lips and grinded her teeth. The cop's unconscious eyes flew wide open, driven by agony that the human brain was not wired to withstand. "You are an animal," she sobbed at Li-Mei.

"And you are welcome," said the Asian. She caressed Sylvya's temple with the gun's muzzle and pulled the trigger. The nurse's last thought in life was about Colton – how wonderful it would have been if he had met Sadie and Dallas and how he would have loved them.

Li-Mei wiped the gun clean and tucked it in Natt's hand then collected the syringe and needle from where the nurse had attacked, careful not to leave her fingerprints, next to Sylvya's. She ruffled Natt's hair, glistening with a sleeping person's sweat and plunged the needle in the back of his skull. For a moment, she held the syringe still, then spun it for two rotations. A memory from a biology class when she was six, washed over her, when she had lobotomized a dozen unsuspecting frogs. Pithing was the correct scientific term, she recalled, and it worked as well on cops as it had on amphibians. The syringe stuck out of Natt's head like a plastic mullet. He rolled his eyes and died in his sleep. Defiance Day was two days away.

one day till defiance day (66

Defiance Day Eve descended upon Seattle with clemency, reducing the wait to one final morning. Colton had turned himself in but this time it was different. He wasn't seeking shelter or bailing out. Defiance Day was tomorrow and he was reporting for his lawful obligation.

He had run from the warehouse and Li-Mei, without looking back, until reaching the first police precinct on the way. He had completed the digital check-in form, filling out "Sacrifice" in the "Vote Designation" box and thinking he had to be the only Sacrifice vote in Seattle coming from a deserter. He sat on the bunk of his detention cell and asked for a visit from his Vote Recipient: a legal right of a Sacrifice voter on Defiance Day Eve.

Yana arrived before ten-pm, accompanied by four ULE embassy guards who waited outside the cell. When the door closed, she gave him a hug and sat next to him on the bunk.

"Mom told me about it," she said and pressed Colton's fingers against her cheek. He held his breath, as if afraid not to break any part of what was taking place. She looked at his motley eyes and smiled. "Your eyes are the same color as mine," she said, "or is it the other way around?"

"I see your old man amuses you."

"You're not that old."

"Thank you for the second chance, patte," he said, lost in the geography of her face and reverse-engineering her features, from the toddler he remembered, to the girl sitting next to him.

She nodded in the blue-ink silence. "You afraid?" she said.

"A little... How about you, Ms. Would-Be-Teenager? You all right? When I get up there, with the other guys who sacrificed," his eyes shot upward, "don't embarrass me by getting pregnant until you're at least sixteen, OK?"

Yana punched his shoulder. "You're gross. No wonder Mom dumped you." She rested a hand on top of his and it made him feel like she was protecting him somehow. "When you head out tomorrow and when you sit in their... chair, their pump or whatever it is, will break and they'll have to postpone until a different time. I know it... and by then... people may have grown tired of killing."

"You'll be fine without me, patte," he said. "The world will get better by trading someone like me for someone like you."

"I don't want you gone... and I don't want today to end."

Colton cupped Yana's cheeks and straightened her eyebrow. "You should know," he said, "I'm the happiest I've ever been. In the whole world. All the days I have left in my life I would have traded for your forgiveness."

Yana's head shook. "My forgiveness is yours... there's no need to trade for it."

"You're like this beautiful sketch that will turn into a painting, one day. I won't be around when that masterpiece is done, but looking at you now, I see a scientist or an inventor – just like your Mom. And if they vote in the future for who's the best in whatever field you decided to pursue, you could count on my vote. It would never be that close. But my vote will always be yours." He squeezed her hand to feel her touch for as long as possible after letting go.

"Fight for your hope," he said, "like you're fighting now, because if something bad happens... too bad to fix, hope does live on. You think it dies, but it doesn't. It turns dark, with nothing to lose, if you would only fight for it." His face glowed with the light of what he believed worthy to live for, like love and courage and hope. He touched his chest. "Look at me. All these years, my one hope was to see you. Not in a hundred lifetimes did I dream you would give me a second chance. But you did. And now... I'm a king."

The sun was setting in the West. He leaned forward and kissed her cheek. "No matter how low you feel," he caressed her hair, "and today is damn low. No matter how alone or how unbeatable the desperation, remember that hope wins out in the end. And that I will always watch over you."

"Me too, Dad... In my dreams, I'll come to you and tell you about my day. I'll tell you about my friends and any boys I dated and I'll take care of Mom for you."

"Has she told you that your eyes change color?" he said. "Sometimes they're blue, sometimes they're green. Depending on how the light hits them. I'll try to be good enough to see you again, patte."

"You will, because I'll come find you in my next life. Even if I am a ladybug and you are a bear, I'll land on your back to spend time, even if we don't know each other or don't talk at all. And I promise I won't embarrass you in heaven, with the other Sacrificers and I won't get pregnant before sixteen." She closed her eyes and when they opened, Colton saw her promise to remain good, because that's how he would have raised her to be. "Whenever I meet someone else's father, I'll think of you and I'll be mad at God for it. And, one day, when I walk down the aisle at my wedding, you'll walk with me too. I will arch my arm in the air, as if it holds yours, because I will be holding you. On that day more than any other."

As she spoke, Colton nodded, his head keeping rhythm with an inaudible slow beat. He spread the fingers of his good hand at her, in a goodbye wave then pulled them together in a fist.

The ULE embassy guards took her away from his cell and he was left alone.

three days after defiance day (67

A developing mist helped the late December day swallow Seattle's tortured downtown. The city was disappearing for good, like a twenty-first century version of Machu Picchu. Fifteen million citizens had been terminated and any High-Potentials were relocating to Vancouver, BC – the designated US Territory hub in the northwest.

Mitko felt Yana's gaze on his face, hugged her and, for the first time in years, wished he could see. He imagined she had the eyes of a blue morning.

"Can we go to Kerry Park, please?" she said.

"You should ask your Mom, first."

"She said I could, if you took me."

"Let's go then."

"I wish Dad could come, too."

"He would have loved it," he said.

"Does it hurt to die by suffocation?"

"Not for him. They sedated him first. Then he died in his sleep."

"I wish we had spent more time together."

"As long as you remember him, he'll always be with you."

"What was he like?"

Side by side they strolled past the gates of the ULE embassy. Mitko walked in silence, thinking of an answer and Yana took his hand. They reached Kerry Park after a few minutes, more a city viewpoint than an actual park with trees. Mitko sat on a bench, placed Yana on his knee and patted her shoulder with a hand. She pressed close to him.

"He was a fearless man who made everyone around him braver." Mitko hadn't known Colton well but wanted Yana to remember her father the way daughters should remember fathers. When love was concerned a white lie was as good as the truth. "Like Crazy Horse, on a Brave Run in front of General Custer's men. Your Dad was the same. He protected you and your Mom. Most of all, you. He was your guardian, a refugee sentinel, he called it, who looked over you, no matter the odds."

"He never told me that."

"He gave his life for you in a flash." Mitko snapped his fingers. "Most Sacrificers have second thoughts, you know. But when it came to you, he decided in less than a second. That's how much he loved you."

Yana's voice shook. "He told me I had made him the happiest man in the world."

"You were his heart and when he talked about you…" Mitko whistled, "his face streamed love. Even a blind man could see that. He made you the heroine of all his stories and now I see he didn't exaggerate… other than the unicorns, that is." His laughter sounded like a tender Chopin sonata.

"The unicorns?" Her question teetered between curiosity and sadness.

They left the bench and headed down a gravel path that turned into a paved alley. "I'm not sure I should tell you," he said.

She stomped a foot on the asphalt. "You have to."

"Oh, well. He told me your spit was as powerful as unicorn tears."

"That's gross… and incorrect. My spit doesn't heal cuts."

"How do you know? I can nick my thumb to give it a try."

Yana stopped and looked up at Mitko. "I like spending time with you," she said and hugged him.

He hugged her back, stooping his shoulders and locking his hands around her to make the embrace warmer. He didn't know how else to give her comfort.

five days after defiance day (68

It felt to Sarah like it had started to snow inside the Starbucks on the Fourth Avenue bridge, as the supple woman approached her.

"The world's algae whisperer," the woman said without looking at anyone else in the café, "or should I call you the Mona Lisa of renewable energy?"

"Do I know you?" Sarah's hand dipped inside her purse, fingers resting on a pepper spray.

"Put your hands where I can see them, Dr. Perkins, or I won't be held responsible for the consequences." The woman was slender, with a figure like a human steel rod.

Sarah's hand abandoned the purse and rejoined the top of the table.

"Thank you, Doctor. You might have heard of me as Agent Taxi."

"So you are the one... The one who Colton defeated." Sarah's words swam in sorrow.

Li-Mei smiled. Her gaze drank in the scientist with measured sips. "A visionary general is not she who wins one thousand battles, but she who wins the battle without the world knowing there was a battle fought."

"Don't patronize me, agent. I did as your superiors asked."

"So did I, Sarah. And we both chose well."

"I didn't, because he beat you."

"You have your kid and we have your algae formulas. How did he," Li-Mei raised air-quote fingers, "beat me? And don't tell me it's about him winning Yana's love, because you see, I don't believe in moral victories." The setting sun bathed the coffee shop's cedar floor with a yellow glow.

"I should have had more faith in Colton..." Sarah covered her eyes. "I should have known he would survive you. It's just that... when that voice called, the day after Yana was earmarked, offering me to turn over my algae work in exchange for sparing her life... I would have given anything." She looked at Li-Mei. "Was it you who called me?"

"That's not important, Sarah. No one could blame a mother for doing what she must to save her daughter's life."

"I blame myself," Sarah said, "because he did outlast you and died on his own terms... not yours."

"Do you really think a one-handed, broken man could have defied the China Territory?"

"He did survive you, didn't he?"

"You believe I kept him alive for more than thirty days because I couldn't kill him? I expect more from your Hi-Po IQ, Dr. Perkins."

"Why didn't you kill him then?"

"You had agreed to our terms." Li-Mei smiled. "Don't get me wrong, it would have been glorious to assassinate Parker. But after your consent, murdering him became optional."

Sarah moved to the edge of her chair. "And had you killed him? How would my Yana have lived?"

"A Chinese citizen would have sacrificed for your daughter a moment before the voting deadline. We're honorable people, Doctor. A deal is a deal."

"A deal is a deal," Sarah said. "It makes me sick. Why do a deal at all? Why did the Chinese send you here to assassinate our people?"

"I'm not the only one who was sent. Hundreds like me canvassed the world to remove the loved ones of all non-Chinese High-Potentials." Li-Mei looked around the café then back at Sarah. "While the ULE thought it ruled the world under the façade of global unity, the China Territory pooled its resources: money, patents and real estate to bribe certain ULE senators and get the High-Potentials list."

"No senator has full access to the list. It's the most confidential piece of information there is."

"We did what we had to, Doctor. We gave as much as required to whomever we had to, to get everything. Try saying "no" to becoming the new owner of the GDP of China in exchange for a list that wasn't even yours."

"So a handful of senators now control China's wealth and real estate?"

"Correct, but we control the world's brightest and most promising minds. And we set out to eliminate the loved ones of those High-Potentials who weren't Chinese." Li-Mei stretched in her chair. "The ULE is a chimera, you see. Our world is devoid of resources and bound to break apart again. And the country who controls the world's brainpower will own all other resources in the end."

Sarah stared at Li-Mei without seeing her. "You couldn't assassinate the heavily guarded High-Potentials, so you went after their loves. Or blackmailed the Hi-Pos to turn over their research instead."

"Now you understand. Breakthrough research is impossible if your daughter or a husband or a mother is about to be executed. Of course, we tried to avoid shedding blood where we could."

"Like with me and Yana..."

"Like with you and Yana," Li-Mei nodded, "we gave the High-Potentials with access to technology we couldn't discover ourselves the chance to turn it over in exchange for saving their loved ones."

"What if the world had found out about your plan?"

Li-Mei smiled. "The risk was high and we had to stage all deaths as accidents. Like I quoted Sun Tzu – we had to keep the battle secret, otherwise winning it would have been impossible. But it was worth it – Mission Dizang has delivered technology and innovation to China that will cement our global dominance over the next several generations."

"And what if I go public with this news tomorrow?"

"I will pretend I didn't hear you ask me such a stupid question, Doctor. Please, don't make me think any less of you than I already do."

Sarah's face had aged years since the conversation started. "You'll find the complete Project Atlas blueprints here." She dug a data stick out of her purse and threw it at Li-Mei.

The Chinese snatched the flying object mid-air and shook her head. "You were supposed to send the data via an encrypted transmission."

Sarah spoke like she had not heard her. "In a month, I'll resign and recommend Atlas for termination. And the US Territory will end up with garbage. Tell your superiors the blueprints on this data stick work just fine."

"You'll always have a home in the East, Doctor. Imagine heading a renewables program, several times larger than anything you've seen in the West. Imagine Yana, safe and healthy by your side... Forever."

Sarah started to respond, then changed her mind. She stood up and headed for the door and a future with Yana – with no High-Potentials and no Defiance Days... like Colton would have wanted her to do. She turned. "You know what? Screw moral victories – he did beat you and we both know it. The broken man, as you called him, pushed your damn Chinese empire into the sea."

Li-Mei smiled again, small white teeth dueling with the outside dusk, and waved a polite goodbye. In the café, the yellow sunlight had morphed into burnt orange. A cricket was dying somewhere with a song, his closing gift to the December night and to the world.

twenty-four days after defiance day (epilogue

Yana's hands danced in the projectors' glow. The three days of competition had led to a finale with the trappings of cattle slaughter. No pundit could have predicted the ULE Classical Prodigy coming down to these last two: a future virtuoso, eighteen-old Yaohua Ling and this eight-something white girl.

Yaohua was a lock to win, even if they forced him to play with his toes. Some would say he didn't have flair, but like an exacting parent, he tended the same to all notes, playing at uniform discipline and without deviation. He had just finished with his usual untouchable perfection.

Yana was going at it now. In the front row, Mitko leaned forward, the room spinning in his head; her first notes hitting him like a sledgehammer. The rendezvous of the piano with her fingers inside the Tennessee Symphony Hall on this brittle January morning filled his conscience with a déjà vu from his own youth. He leaned closer to the music and the fair-haired girl he had never seen, wishing to stop time or, at least, bottle the sensation and pop the cork on the wistful days when his physical and figurative darkness got too heavy to bear. In her unmistakable brand he detected his own influence; pieces of him from old concert halls in capitals long forgotten. She was better than he had been at her age, maybe better than he ever was. But he didn't mind one bit and as she played, he saw color in the forefront of his brain. In his mind, her music blossomed in hues of lavender and silver, like a stream cascading from a snowy mountaintop.

Thunderous applause sucked him back into the hall where he, too, stood up and clapped and where Yaohua was a dead man. Afterward, he waited for her in the lobby. She ran to him, thumping footsteps approaching from one side.

"Sorry I'm late," she said, out of breath. "Mom held me up. And others too."

"Of course they did, Miss Champion of the United Lands of Earth. You played beautiful. Chopin himself would have said so if he heard you."

Yana grew silent and Mitko didn't need eyes to tell she was blushing. "I so wish he were here too. Do you think he would have liked hearing me play?"

"More than anything in the world."

"I'll let you in on a secret," she said. "Tonight I played for him – from the first note to the last."

Mitko cleared his throat. "I, too, will tell you a secret. Tonight he was here and heard everything, from the beginning to the last note. Maybe he sat next to you while you played. Or helped turn your music sheets, you know how they stick sometimes and mess with your rhythm. Maybe he's in this lobby right now, sitting a couple of tables away and taking you in."

"I don't want him a couple of tables away. I want him here," her hand rested on the empty chair next to her, "so I can tell him about my concert."

"You always can... whenever you have a free moment. You can talk to him about anything else, too, and he'll listen, I promise. Then he'll use his super powers to help you... if you needed help." Mitko's hand reached out and she held it with two palms. "The only favor you could give him in return is think of him, from time to time. And one day, many decades from now, when your turn comes to go up, he'll be waiting with a grin as wide as the sun. He changed the way of the world for you. He'll do the same with the heavens, too."

"I don't want to wait that long."

"He'd want you to wait, and will visit your dreams in the meantime."

Yana leaned closer and hugged the blind man tight. "When will you come visit us in DC?"

"As many times as you'd have me."

"I'll show you around... DC is pretty when the cherry blossoms come out."

"I'll hold you to it."

"I love you, Mitko," she said.

"Thank you for saving my life, kiddo."

She nudged her head on his chest and listened to his warm, steady heartbeat. Tennessee was getting ready to welcome the new day.

seven years and thirty eight days after defiance day (post epilogue

The figure formed in mid-air. It shifted into view and took the shape of an approaching man, one foot in front of the other. Under his footfalls the street slept, lulled by the soft moonlight. Yana couldn't see his face yet. From afar, his silhouette seemed familiar, but she shook the thought off. Behind him, the moon formed a near-perfect circle and time slowed to a crawl. She swallowed then heard church bells inside her head, even if she had lost her faith since she was a child.

The approaching man smiled. "How are you, patte?" he said and hugged the speechless teenager. Yana clung to the embrace, while grief tumbled from her chest in a silent avalanche. The man held her, like a pillar.

"I've missed you," Yana said, refusing to let go. Colton caressed her left cheek, with the back of his hand, then the right cheek with his palm. He straightened a lock of her hair. "I've been going to bed at nights hoping to see you in my dreams," she said.

"I know... I've been watching you."

"But you don't come to me."

"Just because you can't see me, doesn't mean I'm not with you."

"I have so much to tell you. It's been so long."

"Then tell me."

"At times, I miss you more than I can bear."

"Time will remove the pain."

"How could it? How can I forget my Dad who saved my life when people, God and providence itself had looked away?"

Colton smiled. "There's a lake in the Andean mountains where the Incas built their empire a thousand years ago. And where the bluest waters in the world shook hands with the bluest skies and the clouds threw white fireworks in the middle. This lake, Titicaca, protected its rich reserves of trout and gold with oxygen deprivation and laid so high in the mountains, that any newcomer needed months to learn how to breathe right." Yana didn't understand, but that was OK. Dreams held no allegiance to logic. Dreams were about the company you kept. "The ancient Inca gods, people said, stuck their fists down the foreigners' throats and squeezed their lungs. Those who survived the months-long asphyxiation saw the lake with different eyes. You are going through the Titicaca suffocation too, but will reach the all-blue dance, in time. I'll come to you then, without making you feel sad, and we'll marvel at the waters together."

"Why can't you be alive? Why didn't God save you for me?"

"Don't say such things. You are safe, and that's what matters."

"I'm not saying this God is bad or indifferent. I'm not even saying he isn't a good God. But if you asked who is more deserving, between this God and you, only a fool would confuse the answer."

"My love for you is deeper than that Inca lake and higher than its altitude."

"Tell me what to do." Yana held Colton's hands and shivered. "I don't want to wake. Tell me what to do, Dad."

When she woke in the morning, she had forgotten the dream. Her pillow was soaking wet, which likely meant the AC had broken again and she had slept hot. But she also felt alive and happy, and full of hope.

my deepest thanks go to:

Kerry Dimitrov – for your unconditional love, always;

Ekaterina Dimitrova – for making me the person I am today;

Kendall Meadows – for being my freshman English teacher;

Jenn Seadia – for being my first editor;

Yoana Nikolova – for drawing Yana's picture book, apologies it didn't make it in the final draft.

Thank you from the bottom of my heart, I couldn't have finished this project without you.

Made in the USA
San Bernardino, CA
18 May 2015